UNORTHODOX LOVE

UNORTHODOX LOVE

A Novel

HEIDI
SHERTOK

alcove
press

Published in the United States by Alcove Press, an imprint of The Quick Brown Fox & Company LLC.

Alcove Press and its logo are trademarks of The Quick Brown Fox & Company LLC.

Library of Congress Catalog-in-Publication data available upon request.

ISBN (paperback): 978-1-63910-376-8
ISBN (ebook): 978-1-63910-377-5

Cover illustration by Ashley Santoro

Printed in the United States.

www.alcovepress.com

Alcove Press
34 West 27th St., 10th Floor
New York, NY 10001

First Edition: July 2023

10 9 8 7 6 5 4 3 2 1

To my husband Daniel whom I love with all my heart
(and because he's a firstborn so everything has to be about him).

And in loving memory of Mary Beth Bergum
(March 18, 1985—October 6, 2022)

CHAPTER ONE

"People will stare. Make it worth their while."
—*Harry Winston*

On the scale of catastrophic things in the world, being a twenty-nine-year-old virgin isn't that bad. It's not like losing a loved one or getting robbed at gunpoint or being thrown in prison for a crime I didn't commit, or anything else that requires therapy and a good lawyer. Which is why if tonight's date ends up being a total disaster, I'm going to be just fine. Repeat: *I am going to be just fine.* I will not curl into a ball on the floor and imagine dying as an old maid, then go to the kitchen and finish off a tub of ice cream. In fact, I will not even think about the cookie dough ice-cream sandwich that gazes at me with seductive eyes every time I open the freezer.

The light turns yellow, and my foot gently pushes the brake until the car comes to a stop. My fingers tap the steering wheel restlessly. I always feel a little sick to my stomach before a first date, and tonight is no exception. You'd think after ten years that I'd get used to it, that the swirling motion in my gut would eventually relax, but no such luck. At least I got a great picture of my outfit to put on Instagram with hashtags #JewishDateNight and #ModestFashion.

When I first started sharing fashion trends with a modest twist on my Instagram account, it was just something fun to do with my family and friends—to share ideas of cute outfits that also flattered our figures. Because in my opinion, modesty *is* sexy. But I certainly never imagined that it would grow to have the twenty-two thousand followers it currently has, including women from all over the world. And they're not all Orthodox Jews either—there are Muslims, Mormons, Jehovah's Witnesses, Pentecostals. It's also become a sisterhood of sorts, a safe place to talk about our struggles (*"Horseback riding with a skirt? You've gotta be kidding me!"*) to our praises (*"The dermatologist said I have virgin skin—no skin cancer here!"*)

I glance at my makeup in the rearview mirror to check that nothing smudged, then remind myself in a stern, feminist tone that I am a strong, independent woman who doesn't need a man to complete me or to notice how my eyeliner brings out the flecks of green in my eyes.

But it would be nice to have someone who could fix stuff around the house. And kill spiders and boxelder bugs. Oh, and carry in the heavy groceries.

Forget a husband—maybe I just need a manservant. I bet—

A loud honk interrupts my thoughts, and I realize that the light has turned green. Crap.

I steer my car into a parking spot and shut off the engine. Tonight's date is a New Yorker named Yoav Bernbaum, and from casually stalking his Facebook profile and Instagram account, I know that he has short-cropped brown hair, a curly beard that reaches his neck, and turquoise glasses shaped like stop signs. I didn't find any scandalous pictures, although there were a surprising number of his mother, which was sweet. Or disturbing. I keep going back and forth on that one.

But his job sounds interesting. My matchmaker, Mrs. Zelikovitch, was vague as always, but she said Yoav is the guy everyone calls when there's been a homicide or other crime scene. Which is perfect because I recently started watching *Criminal Minds* on Netflix, so at least I'll be able to talk shop with him, if nothing else.

I push the lock button on my keypad and head toward the coffee shop. I used to think there's a soulmate for everyone, but it's been ten *loooong* years of looking, and I'm starting to think that I must be the exception to the rule.

A golden retriever that's leashed to a table outside the café perks up when she sees me. Her tail sweeps the ground in quick strokes as I bend down to scratch the fur behind her ears and then she rolls over for a tummy rub.

Maybe G-d was distracted the day He assigned soulmates, and accidentally skipped me. Or maybe I was the distracted one, backstroking through the clouds and making dead people jokes, and totally forgot to get in line.

Yeah, that must've been it.

With a resigned sigh, I give the dog one last scratch, then move toward the door. The scent of freshly ground coffee beans and the cafe's famous cheese croissants greets me as I walk inside. My eyes scan the room, taking in the exposed steel beams, brick walls, and upholstered banquettes. The place is crowded with hipsters sporting neon tops, distressed jeans, and lace-up vegan combat boots, so the lone man in a business suit and black velvet yarmulke is easy to spot. I maneuver through the maze of people and furniture until I arrive at his table. Yoav picks intently at a piece of skin under his thumbnail and doesn't seem to notice me.

"Hi." I smile, setting my fake Prada handbag on the table. "You must be Yoav."

The man glances up. "I'm sorry, but you have the wrong person."

"Oh!" I'm taken aback and more than a little confused since this man looks just like Yoav's picture; maybe he doesn't know who I am? "I'm Penina Kalish."

An awkward silence settles in the air as he gazes at me uncomprehendingly. I clear my throat and add, "It's just that you look so much like the guy I'm supposed to be meeting here tonight for a date . . ."

"Look, you're more than welcome to sit down and schmooze," he says, gesturing toward the seat across from him. "But just so you know, I'm married with five kids."

The blood drains from my face. *I am such an idiot.* "Oh my gosh. Definitely the wrong person—I'm sorry." I grab my purse and turn to go.

"Gotcha!"

"What?" I wheel around, my eyebrows raised in confusion.

"It's me—I *am Yoav*!" He grins and spreads his palms out. "Oh man, I can't believe you fell for that. You should have seen your face!"

My fingers clench my purse as I mentally list all the reasons why I shouldn't whack him over the head with it. Too many witnesses for one thing.

His grin fades as he catches my facial expression. "Hey, I'm sorry—it was just a joke." He pauses, then says, "I forgot that not everyone has a sense of humor."

How is that funny? And anyway, I have a great sense of humor. At the moment I'm picturing him slipping on a banana peel and banging his head as he crashes to the ground.

"I bet you'll go home tonight and laugh about it afterward." He grins. "I know I will."

I glance around the room for hidden cameras, hoping this is one of those reality shows that try to freak innocent people out, but I don't see any. I sigh. If I didn't have to worry about my reputation in the dating world and the impression it would leave on the matchmaker, I'd have been halfway home by now. The problem is, I have enough stacked against me without people saying I bail on my dates before they even begin.

"Can we start over?" He lifts his palm. "No more pranks."

Pranks as in plural? Dear G-d, how many had he planned? Did he plan? I force a smile that's so wide it's almost painful. "Sure."

"Great, great." He grins broadly, obviously pleased with himself. "So, what can I get you to drink?"

Since coffee is the only thing that's kosher here, I say, "An iced coffee please. Decaf," I add.

"Alright, I'm on it."

I watch him weave his way to the front of the store, tripping over a chair in the process before apologizing profusely to the man in it. I shake my head and sigh. Maybe he's nervous. My head starts to pound, so I open my purse and take out the emergency Tylenol I carry with me and dry-swallow two. I just met the guy, and he's already given me a stress headache.

I take out my phone to text Libby, my big sister, mother of five, and number-one go-to person for all things in life.

Am two seconds away from running out on this date

After a short pause, my phone bleeps.

LOL. What's stopping you?
Jewish guilt. My reputation.

I watch the gray dots dance on the screen as she types back.

Matchmakers r overrated. All u need is Tinder.

I laugh and start typing a response.

"Uh-oh. Cheating on me already?" Yoav places my drink on the table, then sits across from me on the teal velvet banquette and tilts his head.

"No, just texting my sister," I say, and put my phone away. "Thanks for the coffee." I murmur the Hebrew blessing and take a sip. "It's delicious."

"Can't go wrong with Columbian dark roast." He takes a swallow and murmurs, "Mmm, so many flavors." He lowers his cup and gives an impish grin. "Want to try some of mine?"

Hell to the no. "No, thank you."

He looks so disappointed that I have to remind myself not to be taken in by sad puppy-man eyes, especially when it comes to swapping spit. Since Orthodox Jews aren't allowed to touch people of the opposite gender, sharing a drink is like getting to second base, so to speak.

"So Yoav," I say, trying to move the conversation along, "what do you do for a living? Mrs. Zelikovitch said you're the person everyone calls when there's been a homicide or other crime scene."

He takes off his glasses and wipes the lenses with his shirt. "Yeah, I'm their guy alright."

When he doesn't continue, I say, "So, you're a detective?"

"Hah!" he laughs. "No, no. I'm just the cleaner upper."

I have no idea what that means. "What does that mean?"

"I clean up people's spilled guts and stuff after they've been killed or committed suicide. And lemme tell you something," he says, shaking his finger, "it's a thankless job. The police order you around like you're their bitch; the family is all emotional and crying—whatever. And it's not like the corpse is grateful." He shrugs. "Whatcha gonna do? It is what it is. So," he says, nodding, "what do you do?"

I swallow. "I work at a jewelry store."

"Hah!" he barks, then takes a drink. "Jewelry store, huh? I guess you didn't go to college either."

"I went to a community college." A couple walks past our table, holding hands and laughing, and something in my heart pinches. It feels like envy, and I shake the thought from my head. "I majored in English."

He smirks. "What a waste of money. Why did you even bother going?"

"The plan was to be the next Jane Austen," I explain, hating this part of the story. "But it took me forever just to write a paragraph and when I finally finished, I realized that it wasn't even a good one." I tilt my head and purse my lips. "I emailed it to a friend of mine and asked her what she thought. She said I should probably take up knitting."

Yoav slams his hand on the table, causing some of my coffee to spill. "Now *that*," he declares loudly, "is funny."

Glad one of us is having a good time.

"What do you do in your spare time?"

He gazes at me suspiciously over the rim of his cup, as though this is a trick question. "What do you mean?"

I repress the sigh that so badly wants to come out. "Like," I say, waving my hand, "what do you do for fun?" He stares at me blankly, so I add, "Do you have any hobbies?" Besides pranking your dates.

"I smoke. I drink." He squints his eyes like he's concentrating really hard, then says, "Does eating count?"

I sigh. "Sure. Why not."

"Do *you* have any hobbies?" he says, crossing his arms over his chest.

"Yes," I reply immediately. "Well, maybe not hobbies per se, but I like going for walks around the lake with my friend, and I hang out with my nephews and niece." My eyes light up and I straighten in my seat. "Oh, and I love watching old movies! You know, those black-and-white ones with stars like Gene Tierney and Humphrey Bogart and Paul Newman—"

"Honestly, I don't have a lot of spare time," Yoav says, cutting me off. "My work hours are pretty long. And when I'm not working, I'm volunteering at Shriners Hospital."

"Really?" My eyes widen in surprise. Maybe this guy *is* my soulmate after all. He's obviously got a good heart if he volunteers. "I do too!" I say excitedly, clutching my heart. "I also volunteer at a hospital."

"Oh yeah?" he says, bringing his cup to his lips. "Do you like it?"

"I *love* it. I get to cuddle babies in the NICU. It's the best. What do you do?"

He finishes swallowing, then clears his throat. "I'm a clown."

"A clown?" I repeat, not sure I heard right.

"Yeah. I have to wear this ridiculous costume with a Ronald McDonald nose and act like a dork."

My eyebrows lift. "That's . . . interesting. We don't have clowns at my hospital." Which is only a good thing, if you ask me. I don't know what it is about them, but clowns give me the creeps. Maybe it's the poorly applied makeup. "Do you put on shows?"

"Yeah. But I only have a few weeks left and then I'll be moving on."

I use my straw to stir the coffee. "You want a different volunteer job?"

"Hah!" he laughs and blots his lips with a napkin. "Nah, I'm finished with volunteering. I just did it because it looks good on my résumé. Unless—" He slaps his forehead. "Oh, I almost forgot. Ma made us her famous brownies." He reaches into a plastic shopping bag and pulls out a Tupperware container that has a mini notepad attached to the top that says in big scrawling print: *To my future daughter-in-law, with love.* He points at the note and chuckles. "She's the best. I tell her all the time that if she weren't already taken, I'd marry her myself."

I laugh weakly. That's not creepy at all. Nope.

When he removes the lid, a strange scent assaults my nose, but I can't pinpoint what it is. It smells like cocoa mixed with death.

"Mmm," Yoav, closes his eyes and sniffs appreciatively. "Don't tell anyone," he says, glancing around furtively, "but mayonnaise is the secret ingredient."

I throw up a little in my mouth. Mayonnaise and I go way back, but not in a good way. Just thinking of its smell and texture causes me to break out into a cold sweat. There's got to be hidden cameras in here, and I start glancing around the room for them because it seems like too much of a coincidence for him not to have known. I admit it's weird (okay fine, *I'm* weird), but I *detest* mayonnaise as though it were its own entity with

7

evil intentions. It's squishy and goopy and jiggly and—I shudder. Why would anyone ruin a perfectly good brownie by adding that poison?

"Something wrong?" Yoav asks with a slight frown when he sees me cringe.

I shake my head, scooting as far away from the offensive item on the table as possible. There's no nice way to explain that his precious mother's famous recipe makes me want to hurl. I almost laugh, hearing my matchmaker's voice in my ear, telling me for the millionth time that honesty is never the best policy when discussing your date's mother.

"I'm not much of a brownie person. Thank you, though," I say, clearing my throat.

"Have a bite or two," he says firmly, pushing the Tupperware forward until it's directly in front of me. "My mother made these especially for you." He watches closely as I take a bite, then asks, "Well? What do you think?"

I think you and your mother are trying to kill me. "Ish sho good." *Don't think about the mayonnaise, don't think about the mayonnaise—*

His phone suddenly rings, and while he checks the screen to see who's calling, I reach for a napkin and spit the brownie out.

"My mother's FaceTiming me." Yoav looks up from his phone. "Do you mind if I get it? She gets worried if I don't pick up by the third ring."

A sigh escapes me. "Sure, go ahead."

"Thanks." Yoav's finger swipes the screen, and he grins widely. "Hi, Ma."

"Hi, baby boy."

I choke on my drink and pound on my chest, trying not to laugh. This is too much. First the prank, then the mayonnaise brownie, now *baby boy.*

"Who's coughing?" she asks. "Is it the girl? Is she there?"

"Yes. She's here right now, actually." He winks.

Did he just wink at me? And why is he wiggling his eyebrows like that? It's like Morse code of the face, but I have no idea what he's trying to tell me.

"Oh good," she says. "Listen, I won't keep you, but tell me quickly, did the brownies turn out good?"

"Are you kidding? They're as amazing as the woman who made them." He grins.

I suddenly feel like the third wheel here. Maybe I could slip away without being noticed.

"How about the girl?" Yoav's mother asks. "Did she like them?"

Yoav motions toward his phone and mouths something to me, but I can't make out what it is.

Without warning, he turns the phone toward me, and I suddenly find myself staring into the beady wide-set eyes of an older woman in a turquoise headscarf.

Oh dear G-d, it's the progenitor herself.

"Um, hi." I smile widely, feeling like a deer in headlights. I've been on a lot of dates in my life, but this is definitely a first. And hopefully, the last.

"Hi, sweetie. I'm Yoav's mom."

Then you have a lot of explaining to do. "Nice to meet you. I'm Penina."

"You're as pretty as your profile picture!"

I laugh nervously. What picture was that? I don't even remember. "Thank you. And thanks for the brownies. They're delicious."

"Good, good, enjoy! My son loves desserts, but he's hopeless in the kitchen. Do you bake?"

This woman moves impressively fast, but the last thing I want is her getting any ideas that I'll be helping her son out in the kitchen. Or anywhere else. "Love that *tichel*!" I say, pointing to her headscarf in a desperate attempt to distract her. "Did you get that in a store or online?"

She looks down at her shoulder and touches the fringed cloth, as if to remind herself which one she's wearing. "Neither, it's from my neighbor down the hall, the one in 21B. She died a few days ago."

Yoav turns the phone back to him. "So sad. She made great pineapple kugels. But not as good as yours," he adds. "No one can measure up to your cooking."

"Oh, you!" She titters like a schoolgirl. "Anyway, that's how I got the *tichel*. The family was cleaning out her apartment and made a pile of things to donate to charity, so I took it."

Er . . . questionable ethics? My eyes dart in Yoav's direction, but he doesn't seem particularly concerned.

"I should go, Ma, but I'll call you later tonight." He promises to call her by nine PM, then hangs up the phone and looks at me. "Now you can tell people you've met my mother!"

Oh dear G-d. I stare at him for a beat. "Sure could," I reply, managing a limp smile.

He tears off a piece of brownie and pops it into his mouth. "People always tell me not to bring this up on a first date, but I've got a good feeling about you." He finishes chewing, then leans forward and lowers his voice conspiratorially. "You know how in China, people live with their parents? Well, that's always been my dream. My mother and wife living under the same roof, cooking meals together in the kitchen."

I stare at him and wait for the part when he breaks into hysterical laughter, then tells me it's a prank.

"I know my wife will grow to love her as much as I do." His eyes travel down to the napkin with my brownie on it. "Are you going to eat the rest of that? Because I'll have it if you don't want it."

I'm willing to bet this guy doesn't have a soulmate either. Unless, of course, his mom counts. I push the dessert toward him, and he tears off a piece and pops it into his mouth. A crumb gets stuck in his beard, and I motion toward it. "You've got something there."

"Oh, I'm saving that for later." He winks.

And now I'm struggling not to dry-heave for the second time tonight. Keep it together, girl. Deep breaths, everything is going to be fine. But as I stare across the table and watch Yoav devour the brownie, I start thinking about reincarnation. Every time I find myself in a bad situation, I figure it's punishment for something I did wrong in a past life. Although I can't figure out what I could have done that was bad enough to meet this guy. Murder, perhaps.

I can't do this anymore, I realize with sudden clarity. I can't keep going on dates like this, pretending it could lead somewhere when, in reality, I'd sooner walk naked across the Sahara Desert without shoes, water, and a GPS than marry someone like Yoav.

My mouth opens, and the words fly out. "I'm sorry Yoav, but this . . . you and me," I say, gesturing between us, "it's not going to work out."

"Whoa, whoa, girl," he says, as though I'm a spooked horse. His eyes widen and he stops eating. "Where is this coming from? We've hardly said two words to each other."

"Still, I can tell that it's not—"

"Is this about my height?" he says sharply. "I'm no basketball player, but five foot six isn't so bad for a Jew."

I bite down on my cheek so as not to laugh, and stand up and reach for my purse. "I promise, I didn't even notice your height."

"Then what's the problem?"

Run, Penina! Head for the door and don't look back. There's a warm fuzzy blanket and a new season of Schitt's Creek *waiting for you at home . . .*

Unfortunately, my mouth suddenly *no comprende ingles* from my brain. "Your prank wasn't a great start, to be honest."

He frowns and crosses his arms. "Agree to disagree. Anything else?"

Yes, but I'd sooner poke out my eyeballs than stay and list all of them.

He leans forward. "What is it? Tell me."

"Your mother," I say slowly and a little painfully, "she seems really special—"

"She is."

The back of my neck starts to itch, and I reach around to scratch it. "But the idea of living with her and cooking together in the kitchen is . . . a bit much. For me. But anyway," I say quickly as his eyes narrow into tiny slits, "I'm sure you'll meet that special someone soon. And what a lucky woman she'll be," I add, sure to maintain eye contact. I've watched enough of those true crime interrogations to know that people often look away or blink when saying something that isn't true, so I've trained myself to stare straight into someone's eyes when lying.

"She will," he snaps, pushing his glasses further up the bridge of his nose. "You have no idea."

"Oh, I have an inkling," I say, inching backward from the table. "Nice meeting you, Yoav. Have a good night."

I turn and head toward the door as fast as my three-inch stilettos can carry me, and step out into the cool night air. I unzip my purse and pull out my key fob as I move toward my car. I know I'm going to get an earful from my matchmaker at some point in the next few days, and she'll lecture me about being too picky. She once told my mother I'm "high maintenance" after I flat-out refused to date this guy whose *kids* were older than me. And to be honest, it's not like she's sending me such keepers. In the last year alone, she's set me up with a guy who already had three failed marriages behind him and seemed to carry a very large chip on his shoulder against women. Then there was the hypochondriac who insisted on showing me his rash and asking if the mole on his face looked cancerous (I spent the majority of the date researching the internet for a diagnosis despite the fact that I'd never been to medical school). And let's not forget the guy that was convinced the government was trailing his every movement, to the point where he barely left his home, and my matchmaker's response was, "It's a temporary situation. Once he's married, his wife will keep him on his meds and he'll be fine." I hung up on her that time, then pretended we got cut off when she called me back.

I was cautiously excited about the last guy she set me up with, who ran a farm and seemed nice and normal, but then I visited and discovered that he was growing cannabis and cooking crystal meth in his basement. On my way out, his friend called and said the Mexican cartel guys were on their way and that "shit was about to get real." I've never driven so fast in my life.

A gust of wind causes some strands of hair to get stuck in my lip gloss, and I take a tissue from my purse and wipe it off. I've come to realize that Mrs. Zelikovitch is basically a used car salesman in disguise and talks up the men so much that if you didn't know any better, you'd think you're about to meet a Chris Hemsworth look-alike who's as rich as a Saudi prince and as chivalrous as a hero in a romance novel. But then you meet the guy and discover he's average-looking at best; between jobs—*"but it's fine because my parents support me anyway"*; and angrily rants about a restraining order that prevents him from contacting his ex-wife. The truth is that Mrs. Z's matchmaking success stories are few and far between, but after the last matchmaker passed away, there was a need for someone to take over and fulfill that role, and she eagerly volunteered. She's not my ideal version of what a good matchmaker is, especially when she reminds me in faintly pitying tones that I'm no prize either and have no right to be picky. Her favorite expression is *"Beggars can't be choosers."* She once said that the whole point of getting married is to have kids, so I'd be lucky if anyone was interested in me, then patted my hand as if to soften the blow.

I climb inside my car, turn on the ignition, and reverse out of the parking space. Obviously, *normal* Orthodox Jewish guys would never date me, not with my infertility problem, but I'd like to think there's someone out there that's between normal and needing to check in with a parole officer once a week.

I sigh and turn on the defroster. The worst part is that I don't even blame the normal guys. Why be set up with a stranger who can't have kids rather than a stranger who could, especially when the commandment to be fruitful and multiply is taken so seriously in our community. Of course, they wouldn't want to date me. I wouldn't want to date me either.

Then again, I can make a mean cheese omelet, and not to steal Kelis's line, but my challah could definitely bring all the boys to the yard, if you know what I mean. The recipe isn't bad either.

I brake at a red light and flick on the windshield wipers. Everyone, from my rabbi to my family, to my therapist, have all said that my life has just as much value as any other human's, barren or not. The logical part of my brain agrees with them, but the emotional part has its doubts and whispers things like *Of course, they're saying that—it's their job to. That doesn't mean it's true.*

I turn on the radio and raise the volume to Olivia Rodrigo's "Good 4 U," and try to bury the despair that's struggling to surface. Driving through Uptown helps, since it takes a concerted effort to stay alert and avoid getting shot.

My phone rings, and like an idiot, I answer without checking to see who it is. "Hello?"

"Penina."

Crap. I knew Mrs. Z would be calling, I just didn't think it would be this soon. She didn't give me time to come up with a good excuse or empty my bladder. The woman has no heart.

"I can explain," I swallow.

"Listen Peninaleh," she says. For some reason, I always hear *The Godfather* movie music playing in my head when she talks. Maybe it's her gravelly voice. Maybe it's the way she smiles and pats my cheek as she tells me there's nothing wrong with dating a man three times my age. "I know you're a good person and you didn't mean to hurt poor Yoaveleh's feelings," she says, clearing her throat. "But I just got off the phone with his mother. She said he was crying."

Crying? I didn't think he'd be *that* upset.

"Yoav is very hurt that you ran out on him."

Yeah and my taste buds died a small death tonight, so that makes us even. "I'm sorry to hear that." I switch to the right lane to let the car tailing me pass.

"What I always say is, even if, G-d forbid, your appendix is about to rupture, better you should pass out than leave a date early. Embarrassing a Jew is the same as killing him."

And allowing your appendix to burst is basically suicide, but that's okay? I glance out the window and see a guy on his motorcycle with his bulldog in the sidecar, wearing matching leather jackets. I'm not sure what this says about the current state of my mental health, but I'd give anything to switch places with that dog right now. The light turns red and I brake to a stop.

Mrs. Z heaves a sigh. "I know you're usually a good girl, Peninaleh. We'll chalk this one up to PMS, alright?"

Lord have mercy. I brake at the red light, then bang my head repeatedly against the steering wheel. I've explained to Mrs. Z a million times that I don't get PMS because I don't get periods because I'm infertile, but she has some kind of block against retaining this information. *"Alrighttttty* then," I say brightly, picturing the GIF of Jim Carrey's face.

"And listen, the next guy I have lined up for you is top of the top. USDA prime. Everything you could ever dream of and more."

Funny. She said the same thing about the sex addict that had done time in prison, but details like that tend to slip her mind. "I appreciate that," I say, treading carefully. "But I think it's time for a break. It's been ten years, and I—"

"Absolutely not, I won't hear of it. You think this is how Olympic gold medalists talk?"

I wouldn't know, and I'm pretty sure she doesn't either. I pull into the parking lot of my apartment building and squeeze into a spot. "It doesn't have to be a long break," I say, killing the ignition. Just a decade or two.

She mutters in Yiddish under her breath, something along the lines of my *fakakta* behavior and how real life isn't *The Bachelor*.

My lips twist into a surprised grin. Of everything that's happened tonight, Mrs. Zelikovitch mentioning reality TV is possibly the most disturbing. Not that Orthodox Jews don't watch television—although some don't—it's just that she doesn't strike me as the type who would. But then she also has twelve children and I can't imagine her doing . . . *that* either.

"Kay, one minute," she murmurs in a distracted voice. "Hold on, hold on."

I open the door to my building and briefly consider using the stairs, but after today's insanity, I've earned an elevator ride. And who knows? Maybe, just *maybe* we'll get disconnected.

"Almost done . . . Alright. There! It's out of my hands now."

I use my elbow to press the "Up" button because, you know, germs. "What do you mean?"

"It's up to G-d and Zevi now."

G-d I know, but who's the other dude? The doors open and I step inside, then press the button for the fifth floor. "Who?"

She starts to say something, but gets cut off. "I'm getting another call, but he'll contact you soon. You're going to love this guy. *Zei gezunt.*"

"Wait! Don't hang up—hello? Hello?"

I stare at the phone in disbelief. What part of *taking a break* did the woman not understand? I lean my forehead against the door of my apartment and take a long, deep breath, trying not to scream. It's not a big deal, I tell myself as I unlock the door. If this Zevi guy calls, I'll just tell him I'm not interested.

And if worse comes to worst, I could change my phone number, book a one-way ticket to Bora Bora, and live off coconuts for the rest of my life. So, I have options.

After I shower and change into pajamas, I open a dresser drawer and lift a pile of T-shirts to reach the letter that's hidden beneath. Although *letter* probably isn't the right word for it; it's just a small note that Libby wrote and slipped under my bedroom door nearly fifteen years ago following the news of my diagnosis.

Wrapped in a cozy chenille blanket and a mug of hot cocoa on my bedside table, I go under the covers and begin to read.

Dear Penina,

I hear you crying from your room, and I wish I knew what to say to make you feel better. If I could switch bodies with you, I'd do it in a heartbeat. You're a really good person and a great sister (most of the time), and you definitely don't deserve this. BTW, doctors don't know everything. Miracles happen all the time, and there's probably some brainiac scientist right now inventing a solution. Plus, there's always adoption. And don't forget that I'm going to need tons of help raising my kids—you know how I feel about dirty diapers. 😖

I heard you tell Mommy that no one will want to marry you now, but that's not true! Everyone has a soulmate and I bet yours is ridiculously good looking and filthy rich. You'll probably go on exotic vacations and make the rest of us jealous. I'm already mad just thinking about it.

And trust me, you will be happy. I feel it in my gut!!! Don't give up on your dream, because it's still there waiting for you. You got this.

Love,

your wise, big sister,

Libby

Even though Libby's prediction didn't end up coming true, there's still plenty of joy in my life and tons to be grateful for. I couldn't have asked for a warmer, more supportive family. My parents are healthy and happily married, and my four nephews and one niece are as dear to me as if I had given birth to them myself. Every morning, I wake up excited to go to work and I'm just as excited to get back home by the end of it. Between keeping up with friends, volunteer work, scouring stores for that next belt or purse to pull an outfit together, I barely have time to simply relax and watch one of my favorite old Hollywood movies, much less obsess over the fact that I've never fallen in love. It's not something that keeps me up at night. If anything does, it's the image of Mrs. Z's face's looming over mine as she pontificates all the reasons why I have no right to be picky. And if you ask me, anyone whose been dating for ten years deserves a gold medal because—as the good Lord only knows—it's *brutal* out there.

CHAPTER TWO

"I wanted to send a message that it's ok to be a woman and be fragile, but it's also ok to have a layer of armor, because you need it."
                                                        —*Irina Shabayeva*

"Why can't carrots taste better?" I ask the squirming preemie in my arms, even though he's clearly lost interest in the conversation. I reposition him so his head is against my chest, and pop the pacifier back in his mouth. "Someone should invent a vegetable that tastes like pizza or barbecued ribs. What good are scientists if they're not inventing things that we actually need? They can't all be trying to find the cure for cancer, right?" I hug his body closer to mine and smile down at him. "What do you think, Antwon?"

"He thinks you're nuts," Delilah, the head nurse, comments as she walks by.

I roll my eyes. The good thing about Delilah is that you never have to wonder where you stand with her, unlike the rest of the nurses here who are "Minnesota nice," meaning they'll smile and be nice until you turn your back, at which point they'll pick up an ice pick and stab you to death.

Metaphorically speaking, of course.

"Didn't you say you're going on a date tonight?" Delilah says, reaching beneath the clear bassinet for a diaper and wipes.

I pretend not to know she's talking to me. After all, in theory, she could be asking any of the other four nurses here, but Delilah takes a special—some might call it *sadistic*—interest in my dating life. I'm the only Orthodox Jewish person she's ever met, and she loves to ask questions about my religion, especially risqué ones to shock me. She can't get over the fact that I've never held hands, much less kissed a guy, and takes every opportunity to remind me how sheltered I am.

"Penina," she says, louder this time. "I know you heard me."

"In my defense," I whisper into Antwon's ear, "I thought she wasn't working today." His eyelids briefly open, revealing a pair of hickory-brown eyes that seem to express sympathy, although that could be my imagination.

Janie, a fresh and pretty young nurse, looks up from her computer. "Speaking of dates, I went out on Friday night with this guy and it was so . . . so . . ." She scrunches her pert nose and taps her cheek. "Traumatizing."

I instantly perk up. I'm usually the one with the awful date stories, so it's a relief to finally share the stage. "Really?"

Delilah leans against a supply cabinet and folds her arms, bemusement written on her face. "Get talking then, we don't have all day."

Janie holds up a finger, then finishes typing something on the computer. I've noticed how often the nurses document in the NICU, everything from weigh-ins to feedings, to how many wet diapers there are. I wouldn't be surprised if they documented sneezes and farts as well.

"Okay, so," Janie says, turning around to face us, "at first, the date was fine. Not great or anything," she adds with a shrug, "but nothing out of the ordinary. Until we got to his place and then it became a *total* nightmare."

"What did I tell you about sleeping with men on the first date?" Delilah demands, then continues before Janie can answer. "They'll think you're booty material, that's what. They'll think they can come and go in your life whenever they feel like it. Don't be going around acting thirsty." She puts her hands on her hips then nods her chin at me as if I'm the Lennon to her McCartney or the Harry to her Meghan. "Right, Penina?"

"Don't look at me, I'm just the virgin," I say, shaking my head. "I know nothing about booty calls. The most action I've ever gotten was when the UPS guy gave me a wink after I signed for a package." I release a happy sigh, remembering how cute he was with his curly blond hair and tight brown shorts. "That wink kept my heart pounding for days."

"Girl." Delilah purses her lips and shakes her head, clearly at a loss for words.

"You don't get out much, do you?" Janie says, tilting her head in sympathy.

I laugh and gesture at the room with my free hand. "This is about as exciting as it gets." Delilah grimaces, as though she's in physical pain, and Janie facepalms.

"Anyway, back to my date," Janie continues, when an alarm goes off, interrupting her. She crosses the nursery to check on the baby, scans the computer screen that lists its vitals, then readjusts a sensor on its foot.

The first time I volunteered here, I got freaked out every time an alarm went off, but I came to understand that there are a lot of false alarms in the NICU because of the highly sensitive equipment monitoring the babies.

"Where was I?" Janie murmurs, wiping antibacterial foam between her hands. "Oh yeah," she nods. "The cat."

"The cat?" Delilah and I repeat, glancing at each other.

Janie nods. "He has a personality disorder and schizophrenic episodes, but of course I only find that out *after* he pees all over my purse."

I lift up my hand. "I'm sorry, but are we still talking about the cat?"

Delilah claps her hands and hoots with laughter, while Janie rolls her eyes. "Yes, I'm still talking about the cat," she says, then heaves a sigh, like she's regretting having opened her mouth in the first place.

"Sorry." I wave my hand with a flourish. "Carry on."

"So, we're getting pretty friendly with each other on the couch, and other than the cat making weird noises every now and then, everything was fine." Janie takes a big breath, then continues. "But then he says, 'Ever been in a threesome?' And then before I have a chance to say anything or run for my life, he whips out this sex doll from behind the couch and says, 'Meet Désirée.'"

My mouth drops open.

"I don't even—I can't . . ." Delilah shakes her head.

"Wow," I say to Janie with newfound respect. "That's really messed up."

She slices the air with the palm of her hand and nods. *"Right?"*

Antwon starts to fuss, so I stand up and sway from side to side. "I've had a lot of bad dates," I say, "but none that included a French sex doll. Did she have an accent? I hope she was pretty at least." I pause swaying to readjust a corner of the baby's blanket, then add, "How realistic are these things, anyway?"

When Janie doesn't answer me, I look up and see that her face is flushed a deep ruby red and she's twisting her hands together so hard that her knuckles have turned white. My eyes cut to Delilah, who's wearing a deer-in-the-headlights expression, something I'd never have thought I'd see on the unflappable head nurse.

What in the—Did I say something offensive? Should I not have asked if the sex doll was attractive? I mean, beauty is in the eye of the beholder, so what she might consider pretty in a sex doll, I might disagree, but why is that such a—

From behind me, someone clears their throat, and I nearly shriek from surprise. With a sense of dread and a pit in my stomach, I turn and glance over my shoulder. A group of strangers and one NICU doctor and a hospital administrator are gathered, looking, for the most part, uncomfortable, although a couple of them seem amused. I inhale sharply as I belatedly recall Delilah mentioning that a group of benefactors were going to tour the NICU later today. She must've misunderstood the *later* part.

It's not that big a deal, I tell myself, keeping my eyes firmly fixed on Antwon's sweet face. Yes, a bunch of bigshots heard us talking about threesomes with sex dolls, which admittedly isn't the most professional topic of conversations, but at least I'm a volunteer. None of those people sign my paycheck, and it's unlikely that I'll run into them again. Unlike Delilah and Janie.

"Is now a good time?" The hospital administrator clears her throat and idly fingers the ID badge she wears on a string around her neck.

Delilah collects herself like the consummate professional she is, and warmly introduces everyone, which unfortunately includes me.

"And this is one of our volunteers from our cuddle program." Delilah grins broadly and gestures to me. "Often, the parents here have other children at home or medical issues of their own that prevent them from being here twenty-four seven, and human touch is more powerful than people realize. When preemies are held, they feel secure and loved, and it also helps them grow and recover from their physical problems."

My cheeks flush under everyone's gaze. *Get it together woman— they're looking at the baby, not you.*

Except for one man who is definitely looking at me. He's about a head taller than the others, and his tanned skin and coal-black hair starkly contrast with his amber eyes. The stubble protruding from his cheeks and chin masculinizes an otherwise too-perfect face. His body looks hard and athletic; broad shoulders taper to a trim waist and long defined legs.

I don't realize I'm staring until the man's eyes lock with mine a second time. I look away, embarrassed, and my heart starts to pound abnormally fast. See, this is the downside of being a twenty-nine-year-old virgin. I'm so starved of physical intimacy—physical anything really—that when a good-looking man walks into a room, I lose my mind a little.

The tour moves on and I breathe a sigh of relief, but every few minutes I feel the man's gaze on me. Is there something on my face? Dried baby spit perhaps? Formula, breast milk, boogers? The possibilities are endless, really.

I stay for another ten minutes until Antwon's mother shows up to nurse, then wave a quick goodbye to Delilah, who's still schmoozing with the benefactors, although the handsome guy is noticeably absent. Maybe he's with one of the nurses that had circled him earlier, like vultures sizing up their prey. A guy that good-looking probably has to fight off women everywhere he goes. I shake my head and smirk. His poor future wife; I pity her already.

The volunteer room is roughly the size of a janitor's closet, but large enough to house a few lockers and a small refrigerator. I grab my purse from the locker and scribble my name on the log-out sheet, then check the clock on the wall for the time. Something niggles at the back of my brain as I jot 10:22 AM, but I don't know why. I run down the list of things I have to do today besides getting ready for tonight's date, such as shop for groc—

My phone rings, and I instinctively know it's my mother because my intuition is sharp like that. The phone is hiding at the bottom of my purse, nestled between my fake Prada wallet and first aid kit and the screen flashes my older sister's phone number. So much for my intuition.

"Hello?" I press "Speaker" and start unbuttoning my volunteer jacket.

"Oh good, you're not dead."

My fingers stop moving and I squint at the phone. "Um . . . Was I supposed to be?"

"Of course not. I'm just wondering why you aren't here yet." There's a clattering sound in the background, like dishes being plopped into the sink. "You're normally a few minutes early and it's not like you to forget." A pause. "Did you forget?"

A bad feeling starts at the base of my spine and trickles up to my neck. I unzip the inside pocket of my purse and pull out my keys. "Forget?" I repeat, stalling.

"You promised last week that you'd take the boys to their swimming lesson this morning, remember? Well"—she puffs out a sigh—"clearly you don't."

Crap! "I'm such an idiot—I'm sorry," I apologize, grabbing my purse. "What time does it start, again? A quarter to eleven?" I open the door and burst into the hallway.

"No, don't worry about it," she says, sounding exhausted, and the baby starts to cry. "I'll see if Natan can take them. Or maybe Fraydie."

I turn the corner and shoulder my purse strap. Natan, Libby's husband, is at his weekly Torah learning study group, and as for our younger sister, Fraydie—well, she sleeps like the dead during the weekends, so that's not going to happen. Short of a zombie apocalypse, nothing could get her up before noon.

"No, I can still make it," I pant, dodging an orderly pushing a pregnant woman in a wheelchair. "Especially if I pretend that red lights are suggestions instead of the law—"

Oomph!

Pain. Everywhere.

I blink, trying to get my bearings, when a pair of hands grab onto my arms to steady me.

"Whoa," says a very deep, very male voice. "You alright?"

I tilt my head and gaze up, up, up into the face of the handsome man from the NICU. He's so ridiculously tall and broad shouldered and hard that I might as well have run into a brick wall. Or a tank.

Up close like this, he's even more outrageously handsome, the kind that should come with a warning label for causing asthma attacks. At the very least, he ought to carry a defibrillator around for those with weak hearts. Mine, it seems.

His eyes are a surprising medley of colors—amber, brown, green, and flecks of gold, and there's an intensity in them as they search my face. His lips are full and plump, with a slight indentation on his bottom lip, and there's a cleft in his chin that is swoon-worthy. He looks a lot like Paul Newman from the 1961 movie *The Hustler*.

He swallows and his Adam' apple jumps with the movement. He smells *amazing*, like a woodsy forest dotted with pine tress and a waterfall and Giorgio Armani cologne models lounging around shirtless, eating grapes. I want this scent in my car, in my apartment, on my clothes. I want to put him in my pocket and bring him everywhere I go, like my own personal human deodorizer—

"Are you dizzy?"

Even his voice is sexy. It's deep and confident and kind. His hands tighten around my arms, almost primal in their touch, and a small puff of air escapes my lips.

"When was the last time you had something to eat? You're very pale."

I blink and shake my head, feeling as though I'm waking up from a dream. "No, no. I'm fine. Sorry," I mumble, taking a step back in an attempt to break free.

The man's hands loosen their hold and then drop altogether. He looks like he's about to say something, but stops to consider; he seems like someone who weighs his words carefully.

"I'm totally fine. A hundred percent." I nod, as if to emphasize how completely normal it is for me to go around crashing into people. I resist the urge to facepalm since he's watching, but *oh my G-d. I should not be allowed in public.*

I give a little wave over my shoulder, then take two steps and nearly collide into an IV pole that was left in the hallway. "Whoops," I squeak, sending up a silent prayer that the man hadn't seen that.

Please, pleaaase let him not have seen that.

The man's deep voice carries across the hallway, and his rich, sexy baritone tickles the backs of my knees. "Are you sure you're okay?"

I hate my life.

I turn around and smile widely. "Never been better," I chirp, bringing my index finger and thumb together. Something warm unfurls in my chest at the concern on his face, but I stuff it back down before it has time to take hold. I allow myself one final glance—seriously, this man belongs on a calendar or a movie screen or a fertility clinic—stop it, Penina! Focus!

"Penina?" Libby says. "Are you still there?"

"Yes, sorry. I'll be there soon," I tell Libby, running toward the elevators. "Well, soon-ish."

"No, it's okay," she says, sounding distracted, and I can hear my nephews fighting. "I already texted Tatty, and he's on his way."

I stop running and pause to catch my breath. I had forgotten that our father's business trip had been canceled. "Oh, okay," I say, wiping sweat off my forehead. "I'm really sorry."

"Oh, stop," she says firmly. "It's my fault—I should've reminded you. Okay, listen, I've got to run, but call me later. I want to hear all about the date you had the other night."

I release a deep sigh that comes from the bottom of my soul. "Okay, talk to you soon."

As I make my way toward the parking ramp, I think about that horrible date. It's funny, in a way, the lengths people will go to for the people they love. My family wants nothing more than to see me happily married, even though I (mostly) gave up on that dream a long time ago—twelve years ago, to be exact. When the doctor said I'd never be able to have children because my uterus was too small, my whole worldview shattered. I expected marriage and babies as though it were my birthright. So much of my identity was centered on my future motherhood that when I was told at the age of seventeen that I would never have children, I felt devastated and more than a little angry. Not only did this mean I couldn't have children, but I also knew that no self-respecting Orthodox man would want to date me.

I unlock my car and climb inside. Yep. I called that one.

I take a left out of the parking ramp and head onto the main street. But that's in the past. I've got a job I love, friends and family that I'd give my left arm for, my fashion-influencer gig. My life is busy and full. What more could a girl want?

A pair of piercing amber eyes and strong hands steadying me flashes across my mind. The stubble grazing his cheeks and his lips—

No. Bad Penina. Do not go there. "I refuse to let you go there," I say aloud.

I turn on the radio and absently flip stations. Why am I still thinking about a nameless man I met for half a second? Sure, he was handsome and everything, but at the end of the day, he's just any other person you see once in your life, then never again.

And for some reason, that thought makes me absurdly sad.

CHAPTER THREE

*"You can use fashion to emulate what's happening in the world or
what you want to happen."*

—*Elisheva Rishon*

One week blends into another, until the memory of the good-looking
benefactor grows dim enough that I no longer find myself holding my
breath in the NICU or anywhere else in the hospital. And for all of Mrs.
Z's talk about this perfect Zevi guy, he never did end up contacting me,
so it appears there is a G-d after all.

I angle the mop against the kitchen counter, then lift the front of
my shirt to blot my sweaty face. I'm still not quite sure who's responsible
for turning the holiday of Passover into a miserable cleaning festival, but
I'd love an hour alone in a locked room with that guy. The only fun part
was the challenge of putting together an outfit for cleaning the house,
and I settled on a cute jean jumper with suspenders and a bandana in
my hair. For jewelry, I chose a locket necklace and charm bracelet. It's
Molly Ringwald from *The Breakfast Club* meets Eleven from season
three of *Stranger Things*.

"I can't find the ketchup," Maya says, poking through my refrigerator. "How do you expect me to eat pizza without ketchup?"

I invited Maya, my coworker and friend, over to eat the non-kosher-for-Passover food so it wouldn't go to waste, but I'm definitely having second thoughts.

"And why do you have one percent? That's fake milk," she complains. "I'm going to need a vat of chocolate syrup to get that down my piehole."

I wipe the sweat off my forehead, using the back of my sleeve. Maya is one of those freaks of nature who can eat whatever she wants and still look amazing. If she weren't my best friend, I'd hate her.

I pick up the mop and swish it inside the bucket of cleaner. "I'm a little busy here, if you haven't noticed."

"Why are you cleaning so much anyway? You're acting like the poster child for OCD."

"Because," I say through gritted teeth, "I have to get rid of all the *chametz*."

Maya shuts the refrigerator and pulls out a chair from the table. "That means 'bread,' right?"

"Food that has leavening agents."

"Leavening agents? You're so weird," she says, as though I'm the one who made these things up. Maya's mom is a Sephardi Jew, and her father is a Protestant from Sweden, which is how she ended up being a tall blonde with olive skin and dark brown eyes. And since she observes both Jewish and Christian holidays, she snags twice the number of presents every December.

Maya takes a bite of pizza and chews with her mouth open. "You know what your problem is? You need a cat." She holds up a hand to stop me from interrupting her. "Mr. Darcy died over a year ago. It's time to move on."

"I have moved on," I say, attacking a stain with my fingernail. "I bought a plant."

"Plants are not pets, hon. You need a warm, furry body that cuddles against your body and purrs. Someone who loves you unconditionally."

I shift so I'm resting on my haunches and rub the crick in my neck. So maybe I haven't moved on since burying Mr. Darcy, but it's not that simple. He was my everything—my sleep buddy, movie companion, entertainer, secret keeper, and even security guard at times. It would feel wrong to have that with another cat, and besides, I don't have it in me to bury another one. I get too attached, too emotional, and—

"Are you crying?" Maya asks, putting down her pizza crust. "I'm sorry, I didn't mean to upset you. I just think everyone should have a cat or dog or hamster. It keeps you distracted so you don't notice how lonely and miserable your life is."

What the hell? I narrow my eyes at her and say, "But I'm not lonely or miserable. I'm *happy*. Why is everyone so obsessed about me being single?" I wave the dirty rag in my hand and add, "I'm sick and tired of people treating me like I'm a disease that needs to be cured. You're single. Are you lonely and miserable?"

"Apples and oranges," she says, shaking her head. "My options aren't limited like yours."

"And Mr. Darcy isn't replaceable," I continue irritably, dipping the rag into the bucket of sudsy water. "He was the finest, most majestic cat that ever walked the face of the earth."

Maya stops chewing. "He peed on my shoes and used my body as a scratching post."

"Did you know that Joe's son is coming to town?" I say, swiftly changing topics. "Joe said he can hardly remember the last time he came in for a visit."

Maya's eyes immediately brighten. "The hottie with the angry eagle upper arm tattoo?"

I squeegee the mop and reply, "No idea. Also, creepy." There are a couple of family pictures framed in Joe's office, but apparently Maya studied them a lot closer than I did. The intercom buzzes, startling both of us.

"Are you expecting someone?" Maya asks.

"No." I put aside the mop and press the intercom button. "Hello?"

"Hi. It's me."

I wrinkle my eyebrows in concern. Usually Libby gives me a heads-up before dropping by, just to make sure I'm home. Maybe she was nearby. "Come on through, Lib," I say, pushing the buzzer to let her in,

"Which sister is she again?" Maya asks. "The one that's married to the Russian dude?"

"Israeli," I say over my shoulder, heading to the front door to unlock it. It took some time getting used to my brother-in-law, Natan, and his inherent "Israeliness," specifically the way he lets everyone know exactly what he's thinking the moment he's thinking it. Just the other day he said to me, "Penina, why you wear such ugly hat? You scare the men like this, no?" He is, however, a very devoted husband and father, and funny too (when he's not making fun of my fashion choices).

"Is she here to eat or to clean?" Maya asks, reaching for a napkin from the holder. "Because I'm eating just fine on my own."

I glance over my shoulder as I wet a paper towel under the kitchen faucet. "I see that," I snort.

My apartment door creaks open, and I call out, "Hey, Libby, we're in here. Come in and keep us company. I'm slaving away here while Maya is doing absol—" I stop suddenly, catching sight of Libby's face. Her eyes are red and watery, her lashes dripping with tears. I shut off the faucet, my heart galloping in fear. "What's wrong? What happened?"

She shakes her head. "Sorry, I should have called. I didn't realize you had . . ." She lifts a hand toward Maya, and it doesn't escape my notice that her hand is trembling.

"Is someone hurt?" I ask, swallowing back a lump of fear.

She shakes her head and gives a limp smile. "You and Ma are always so paranoid."

My heart slowly, *slowly* returns to its normal pace. My sister's right, but show me a Jewish woman who doesn't start her day expecting a cataclysmic tragedy, and I'll show you a convert. Seriously, the first thing we do every morning is say a prayer of thanks that we didn't die in our sleep, so it's only natural that by the afternoon we're on high alert.

Maya stands up and brushes the crumbs off her pants, so I'll definitely be recleaning that section. Wonderful.

"I just remembered I have somewhere to be," Maya says, displaying a surprising amount of tact. "Mind if I take some of these snacks with me?"

"Not at all," I reply with a smile, hoping to convey that I appreciate her timely exit. "Let me grab some bags." I hurriedly pack up the rest of the *chametz*, thank Maya for her "help," then return to the kitchen to make some coffee.

As I wait for the water to heat up, I observe Libby as she shrugs off her sweater and arranges it over the back of the chair. Her hands shake slightly resting on top of the table, and then she clasps them together as if to stop the trembling. Her beautiful diamond ring glistens under the fluorescent lighting, and I think of the phrase *"Diamonds are a girl's best friend."*

But as much as I love diamonds, it's Libby who's my best friend. We've always been inseparable. Perhaps it was because we were born so close in age, only twelve months apart (although as kids, Libby often reminded me that she was born first). Despite her "firstborn right to boss me around," attitude, she'd been my constant companion and playmate, and she had a way of convincing me that I was stronger than I gave myself credit for.

She was the one who helped me learn to ride a bike and taught me to swim when I was afraid to go underwater, and she was the one who yelled at my friend for making fun of the fact that I sucked at math, specifically anything that had to do with arrival times of trains labeled "A" and "B." Isn't that what Siri was invented for?

When we got older, we experimented with makeup, giggled about boys, and snuck into R-rated movies. She was in the passenger seat when I rear-ended the neighbor's car, then came with me to apologize despite my best efforts to convince her that we should do a hit-and-run.

She didn't have to do any of those things, but she did anyway, and I loved her all the more for it. Libby has always been there for me, and now it's my turn to be there for her.

"How bad are we talking?" I ask gingerly, adding creamer and two teaspoons of sugar to her coffee, the way she likes it.

"I don't want Ma or Tatty to know," she says, smoothly evading my question.

Pretty bad, then. It's never a good sign when Libby wants to keep something from them. They're as supportive as parents can be, but they also worry like crazy.

"I won't say anything." I swallow, thinking back to all the times my sisters have confided in me, the most recent one being when Fraydie caused my parents' microwave to explode. And for the record, that did not end well for either one of us.

"So," I say, nudging when she doesn't continue talking. "What is it?"

"We're going to lose our house," she says in one quick breath, fingers clenched around her untouched mug.

"What?" I feel poleaxed and for a moment can't think of anything to say. In the eight years Natan and Libby have been married, he's gone through several jobs and career changes, but I thought he had finally found his niche with this latest project, a pet spa and hotel, complete with a masseuse and indoor pool. Obviously, I was wrong. "What happened?"

Her shoulders drop in defeat, and the dark circles under her eyes imply she hasn't slept in days. I knew her nights were hard, but I put it down to the baby getting her molars in. A pang of guilt hits me square in the chest. I should've paid closer attention. I should've noticed that something wasn't right.

"I don't really know," she confesses. "He doesn't like talking about it. I mean, he did in the beginning. Remember how excited he was?"

I nod warily. Natan's only consistency in life seems to be his inconsistencies, in the form of project after project, all of which required lots of seed money that eventually disappeared into some black hole of doom, never again to be recouped. I don't know if he's truly been unlucky or simply made poor choices, but it's becoming painfully clear that his entrepreneur days are fast coming to an end. Funny how he can be so successful in one area of life, as a loving husband and father, yet fail miserably in another.

"I told him he had to stop borrowing money from people, so he used our house as collateral instead." She glances down, embarrassed. "I was scared to say no, and he was so convinced this would work."

I swallow, still trying to wrap my head around this. "What are you going to do?"

"I honestly don't know." She threads her fingers through her curly hair and frowns.

"Bankruptcy isn't an option because we still wouldn't have money to pay our mortgage."

My chest grows tight and it gets harder to breathe. *Don't panic*, I order myself. There has to be a solution . . . it just hasn't come to us yet.

She takes a deep, shaky breath before continuing. "I love him, Penina, I do, but . . . I can't take the constant stress," her voice cracks as she breaks into tears, covering her face with her hands. "I love my house."

Just the thought of them losing it causes my throat to thicken. That house is more than just bricks and mortar—for Libby and Natan and the kids, it's a treasure chest full of memories. It's the place where Natan and the boys spent an entire summer building, then destroying, then rebuilding a treehouse in the backyard. It's the place where Libby defied everyone's advice by painting a mural across the breadth of the nursery wall, then dared anyone to call it ugly in her presence. It's the place where the boys collided heads wrestling on the kitchen floor, only to have the neighbor's Newfoundland jump on top of them. It's where countless birthday parties, anniversary celebrations, and family dinners took place.

"Shh, shh, everything is going to be okay," I say, getting up from my chair to hug her. My stomach tightens, and I feel a surge of anger at Natan for putting her in this position. "Don't worry. There's got to be a solution," I say reassuringly, though I have no idea what. At the moment, hiring a hitman to take Natan out seems like a good start, but then I remember how costly they are. Besides, I've seen enough movies to know that hitmen always rat on the people who hire them, if they get caught. It's like there's no code of ethics with these guys.

I hesitate, then say, "Are you sure you don't want to tell Ma and—"

"No," she says firmly, shaking her head. "It's not fair to put them under more strain, financial or otherwise."

"Okay." I bite my bottom lip. "How much time do you have left before it goes into foreclosure?"

"Three months." She sniffs, grabbing a napkin and dabbing at the corners of her eyes.

"How much money would it take to save it?"

She rubs her eyes. "Natan said he'll figure something out, which probably means it's so much he doesn't want me to know. He'd sooner die than admit it, but I think he feels he's less of a man because of this."

I just manage to hold myself back from agreeing with that sentiment when her phone suddenly buzzes from the kitchen table. "It's Natan." She frowns. "I should answer. He's worried about me."

"Go for it." I pat her shoulder and head to the other room, to give her privacy. I slouch onto my favorite armchair that I got for a steal off Craig's List and type the words *Foreclosure laws in Minnesota* into Google's search engine. I catch snippets of conversation (hey, it's not my fault that I have freakishly good hearing), but it's mostly a lot of sighing and "I know" and "Yeah" except for one notable "He ate *what?*"

She hangs up soon afterward and rushes out of the kitchen, throwing on her sweater. "I have to run. Natan found Binyamin eating dog kibble. Thanks for letting me cry all over you," she says, holding her arms out for a hug. "You're the best."

I squeeze her tightly, inhaling her trademark perfume that smells like lilies and watermelon. "I wish I knew how to fix this."

"I know you do." She takes a step back, and her arms fall to her sides. Her normally infectious smile seems forced and her pretty brown eyes lack their customary luster. "But some things are too broken to be fixed."

After one last quick hug, she hurries out the door, leaving me to wonder if she was referring to her house or her marriage.

CHAPTER FOUR

"True beauty in a woman is reflected in her soul."
—*Audrey Hepburn*

I open the break room's refrigerator, toss in my lunch, then head to the coffee machine to get some caffeine into my system. Three months isn't a lot of time to come up with a solution to save Libby's house, and I tossed and turned all last night thinking about it. Losing it is *not* an option. I'll chain myself to the floorboards and swallow the key if I have to.

I rub my eyes and blink at the Styrofoam cup in my hand. For as long as I can remember, I've been my family's go-to person for every crisis, big and small. My father's great, but he works long hours as an accountant, and my mother can only handle stress in minute dosages. So when my grandfather had a stroke a few years ago, I was the one that cooked kosher meals and visited with him every day, and when Libby had postpartum depression, I babysat so she could catch up on sleep and get therapy. And when my younger sister, Fraydie, went ballistic because her school project got destroyed the day before the science fair, my fingers were the ones covered in superglue trying to mend it.

I take a sip of coffee and shudder. Is it possible that the coffee here is getting worse, or is it just my imagination?

"Penina!"

So much for my break. I drain the rest of the coffee down the sink, telling myself for the umpteenth time to stop worrying, but it's no use. Once my brain gets stuck on a bad thought, it grabs onto it like Velcro and refuses to let go. Which would be fine if it led to a solution, but all it's done so far is replay the worst-case scenario over and over again in my head.

"Joe is doing this to spite us." Gina, the store manager, punches the code into the store's stainless steel safe. The vault door swings open, revealing millions of dollars' worth of jewelry. Cultured pearls, precious gemstones, and diamonds of varying cuts and clarity shimmer against the backdrop of black velvet trays.

"Doing what?" I ask, confused. Gina often begins a conversation as though we're already in the middle of one, and it's disorienting at the best of times, but currently I'm only running on three hours of sleep, if that.

"Cancer." A frown tightens her lips as she hands me a tray. "Mark my words, Penina, Joe Kleinfeld is dying to spite us all."

The scary part is that she isn't joking. Gina's paranoia supersedes all logic. She assumes everyone's out to get her, from the skateboarding teenagers in her neighborhood to the hearing-impaired bagger at the grocery store. In the past, I've tried to—as casually as possible, of course—ask whether she had any head injuries as a child, but she insists nothing like that happened. The closest she came was when she broke her femur during an ice-skating birthday party.

"The thing about cancer," I say, accepting the second tray of jewelry extended toward me, "is that it just happens to you. You can't get it to teach people a lesson."

"Oh, you naive child. Cancer is science and if anyone could manage it, it's Joe." Gina's lips compress into a thin line while passing a third tray to me before balancing two of her own. "He knows this store will fold the moment his son takes over. And with the way the jewelry industry is nowadays, with everyone buying online, it's a recipe for disaster. Joe always had it out for me, and now he's going to die so we can all lose our jobs."

I follow her to the showroom, carefully balancing the trays of jewelry and doing my best not to trip over my three-inch-heel Stella

McCartney knock-offs. My hot-pink flower dress is on the long side, which doesn't help either, but it's cute, so I figure it's worth the risk of falling and breaking my neck.

I think back to the tidbits Joe had shared about his son. "Isn't his son a really successful business mogul?"

"*Please.*" Sixty-something-year-old Gina rolls her eyes like an irate teenager. "Being a financial analyst for a Fortune 500 company hardly qualifies him to take over this store. If Joe was smart, he'd have asked me to take over. But no," she continues, jabbing a key into the display cabinet's keyhole with unnecessary force, "he chooses his playboy son instead, who wouldn't know a Painite if it hit him between the eyes."

Interesting. Joe never referred to his son as a playboy, but then, what father would? "Mmm," I say, which is my standard reply when I don't have an opinion but don't want to endorse someone else's.

I'm arranging a three-strand pearl necklace inside a display case when a pair of headlights flash into the store.

"Late. Again," Gina mutters, glowering toward the window overlooking the store's parking lot. Maya's bright red BMW coupe comes to a stop, and she emerges from the car, swinging her blond hair over her shoulder like there's a hidden camera crew filming a shampoo commercial. According to Maya, she had come *this close* (her forefinger almost touching her thumb) to becoming the next hottest thing in Hollywood, but the bastards in charge are blind and deaf when it comes to true talent.

Gina unlocks the front door and pushes it open. "What's your excuse this time?"

"I hate to say this, Gina," Maya says, breezing through the entryway and pushing her sunglasses to the top of her head. "But you only have yourself to blame. If you hadn't bitten my head off for coming in late on Friday, then I wouldn't have had such trouble falling asleep last night. I only got three hours—if that—which is why I slept through my alarm this morning." She glances my way and gives me a discreet wink before turning back to Gina.

I dip my head and smile. One of Maya's best qualities is the way she can ignore her haters. Gina, of course, being at the top of that list.

Gina mutters something about disrespect and millennials, then leaves us to do her own thing, which to my knowledge involves drinking copious amounts of coffee and gossiping over the phone with her friend.

"She should try doing reverse psychology next time," Maya says. "She might get better results."

"*Might* being the operative word here." I smirk. "How was the rest of your Sunday?" I ask as we make our way toward the safe.

"Awesome! I met the most amazing man." She points a red fingernail toward a large tray of jewelry, and her gold bangles slide down her arm. "Give me the heavy one. I'm trying to tone my biceps."

I pass her the weighty tray, then grab a lighter one for myself. "Tell me more about Mr. Amazing."

She breaks into a wide smile that reaches her chestnut eyes. "I met him at the gym. He's gorgeous and sweet—sensitive but macho, you know? Plus, he has a normal job with health insurance. A real grownup, unlike Cam," she says, referring to her ex, who spends the majority of his time playing video games and smoking weed in his parents' basement. "The only problem is"—she pauses, sucking on her bottom lip—"I'm not exactly sure if he's single."

Maya reminds me of Scarlett Johansson—a bubbly, beautiful blonde, although she never stays too long with the same man. We march down the hallway, and I glance at her over my shoulder. "Can't you just ask him?"

She looks at me like I'm nuts. "Why don't I just throw myself at his feet and beg to carry his babies with a big ol' "Desperate" sign plastered to my chest?"

"So . . . that's a no?"

"That's a hell to the no," she confirms. "Nothing scares away a guy faster than letting him know you're interested."

It seems counterproductive, but what do I know? I'm hardly an expert on the nuances and mind games of secular dating. In my community, you're set up by a matchmaker once both sets of parents agree to the match, at which point you meet the other person with the express purpose of dating for marriage. "Meet-cutes" happen from time to time, but the intention to marry is still there.

"Why is that, anyway?" I ask, transferring the jewelry onto a display pedestal.

"Honey, if I knew the answer to that, I could have had three husbands by now," Maya says, arranging a row of diamond tennis bracelets across a velvet pillow.

"Have you tried googling him?"

She shakes her head. "I don't know his name, and I didn't want to freak him out by asking. I mean, I just met him for the first time yesterday, and Caroline says I give off an intense energy, and it scares guys."

"Who's Caroline again?" I mentally run through the list of people Maya has told me about, but don't recall that name. "Is that your cousin from New York?"

"No, that's Carrie." She reaches for a sapphire bracelet, then clears her throat. "Caroline is my psychic."

"What?" I laugh, looking up at her to gauge whether she is being serious. It's sometimes hard to tell with her. "You're not serious."

"The woman is a friggin' *genius*," Maya says defensively. "All I had to do was tell her my name, spread my legs open, and she literally knew everything about me."

I blink, unsure that I've heard correctly. "Spread your legs open?"

"Not like *giving birth* open," she explains with a wave of her hand. "Just open enough so she could read my aura. It's hard to read someone when their legs are closed, you know?" She reaches for another piece of jewelry. "Anyway, it's better to just be in the friend zone for a while. Then the information comes out naturally. And if he does have someone," she shrugs, "no harm done, but if he doesn't, then I can move on to phase two."

I grab a roll of paper towels and a bottle of glass cleaner. "Asking him out?"

"Phase two," Maya says, lifting a finger, "is figuring out whether he's straight or not. You can't move on to the other phases before figuring out that one."

I raise my eyebrows. "How many phases are there?"

"Eight, according to Caroline."

"Eight?" I roll up my sleeves and squirt some glass cleaner onto the display cabinet. "Secular dating takes too much work. People should just . . . I don't know"—I gesticulate with the soggy towel—"wear their information on a sticky tag attached to their shirts. It would save everyone a lot of time and heartache."

Maya moves to the next display case and unlocks the door. "Spoken like a true Leo."

My eyes roll of their own volition. Maya takes zodiac signs as seriously as a religious zealot, the horoscope being her bible.

"Five more minutes till opening," Gina shouts from her office.

I glance out the window and see a Porsche convertible turn into a parking spot. Gina's footsteps echo across the tile floor before coming to a stop in front of the mahogany doors.

"Want to do rock paper scissors for this guy?" Maya asks, dipping her head in the direction of the Porsche. Once in a while we'll play a round of that to vie for a customer since this is a commission-based business.

"Nah, you can have him," I say, collecting the empty trays. Maya needs the high-end customers to feed her high-end boutique habit (especially after the recent devastation of her parents cutting off her allowance), whereas I'm perfectly content getting my clothes from secondhand or resale stores. I like the challenge of putting together a modest, fashion-forward outfit while keeping to a budget because that's what my blog is all about.

"That won't be necessary," Gina says, walking into the showroom. She moves to the storefront window and squints through the glass. "It's Joe's son." She nods, turning around to face us. "The one taking over the business."

"Wait—*what*?" Maya's eyes go round with shock. "What happened to Joe?"

"Cancer." Then I add with a head tilt, "Some say it was intentional."

Maya looks confused. "What was?"

"The cancer," I reply.

Maya waits until Gina isn't looking, then makes a circling motion with her finger next to her head. "Wait, doesn't the son live in New York?"

"I guess not anymore," I say, glancing at the clock. The store is supposed to open soon, and we still haven't finished unloading the trays. I try to work twice as fast since it's clear that Gina's and Maya's attention is more focused on the new owner making his way inside than getting the showroom ready.

The door opens, and a large gust of wind blows inside. "Welcome Sam," Gina purrs, stepping back. "Come in and I'll introduce you to the staff."

I choke back a laugh as I turn around—the "staff" being Maya and myself. This should take all of thirty seconds.

A tall, handsome man with broad shoulders and tan skin glances around, every gesture and look exuding an easy confidence. He's huge and gorgeous, and when I get a better look at his profile, my heart stops.

Oh my G-d. It's him. The wall that I had crashed into. Benefactor guy. I blink a few times to make sure my eyes are working while my body continues to have a mini heart attack.

This is *not* okay. It's downright unnatural. He's supposed to be the sexy, mysterious stranger that I had made peace about never seeing again. *Except now he's here* and *he's my new boss? That's just . . . messed up.* I glance up at the ceiling and send a telepathic message to G-d, letting him know that this isn't funny and to wake me up from this nightmare. Immediately.

"I think I'm in love," Maya whispers, sucking in a deep breath. "I want to marry that man and have his babies. I want to buy a house with a white picket fence and get a golden doodle. I want to wipe his brow when he's sick and give him sponge baths."

Apparently, I'm not the only female affected by him. I rub my temples and start to pace. This is going to be *so* awkward. Like the mothership of all awkward. Except . . . is it possible that he won't remember me? Maybe he meets so many people as a benefactor/hot guy that his brain can't catalog all of them.

They're coming over. *Oh G-d, I feel sick.*

"These are our sales associates, Maya and Penina," Gina says, leading him toward us. "Ladies, this is Joe's son, Sam."

My breath catches in my throat. Sam. His name is Sam.

I can tell the moment he recognizes me because he does a double take, and his mouth opens slightly. For a moment, he simply stands there staring at me while I pretend to be fascinated by the three-strand pearl necklace across the room.

"So nice to meet you," Maya says, stepping forward to shake his hand. She's in a low-cut sweater that showcases her ample cleavage, paired with tight pants and alligator pumps. If she's serious about having his babies, she couldn't have worn a better outfit to get a head start. "If you have any questions or need anything at all"—she pauses and bats her eyes meaningfully, probably envisioning giving him a sponge bath—"please don't hesitate to ask."

"Thanks," he murmurs, and to his credit, doesn't glance down at her chest, even though it's practically jumping up and down, screaming for attention. Then he turns and takes a step toward me. "I didn't catch your name." His eyes connect with mine, and the air in the room turns stuffy, as though the oxygen had been replaced with a thick blanket, making it difficult to breathe. Blood pounds through my veins, and I have to lean against the display counter as a wave of dizziness hits me like a tsunami (and trust me when I say that fainting isn't cute in real life the way it is in the movies). I take a deep breath and try to imagine how he'd look several decades from now, bald and pot-bellied and stooped over. Except it isn't working. My normally strong imagination is scoffing at the very idea that Sam would be anything other than an older version of himself, still managing to cause heart attacks among all the little old ladies in the nursing home.

"Penina," I say, then clear my throat because my voice is unaccountably hoarse. On the bright side, though, I'm still fully conscious. So, that's a win.

"Penina," he repeats. "Is that Hebrew?"

Crap, is he expecting a dialogue? I've stayed upright and told him my name, which is pretty impressive, given the shock. I see no reason to push my luck here. "Yes, it means 'precious stone' or 'pearl.'" I should quit while I'm ahead, but a part of me can't resist adding, "Fitting for the job, right?"

"It's perfect," he says quietly, in a way that makes me think he wasn't just talking about the connection between my job and my name. Which is completely absurd and most definitely in my head since he doesn't even know me.

He extends his hand toward me, and I stare at it in panic because I'm not supposed to touch men. Especially not men that look like sin on a stick (okay, I made that part up, but you know what I mean). Handshakes, though, are kind of a gray area, especially if someone is at work, and I've shaken hands with lots of men before, just never with *him*.

Stop being a weirdo and just do it! It's a quick skin-to-skin moment that is completely devoid of all sexual intent, the very definition of asexual. *Totally* innocent. Platonic with a capital "P." Just get in there and get it done—don't overthink it.

I exhale a breath and throw my hand into his a little more violently than what I'm sure is considered normal. Luckily, he's strong and easily grasps it firmly within his, his fingers curling over mine. A current so powerful and electric that it's almost painful charges up and down my body, and I look up at him, wondering if he feels it too.

Stop being crazy, Penina. This is your new boss, not Prince Charming, the Fifty Shades *version, here to save you from the clutches of your evil stepmother* (although Gina would make a great villain, and I wouldn't put it past her to trap me in an attic if my chores weren't completed in time). I gaze down at our intertwined hands, noting how his is about twice as large and much warmer, practically a mini heat generator. And according to Maya, the size of a man's hand is indicative of the size of—

I blush and start to sweat. Shouldn't he have let go of my hand by now? How many seconds is considered normal for a handshake, and why don't I know this information? I tentatively pull back, but he's got quite the grip.

"I believe we've met before," he says with a slight arch of one eyebrow. He's so close that I can see each individual stubble on his five o'clock shadow, and he's even more handsome than I remember. There's something about the way he looks at you that makes you feel like you're the only person in the room. Possibly the only person in the universe.

"Really?" I say, pretending not to remember. I don't know why I'm lying—maybe it's a survival strategy? Or maybe I'm not getting enough oxygen to my brain to make good life choices? "I don't know. I probably just have one of those faces."

"No, it was definitely you. I remember because you were talking about having a threesome with a sex doll while holding a baby in the NICU."

Gina and Maya gasp, and I quickly say, "No, it wasn't like that. I mean, it was, but *I* wasn't the one who had the threesome—it was a nurse. But it wasn't a real threesome—"

"Glad your memory came back," Sam says, and that's when I realize I had walked right into his trap.

"The NICU?" Maya says, confused. "What were you doing there?"

"How is it considered a threesome if the third person isn't even real?" Gina says to me, as though I'm the expert on this topic.

"Why were you in the NICU?" Maya repeats, looking at me like I'm a stranger.

"Just, you know . . . passing through." I cough. My volunteer work isn't exactly a secret, but all things being equal, I'd rather no one find out that I hold babies in my spare time to fill up the gaping hole in my heart. Even *I* think that sounds pathetic, even though it isn't (maybe a little). Sam stares at me curiously, but doesn't contradict me.

"Passing through," Maya repeats, tilting her head. I remember too late that she once told me that I was the worst liar she'd ever seen. "Do you do that often? Don't they have security to handle people like you?"

I realize that Sam is still holding my hand, and when we make eye contact again, he quickly drops it, as though it's about to burst into flames, and takes a few steps back. My hand still tingles from his touch, and I clasp it in my other hand, trying to shake off the unfamiliar feeling coursing through my body. *Damn you, pheromones!*

"I'm not sure," I say, blanching at the lies that keep coming out of my mouth. The NICU ward, in fact, has lots of security in place to prevent kidnappings. Even I, who have been cleared and had my background checked, am unable to get into the actual nursery until a nurse visually checks through the glass window to make sure it's me instead of someone masquerading as me.

"Penina, when did this alternative lifestyle start?" Gina asks. "I never, *never* would've thought that you of all people—"

"And your dad?" I blurt, turning to Sam, before Maya or Gina can ask more probing questions. "How's his cancer going?" I say, then immediately cringe. OMG, I can't believe I just did that—*how's his cancer going?* As if I was asking whether his golf swing was improving or something. *G-d.* If I could only go back in time and redo the last five minutes, I'd tell myself to go ahead and faint.

"He's doing really well, according to the doctor," Sam replies smoothly. "He's probably going to outlive us all."

Gina emits a falsetto laugh and slaps her hands together. "Well, isn't that just the most *wonderful* news!"

I briefly frown at Gina, then turn back to Sam and say, "That's awesome," and Maya raises a fist and shouts, *"Yesss!"* And unlike Gina, we actually mean it.

"Cancer can be tricky, though," Gina muses, looking thoughtful. "You never know when things can . . . *change*. I'll keep him in my prayers." I cringe. That can't be a good thing. I wouldn't put it past her not to pray for his recovery and to wish instead for delayed torture. "And take as much time as you need to be with him," she continues. "The store pretty much runs itself at this point."

I try not to snort, but fail, and Sam briefly glances at me. "Thank you. I'll keep that in mind."

Gina nods, satisfied. "Let's go, ladies," she says, clapping her hands like a cheerleading captain pumping up her squad. "There's work to be done."

"Nice meeting you, Maya," Sam says with a tilt of his head, then turns to me. "And nice to formally meet you, Penina." He hesitates, then adds, "I have a meeting at the hospital later this week. Maybe I'll see you there . . . if you happen to be passing through."

He grins as my face radiates heat, and two things become instantly clear: First, Sam has a sadistic sense of humor, and second, he isn't afraid to use it.

Lucky, lucky me.

CHAPTER FIVE

"Care for your clothes like the good friends they are."
—*Joan Crawford*

It's the first night of Passover, and my parents' dining room looks picture-perfect. Everything gleams and sparkles, from the crystal chandelier and candlesticks to the myriad of sterling silver kiddush cups with their matching plates. My great-great-grandmother's tablecloth, an old-fashioned, off-white curlicue design, is one of the few items that came from her childhood home in Lithuania, and every time I set the table with it, I imagine how proud she'd be knowing it's still being used.

Despite all the cleaning and cooking that comes with preparing for this holiday, it's always been my favorite one to celebrate. It's the one time of year that my extended family members get together, some of them coming from as far away as Israel or the not as distant Tri-state area to observe the eight-day festival.

And best of all, it's an opportunity to dress up. I view that as a good thing, although most every other woman I know vehemently disagrees. How someone doesn't enjoy wearing a fancy dress and high heels along with jewelry and smoky eyeshadow is beyond me. My mother says I'm an aberration of nature every time I wobble into a room wearing sky-high stilettos. She likes to remind me of all the possible ways I'm causing permanent damage to my feet—unless she happens to need something from one of the tall shelves in the kitchen or pantry, in which case, she's all smiles and grace.

Tonight, I'm in a mauve wrap dress with rose gold earrings, and my hair is held back on one side by two golden leaf clips. I kept my makeup on the simple side except for my lips, which are painted a deep, vibrant red, and my shoes are cappuccino-colored suede pumps. It's *Breakfast at Tiffany's* meets The Frock NYC meets Margarite Bloom.

I gaze around my parent's table and smile at the hodgepodge of relatives, from the very young to the quite old, plus a few nonfamily members that my mother had convinced to join us. My mother, bless her heart, isn't content unless she has a few non-Orthodox Jews at our table for every Shabbos and holiday meal. Our particular branch of Judaism believes that every time a Jew fulfills a commandment, no matter how trivial it may seem, that person's soul becomes closer to its Creator—even something as small as saying "Amen" to a blessing. And because it's also a commandment to be extra kind to widows, orphans, and poor people, my mother isn't happy unless we have some of those too.

"You want more wine?" Natan turns to Libby, gesturing to her favorite cabernet. He's always been an attentive husband, but tonight he's even more solicitous than usual, though it doesn't take a genius to figure out why. "Come, give me your cup."

"I can pour for myself," Libby replies tightly. "Thank you," she adds as an afterthought, as though she doesn't want to appear rude, just slightly miffed.

Natan's face falls ever so slightly as he passes her the wine. My heart breaks watching these two—I have a hard time staying mad at anyone for very long, but I'm lazy like that. Libby, on the other hand, can go a while before she breaks.

I think back to the only time our parents grounded us. Libby's friend convinced a group of us to break into the Orthodox boy's high school and do some light vandalism, which involved copious amounts of shaving cream and honey (it was *hilarious* and totally worth getting grounded). But Libby didn't agree. She was so upset about being grounded that she refused to talk to our parents for two weeks straight. I agreed to do the same, but only lasted about ten minutes before breaking down and asking my mother what was for dinner.

I'm still irritated of course that Natan landed them in this situation, but after the initial wave of fury (where I may or may not have googled the price of hiring a hitman) passed, I'm focused on trying to find a solution, both for their house and their marriage.

"How are your parents, Natan?" I ask, attempting to fix the tense silence at our end of the table. "Is your dad doing better? He had a knee replacement, right?"

Natan's soulful dark eyes glance in Libby's direction for just a moment. "Yes, he much better. My mother doing a lot of work that he normally does, and now she says she needs knee surgery, but I—"

"Please pass the saltwater, Penina," Libby interjects loudly.

I catch the hurt look on Natan's face and he glances down at his plate, like a scolded puppy. I sigh and hand her the bowl. "What were you saying Natan?"

"Nothing," he mutters, shaking his head. "Not important."

"Neither is losing our house, apparently," Libby murmurs under her breath, stabbing her boiled egg into the saltwater.

I kick her under the table, but accidentally end up hurting the Russian widow beside her instead. "I'm so sorry—I meant to kick my sister," I say, then recall that her English is even worse than my Hebrew, so I point to Libby and say, *"Cyka."* My Russian vocabulary is limited to curse words since I was taught by a nine-year-old, so "bitch" is the closest thing to "it was her fault." Unfortunately, both the widow and Libby gaze at me like I've lost my mind.

"I'm hungry," Asher, my six-year-old nephew pipes up from his seat further down the table. "When does the real food come out?"

A college student that my mother had met in the grocery store, as he stood confused by the boxed matzo ball soup packages, glances up from his Haggadah, the storybook of the Exodus. "Oh, so this isn't the whole meal?" he says, clearly relieved.

My mother laughs. "No, I'm not sending you home with only matzah and lettuce in your stomach. We'll eat right after we're done with the story part."

The college student visibly brightens. "Great! Not that there's anything wrong with only matzah and lettuce," he quickly adds. "I'm full just from eating this."

My mother smiles while my uncle from New Jersey, who's infamous both for his sarcasm and for trying to speed the seder up, says, "Don't worry. We've got at least three hours to go before the meal is served. Plenty of time to work up an appetite."

"You're scaring him," my mother says.

"Nah," the college student says, chuckling. "I know a joke when I hear one."

My entire family laughs, knowing full well that it will be *at least* two hours before the meal. What can I say? To be a Jew is to suffer.

"It goes by fast," my father says, patting the confused young man's shoulder.

"Still hungrrrrry," Asher reminds everyone.

"Come with me, *yingelehs*." My mother stands up from the table and motions to the boys. "I'll get you something to eat."

As my father instructs everyone to break their middle matzah, I stand up from the table and follow my mother into the kitchen. My nephews are adorable, but definitely a handful, and my mother never realizes she's overdoing it until her back goes out or her arthritis gets worse.

"Who wants meatballs?" she asks, ladling some onto a plate.

"Me, me!" the boys shout, jumping up and down.

"It's okay, Ma—I got this," I say, taking the oven mitts out of her hands. "Go sit down and relax. I'll take care of the kids."

"You sure?" She's a whirlwind of motion, pulling bowls from the cupboard, stirring the pot of chicken soup, running utensils under the sink.

"Positive," I reply, taking the bowls from her.

"How's everyone doing?" she asks, giving me a warning look. By "everyone" I'm assuming she means Libby and Natan, who she knows are sitting near me. My mother is one of those people who can tell how a person is feeling just by looking at them, although to be fair, Libby was never that great at concealing her emotions. Same as me—must be one of those genetic abnormalities.

"Eh. So-so," I reply, pulling out a tray of hot dogs. "I'm a little concerned. Here, boys, give me your plates."

My mother ends up staying to help, even though I tried my best to shoo her away. After the boys leave the kitchen, carrying plates laden with food, she covers everything up and puts it back in the oven to keep it warm for the adults.

"You're supposed to be relaxing and entertaining your guests," I say, grabbing the last few dishes before she can. "I know my way around your kitchen."

"I know, I know," she says, shutting the refrigerator. "I just can't help myself. By the way," she says, glancing around, then lowering her voice, "do you know why Libby is upset?"

I rub the back of my neck and try to figure out how to respond. I don't want to lie, but I also don't want to betray Libby's confidence. A big part of me—okay, fine, *all* of me—is dying to unload this onto her. It's not easy to carry the responsibility of this burden alone. "Do you?"

She shakes her head, wrapping tin foil over an aluminum pan. "It's probably nothing. Maybe the baby's been keeping her up at night."

My mother has always been of the opinion that a good night's sleep is all that separates rational people from those that are institutionalized, and while I agree that sleep is important, I don't think it's the end-all to problems. Especially not in this case. "No, I think she sleeps through the night now," I say, folding down a corner of aluminum covering the brownies. "Maybe you could try talking to her," I suggest, leading the witness.

My mother ladles chicken soup into a bowl, then hands it to me. "I'll try. Here, give this to Savtah," she says, referring to my father's mother.

I place the soup in front of my grandmother and pull up a chair to feed her. Between her Parkinson's and hearing issues, she needs a lot of assistance with self-care.

When I next glance at Libby and Natan, I'm relieved to see that Libby is trying not to smile as Natan whispers something in her ear.

"Does it taste good, Savtah?" I ask, dabbing the corners of her mouth with a napkin.

"What?"

"Does it taste good?" I repeat loudly.

Her eyes run over my face. "Cause a paste hood? What on earth?"

I gaze helplessly at my grandfather, who fortunately still has his hearing and marbles (but unfortunately for the inhabitants of Minneapolis, also a current driver's license). "Just nod and smile, at her Peninaleh," he says.

I follow his advice, and my grandmother continues eating in relative contentment. Sometimes I wonder if she's putting us on and can, in fact, hear perfectly fine. I wouldn't blame her if she did—I actually think it's a pretty brilliant way to stay out of drama. As soon as I turn eighty, I'm going to make sure that I'll have hearing issues and some walking issues too. Man, I can't wait to use one of those scooters with an attached basket. I've been eying those babies for years now.

But in the meantime, my hearing and balance are perfect, which means I'm in for lots and lots of drama.

*　*　*

Two days later, I'm driving to work, trying my best to see as sheets of pouring rain slam against my windshield. It's a slow, painful drive, with lots of traffic delays and more than one accident. People are taking out their frustration by tailgating and honking, and on several occasions, waving the middle finger. Okay, fine—that might have just been me.

I walk inside the store and run a hand through my wet hair, already regretting the time I spent earlier curling it. There's twenty minutes of my life I'll never get back.

"Jeong is quite literally the stupidest person I've ever met," Gina says by way of greeting as I shrug off my raincoat.

"Mmm," I say, seriously doubting the validity of that statement. Jeong, Gina's daughter-in-law of two years, graduated with a bachelor's in business administration from Wharton, a school that isn't exactly known for producing dummies.

She brushes past me, wearing a pinched expression and balancing three trays of jewelry.

"And she's selfish," Gina continues with an angry glint in her eye. She pauses, then waves a bloodred lacquered fingernail toward me. "I wish Will had married a girl like you. You would have been my dream daughter-in-law."

My breath catches in my throat, and I place a hand over my heart. I think that's the nicest thing Gina has ever said to me. "Thank you, Gina," I say, touched. "What a lovely thing to—"

"You're just so easy to manipulate," she continues, rubbing one of her rhinestone hoop earrings. She catches the expression on my face through the reflection of the mirror and says, "What? It's a compliment. It means you're innocent."

Uh-huh. At least I know it's Gina now and not some alien that abducted her body.

I head toward the showroom and begin setting up for the day. A few minutes later, the front door swings open, and I know without looking up that it's Maya, since she shows up for work every day ten to twenty minutes after she's supposed to. "Good morning, sexpot," I call out, using her high school nickname.

The extremely rare Orissa alexandrite necklace gleams brilliantly from its velvet cushion. Watching the gems change from their vibrant green to red under the incandescent built-in light of the cabinet is so awe-inspiring that it's a borderline spiritual experience. If you're a jewelry freak like me, that is.

"Hello, Penina," floats a deep male voice.

I startle and bump the side of my head against the belly of the glass display. *Holy mother of G-d, that hurts.* I lift my head and look into a pair of iridescent amber eyes belonging to none other than Sam Kleinfeld.

"You okay?" In a Prussian-blue button-down shirt and fitted suit pants that emphasize his trim waist and hug his tall, muscular legs, he could easily grace the cover of *GQ* magazine.

He must think I'm the clumsiest person he's ever met. I've had head injuries in front of him twice now. Resisting the urge to rub the aching spot on my head, I respond, "I meant to do that."

His lips twist at the corners as though he's trying not to laugh. "There's probably ice in the refrigerator."

"I'm fine," I say, ignoring the pain. Besides, I've got a stash of emergency Tylenol and ibuprofen in my purse that I'll take as soon as he leaves. This is the first time he's been back in the store since the introduction two weeks ago. Between his other businesses in New York and helping take care of his dad, he made it clear we wouldn't see him very often. I guess I had assumed "not very often" meant once every three months, not every two weeks.

His eyes dip to the center of my blouse and widen before quickly shooting away.

Um . . . okay . . .? I don't think my chest is worthy of such an alarming knee-jerk reaction, but maybe I'm underselling myself.

Sam clears his throat and crosses his arms against his chest. His face, I can't help but notice, has turned pink. "Your . . ." he starts to say, then stops.

"What?" I tilt my head.

He rubs his hand over his face and exhales deeply. Then, keeping his eyes firmly on mine, he says, "It's your shirt. The buttons are, uh . . ." He breaks off and makes some vague hand gesture.

I glance down and see in horror that the two middle buttons have come undone, exposing my lacy black bra.

Oh. My. G-d.

I quickly turn around and button them, feeling exposed in more ways than one. This must be a record-breaking awkward first day of work with a new boss encounter. First, I call him sexpot, then I bang my head, and then he gets an eyeful of my cleavage, all within the first five minutes of his arrival.

Impressive work, Penina. Well done.

"Sorry, I'm not usually this . . ." I trail off, buttoning the last button, then turn back around. How can I make him understand that my DDs push against buttons without saying that my DDs push against buttons? "The problem is that I've never worn this shirt before, and sometimes with new shirts, I don't know whether—well, you wouldn't understand," I say hurriedly with a wave of my hand. He leans his hip against the counter and tilts his head, listening intently. "It's a female thing. A female anatomical–type thing. Have you ever studied anatomy?" Clearly, my normal brain is out on break, and the backup one has no social skills.

There's a delayed pause, as though he's struggling to process what I said or struggling to come up with an appropriate response. Truthfully, I don't blame him. I'm a walking, talking disaster of a train wreck. Maybe it's his fault—yes, let's blame this on him. There's got to be a condition or personality disorder that causes you to say the most embarrassing, awkward things when your distractingly sexy boss is nearby. The Sam Kleinfeld syndrome has a nice ring to it.

He studies some invisible point near my left ear and says, "Would a safety pin help?"

I frown. Safety pins are tools of the devil. "The material is delicate, and I'd rather not poke a hole in it."

His gaze travels from my ear to my eyes. "You'd rather risk the buttons popping again?"

"Well, no. Of course not." Actually, yes, I would. Safety pins cause a lot more damage than people realize; they stretch the material and leave a permanent mark. It's no laughing matter. "But short of going home to change or borrowing your shirt, I don't see a good alternative. And I'm not using a safety pin," I reiterate.

He scowls. I try to arrange my face to appear simultaneously sympathetic and assertive, but it's hard to say whether I'm pulling it off or not. Then, just when I think he's about to admit defeat, he untucks his shirt and begins unbuttoning it.

"*Whoa, whoa.*" I swallow. "Maybe we should talk about this."

"What's there to talk about? You won't use a safety pin, the store's about to open, and Maya is conveniently missing."

"I was kidding about wearing your shirt. I mean, look at you," I protest, gesturing toward him. "You're like, size monster and I'm size human. Not to mention that that blue totally clashes with my lilac skirt, and not in a cutesy way either."

"You'll survive."

I roll my eyes. "I'm not worried about surviving, but I do have certain fashion standards that I try to live up to and—*Oh my G-d!*" I'm paralyzed for a long moment, then turn around faster than the speed of light. My face and hands are all sweaty, and I'm breathing too fast, but I'm trying to recover from catching an eyeful of the most perfect male chest I've ever seen. His tan skin has a trail of black curly hair that leads to his naval, and his sleek abdominal muscles are outrageously chiseled. It's like he decided a six-pack wouldn't do, so he traded it in for a twelve-pack. His body is un-freaking-believable.

"Think fast," he says, and within nanoseconds his shirt lands on the back of my head, then falls to the floor.

I can't believe he's serious about this. There should be laws that pro-tect employees from being forced to wear their boss's clothing. "What are you going to wear?" I ask, putting an arm into the sleeve.

"There's an old windbreaker of my dad's in his office," he says, over his shoulder. "And when I come back, we're going to have a quick chat."

A bad feeling emerges from the pit of my stomach as I button up the shirt. Nothing good ever follows a statement like that. At least he'll be covered up instead of standing there looking like he just popped out of a bachelorette cake.

"So, listen," he says about thirty seconds later, reemerging into the room in a jacket that's at least ten sizes too small. "You're not—" He stops and tilts his head, his eyes running down the shirt of his that I'm wearing. I'd taken the two bottom corners and lifted them to my waist, then tied them into a knot. It's the best I could do on short notice, but it's a far cry from normal looking.

I decide to state the obvious. "We both look hideous."

He clears his throat. "It's cute. I like the . . ." He trails off, pointing to the loose bow at the bottom of the shirt.

I shake my head. Clearly, he has no fashion sense and can never be trusted. "Normally, I enjoy a challenge, but I don't think I'll be posting this particular look on my social media account."

His lips dance and twist, like he's fighting with himself not to laugh. "Do you normally post pictures of your outfits, then?"

I nod and in my best Ron Burgundy voice say, "I'm kind of a big deal."

He laughs at that. "You don't say."

The sight of his grin catches me off guard. It completely transforms his face into something indescribably bewitching, making him seem more human and less of an authority figure. His grin falters as his eyes remain on mine, and I wonder what he's thinking. My eyes feel dry and itchy, and I'm trying to remember if I took my Zyrtec this morning.

"What did you want to talk about?" I ask, rubbing the corner of one eye.

"Right." He blinks and exhales heavily, then runs a hand through his hair. He seems to need a moment to collect himself and gather his thoughts. "Penina, in the workplace, there is a certain level of ethical conduct. Not just in appropriate actions and how we dress, but in the way we talk as well."

Is he for real? My eye starts to burn, and I rub it more vigorously. "You're giving me a speech on ethics when we both know you're naked under that jacket?"

He presses his lips together, either to repress laughter or curse words. "I'm going to ignore that."

"I didn't do anything wrong," I say, mainly to myself. "Is this about my shirt?"

"No, we've moved on from that," he replies. "It's because you called me a sexpot when I walked in this morning."

My jaw drops and I might have made a squeak of protest, but I can't be sure. "No, no, no, that's not what I—"

"I'm not finished," he says, cutting me off. "Any sexual references— be it with humans or dolls—do not belong in the workplace. What you do in private is your business, but when you're here you represent the company. Make sense?"

My ears and face feel infernally hot, and my hands squeeze into fists at my sides. How dare he bring up the sex doll orgy again? I mean, he didn't even give me a chance to explain! He's acting like some brutal tribal dictator–slash–communist. He should have *asked* me about it, asked if there had been a misunderstanding, which there obviously was!

He pauses, then says, "Do we have an understanding?"

I gape at him. *Do we have an understanding? Am I supposed to click my heels together and salute?*

"You can't be serious," I say.

"Oh, but I am."

I point to my face. "Look me in the eye and tell me you actually think that I was calling you sexpot."

"I actually think you called me sexpot," he says without breaking eye contact.

I stare at him incredulously. Do I look like someone who has sex with dolls and who would be dumb enough to call my boss a sexual nickname? "This is ridiculous—I don't even know what a sexpot is! You can't put sex in a pot and cook it—"

He interrupts with, "Again, not appropriate. Look, I know this is uncomfortable—"

"For you, maybe. I'm not the one being a total *idiot*."

He drums his fingers on the counter. "Penina."

"Samuel."

He drags his hand down his face and mutters something that sounds suspiciously like "fuck my life," but I can't be sure. We have a silent stare-off, but it's hard to say who's winning because we've both blinked several times.

The door bangs open and Maya trills, "Mama's home, bitches! Guess what? I have the best news." She walks into the room, only to stop short at the sight of Sam leaning against a display counter in a windbreaker several sizes too small. Her jaw goes slack. "Oh! Hi there."

"Hello, Maya." Sam nods. "Everything alright?"

"Of course! Everything is great." She sees me and waves, but I'm too agitated to do more than a half-hearted floppy arm movement. And then I realize that everything will be okay because Maya knows the truth.

"*She's* the real sexpot!" I exclaim, pointing to Maya. "She had this nic—"

Sam gives me a disappointed look. "Did we not just agree that that word does not belong in the workplace?" I open my mouth to argue, but he puts up his hand to silence me—which I don't think anyone has done to me since grade school—and says to Maya, "Your family is doing well?"

Her fingers pause from unbuttoning her coat, and she looks up at him, startled. "Um, I think so. Last I checked. Of course, it's been awhile since I spoke to Big Timmy, and I haven't seen Aunt Jennifer since Mama June had nine puppies. And obviously, I won't have anything to do with the twins on account of what happened last Thanksgiving. I mean, I forgive Uncle Bobby for spiking the lemonade and forgetting to tell everyone, but how . . ."

"Does she come with an 'Off' button?" he murmurs to me in an undertone as she continues to babble.

"She only does this when she's nervous," I whisper back. "Which she rarely is." I decide to hit him where it hurts. "You're very intimidating."

He dips his head in acknowledgment. "Thank you."

"That's *not* a compliment." I glare at him, but he doesn't notice because he's approaching Maya.

"How's your car?" he asks when she pauses to take a breath. "Is it working?"

Maya throws me a look that screams *"Help,"* like she knows this train is about to derail off the tracks, and only I can save her. Unfortunately, I've got my own problems. "Uh, yes," she says in a low voice, her eyes darting nervously back at him, "although sometimes it makes a sputtering sound, and then a blue light shows up on the dashboard, but I have no idea what it means; it's like an inverted triangle—"

"So," he interrupts impatiently, glancing at his Rolex before fixing her with a steely gaze. "So, there's no good reason you came to work forty-five minutes late."

Maya sucks in a quick breath, and I cringe in sympathy. I can practically see the inner workings of her mind as she struggles to invent a good excuse.

Sam rocks back on his heels. "Look, Maya. I know that it can be difficu—"

"It's Gina!" she blurts. Sam lifts one eyebrow and pauses, which she takes as an invitation to continue. "She's always making such a big deal about what time I come into work, and it really stresses me out. It's affecting my circadian rhythm and my interpersonal relationships. It's even affecting *my health*," she says, then fake coughs into the crook of her elbow.

She's laying it on a bit too thick, in my opinion, but I put on a sympathetic face to make it look like I believe every word.

"Interesting," Sam muses, stroking his cleft chin. "Penina doesn't seem to have this problem."

True. I may call my boss sexy pet names and flash my cleavage, but at least I show up on time. Yay me.

"That's not really a fair comparison, though, because Penina has a spectacularly dull life." She turns to me, cups a hand against her mouth, and stage whispers, "No offense."

My jaw tightens. "None taken."

"See, I have to balance work, friendships, my very active love life, an online shopping addiction, my psychic readings, insomnia." Maya pauses to take a deep breath, then slowly exhales and pinches the bridge of her nose. "I seriously have a lot on my plate right now."

"Let me see if I have this straight." Sam runs his thumb across his full bottom lip, looking thoughtful. "Penina comes in on time only because she doesn't do anything outside of work. She wouldn't be . . . oh I don't know"—he shrugs—"volunteering at a hospital, comforting sick children. Nothing like that."

I gaze at the ceiling. He's going to lord this over me for the rest of my life now that he knows it's a secret.

Maya nods. "Exactly. Not that there's anything wrong with being boring," she adds, throwing me a bone.

"You're too kind," I say, narrowing my eyes.

Sam runs one hand through his thick, dark hair, then thrusts it into his pants pocket. "Listen," he says, looking between Maya and me, "it's important that everyone comes to work on time, every day. If there's something going on that makes that difficult, then let's talk more about it. Alright?"

"I'd love to talk about this further with you," Maya purrs, walking seductively toward him in a black bodycon dress that leaves little to the imagination. "Name the time and place, and I'll be there."

I thought she'd said nothing scares guys away faster than letting them know you're interested, and she couldn't have been more obvious had she jumped onto his lap stark naked. Maybe her hormones took over. Her earlier theory must be right, though, because he says nothing. Instead, he literally turns around and walks away.

"Oh, and Penina?" he says, stepping back into the room.

Crap. "Yes?"

"Remember to call me Mr. Kleinfeld, not"—he cringes and makes a circling hand motion—"you know."

My mouth opens and closes like a gaping fish. Dozens of words are on the tip of my tongue, but by the time I'm ready to use any, he's already turned and walked away. I look over at Maya, who's humming as she hangs up her coat, obviously moving on from Sam's lecture.

Honestly, I kind of wish I had just come to work late too.

CHAPTER SIX

"Fashion should be a form of escapement, and not an imprisonment."
—*Alexander McQueen*

The smell of grilled hot dogs and hamburgers wafts through the park as our synagogue's members line up at the buffet table for the annual *Lag Ba'omer* celebration. It's all very Fourth of July, with its barbeques and bonfires, and you'd never know it's to commemorate the death of a beloved ancient rabbi, instead of a celebration of declaring independence from Britain. And like all synagogue dinners and events, I'm one of the steadfast volunteers who can be counted on to prepare food, serve it, and help with the cleanup. Plus do the things that no one else wants to do—like drive a pair of dentures back to an elderly congregant at ten o'clock at night because he left them in a jar inside the men's bathroom. On a shelf above the urinal. Normal stuff like that.

I'm feeling nice and summery in a red Bishop sleeve top coupled with a floral bubble skirt and platform hot-pink sandals. I kept my accessories on the simpler side, with a pair of threader earrings and a few gold rings. But even though I'm dressed for success, I am sick and tired after a night out with five of my old college friends and some of their spouses/partners. We met at a bar/restaurant in Golden Valley, where I nursed a pale ale while everyone else ate mouth-watering burgers and steaks and fries—except for one vegan friend who nibbled at a salad. Despite the fact that I was being tortured by the tantalizing nonkosher food, it was so much fun catching up with everyone. I love how the passage of time doesn't affect the comfort level among us. We're just as goofy and immature as the days when we shared English and psychology classes, and I hope we'll always have this easy connection, even in old age.

"French fries?" I ask Mr. Blau, a pair of tongs in my hand.

He nods and holds out his plate. "How've you been, Penina?"

"Great, thank G-d." I put a big helping of French fries on his plate. "How are you?"

"Not bad. Not bad." He gestures toward his paunch stomach. "I'm supposed to be watching my cholesterol and getting more exercise, but other than that, can't complain."

"Nice," I reply, and scoop up French fries for the next person in line.

"Did you know my Tamar had her fourth a few days ago?"

"Oh yeah?" I look up and smile. "Mazel tov! Boy or girl?"

"Girl." He scratches the side of his head. "Remind me now, were you in her class? Or was she above you?"

I'm pretty sure he knows, but why not humor the guy? If it makes him happy to point out that his daughter is happily married with four children while I'm over here single and childless, then I'm only too happy to accommodate. "She was two grades below me."

"Below you, eh?" The line of people is growing, but he doesn't seem to notice. "Well, one day by you, G-d willing." He takes a few steps forward and I'm about to breathe a sigh of relief, when he turns back and adds, "Miracles can happen."

"Amen," I mutter, thinking it's a miracle his family hasn't "accidentally" deserted him in the middle of nowhere on a cold Minnesota winter night.

The next hour creeps by as I make small talk and give out food. It's a small community, and most everyone has known everyone since childhood, so it feels like one big family in a lot of ways. Which is, you know, good and bad. Good because you know they'll have your back if you need help or support, but bad if you don't want people knowing your business. Just the other day, for example, everybody and their mother heard that the rabbi's son was smoking pot in the shul parking lot before the kid could even finish his joint. Or when Yoeli Horowitz had a mental breakdown and temporarily left his wife of twenty years because he fell in love with a dental assistant.

Between servings, I catch a glimpse of my nephews running toward the playground, with my mother and Libby close behind, talking to each other. My stomach sinks as I picture Libby and Natan and the kids forced to move into my parents' shoebox of a house. I've scoured the internet, trying to come up with ideas to make a lot of money fast, but so far cheating at bingo or stripping at Bar Mitzvahs is all I've got.

I jump in surprise as the fabric of my shirt is pinched, then hear a familiar voice say, "Hide me."

I twist my neck around. It's Fraydie, and there's panic reflected in my sister's pretty hazel eyes. "What—why?"

"Because," she hisses, peeking through the armpit of my sleeve, "the yenta of the village is harassing me."

"Who?"

"*Mrs. Zelikovitch*—who else? Oh shit, I think she saw me." Fraydie drops to the ground and crawls under the buffet table like a commando under fire. "I'm not here," she whispers, piling a stack of cardboard boxes in front of her. "If she asks, tell her I've moved to Alaska and joined a Buddhist colony."

"I think you mean a monastery."

Fraydie makes an impatient noise from the back of her throat. "Not the time, Penina."

Fraydie always does the unexpected, but this is a bit much, even for her. "Just tell her you're not interested," I say. Fraydie isn't exactly shy about telling people what she thinks, so I don't know why she's suddenly acting like a fugitive on the run.

"As if! You think I haven't tried?" she says, the visible part of her head shaking. "That woman doesn't take no for an answer."

Well . . . can't argue with that. "I didn't know she was trying to set you up," I say, wondering why I feel surprised. I was Fraydie's age, after all, when I began dating—I guess nineteen seems so young now that I'm nearing thirty.

The head rabbi and his assistant approaches the table, and I smile in greeting.

"This is the first time she's done it," Fraydie replies, not bothering to lower her voice, "and the guy is like a hundred years old. He probably needs to OD on Viagra just to get it up."

I kick her to let her know people can hear what she's saying, but instead she yelps, "Ouch, that hurt! What the hell is wrong with you?"

There's an uncomfortable silence as the rabbi and his assistant glance at each other.

"Wow, weird podcast," I say, and pretend to laugh. "One sec while I shut that thing off." I duck my head under the table and gesture wildly to Fraydie to keep quiet, before popping back up. "French fries?" I offer brightly, waving the tongs.

After that, Fraydie is mercifully quiet for a while, and eventually the buffet line slows down enough that I'm thinking about making a plate for myself, when I spy Mrs. Zelikovitch approaching, her long blond wig at odds with her eighty-something-year-old face, not dissimilar to how E.T. looked playing dress-up. The red pearl necklace she doesn't leave home without is wrapped around her neck, and she's in a sweater and wool skirt despite the unseasonably hot temperature. She comes toward me slowly, like a nightmare in slow-mo, waving her cane at me as though it's a weapon. "Hello, Peninaleh. Tell me, tell me, how are you and Zevi getting along?"

Not this again. The Zevi guy had recently contacted me out of the blue, and though I explained very nicely that I'm taking a break with no end date in sight, he hasn't given up. There are currently three voice messages on my phone and five texts that I have no intention of responding to, but you have to give him credit for being persistent. "We're playing phone tag," I say evasively.

She narrows her eyes in suspicion and says in a sticky-sweet voice, "Don't play too long, Peninaleh. It's not every day that someone of his caliber is willing to date someone like you."

So glad she doesn't feel the need to sugarcoat. "French fries?"

"Where's your sister?" She holds out her plate and looks around. "I thought I saw her—Fraydie," she clarifies, since Libby is, after all, of no use to her.

I try to think of a way to answer that doesn't involve lying. "Is there something you needed to tell her?"

"Well." She shrugs. "I already told your mother, but I might as well tell the whole family—why not?" She takes a bottle of ketchup and flips open the cap. "I've got a fantastic guy, top of the top. Easily a multimillionaire." She tips the bottle upside down and squirts some out onto her plate. "He's fifty-two, but he's looking for someone very young, someone to have more kids with." She puts down the ketchup bottle and glances up at me. "That rules you out."

"Darn it." I snap my fingers and try to seem sad. "He doesn't really sound like my sister's type, though. I think she's hoping to find someone closer in age. When she does decide to start dating," I add.

Mrs. Z pauses like she doesn't know what to make of my response. In her mind, a millionaire is everyone's type, no matter the age difference. "Anyway. Your sister is how old?"

"She'll be twenty in two months."

"*That* old?" She frowns. "I think he was hoping for eighteen or nineteen. I'm going to have to check with him to see if that's okay."

There's a crashing sound under the table, and Mrs. Z and I look at each other. "Squirrel," I say after a beat.

"Anyway"—Mrs. Zelikovitch picks up her plate and says over her shoulder—"keep me posted about Zevi."

"You betcha," I reply, waiting until she's safely seated at a picnic table before checking on Fraydie. A cardboard box under the table had crashed open, and about a hundred plastic spoons are dispersed over the ground. "What happened?"

"My temper happened," Fraydie replies, reaching forward on her hands and knees to help me gather the spoons. "Seriously, what kind of pervert wants a child bride, and what kind of sicko makes it happen for him?"

I lean back and wipe an arm across my hot forehead. "Is this a trick question?"

"And who's Zevi?" she continues, throwing spoons back in the box. "I bet he's a real prize if the yenta found him."

"I know, right?" I snort. The thing is, even though I'm not interested in dating, he does leave some pretty funny messages. And I like his voice—it's deep and masculine, sort of like Sam's. Except without the condescension and murderous undertones. Speaking of Sam, he comes to the store a few days a week now, despite him saying he's got a lot going on. Mostly he stays in his office doing conference video calls that probably involve high-level intimidation, but the energy in the store has changed. Not in a good way either.

I frown and stare off into the distance. What happened to the sweet man who rescued me in the hospital hallway? It's like there are two different versions of him, but I only get to see the stern, demanding one. Even Gina, who is no shrinking violet, seems scared of him.

"I need to get out of here—my legs are killing me," Fraydie says, poking her head out. "Am I safe? Where is she?"

I tent my hand against the blazing sun and see Mrs. Z at someone's table, gesticulating wildly. "At your three o'clock."

Fraydie looks at me blankly. "Huh?"

"You're safe," I say, then glance back at Mrs. Zelikovitch. "But you better hurry."

"Okay. Oh, and I have a secret I'm not supposed to tell you, but I'll let you guess." She scrambles out, then grabs my hand and tugs me along beside her, half crouching, half running toward the other end of the park.

I don't think Libby's dumb enough to have confided in Fraydie, but maybe the stress of losing her house got to be too much for her. Fraydie, in all honesty, couldn't keep a secret even if her mouth was gagged and her life depended on it. The only person worse than her is my mother, and I can't count the number of times they've spilled each other's secrets. "What is it?" I ask once no one can see us.

Looking scandalized, she says, "I can't just tell you! You have to guess."

I tilt my head back and groan. "Or you could save us both a lot of time and aggravation and say whatever it is you promised not to say."

"How would you like it if I just blurted out one of your secrets?" She shakes her head, the ends of her ponytail swishing over her shoulder. "It's not nice."

I roll my eyes at her twisted logic. "Is it someone we're related to?"

"Yes." She nods. "A female. A married female with children."

I sigh. "*G-d.* I can't believe Libby told you."

Fraydie has the grace to look slightly guilty. "Well, she didn't exactly."

"Was it Natan?"

"Technically, it was the trash can."

Say what? I am so confused. I lean against a tree trunk and cross my arms. "What do you mean?"

She leans forward. "I found a pregnancy stick in Libby's bathroom. And"—she pauses, staring at me meaningfully—"it was positive."

OMG. That brings the count up to six kids. I sink to the ground and close my eyes. *Don't panic, Penina. I repeat, do not panic. Just because there will be one more mouth to feed and another body taking up space doesn't warrant a complete nervous breakdown.*

"The only other person I told was Mimi because she was there anyway."

I groan. Mimi is our fourteen-year-old cousin on my mother's side, and even though she's quiet and discreet, it's still one more person that Libby and Natan wouldn't have wanted to know.

"Mimi was helping out with the kids, so it's not my fault I told her since I obviously had to share the news with someone."

I roll my eyes at that. Leah, like most Orthodox Jewish women, waits until the three-month mark before announcing her pregnancy. I stare off into the distance, wondering how much money I could make as a crystal meth cook despite the fact that (A) I can barely manage the simple stuff like noodles and boiled eggs, and (B) I have no connections in that world. It's not like I could make a cute reel for my TikTok account, with Bachman crooning in the background, "She's So High" while, wearing a biohazard suit, I wave at the camera.

"Pen, can I ask you something?"

Fraydie's voice is uncharacteristically serious, and I'm immediately concerned. "Of course. Anything."

"What if . . ." She plucks weeds out of the ground and keeps her eyes down. "What if it wasn't Libby who was pregnant? What if the test belonged to someone else?"

The hairs on the back of my neck stand up the way they do when I get a bad premonition. "Like who?"

"Hypothetically, what if it belonged to someone related to you? Someone who's still a teenager?"

My heart literally stops, and my eyes drop to Fraydie's stomach. There's a slight bulge that hadn't been there a month ago, and my hand flies to my mouth. *"Oh my G-d,"* I whisper.

"Don't freak out," she says, glancing around as if afraid someone is eavesdropping. "I said it's only hypothetical. It could belong to Libby."

"Uh-huh." I nod robotically while freaking out inside. Of course it's not Libby's test. I had forgotten how a few months ago Libby was complaining about how her new IUD was making her bleed. Blood and I aren't a good combination, so I had covered my ears and run out of my parents' kitchen.

I'm used to helping my family out, but I've never had both of my sisters be in a crisis at the same time. And these aren't small crises either—they're huge, life-altering ones. I lie down on the grass because it's impossible to faint lying down.

"Who's the father?" I ask suddenly, turning to look at her.

She lies down next to me and closes her eyes. "Hypothetically, this person slept with more than one boy, so she isn't sure."

More than one? I'm still struggling, trying to grasp the fact that Fraydie is no longer a virgin, has had sex outside of marriage, and now I find out that she's had more than one partner too. *"How many were there?"* I ask in a horrified voice, turning on my side to stare at her.

"Three."

My eyes widen. This is unbelievable. I can't even begin to know how to deal with this—

"Wait, no. Sorry, I forgot about one. There were four." She nods, unaware of my mouth falling open. "Definitely four."

I put my hand over my chest, which is getting tighter by the moment. She's going to be one of those people who end up on the *Dr. Phil* show, crying about her childhood. And then there will be a big reveal at the end, where the studio audience and the rest of the country finds out who the biological father is.

And who is supposed to raise this baby? Fraydie can't do it. The girl can barely manage to keep the days of the week straight. I wouldn't trust her to take care of a houseplant, much less a living, breathing human being. My parents will have to do it while Fraydie probably continues to have reckless sex behind our backs. There's no controlling her. Maybe Dr. Phil is our only hope.

Keep it together. Breathe in . . . and exhale.

My phone suddenly pings, but I'm too distraught to see who it is. Fraydie, on the other hand, is acting like nothing is wrong, and she bursts into laughter after glancing at my phone.

"Who is Zevi? He's hilarious." She holds the screen up, and I see a picture of a yacht with the inscription *Hot Jew Boy* on it. Despite everything going on, I laugh.

"Anybody with a boat like that has to be awesome," she says, handing the phone back. "I'll take him if you don't want him."

"I want him," I say quickly. She's had enough men already, if you ask me.

"If that's the kind of boat he has, imagine his house. I bet it's one of those huge contemporary mansions with its own garage park."

And that's when it hits me: this supposedly gorgeous and wealthy man could be the answer to Libby's problems. And who knows? It's not impossible that I might fall in love. I enjoy listening to his messages; he definitely has a great sense of humor, unlike another man I know.

Ahem, Sam.

"Are you sure you want him?" she says.

"Fraydie," I say, my fingers already tapping out a response to his text, "This one is all mine."

CHAPTER SEVEN

"You can see and feel everything in clothes."

—*Diana Vreeland*

A week has passed since learning Fraydie's "hypothetical" news, and since she's sworn me to secrecy, I haven't said anything. But it's only a matter of days until the whole family hears about it. At work the next day, I have trouble concentrating because I'm so nervous about meeting Zevi. There's a lot riding on this date, especially because in my mind, we're already married, saved Libby's house, and bought ourselves a nice mansion (what can I say? I'm a fast operator). We've spoken on the phone a few times, but he already feels like someone I've known my whole life. We also have the same taste in music and—get this—he actually *enjoys* shopping for clothes! If he's not my soulmate, then I don't know who is.

He's flying in from Manhattan next week, which leaves me five days to research and come up with a game plan on how to make him fall madly in love with me. Google recommends a lot of eye contact and laughing, which seems absurdly easy. Maybe I should ask Libby for advice since she had lots of guys wanting to marry her. Although I don't want to bother her since she's got so much else going on at the moment.

I take a deep breath and roll my shoulders. It's going to be fine, absolutely fine. I will marry Zevi, and save my sister's house. I will sell his yacht if I have to (although I'd rather not since it does have a hilarious name).

But what if Zevi doesn't like me? My breath gets trapped in my throat as I consider that very real possibility. Maybe I'll ask Maya for suggestions as she's constantly falling in love, Sam being her latest. She invents excuses to talk to him and does a lot of hair tossing and giggling when he's around, not that it seems to be working. Or if it is, I can't tell. But he's made it clear from day one that he separates his personal life from his work life, so if Maya wants a real shot with him, she should probably quit.

I place the vintage diamond ring under the microscope and grin, recalling her theory about him. At first, she was insulted by his abrupt mannerisms whenever he spoke with her, glancing at his watch and cutting her off mid-sentence more than once. I mean, he treats everyone this way, but I don't think the twenty-three-year-old blond beauty often gets the brush-off. Her psychic convinced her that he's desperately attracted to her but is scared of rejection, and that's the reason he keeps his distance.

I don't know if that's true, but either way, that psychic is a genius. Anyone who can convince people to fork over three hundred dollars for an hour's worth of conversation is obviously doing something right. I should've skipped college and created a 1-800-dial-a-psychic hotline myself.

I briefly stand up and wiggle my skirt back down. I made a poor life choice a few weeks ago by ordering a bunch of cheap clothes off this website, and now I'm suffering the consequences. I'm in a black two-piece suit, but the skirt rides up if I take more than five steps at a time. There were even some nasty comments on my Instagram page about it not being modest, although I did my best to explain to everyone that it's the designer's fault, not mine. At least I'm not flashing my cleavage.

I pick up a probe and start checking for bent prongs or loose stones. Despite our rough start, Sam isn't that bad as far as bosses go, although it probably helps that he mostly stays in his office with the door shut.

At first, having him around all the time made everyone super tense, but we're slowly returning to normal—a new normal, that is. It's funny how one person can bring out so many changes in people. Maya comes to work on time every morning and is super helpful. Before, I was always the one to work late and to lock up, but Maya has done it twice now. Both times Sam had been in his office, so that probably had something to do with it, but I'm sure not complaining. And Gina does less talking on the phone and more actual work.

I switch on the ultrasonic machine and put the ring inside. Even I have changed in a way, although mostly through avoidance. I admit I've been a little paranoid ever since the sexpot incident, and Maya's little jokes about sexual harassment in the workplace definitely aren't helping. My coping mechanism is avoidance. For example, when Sam walks into a room, I try to leave. If he speaks directly to me, I make sure to keep my answers very brief and professional, nothing that can be misinterpreted as perverse. I'm always two steps ahead of the mind game we play, the one he doesn't know he's competing in.

It's all so exhausting.

I pull the ring out as Maya bursts into the room, clasping her hands together prayer style. "Penina, can we trade places? I can't handle the customer out there. I'm about two seconds away from throttling her."

"Sure," I say, handing her the ring. "This is ready for a soak." I gaze at her back as she places the ring in the soaking container. "What's the deal with the customer?"

Maya plops down on the stool I had just vacated and rolls her eyes in exasperation. "Ugh. She's a looker. And she wants to look at *everything*."

For Maya, selling jewelry is all about the sale and the three percent commission that comes with it. Unfortunately for her, a good portion of people wander into the store just to look. Maybe they're bored or curious, or don't have the money yet, but whatever the reason, they keep their wallets shut tight. Maya has a habit of pawning these customers onto me, and unless I'm strapped for money, I don't really mind. It's not hard to show them jewelry and answer their questions, and they usually come back when they're ready to buy. There's something really satisfying about helping people find that perfect piece of jewelry to mark a special event in their lives, like an engagement or a special anniversary, and it feels amazing to know that I played a role in that.

In one corner of the showroom is a heavily made-up woman whose cheeks and forehead are stretched unnaturally tight. When she sees me, she tilts her platinum-blond head and assesses me from head to toe, probably trying to determine whether I'll be more patient than the last woman who helped her.

"Hi," I say, smiling and extending my hand. "I'm Penina. Maya had to take care of something in the back, so I'll be taking over. What can I help you with today?"

"I'm looking for a gift for someone. A man," she adds, clearing her throat. "Not anything too special. Maybe cufflinks or a watch."

"Sure," I say, gesturing with my hand that she should follow me. I pull off my black wrist coil bracelet when I reach the men's accessories display case, and select a key. I tug my skirt down again, even though I know it will inch up again the moment I move. "We have some stunning new watches by a local designer. Is there a particular style or color you're thinking of?"

"Not really." She frowns, her carefully styled head bent over as she peers into the glass case. A stray lock of hair falls loose from her chignon, brushing against her cheek. She tucks it impatiently behind her ear, then points to a yellow gold and steel watch resting in the front row. "That one is very nice. How much is it?"

I unlock the door and reach inside. "One thousand five hundred dollars," I read from the tag hidden underneath the box. I hand it to her and add, "It's eighteen-karat yellow gold with sapphire crystal. It's also water resistant—a definite plus for those rainy days."

The woman runs her finger over the bracelet, stroking the tiny grooves in the bezel. "I don't know." She sighs, a worried crease settling between her brows. "I wish I knew my nephew's taste better. Do you have cuff links?"

"We do." I smile, moving to the next display case. "It's always tricky shopping for someone else, but I can show you some pieces that match most styles. There are some very cool tie clips as well, which could work too."

The woman points to a pair of octagonal-shaped crystal cuff links. "May I see those?"

I bring out the black velvet box from the display case and place it on the glass counter. "You picked one of my favorites. These are stunning Swarovski crystals set in white gold. They're so pretty that I've been tempted to buy a men's button-down shirt just to wear them," I joke.

She moves her lips into a vague semblance of a smile. I can't put my finger on it, but there's something about her that's a little . . . off. Is she depressed? Except don't depressed people stay in bed all day and eat ice cream straight out of the carton? Or maybe that's just me after a bad date.

I spend the next twenty minutes showing her every piece of men's jewelry in the store, but she still hasn't made up her mind.

The woman shakes her head. "Sorry, I'm not usually so indecisive. I guess it's just one of those days."

"Take as much time as you need," I say. "And don't worry about making a decision today," I continue, glad that Gina isn't around to hear this conversation. Or Sam, for that matter. "A lot of people like to think over their options before coming to a decision."

Without warning, a tear slides down the woman's cheek, but she quickly flicks it away with her finger, probably hoping it would escape my notice. Only it didn't, and now more tears are rolling down. I quickly reach for the tissue box underneath the cabinet and hand it to her.

"I'm sorry," she sniffles, pulling several tissues out and dabbing at her watery eyes.

"Don't be," I say, waving my hand dismissively. "We keep this place full of tissues for a reason." Specifically for Gina, who is allergic to everything and has a constant runny nose, but, nonetheless.

Speaking of the devil, Gina walks into the room, followed by Sam, who hovers nearby, making me conscious of the fact that my legs are on display.

The woman dabs at her runny nose. "It's just . . ." She pauses, rubbing her temples. "It's been a rough couple of months. To say the least."

I nod, waiting. They say hairdressers are like therapists, but you'd be surprised by the number of people who walk in here and tell me their problems.

"It's a long story, I don't know why I said anything. I should probably get go—"

"It's okay. I don't mind listening. As you can see, we're not too busy at the moment, and it might make you feel better to talk about it."

"You're too sweet." She smiles, but it doesn't reach her eyes. "Okay. But stop me anytime you want." She takes a deep, fortifying breath. "My husband served me with divorce papers a few months ago. I was completely shocked. I thought we were happy. He wasn't home much of the time, but that was the nature of his business." She sighs and looks away. "Married for over forty years. Here, I thought this was one person I knew even better than myself, and yet I was completely blindsided."

I wince. "That's rough."

"Yes, so . . . I don't know." She shrugs, sniffling. "It's hard to trust anyone anymore. Even myself." She pauses and glances down. "Especially myself."

My heart breaks watching her. I can practically *feel* the sadness coming off her in waves. And even though she's a stranger and I don't know any of the details, I can't stand to see her in pain. "You know what?"

She lifts her watery eyes. "What?"

I walk around the counter and take her hands in mine. "I feel bad for your ex. I *pity him.* He lost the trust of a loyal woman—a woman whose heart loves to love. And that's a lot more rare and precious than people realize." I give her hands a small squeeze. "Never forget that you are worthy—You're worthy of love and loyalty and all the blessings in the world. You deserve to find true love and build a happy home together, filled with laughter and children, a roaring fireplace, and maybe a dog or two—" I break off at the curious expression on her face and realize I was talking about my own fantasy. "Anyway. You are worthy. Promise me you won't ever forget that."

Gina walks by and rolls her eyes, letting me know in no uncertain terms that she doesn't approve of this kumbaya moment.

The woman's bottom lip trembles as she nods. "I promise. Thank you. I really needed to hear that."

We hug each other and I end up showing her some more jewelry, although she doesn't buy anything. When she's ready to leave, I insist on walking her to her car, where we hug one more time.

When I return inside, Sam, Gina, and Maya face me like a shooting squad.

"What the hell was that?" Gina asks, lifting a hand and making a vague circular motion.

My eyebrows draw together. "Empathy?"

"Yeah, we don't do that here," Gina says, as if I had just admitted to smoking a joint or stealing someone's coffee mug.

I tilt my head and feign confusion. "We don't do empathy?"

"Correct."

"Even though her husband divorced her out of the blue, and now she's having trust issues—"

"You're still doing it." Gina briefly closes her eyes and pinches the bridge of her nose. "How many times do I have to tell you that we are not a psychiatric office?"

I lift my palms and try to look innocent. "I don't know. Two or three?"

"This month alone, maybe." Gina turns to Sam. "She's impossible. She's more interested in comforting people than selling jewelry."

He gazes at me with an unreadable expression, and I feel my traitorous body blush under his watchful attention.

"Gina," he says, "I'll need you to cover for Penina this morning."

My heart gets lodged in my throat. Cover for me? What exactly is he planning? He wouldn't drive me out to a deserted forest and kill me because I showed empathy, would he?

"I still think you should take Maya," Gina says.

"Yes." I nod enthusiastically, even though I have no idea what we're talking about. "I think so too."

He ignores both of us, puts his phone in his pocket, then lifts his chin toward me. "We're going to hit a few stores. I'll tell you more about it in the car."

That's literally what a murderer would say to lure someone who loves to shop into his car. And being alone with the man I once called a sexpot isn't exactly my idea of a good time;—he's just too . . . testosteroney, too intense, too *alpha*. I prefer being around effeminate men who smile and know how to make polite conversation.

"Shoot, I wish I could," I lie, "but my schedule is chockfull this morning." I point to Maya and add, "She's bored."

He narrows his eyes. "Busy how?"

"Repairs, cleanings. Phone calls." I blow out a puff of air and lift my hands in a show of frustration. "I'm up to my eyeballs here."

His head tilts slightly. "I'm sure it's nothing Maya and Gina can't handle."

"Well, I don't know," I say, scratching my neck, which is heating up from stress. *Why is he being so stubborn?* "I'm already in the middle of this one really complex repair—"

"Penina." Something about the steely expression in his eyes tells me he's not the kind of guy to accept no for an answer. "I'll meet you out front."

"Like now?" I swallow. I'm pretty sure that whatever is about to happen isn't in my job description.

"Right now." He nods goodbye to Gina and Maya, then heads outside.

I glare at his retreating backside. Just because he's my boss doesn't mean he can order me around.

"You're so lucky," Maya says wistfully, watching me grab my purse. "Enjoy every moment for my sake. Savor him like"—she licks her lips and waves her hand—"like a fine wine. Or chocolate cream mousse pie."

Apparently, we have very different ideas about Sam's intentions; while I'm picturing him stabbing me to death, she's envisioning a romantic tryst. "Yeah, that's not going to happen," I say, heading toward the door. "Bye, guys. Wish me luck."

I get the feeling I'm going to need it.

CHAPTER EIGHT

"Give a girl the right shoes, and she can conquer the world."
—*Marilyn Monroe*

Outside, the rain has calmed to a steady drizzle, and glimpses of a brilliant spring sun peek between the clouds. I find Sam leaning against a shiny silver Mercedes-Benz SUV, twirling a key fob in his hand. Something changes in his eyes when he sees me, a subtle shift in the color or a darkening of the expression. I don't know what it means or if it means anything at all, but it feels intense, and I remind myself to breathe.

He wordlessly gets in the car, and I do the same. The interior is sleek and modern, with piped leather seats, a gleaming wooden console, and enough screens and buttons to fill up a spaceship. The car reeks of money—or whatever it is that makes new cars smell so good. Between Sam's hypnotizing scent and the new-car smell, my body relaxes, and a happy sigh escapes me as I buckle my seat belt.

"You okay?"

I glance at him. "Yeah. Why?"

He places a hand over the back of my seat as he reverses out of the parking spot. "You moaned."

What? I didn't moan—I sighed. *It was a sigh.* At least, I think it was?

"No." I shake my head emphatically. "I didn't."

He removes his hand from the back of my chair and puts the car into drive. "If you say so."

"I do," I reply firmly, clasping my hands in my lap.

He guides the car out of the parking lot, and just when I think he's moved on, he adds, "Let's not make that sound again, whatever it was."

I fan my suddenly warm cheeks with my hand. Oh my G-d. *It's happening again.*

I take a deep breath through my nose and slowly let it out. I've never liked confrontations, but there are times in one's life when the air needs to be cleared. It's one thing to be falsely accused, but it's another when the accusations keep piling up. For the sake of my integrity—and my *sanity*—I have to say something.

"Mr. Kleinfeld, I need to tell you something, and it comes from the most truthful, honest part of my heart. And I'm not telling you this to hurt your feelings or to offend you in any way—only to clear up a misunderstanding."

The traffic light turns yellow, and he brings the car to a stop. He turns to face me. "Go ahead."

I take a deep breath and plunge in. "When we first met and you over-heard me talking about"—I pause and cringe—"the doll orgy thing, it was Janie the nurse telling us why she ran out on her date. And that day I called you a sexpot, I didn't know it was you. I thought it was Maya—it was her nickname in high school, but you didn't give me a chance to explain. I don't want you to think"—I glance away and swallow—"that I have a thing for you, but then it seemed weird to bring it up, so I didn't. And just now, I made a noise because I like the smell of new cars, but it wasn't *that type of noise.* I just . . ." I stop and run my hand through my hair. "I don't want to give you the wrong idea. You know?"

The light turns green, but he's watching me so intently that he doesn't realize it until the car behind us honks. He steps on the gas and says brusquely, "Understood."

Well, that went . . . not exactly great, but it could've been worse. He could've called me names and fired me or brought me to a quiet, abandoned rooftop somewhere and pushed me off the edge. Actually, that could be where we're driving to.

Still, though. It would've been nice if he'd have said more than one word in response. That's the cornerstone of good, honest communication. Everyone gets a chance to speak their truth and release whatever negativity they've been holding onto. I guess his truth is no more than three syllables at a time.

The seconds tick by and neither of us speak. We stare straight ahead and sit in uncomfortable silence. G-d, I hate this! Why isn't he saying anything? Did I offend him? Did I hurt his feelings?

So I do what I always do in an awkward situation: I vomit my innermost thoughts despite the fact that historically it only ends up making things that much worse.

"There's nothing wrong with you, of course," I say, cringing at the bizarre words falling out of my mouth. "It's just that you're not my type."

In the silence that follows, I glance up at the ceiling of the car and wish for a bolt of lightning to strike me dead.

"What is your type?" he asks, glancing at me from the corners of his eyes.

This is what you get for opening your mouth, Penina. Hope you're happy.

"Well, at a minimum"—I lick my lips and notice his eyes follow the movement before returning to the road—"someone who has a job and isn't addicted to drugs or alcohol. Or gambling. And who hasn't been to jail for not paying child support or for exposing himself in a women's locker room."

"You really believe in setting the bar high, don't you?"

I smile wryly, not revealing that these are all real-life examples over the last ten years. "Those are entry-level conditions. If I was going to be picky, then I'd specify a stable job with good health insurance." I pause, then add, "And who always files his taxes on time."

He shakes his head like he feels sorry for me.

"And, of course, he has to be *kind* to people," I say, glancing pointedly at him, "and be considerate of everyone's feelings."

"So, your dream man," he says, turning the steering wheel, "is a woman that works for the IRS."

I blink. I'm not exactly sure how he came to that conclusion, but I'm going to ignore it. "And it would be great if he had a sense of humor and was intelligent. So, you see"—I breathe out a puff of air—"you don't fit the bill."

Silence.

"Except as a boss. You're totally my type as a boss." Why, *why* can't I stop talking?

He turns on the signal and switches lanes.

"I'm sure I'm not your type either," I continue helplessly. "I bet you only date Victoria's Secret models."

The traffic light is red, and Sam brakes to a stop. I look at him, only to find that his eyes glance at my thighs, which are on full display because this skirt has it out for me. He quickly looks back at the road, and I try to wiggle the material down as much as possible. The moment I get home, I'm going to burn this skirt.

"There's a sweater in the back," he says. "You can use it to cover . . ." He makes a vague hand gesture.

"Yep," I say, unclipping my seat belt. And just when you think the car ride from hell couldn't possibly get worse, it does. I lean against the middle console and twist my body so I can reach the black sweater folded neatly on the seat, but there's a frustrating gap of space preventing me from getting it. I scoot further onto the console, when the car suddenly lurches forward, and I tumble into the back seat with a cry of surprise.

"You okay?"

I ignore the question and reposition myself so my underwear isn't on full display. "What was that for?"

"The light turned green." He glances at me through the rearview mirror. "What did you expect me to do?"

For an intelligent man, he is frustratingly, *irritatingly* dumb. "Uh, warn me?" I say through clenched teeth as I buckle my seat belt. "Give me a heads-up? Something along the lines of '*Hey Penina, the light turned green, maybe you want to sit back down*'?"

"Okay." He nods. "The next time you come to work without a skirt on, and need my sweater to cover up, I'll be sure to do that."

My mouth opens and shuts, then opens and shuts again. I slip my hands under my thighs, to prevent myself from strangling him.

It's quiet again, but I'm too angry to care. I hope he chokes on the awkward silence.

Seven minutes go by, but I still refuse to break down and say something.

"I'm sorry," he says, looking at me through the rearview mirror. "I shouldn't have made that comment about your skirt. I was out of line."

"Thank you," I say stiffly. "And I'm sorry for losing my temper and fantasizing about killing you."

He smirks. "I'd love to see you try."

"Don't tempt me," I mutter. At the red light, I unbuckle and climb back—not very gracefully—into the front seat. "So, where are we going?"

He pulls down his sun visor and flips on his sunglasses in one swift, fluid motion. "I thought we'd visit some jewelry stores in Edina."

"Ah, the high-end stuff," I nod. "Why?"

"I want to check out the layout of these places. Compare pricing and payment plans. Get a feeling for what we're up against."

I unzip my fake Louis Vuitton purse, take out my water bottle, and unscrew the cap. "Are they expecting you?"

"Hell no." He flicks on the signal. "This is going to be a covert operation."

Covert operation? "What exactly did you have in mind?" I tilt the bottle to my lips and take a gulp.

"We're going to pose as an engaged couple shopping for a diamond ring."

The water trickling down my throat takes a sudden detour down the wrong pipe, making me cough uncontrollably.

Sam glances at me. "You okay?"

I give him a thumbs-up even as my coughing escalates to wheezing. From past experience I know that my face is turning an unattractive shade of purple and that my eyes are starting to tear up. Why is it that the more I try to stop coughing, the more out of control it gets?

"You don't look good," Sam remarks in the casual tone of someone commenting on the weather. "Want me to pull over?"

I shake my head. But then the contents in my stomach suddenly clench, and I have a terrifying thought: *What if I vomit?* What if his new-car smell gets replaced by my leftover-breakfast-of-cereal-and-milk puke smell? *Ugh.* I start flapping my hands in the direction of my window, hoping he'll get the hint to pull over.

He does and quickly maneuvers the car to the shoulder of the highway. The moment he puts the car in park, I jump out and dry-heave onto the hard concrete. In the dizzying haze of trying to get my breathing under control, I become aware of a strong arm holding onto me and another one patting my back.

"Better?" Sam asks.

I nod and try to extricate myself, but Sam tightens his hold.

"Take a few more deep breaths," he says.

"I'm fine," I say hoarsely.

"You don't look fine." He's so tall that the top of my head reaches his neck, and his broad shoulders seem as dense and immovable as a brick fortress.

A strong gust of wind charges toward us, and I instinctively tuck my face against his shirt. Through the thin fabric, I feel the soothing, rhythmic beating of his heart, and the warmth of his body heat spreads to my own.

Step away from the man, Penina. I gently pull free of his embrace and look up at him. "I have asthma and acid reflux. The combination of the two can make me cough and occasionally—if it gets too out of control—vomit."

"That must be tough," he says softly. "Being so fragile."

I frown. "I'm not fragile."

"Uh-huh." Then he pats me on the head like I'm a child.

"Really, I'm not," I insist, feeling a tinge of annoyance. "If anything, I'm more Superwoman than fragile."

Apparently, Sam thinks that's hilarious, because he laughs. "Got it, Penina. You're a total badass. Are you ready to get back in the car?"

I nod, feeling guilty that I let him hold onto me for so long. I climb back in and pull the seat belt's shoulder strap over my chest. Sam starts the car and pulls back onto the highway, and that's when I realize that something more than just guilt is bothering me. Something more than the self-reproach of allowing a man I'm not married to hold me tightly against his chest. It's something more than the embarrassment of having my new boss witness me dry-heave on the side of a highway.

And that's when it hits me—it's *sadness*. I feel sad at the realization that I may never again be held by a man—unless, of course, I make a habit of choking, which I hope not to. I glance at Sam, somehow worried that he might be able to read my pathetic thoughts, but his face is relaxed and unworried as he presses the climate control button on the console.

I close my eyes and take a few calming breaths. I *thought* that I had made peace with the likelihood of ending up an eighty-year-old virgin, but apparently one embrace by a man is all it takes to undo years of therapy.

The worst part is how much I *liked* it. His strong arms cocooned my body as though he were my own personal fortress that would shield me from harm, and for that brief moment in time, it felt as though it were the two of us against the world. I loved the way his skin smelled when he held me close and the way his breath tickled my neck when he spoke.

"Penina?"

I swallow. "Yes?"

"So, you'll do it? Pretend we're engaged?"

"Oh, right. Yes, I can handle that."

But can I handle a future that doesn't include a husband and children? Will I be okay celebrating the weddings of my friends and siblings while I wither into old maidenhood? I want to be able to. I want to be the kind of person that can rise above my envy and rejoice when others have what I crave. And for the most part, I have. I've danced at my friends' weddings and celebrated the births of their babies. I've smiled in pictures and bought presents. I've even pulled all-nighters to arrange decorations for a bridal shower and baked desserts for my friend's son's bris.

I shake my head. I'm being ridiculous. This is probably my body's cry for help for chocolate; nothing more, nothing less.

* * *

"Should we have a backstory?" I ask, tapping my fingernails on the armrest. "In case they ask about the proposal or how we met?"

He nods. "We met at a party, and I proposed a year later over dinner. T-bone steak, medium rare, paired with a nice cabernet." He pauses and squints his eyes. "Bourbon and cigars for dessert."

Right, because nothing spells romance like liquor and lung cancer. "Is that really the best proposal you can come up with? No candles or rose petals arranged into the words 'Will you marry me?'"

He shakes his head and makes a sound under his breath that sounds suspiciously like a snort. "If it's not edible, why bother?"

Because it's pretty and makes you feel all warm and happy inside. I don't care how good-looking or rich a man is, he ought to make some kind of grand gesture when he proposes to a woman. "Leave the talking part to me," I say. "You just stand there and look pretty."

"That," he says, glancing over his shoulder to switch lanes, "is your job."

I blush at the unexpected compliment but quickly brush it off. "It pains me to say this," I sigh, "but you're prettier than me."

He laughs, even though I'm not joking. On days when my skin is clear and I'm not bloated, I *might* consider myself attractive, but I'm still not in his league, which is somewhere between Bradley Cooper and Regé-Jean Page.

"So why aren't you married?" he asks, steering the car up a parking ramp. "There have got to be enough candidates out there who meet your demanding expectations."

I stiffen, surprised by the suddenness of his question. "Oh—I don't know. I guess I haven't found the right one yet."

"And you're religious?"

"I'm Orthodox, yes."

There aren't very many cars, and he easily finds a space. "I always thought Orthodox Jews got married at eighteen."

"Some do, but not everyone."

"Why so young?"

"Since you can only touch someone of the opposite gender if you're married to them, it helps prevent premarital intimacy." Unless you're Fraydie, of course.

He shuts off the ignition. "Hmm."

I glance at him. "What?"

"Nothing," he says absently, and unbuckles his seat belt.

Oh no, he doesn't. I'm not going to let him off that easy. "That *hmm* noise you just made," I say, imitating it. "What was that for?"

"I was just wondering why you haven't been snatched up yet. But," he adds with a shrug, "it's not my business."

The idea of me being a prize, something to "snatch up" is so absurd that I have to stop myself from laughing out loud. I open the door and wait outside while Sam locks it.

He's right—it isn't his business. And I don't really care one way or another what people think, and yet something compels me to say, "I'm not—" I stop abruptly, wondering how best to phrase this without getting too specific. "I'm not a typical Orthodox woman."

Sam rests his wrists on the roof of the car and gazes at me intently. "Penina, you don't strike me as a typical anything."

I grin at that, and then he gazes at me in that way of his, a combination of reluctant fondness mixed with exasperation. Okay, "fondness" might be a stretch, but it's somewhere on the spectrum of not hating.

He clears his throat and says brusquely, "Let's go."

We head across the parking lot and pass an older woman hobbling up to a jazzy sports car. I smile, imagining a gray-haired granny pushing eighty on a highway.

The sun shines brightly through the gaps in the parking ramp, and I reach for my sunglasses, only to realize I left them in the car.

"Shoot, I forgot my sunglasses," I tell Sam. "Can I have the keys?"

He makes an impatient noise as he pitches them toward me. "Make it quick. Our appointment is in two minutes."

I hurry to the car, no longer even trying to tug my skirt down. On my way back, I notice the older woman again, this time by a different car. She leans her cane against the side of the vehicle, then uses both hands to pull the door handle. The car's alarm shrieks at a deafening volume, and the woman startles, grabs her cane, and hobbles away like a criminal caught in the act.

"Do you think that woman needs help?" I say, jogging up to Sam. "She keeps going to different cars."

He glances over his shoulder in the direction I'm pointing, then shakes his head. "No."

"Are you sure?" I nibble on my bottom lip and study her. "She looks confused."

Sam shrugs and slips his phone into his back pocket. "You look confused half the time, but I don't call you out on it."

Ruuude. Still, he has a point. I talk to myself sometimes, and it would be awkward if a stranger came up to me and asked if everything was alright. Unless of course, I did need help, in which case I'd feel relieved.

We set off toward the elevator nearest the parking ramp, although Sam's long strides keep him steadily ahead of me. A car starts to reverse, but instead of waiting for it to finish pulling out, Sam quickens his pace. I roll my eyes. Unlike a normal person, he'd rather take his chances at getting run over than wait a few seconds.

I hear something crash onto the asphalt, followed by a shriek. I turn around and see the older woman, one hand over her face while the other grips the cane. On the ground rests a purse on its side, with items scattered around it: keys, pens, a checkbook, a candy bar, and a travel-size tissue packet.

Stupid Sam. And shame on me for listening to him.

"You go ahead," I call out to him as I turn in the opposite direction. "I'll be there in a minute."

His face turns dark and scary, but what does he expect me to do? Old people are fragile—everyone knows that. If this lady trips and falls while trying to get her stuff off the ground, she might end up with a stroke or heart attack or who knows what, and I'm too young to have someone's death on my hands.

"Hi," I say with a little wave, coming toward her. "Are you alright?"

"Well"—she lifts a hand and gestures to the ground—"my purse fell, and everything is a mess. Other than that, I'm doing just dandy."

I grin at hearing the word *dandy*. Old people are so cute. "That's easy enough to fix," I say, bending down to pick everything up.

"Oh, aren't you are a sweetheart! Thank you so much."

"Of course." I hand her the purse with everything inside. "Okay, this is all of it."

"I really appreciate it. My joints aren't what they used to be." She exhales loudly. "I never appreciated doing something as simple as bending down until it became a five-minute procedure."

I take a moment to study her. She has stooped shoulders and a wrinkled face sprinkled with liver spots, and her eggshell-blue eyes convey defeat, like someone who has had her share of hardships and then some. "Have you tried aquatic exercises?" I ask. "Because my grandfather has rheumatoid arthritis, and he swears by it—"

"Penina," Sam interrupts as he comes forward, a stormy expression on his face. "What do you think you're doing?"

Before I have a chance to respond, the woman turns to Sam. "You have such a lovely wife. I dropped my purse, and she came running over to help."

I open my mouth to correct her, to say that I'm not his wife, that in fact, hell would have to freeze over before I'd marry someone with such abysmal manners, but he replies with, "She's a real saint, alright." Except he doesn't make it sound like that's a good thing.

I focus my attention on the woman. "Was there anything else you needed help with?"

Sam rubs his hand over his face and sighs loudly while the woman says, "Well, since you mentioned it . . . I seem to have lost my car."

I knew it. Sam might seriously fire me over this, but what am I supposed to do? Shrug my shoulders and wish her good luck? Let her wander around aimlessly until someone else happens to notice her? Someone that might think nothing of stealing an elderly woman's purse? *Or worse?*

No, sir. Not on my watch.

"What does your car look like?" I ask, careful to avoid Sam's gaze.

"It's white." She pauses and purses her lips. "Well, my daughter thinks it's more of a cream, but my grandson insists it's white. He's only six, but he's very good with his colors."

"I have a six-year-old nephew," I say, smiling. "Such a cute age."

"Oh, it is," she agrees.

"Make and model?" Sam barks.

I sneak a glance at him, surprised that he's actually willing to help, albeit in a cranky way. The woman blinks. "It's a Ford sedan." She scrunches her nose, then says, "Wait, no, that was my last car. This one is a Honda. Or is it a Hyundai?" She nods her head in quick succession. "It definitely starts with an 'H.'"

Sam rubs his jaw and says tightly, "Great. That only leaves fifteen different brands."

"With three pairs of eyes, we'll find it in no time," I say, mostly to reassure myself.

Sam turns to the woman. "It's in a handicapped spot, right?"

"No, it is not," she replies with a lift of her chin.

He tilts his head back and blows out a long puff of air. "Have you tried pressing the alarm button?"

"It doesn't work," she says, shaking her head. "The battery died, and I haven't gotten around to replacing it."

"Perfect," Sam mutters, and I shoot him a glare.

I touch the woman on her shoulder. "Where have you already looked?"

"Everywhere," she says, waving her arm back and forth. "I'm starting to worry it's been stolen."

Sam's face visibly brightens. "I'll call security."

"Wait, you didn't even *try* looking," I say.

He stares at me, and for a moment I start to wonder if I've pushed him too far, but then he abruptly turns and points to a row of cars. "What about any of those? Have you checked down there?"

"Um, I'm not sure." The woman squints her eyes through her glasses. "I think I see one that might be it."

We head in that direction and pass a couple white sedans along the way, but none of them is hers. The three of us pace up and down the ramp, craning our necks to spot it.

"What a darling outfit," she says, pointing to me. "I wish I could show off my legs like that."

I glance down and shake my head in despair. "It's supposed to stay past my knees, but it refuses to cooperate."

"Well, you know what they say—if you've got it, flaunt it."

"Ladies." Sam claps his hands once. "Can we focus, *please*."

Jeez. Doesn't he know that women can multitask? That's how we can apply makeup with one hand and drive with the other.

There's one last white car near the end of the row, and I hold my breath and silently pray that its hers. She peers at it, then shakes her head sadly. "It's not this one either. I really do think it was stolen."

Sam gives me an *"I told you so"* look. "Probably, since we've combed through the entire second floor. I'll get security—"

"Second floor?" the woman gasps, her hand fluttering to her mouth. "We're on the second floor?"

"Yeah." Sam turns to her with narrowed eyes. "Why?"

"Oh dear." Two pink circles stain her cheeks as she confesses, "I parked on the third. I'm so sorry," she adds, looking flustered. "I must be having a senior moment."

A stunned silence follows, and I quickly try to think of something to say that might make her feel better. "I've been having those since I was twelve."

The woman gives a half-hearted smile but is clearly still embarrassed. Not that I blame her. I'd hate to look like a fool in front of two strangers, especially if one of them was as grouchy as Sam.

"It's fine," Sam says, with a brusque nod. "Glad you figured it out. We should get going, Penina." His face clearly reads, *"Don't even think about arguing,"* and then he smiles at the old lady. "It's been nice meeting you—"

"And obviously, we'll come with you to the third floor," I interrupt, ignoring Sam's sharp intake of breath. "Just to make sure it's really there. Right, dear?" I add, batting my eyelashes.

A vein in Sam's neck visibly throbs, and instead of replying, he bares his teeth.

I hook my arm through the woman's. "I'm Penina, by the way. What's your name?"

CHAPTER NINE

"Fashion is only the attempt to realize art in living forms and social interactions."

—*Francis Bacon*

"There's thirty minutes of my life I'll never get back," Sam mutters as the taillights of the woman's car disappear around the corner.

I smile and fall into step beside him. "Isn't it a great feeling to help someone out?"

"Are you asking for my honest opinion or what you want to hear?"

My smile falters. "Um, it was supposed to be rhetorical?"

"I'll tell you my real opinion," he says, as though there was ever a doubt he wouldn't. "Only masochists think helping others feels good. For everyone else, it's like stubbing your toe against a hard object. You know what does feel good? Helping yourself."

I give him a sideways glance. That's crazy. *He's* crazy. Everyone knows that the key to happiness is helping others—I didn't make this up. It's on keychains and bumper stickers and posters and other stuff. "Maybe *you're* the problem," I say as we approach the parking ramp's elevator. "Has that ever occurred to you?"

He presses the down button, then turns to face me. "Let me get this straight. You think *I'm* the one with a problem?" he says, hooking his thumb toward his chest. The elevator doors open with a *ping*, and he steps inside. "Because I'm not the one that exchanged names and phone numbers with a perfect stranger."

I frown and follow him inside. I press my back against the wall and shrug. "She's a nice woman who needs help with her wardrobe options. There's nothing wrong with that."

Sam shakes his head and jabs the ground-floor button. "It's not exactly normal, either."

I fold my arms and think. Maybe it's not 'normal' to make friends with people I've just met, but I've been doing it my whole life. One of my father's favorite stories is the time he turned his back on me in a store only to find me, aged four, chatting to some stranger with big biceps and tattoo sleeves.

The elevator comes to a stop and Sam and I head out. His stony profile reminds me of a moody male model walking down the runway. Although it's only been a few days since I've known him, I have yet to see the guy be genuinely happy. Or relaxed. It's like his personality only has one setting, and that's crabby pants. He's dedicated and driven when it comes to work, but what does he do for fun? I glance at him again. Maybe he moonlights as a prison guard.

We continue toward the jewelry store in silence. A door with the words "Eternity Diamonds" emblazoned in glittery script comes into view, and Sam stops in front of it. "Listen, Superwoman, if there's anyone in there who looks confused or needs help, do me a favor and keep quiet."

I've never been a violent person, but the image of handcuffing him to a pole and kicking him in the shins is suddenly appealing. *Very* appealing.

He exhales and runs a hand through his hair. "All I'm saying is don't go looking for trouble."

Self-centered, pompous butthead! I don't go *looking* for trouble, but I refuse to turn a blind eye to it.

He opens the door and murmurs, "And remember to act like we're in love."

"Yeah, but it won't be easy," I whisper, walking past him. "I'm not feeling too fond of you at the moment."

"Believe me," he utters softly just above my ear, where his breath tickles my neck, "it's mutual."

* * *

My patent-leather, sling-back heels sink into the plush blue carpet as I take in the large, airy room with its wall-to-wall showcases featuring jewelry on pedestals of differing heights. Necklaces adorn blue velvet displays, and earrings and rings sparkle from slotted ramps. Watches are shown in a rotating clear acrylic case with built-in spotlights. A group of sales associates are talking in a corner, and in the center of the room there appears to be a . . .

"This place has a *bar*?" I gasp as Sam comes to join me. I point to a finished, white, semicircular panel displaying champagne bottles and glasses. "Remind me again why I work for you," I say, moving toward the bar, already imagining clinking glasses of sparkling champagne with customers, "because I'm having trouble remembering."

He leans against a counter and crosses his ankles. "You want a shovel for that hole you're digging?"

I run my hand along the glass, checking out the merchandise. "Does it come with a martini?"

His lips twist into an almost smile, and in that moment, it's like a glimpse into the *real* Sam, the one I first met in the hospital. A human with a sense of humor, instead of the serious, brooding version he is at work.

"Hi there—welcome!" A saleswoman dressed in a white silk blouse and tight red skirt approaches. She's all ruby-red lips and incredible cheekbones, glistening black hair and the kind of curves that inspire dirty song lyrics.

"My name is Carly." she smiles, extending her hand first to Sam, then me. Her eyes linger on Sam's several beats longer than they do on mine, and I wonder if he picks up on the fact that so many women find him attractive. What am I thinking? Of course he does. "Is there something particular I can help you with?"

"Yes, I think we spoke earlier today about engagement rings. I'm Sam, and this is my fiancée"—he pauses—"Prudence. But most people call her Prude for short."

Prude? I narrow my eyes. Two can play that game. I clear my throat and gesture toward Sam, "Most people call him Sordid for short."

Sam simply gives me a dark look that implies I'll be paying for that little comment later.

"Great," Carly chirps with a wide smile. "Nice to meet you, Prude and Sordid."

Sam sighs while I say, "The pleasure is ours."

"It's so refreshing to see a couple come pick out the engagement ring together."

"Prude insisted," Sam replies. "She's very . . ." He rubs his chin and scrunches his face like he's trying to figure out how to delicately phrase something. "Difficult," he finishes.

So, my name is Prude, *and* I have a bad personality. Aren't I a catch?

Carly laughs as though Sam is the funniest person she's ever met. "Luckily, you've come to the right place," she says to me with a wink. "And congratulations! Can I get you some champagne to celebrate?"

"No, thank you," I say, knowing it won't be kosher. Sam refuses too, probably because it wouldn't be up to his standards.

"Alright, then." Carly makes a hand motion. "Follow me, please. Do you have a certain style of ring in mind, uh, Prude?"

"Something sharp that can double as a weapon," I suggest.

Sam lifts an eyebrow and does that almost-smile thing while Carly giggles.

"Kidding." I laugh. "Totally kidding. I actually love vintage-style rings."

Carly makes a follow-me motion. "Wonderful, we have a great selection of those. And what pretty fingers you have," she says, glancing down.

I smile, aware that she's trying to butter me up the way a good sales-person does. Then again, my fingers are pretty nice, so you can't blame the woman for pointing out the obvious. "Thank you."

She pulls out a velvet cloth and smooths it onto the counter. "There are a lot of options here, so we'll have fun figuring out what you like." She unlocks a display case and pulls out several rings. I make the appropriate oohs and aahs until I see one that literally steals my breath away.

"This is the Asscher cut, three-stone halo ring set with a five-carat diamond."

"Not bad." Sam turns to me. "What do you think?"

"Not bad? It's *perfect*," I breathe, picking it up and inspecting it from all angles. The clarity of the diamond, the cut and design—everything about it is mesmerizing. "This is the exact ring I would want if I were—" I stop myself just in time. "If I were shopping without a budget," I say, putting it back down. When I look up, I catch Sam studying me.

Over the next hour, we discuss engagement rings, the quality of diamonds, and payment plans, and we study a few diamonds under the microscope, at Carly's insistence. The three of us are joking and laughing and getting along great, but as they say, all parties have a pooper, and Sam, of course, ends up being ours.

"What about fake diamonds?" he suddenly asks, drumming his long fingers on the counter. "Do you have those?"

Carly's smile freezes. It's probably the first time someone has uttered the word *fake* in this store. "Um, we don't have cubic zirconia, but there are some beautiful moissanite rings here."

"Excellent." Sam nods. "The cheaper, the better."

Words sure to capture any girl's heart. Except Carly's, based on the look of horror on her face.

"Okey dokey," she says, her voice unnaturally high. "I'll be right back with some."

Poor woman. She had probably counted in her head how much this commission would earn her, and then Sam goes and ruins it. We've already wasted so much of her time, and another customer just walked in.

"Actually, we can come back another time," I tell Carly, and then turn to Sam. "We have so many options to discuss. Right, honey?"

"Wrong." He folds his arms and adds, "Unless you want to pay for it yourself?"

"Aren't you so hilarious." I give him a big dopey grin, then face Carly again. "Of course, not everyone gets his sense of humor."

Carly looks back and forth between us and breaks into a grin. "You two are the cutest! Listen," she says, pointing to a set of chairs that face a glass-topped desk. "Why don't you guys have a seat over there, and I'll grab a few of those rings for you to look at. Make yourselves comfortable."

The moment Carly is out of sight, I whisper to Sam, "Don't you feel bad, stringing her along like this? She'll be so disappointed when we don't buy anything."

"No." Sam takes out his phone and starts to type. "Disappointment is part of life."

Profound words for someone born with a silver spoon. I study his model profile and expensive suit and can't help but think he couldn't possibly know what true disappointment is. He probably thinks a traffic jam is a huge catastrophe, whereas I have to figure out how to save one sister's house and marriage, *and* work out who is going to raise my other's sister's love child.

Zevi will rescue all of us, I remind myself. He'll save Libby's house, figure out who the father of Fraydie's baby is and bribe the dude to marry her, and we'll fall madly in love. As long as I'm fantasizing, I might as well throw in a couple of kids for myself too. Maybe a pool and a pony or two. Oh, and definitely that five-carat diamond ring that Carly showed us. Obviously, I'd have to take it off before going in the pool, because of the chlorine, and I probably shouldn't wear it when I ride the ponies either—*are adults even allowed to ride ponies?*

I'm about to type that into Google—how did people know *anything* pre-Google days?—but then Carly returns with a tray full of diamonds. I put my phone away and feign interest in the rings while Sam peppers her with boring finance questions.

A salesman comes over and taps Carly on the shoulder. "Carly, your mom's on the phone. Says it's urgent."

She sighs and rubs her forehead like she's annoyed instead of worried. If that happened to me, I'd have shot out of my chair faster than a bullet. Did she not hear the *urgent* part?

"Sorry," Carly says, placing her hands on the table as she stands up. "Excuse me a minute."

Mr. Congeniality takes out his phone, so I do the same and scroll through my Instagram feed, hearting the comments made on my last post, but Carly's voice is loud, and it's impossible not to overhear the conversation.

"I can't, Mom—you know I'm working . . . I have been, that one guy almost worked out . . . No, I don't want your help . . . Because I know what I'm looking for, and you don't!" she says, her voice rising in volume.

"Don't even think about it," Sam murmurs, eyes still glued to his screen.

"I have no idea what you're talking about." Actually, I know exactly what he's talking about, but it's annoying that he knows how my mind works.

"Whatever's going on," he replies, tipping his head in Carly's direction, "just stay out of it."

I really, *really* don't like his tone. He's talking as if I'm a badly behaved dog with its head in the trash.

I mean, yeah, I was *thinking* about saying something, but still. Not cool.

"She's obviously looking for a guy," I say, inching closer so we're not overheard, "and I was just thinking how cute the two of you would look together, but then I realized she wouldn't want you." I wait a moment to let that sink in. "And do you want to know why?" I ask, crossing one leg over the other.

His gaze briefly lands on my legs before returning to his screen. "Not really."

"Because even though you're disgustingly handsome and obviously wealthy"—I pause again for dramatic effect—"you're not *nice*."

He glances up from his phone. "It's amazing my father never fired you."

"Why would he? We got along great because *he* was nice." I fold my arms and say pointedly, "I miss him."

He opens his mouth to say something but shuts it when Carly reappears.

"Sorry about that," she says with a bright smile that seems forced. "Babysitting issues."

"Babysitting? Oh, I thought—" I glance at Sam, who gives me a smug look. Okay, so I misread the situation. But she still needs help.

"It's hard to find good babysitters," I say. "When I was a kid, I hated mine on principle."

"What principle would that be exactly?" Sam says, pocketing his phone. "That parents should never leave their kids?"

"I'm not saying it was rational," I say, a little defensively. "But yeah. Basically."

Carly fiddles with a charm on her bracelet. "I never liked my babysitters either, which is why I use my mom all the time, but it's getting to be too much for her." She pauses and shakes her head. "Anyway, enough about my problems. Let's talk about these rings—"

"You know," I say, leaning forward, "there's a woman in my neighborhood who babysits a lot. If you're interested, I could give you her number."

"Oh, you're sweet," she laughs, batting her hand, "but don't worry about it—"

"Yes, Prude," Sam says, "don't worry about it."

"Are you sure?" I pretend not to notice the way Sam is glaring at me. "She's really nice. And kids love her."

"Well . . ." Carly hesitates.

"Trust me, your kid will *adore* her."

"I guess it wouldn't hurt." She grins, then throws up her hands. "Why not?"

"Great!" I beam, reaching for my phone. "What's your number?"

Sam lowers his face into the palm of his hand as Carly and I exchange numbers and then babysitting stories. Eventually, he redirects the conversation back to fake diamonds, and after going over the pros and cons of moissanite, he thanks Carly for her time and motions to me that we need to get going. Carly gives us her card, no doubt hoping we'll be back to buy something.

"I've never seen any couple with as much chemistry as you two," Carly grins as she walks us to the door. "How long have you been together?" she asks.

Sam doesn't miss a beat. "Not that long, but when you know, you know." He gives me a fake tender smile. "Isn't that right, Prudence?"

"Absolutely, Mr. Kleinfeld."

He turns to Carly and shrugs. "She's very traditional."

Carly laughs and we promise to be in touch. The minute the door closes behind us, Sam growls, "What the hell?"

I gaze up at him with big lovey-dovey eyes and smile. "You know she's watching, right?"

He glances behind me and breaks into a fake grin. "Shit. Let's go." He grabs my hand and pulls me along beside him, like a caveman on a schedule.

"What are you so mad about?"

"I can't believe you have to ask. That thing about the babysitter," he says, "and then the old lady with the car. And earlier today in our store with the crying customer. It's like you have a Superwoman complex."

At least he's no longer calling me fragile. I shake my hand loose from his grip, and because I'm truly curious as to how his mind works, I ask, "What's so bad about helping people?"

He stops moving and turns to face me. "You do realize that there are millions and millions of people in the world suffering right now, and there's absolutely nothing you or I can do to stop it?"

"I'm three for three so far," I say, lifting my shoulders. "And the day is still young."

He stares me down. "You have to accept the fact that you can't fix everyone and everything. It isn't possible, and you'll exhaust yourself trying."

I shake my head. "Are you saying it's better to look the other way? Instead of helping someone?"

A frown tugs at the corners of his mouth. "Listen, you have a big heart and a drive to help people. But that doesn't mean you're responsible for every person you meet." He pauses. "You have to accept the fact that you can't save everyone, Superwoman," he says in a softer voice. "No one can."

* * *

A week has passed since the jewelry field trip. Sam has been in and out of the office all week trying to spearhead a new business campaign, and Gina has been grumpier than ever. I think as much as she hated Joe, she hates change even more.

Anyway, time to focus on the task at hand—I have a big date tonight, and I need to look my best. It's not every day you get to meet your future husband, who is evidently successful, Orthodox from birth, and has a reputation for being a philanthropist. The only strike against Zevi is that he comes from a divorced home, but even that isn't so uncommon nowadays, which makes this setup all the more suspicious: if he's that amazing, why would he agree to date someone like me?

There's got to be something wrong with him. It's the only explanation. Maybe he's impotent or has a glass eye or is one of those people that hates kids.

I check my eyeliner in the mirror and frown. Shoot. My left cat eye is swooped down instead of up. I reach for the makeup remover in my bathroom cabinet and set to work fixing it.

If Judaism allowed tattoos, I would definitely get permanent eye makeup. Oh, and a star of David on the inside of my wrist—and maybe a strand of pearls around my ankle.

Okay, time to see the overall effect. Moving to the full-length mirror hanging behind my bedroom door, I turn from side to side. Hair? Check. Makeup? Check. Outfit and shoes? Check and check. Perfume? No, but I've got deodorant and pheromones, and that ought to count for something.

I grab my purse and keys and head to our prearranged meeting spot—the lobby of the Viridian Inn in downtown Minneapolis. Maya thinks it's hilarious that Orthodox Jews have dates in hotel lobbies. When I mentioned the location of my date earlier today, she doubled over in laughter and said, "Do you book a room for the second date?"

Ha ha. I have heard stories about overnight dates, but I can't see myself doing that. I'd keep picturing Mrs. Z's face lecturing me about my reputation.

Still, there is some logic to using lobbies as a dating forum—it's unlikely you'll run into friends, and there's nothing much to distract your attention.

Traffic is light, and twenty minutes later I arrive at the hotel entrance. Inside, the scent of freshly cut roses greets me, along with classical music drifting from a self-playing grand piano—I used to be creeped out by those pianos as a child but now, as an adult, find them irrefutably cool. Crushed red velvet furniture and gold-plated cigar tables are artfully arranged beneath waterfall chandeliers. Crystal wall sconces twinkle above freestanding sculptures, and the black-and-white checked flooring instills a distinct art deco vibe or Paris meets SoHo.

I glance around the room, searching for a good-looking guy with a yarmulke, but the only people here are a middle-aged couple with their two kids, and a cleaning woman pushing a supply cart.

"Can I help you?" The woman behind the front desk smiles politely.

"Oh, hi," I say, smoothing my hair back. "I'm supposed to be meeting someone, but I guess he's not here yet."

"Have you tried the bar?" she asks, pointing to the left. "Down the corridor, on your right-hand side."

"Thanks. I'll try that."

I head in that direction, silently regretting my choice of shoes. The high heels make my legs look nice, but take torture to a whole new level. I limp down the hallway, feeling a blister begin to form on my pinky toe. Why can't I learn my lesson? It's like I get amnesia as soon as the pain and bruising go away. And yeah, they make my legs look good, but the limping kind of ruins the vibe, especially when—*whoa!* I slip and my arms flail helplessly in search of something to anchor myself, but there's nothing. I yelp and crash into the wall.

"Uh, Penina?"

I wince and blink my eyes into focus. "Hi?"

My breath hitches and I stare in awe, forgetting to be embarrassed as I take in this man's glorious face and body. He's got dirty-blond hair and chiseled cheekbones, and muscles so ripped they're practically jumping out of his clothes.

It's the closest thing to a spiritual experience I've had in a long time, and I send up a silent prayer of thanks.

"That was a quick save on your part." He smiles as he gestures toward me. "You could have hit your head on the floor." He adds, "I saw the whole thing happen."

Of course, he did. "I love to make an entrance," I say, then immediately blush. *Geez, great line, Penina.*

He chuckles. "I'm Zevi by the way," he says, "in case you were wondering."

The only thing I'm wondering is why a man like this is still single— and interested in dating a woman he knows can't give him children. My eyes briefly run over him, trying to figure out what invisible issue he must have. *Please, don't let it be impotency . . .*

"Your name fits you," I say.

"Yeah?" He grins. "How so?"

"Zev means 'wolf' in Hebrew and you have gorgeous wolf eyes." I blush and look away. *What is wrong with me?* First, he sees me crash, and now I'm hitting on him in the cheesiest way possible. I gingerly touch the side of my head. Could I have had a concussion? "Sorry." I grimace, holding up my hands. "Clearly, I wasn't socialized enough as a child."

Zevi laughs. "Oh my G-d, you're hilarious. Come on," he says, gesturing, "let's find a place to sit."

He leads me to a nestled alcove with blooming evergreens, far enough away from the front desk and main hallway to provide privacy. He makes himself comfortable on a suede tufted loveseat, then offers to get me a drink. "Whiskey, vodka, beer . . . what're you in the mood for?"

I choose one of the red velvet armchairs across from Zevi and set my purse on it. "I'm fine, thanks."

"You sure?"

The first and only time I had a mixed alcoholic beverage—three Sea Breezes, to be exact—I ended up grabbing my friend's phone and calling her brother, to whom I then swore my undying love and allegiance before passing out on the floor. In the morning I discovered that I had actually spoken to his pregnant wife. I've never trusted myself since.

"I'm good, thanks."

"Soda?" Zevi's shoe jiggles, and it occurs to me that he might be as nervous as I am.

"No thanks." I don't want to risk choking and coughing the way I did in Sam's car.

"Okay." His eyes scan the room, like he's looking for someone or something. "So!" he says, rubbing his hands together briskly, "tell me about yourself, Penina. The matchmaker said you're in the jewelry business?"

"I'm in sales." I nod. "I work at a small, family-run jewelry store. It's a great place. I started working there to put myself through college and somehow never had the heart to leave. The people I work with are wonderful." Then I remember Gina and Sam. "Well, one of them is."

Tapping the rolled arm of the loveseat, Zevi smiles encouragingly. "Do you love it?"

"Yes." I nod, leaning forward. "I love finding the perfect gift for people. It's rewarding knowing that you're helping make people happy. Plus, jewelry is fun. I'm like a kid in a candy shop."

Zevi smiles. "Do you have a big collection of jewelry yourself?"

I picture my modest closet and the two drawers within that house my jewelry. "It's not big by most people's standards," I admit, "but what it lacks in quantity, it makes up for in quality."

"I'm the same way," he replies, crossing his knee over his leg. "When I first started working, I ate nothing but Ramen for several months, just to save up money for this one contemporary sculpture."

A kindred spirit! "Was it worth it?"

"Beyond a doubt. There's nothing like working hard for something, to make you love it even more."

Zevi is turning out to be more than just a pretty face; this dude has substance. And there's something incredibly irresistible about a handsome man with character. Unlike Sam, whose life revolves around work and telling people what's wrong with them. Bless his heart.

Maybe this is the guy I've been waiting for all these years. Maybe I won't end up being a spinster. Maybe I'm finally getting a shot at true happiness.

"Every time I pass through the foyer," he continues, "where the sculpture is positioned—it's a reminder to me that anything in life is possible. You just have to be willing to work for it."

"Exactly," I agree, tucking hair behind my ear. "So, what kind of business are you in?"

Zevi crosses his arms against his chest. "I'm a film producer and at times a director."

"Oh! Really?" I ask, taken by surprise. "I could have sworn the matchmaker said you were a businessman."

"Yeah." He smiles sheepishly, eyes drifting away. "I kind of let her assume that."

A prickle of unease courses through me. Why would he lie about that? It probably doesn't mean anything, but I can't shake the bad feeling now that I've had it.

On a completely unrelated note, if I screw my eyes real tight, I can almost make out his six-pack.

"Penina?"

I sit up straight. "Yes?"

"Just making sure you're okay. Your eyes looked a little glazed over."

"Oh!" I clear my throat, trying not to blush. "Sorry." *Geez, focus, woman.* I lean forward. "What kind of movies do you make?"

Zevi's phone vibrates, and he glances at it. "My specialty is high-concept horror."

"High what?"

Zevi taps on his phone, obviously distracted. "It just means it's easily pitched, easily summarized."

Oh, cheesy stuff. He should have just said that.

Zevi spends the next few minutes telling me about the complexities of the industry and everything that goes into making a film successful. I do my best to follow and try to fake it when I can't, but then he starts using words like *anachronism* and *neorealism*, and I'm pretty sure I couldn't even fake it now if my life depended on it. I'll have to do research on this stuff so I don't embarrass myself the next time we get together. *If we do.*

"Penina." Zevi glances up from his phone. "I need to come clean about something."

My stomach dips as though I'm on the log chute ride at the Mall of America. I knew he was too good to be true. He's going to tell me something unbearably awful, that he's not a film producer after all, or he is but they're X-rated and that *he's* a porn star *and why, why, WHY didn't I see this coming?*

He pauses, scratches his head, then looks at me guiltily. "There's someone else here who would really like to meet you."

Someone else? My heart starts to beat so fast it hurts. What are the chances it's a good someone, like a puppy or a kitten?

"Who?"

Zevi rubs the side of his neck, which is turning red from his touch. "My boyfriend."

CHAPTER TEN

"Diversity lasts when it no longer has to be the subject of a story."
—*Robin Givhan*

A thin man with short dark brown hair takes a seat beside Zevi. He's wearing a thick bracelet on his wrist, and on his face rests a pair of Coke-bottle glasses that should look nerdy but somehow comes off as artsy instead. The man reaches for Zevi's hand and gives it a reassuring squeeze, and Zevi responds with a quick peck on his cheek.

It's official: I hate my life.

"I'll have that drink after all," I say, glancing away. Sure, I may end up drunk calling people and pledging my love before the night is over, but it's a risk I'm willing to make. The way I see it, I've earned the right to blur the lines of reality, at least for a little while. Is it too much to ask that for once—seriously, just *once*—I'm not given the short end of the stick? That I might get set up with a normal guy and fall in love? That the person I'm set up with is exactly as he seems?

Zevi leaves to get the drinks, and the other guy—*the boyfriend*—introduces himself.

"I'm Jack, by the way." He lifts his hand in greeting and smiles, revealing straight white teeth. "Sorry about the ambush. You're probably pretty shocked."

Shocked doesn't even begin to describe it.

"Shocked and confused." I laugh without humor. "I'm not sure why I'm here."

"I get that." He nods, stroking his goatee. "I don't want to say too much without Zevi, but trust me when I say, what we have planned . . . it'll be good for you too." He looks at me for a silent moment, then adds with a smile, "Don't worry! Your face is going to light up the room when you hear what we've got planned."

And then it hits me.

Oh my G-d. They want a threesome. I've been recruited for some bizarre Orthodox Jewish orgy, and Mrs. Zelikovitch is my pimp. To be honest, I always suspected there were a few loose screws there, but *this?* No way did I see this coming. Although, let's face it—if anyone fit the job description, it's her.

I glance around the room as my heart races and my stomach curdles. The life I knew just went from somewhat dysfunctional to absolute out-and-out insanity.

"Listen." I clear my throat, and my eyes have a hard time reaching his face. "I'm not into that . . . stuff."

"Oh, c'mon"—Jack laughs—"everyone is into that stuff."

Clearly, he has never met my rabbi or his wife. I shake my head and unzip my purse. "Not me."

"Why do you say that?" Jack says. "You don't even know what it is yet."

I rummage for my car keys and stand up. "I've got a feeling."

"Hold on a sec! At least hear us out before you go."

I shake my head. "No can do."

"See these eyes?" he says, removing his glasses, then batting his long lashes. "They're about to get real wet and teary if you don't sit back down."

Normally, I wouldn't think twice about complying, but these guys are master manipulators and I'm through with being played.

"I'm legit crying right now," he says in a hoarse voice, and his eyes actually fill with tears. *Master manipulators,* I remind myself. But there's still the problem with Libby's house. I gaze up at the ceiling, wondering if G-d wants me to prostitute myself in order to save my sister. Does He do this sort of thing?

"You're our only hope," Jack croaks as a tear rolls down his cheek.

Crap. My body doesn't even give me a choice—it just propels me back into the chair while Jack smiles and crosses his legs, the picture of contentment.

Zevi returns with our drinks, beer for them and hard cider for me.

"For the record," I say, "I'm only hearing you out for the free liquor. But there is zero chance of me signing up for whatever group activity you've got planned. As soon as this bottle is empty, I'm out of here." I murmur the Hebrew blessing, then tilt the bottle back and savor the cool sweetness on my tongue.

"Okay," Zevi says, watching me carefully, like I'm a dangerous wildebeest.

What a date this is turning out to be. As far as dates rank, it's definitely up there with Janie the NICU nurse's last one—

"Hey," I say suddenly, leaning forward, "Have you considered investing in a humanlike doll?"

Zevi turns to Jack and says, "What exactly did you say to her?"

"Nothing that would explain that," he replies with big eyes, gesturing toward me.

Zevi shakes his head as if to clear it. Then he takes a deep breath and says, "Penina, my mother is dying."

"What?" I glance between them, taken aback.

Jack nods. "His mom has heart disease, and the doctors aren't too optimistic that she'll make it."

"Oh no, I'm sorry," I murmur, still unsure where this is going.

Jack threads his fingers through Zevi's, and a pinch of envy washes through me. What would it be like to have that kind of all-encompassing love and support? To know that someone has your back, no matter what?

"Zevi loves his mom very much," Jack says, adjusting his glasses. The overhead light casts a shadow over the lower half of his face, making his mocha-brown eyes seem that much bigger. "Their relationship is complicated, though. Zevi's mother is Orthodox."

Glancing at their entwined hands, I can only imagine how his mother would feel if she were to see this. "And your father?"

"Not in the picture," Zevi says curtly.

Something about his abrupt response makes me think there's more to that story. "Is he alive?"

"Just until I can get my hands on him," Zevi mutters.

Gotcha. We hate the dad. But I still don't understand how I fit into all this.

"The point is," Jack hurriedly carries on, "that Zevi's mother's dying wish is to see him married to a nice Jewish girl."

I glance pointedly at their entwined hands. "I don't see that happening any time soon."

"That's where you come in," Zevi says. "Would you be open to marrying me and living together until my mother passes away?"

I suck in a deep breath and my jaw drops. The shocks keep on coming; any more, and I might pass out. And *marry him? Lie to his family and mine and the whole world?* I feel sorry for Zevi, but this is way too complicated a charade. Is it even *legal? What if I end up in jail because of this?* "Sorry, but I don't want to get involved in this."

"I'll pay you, of course," Zevi says. "Whatever you want—just name your price."

"See?" Jack says, waving his finger. "I told you there's something good in it for you."

He could've just said it was money from the beginning. I tilt the bottle and swallow more cider. "Any price?" I reiterate. Zevi nods. "Five million," I say because it's the first number that comes to my head.

Zevi and Jack exchange a look. "Okay, I think I can swing that," Zevi says.

I stare at him incredulously—it was a joke. I didn't actually think he'd say yes. Now, of course, I regret not going higher. But in all seriousness, five million dollars would solve all of my problems—and by my problems, I mean my sisters'.

"What, um"—I pause to clear my throat—"what would I have to do exactly?"

"Everything a regular couple would do. We'd have a small Jewish ceremony with family and friends. Obviously, you wouldn't be able to tell people the truth. I can't have anyone in my family think it's fake."

I stare at Zevi, then Jack. Are they for real? Because this is legitimately crazy. No, *beyond* crazy. "You want me to fake marry you?"

"No, no," he says, shaking his head, "I want you to marry me for real. It has to be as authentic as possible so my family buys it. We'll do everything by the book."

I gulp. "Everything?"

"Everything," he confirms, and takes a sip of his beer.

"Even the wedding night?" I squeak.

Zevi starts to choke, and Jack pats his back. When Zevi regains control of his voice, he croaks, "Except for that."

Who does stuff like this? It feels like an elaborate prank, and I glance around the bar looking for hidden cameras.

He holds up a finger, signaling he needs a moment, probably for his voice to return to normal. It's funny, because I had been afraid that that was going to happen to me. Oh, the irony.

"And you'd move to New York to live with me," Zevi continues. He leans forward, clears his throat. "I know this is a lot to ask of someone. But if you agree to this, you would be provided with enough money to live comfortably for the rest of your life. You'd never have to work again. And," he adds, "we'd get divorced after my mother passes. This wouldn't be a life sentence."

Something must be wrong with me. This is the answer to my family's prayers, and instead of feeling elated, I'm on the verge of tears. I inhale deeply through my nose and stare at the two of them, trying to stay composed. For once in my life, I thought things were finally falling into place. Here was a man I could fall in love with, get married and live with happily ever after, et cetera. And then, like a bad magic trick, he pulls his *boyfriend* out of thin air, then asks me to marry him anyway!

The disappointment welling up inside me makes it hard to breathe. It's like there's a metal anchor lodged inside my chest, with no way to get it out. I thought I had *finally* been given a shot at love, and for a short while I even felt normal. Not like a girl with a medical defect, but a girl who might be seen for who she is—the real Penina.

Stupid, *stupid* girl.

I tilt the bottle into my mouth and gulp the rest of the cider down.

"Our girl can sure drink," Jack murmurs to Zevi.

"Want another one?" Zevi offers.

I shake my head. A thought hits me, and I ask, "Why me, of all people?"

Zevi's eyes soften and he glances at Jack before answering. "Because you're like me, in a way. You were born differently too. And I figured if I could find someone with a unique set of circumstances, someone who maybe had a hard time getting married herself because she's seen as . . ." He breaks off and gestures with his hand. "Anyway. It just made sense."

I swallow against the sudden lump in my throat. What was he about to say? That I'm seen as what—damaged? Less than? Not good enough?

"And you look like Gal Gadot," Jack cuts in with a grin. "We need someone that can match His Royal Hotness in the looks department," he says with a playful jab to Zevi's side.

"If anything, people will wonder why you haven't been snatched up yet," Zevi says, and I'm reminded of how Sam said those exact words to me.

"She looks a little like Ashira too, if Ashira were brunette, don't you think?" Jack adds.

"Who?" I ask.

"My younger sister," Zevi explains. "Yeah, I can see that—similar bone structure," he says to Jack.

I have to agree to this. I can't *not* do it. I'd have the money to save Libby's house—even buy her a way better one if she wanted. And I could put money down for my nephew's and niece's college funds, buy my parents a new car. I could pay for a nanny to watch Fraydie's baby. *It would change everything.*

So why am I dragging my feet? The word *yes* is stuck in my throat, and it's not coming out.

"Please," Zevi adds. "You're my only hope. There's no one else I can ask that would make it believable. Think it over at least."

Relief rushes through me. Maybe I just need some time to adjust. "I will," I say, causing Zevi's face to instantly brighten. "When do you need to know my decision by?"

"I'll wait as long as you need," Zevi says. He pulls a card from his pocket and hands it to me. His eyes shine with hope, and it pulls at my heartstrings, knowing how much this decision means to him. "Hopefully my mother's condition doesn't deteriorate too fast."

I nod, catching his meaning. Death has its own time line, and it doesn't wait for anyone. I tuck the card inside my purse and stand up. "Well . . ." I smile. "Thank you for the drink. It's been an interesting evening. Definitely unlike any date I've had before."

Both men chuckle. I turn to leave, when Jack says, "Nice eyeliner by the way. Those cat eyes are not easy."

"I know!" I grin, then wave. It's gratifying when someone appreciates a job well done.

Once I'm home, lying in bed, I have a hard time falling asleep. Thoughts race through my head, fast and furious, and the worst part is that I can't share them with anyone. I cover my face with a pillow as moisture gathers in the corners of my eyes. I'm in emotional solitary confinement, and it's torture.

At first glance it seems like a no-brainer: marry the sweet, kind, gay man and collect the money. Money, which by the way, could not only save my sister's house but her marriage too.

On the other hand, this arrangement would end in divorce, which would be one more strike against me in the dating world. I'd be single again, right back to square one except having to carry this huge lie with me for the rest of my life. And I *hate* lying. Although that's probably because I'm bad at it and always get caught.

I groan, throw off the covers, and stare up at my bedroom ceiling. I had thought tonight was my one shot at happiness, my chance at starting a whole new future, a clean slate full of opportunities. But I'm forgetting that this isn't about me. It's never been about me.

It's about Libby.

CHAPTER ELEVEN

"Whoever said that money can't buy happiness simply didn't know where to go shopping."

—*Bo Derek*

"One. More. Store," Sam says through gritted teeth as he fires up the car. "This engaged couple thing is definitely getting old. Some people aren't meant to be brought out in public, and you"—he pauses to catch my eye—"are definitely one of them."

Earlier today Sam appeared in the cleaning room as I worked diligently on a rusted bracelet, and basically kidnapped me. I told him—in very strong language—to take Maya or Gina, but I swear he has some kind of oppositional defiant issue. It's like the more I argue, the more stubborn he gets.

"Pot. Kettle." I unzip my purse and start pulling out a water bottle, when he suddenly slams on the brakes, snatches the purse from my hands, and catapults it into the back seat like it's a bomb about to detonate. I stare, open-mouthed, as my purse briefly hovers on the edge of the back seat before sliding to the floor and landing in crumpled defeat. Sam releases his foot from the brake and resumes driving.

"Do you mind telling me what that was for?"

"It's safer this way."

The man has clearly lost his mind. "What in the world are you talking about?"

"The coughing and choking and gasping for air thing. I do not want a repeat of you bent over on the side of the highway, puking." He turns the car onto Forty-Second Street.

"First of all, get your facts straight. I didn't puke on the side of the highway, I *dry-heaved*. Major difference."

"Whatever it was," he says, braking to a stop at the intersection, "it wasn't pretty."

I stick my tongue out at him, which in hindsight probably wasn't the smartest move.

He looks at me incredulously. "Did you just stick your tongue out at me?"

"Me? I would never do such a thing." I point to the traffic light. "It's green."

"Unbelievable," he mutters, returning his attention to the road. "You are unbelievable."

I get the distinct impression that he doesn't mean that in a good way.

"Do you want to know the last time someone stuck their tongue out at me?"

"Nope," I say, admiring my nail polish. The dark shade of purple is definitely vampy, but goes surprisingly well with my Navajo Red Mountain turquoise ring.

"*Third grade*, Penina. It was Benny Schwimmer, and just so you know"—he gives me a significant glance—"I kicked his ass for that."

I burrow deeper into my seat. I do not want to be his next ass-kicking. Still, I can't resist adding, "I bet you started it."

"Probably," he agrees, and chuckles unexpectedly. I'm taken aback at this rare display of normal human behavior. So taken aback that I'm afraid to say anything in case I ruin it. The next few minutes pass in comfortable silence, the kind that doesn't make me tense up and urge me to speak.

But then he goes and ruins it.

"It's interesting," he says, flipping down his sun visor. "The other night I watched a documentary about Orthodox Jews, and I learned that most of them get married a year or two after high school, and it got me thinking: How come you've never married?"

A pinprick of unease crawls through my flesh. In the time span of five seconds flat, the ambience went from comfortable and relaxed to something that makes me want to cover my ears and run in the opposite direction.

"You're smart and funny. Irrationally, abnormally kind," he adds, unaware of my growing discomfort.

I burrow further down into my seat, wishing I could disappear. He's going down that rabbit hole again, trying to figure out why I'm not married.

"You make sure that Gina's bowl of candy is always full."

I glance at him, surprised that he knew. "That's purely a self-survival tactic. Gina and sugar withdrawal is a dimension of hell you don't want to experience. Sooo . . . what kind of music do you like?" I say, grasping for something else to talk about, something that doesn't involve me being at the center of it.

"I can't figure it out—" He abruptly stops and shakes his head. "Sorry. I shouldn't have said anything. I don't even know why I'm talking about this." He sighs.

Why is he watching documentaries, anyway? He should stick to sports and the news like all of the other men. "Although," he says, turning right into a parking lot, "you're very sarcastic. Some guys find that intimidating. Immature too."

I wave my finger at him. "See, this is exactly the kind of thing that makes people stick out their tongues at you."

He flashes a sideways grin that creases the dimple in his cheek as he maneuvers the car into a parking spot. "I've obviously touched a nerve. My apologies."

If he only knew.

As Sam turns off the car and grabs the fob from the console, I'm filled with a sudden crazy urge to tell him the real reason why I never married. Which is completely out of character because it's not something I talk about, not with anyone. It's not a feel-good topic, and besides, I hate seeing that flash of pity, however brief, in their eyes. But for some insane reason, I want him to know.

"I can't have children."

Sam turns to face me. "What?"

I swallow and look down at my hands. "I never got married because I have this rare condition called uterine hypoplasia. My uterus is too small to ever carry a child."

Silence fills the car, and I glance at Sam curiously. I'm used to people telling me they're sorry by this point, as though my infertility is something they're personally responsible for. Sam's wordless reaction is . . . strange. And unnerving. "See, in your world, it's not such a big deal—"

"*My* world?"

"The non-Orthodox world," I clarify. "People choose not to have kids more and more nowadays. But if they do want children and discover they're somehow infertile—"

"Wait," Sam shakes his head. "Back up a second. What does your infertility have to do with you not being married?"

"Everything." I sigh. "Having kids is super important, so the fact that I can't have any means I'm low on the totem pole."

"But you could adopt."

"Yeah, I could. But it's not so simple," I reply. "For example, if I adopted a boy, I wouldn't be allowed to hug or kiss him after his ninth birthday, or be alone with him in the house. Because we aren't tied by blood. Although, some rabbis might say it's okay, depending on the circumstances. So," I say, exhaling, "while it is an option, it's not something that we take on lightly."

Sam shakes his head and whistles softly. "Wow. I had no idea." He leans his arm on the console and says, "You could adopt a girl."

I nod. "It's something I think about a lot, but—" I hesitate, sucking my bottom lip. "But then those same laws of separation would apply to my husband."

"You don't have to be married to adopt."

"I know. But I feel like I already have my hands full taking care of my sisters and my parents." I twist the gold ring on my thumb. "And if I did adopt one day, I'd want to share that experience with someone. I think it would be better for the kid too."

"Not necessarily," Sam counters. "It's not as though kids from two-parent households have perfect lives. Sometimes they have it worse than the single-parent ones."

"Well—"

"Do you *ever* date?" Sam interrupts.

"Yes," I say defensively, crossing my arms against my chest. "The men just tend to be twice my age and impotent."

Sam pivots so that his entire body is facing me. Peering into his gold-flecked eyes, I see a trace of sympathy, but something else too.

"Is being religious so important to you that you'd rather live a love-less life?"

I open and shut my mouth. No one has ever framed the question quite so bluntly before—at least, no one besides me. "My life isn't love-less, though. I have my family and friends."

"And that's enough for you?" Sam tilts his head, catching my eye. I hate it when he looks at me like that, like he can see straight through my cheerful facade and into my soul. "Is it?" he repeats.

No. No, it's not.

"We should get going." I unbuckle my seat belt and open the door, putting an end to the conversation. "We've got people to spy on."

Sam hesitates, like he wants to say something, but then changes his mind. We head to the jewelry store in silence, and I start to wish I had just kept my mouth shut.

A woman and her toddler approach us on the sidewalk, and the kid's walking style is half drunk sailor, half serpentine. Sam and I take a step back to give him a wider berth, but he still manages to crash into my legs.

"Oh, honey," I say, kneeling down to the boy's eye level, "are you okay?"

"Don't worry—he's used to it," the mother says, scooping up her son and planting a kiss on his cheek. "He slams into people at least once during every outing." She brushes his bangs back with her fingers as she looks us over. "Appreciate this time now, because once you have kids, there's no such thing as an easy errand," she says, rolling her eyes.

Sam and I chuckle politely and continue walking.

"You're good with kids," he says.

Why are we back to listing my personality traits? "Well, yeah," I say lightly, "because I'm one of them. I'm still eight years old in my head."

"And babies too. It makes sense that you hold—" He stops before finishing his thought.

Yes, I hold other people's babies in my spare time because I'll never hold one of my own.

I'm about to change the topic, but then I catch sight of his face. He's wearing that heartbreaking expression I've come to both recognize and loathe.

"Stop it," I say roughly. This time I notice, I don't have to run to keep up with him. It's like the pity slowed him down.

"What?"

"You know 'what.' Like you pity me," I say, and pick up the pace. "I can't *stand* that. You can hate me, spite me, wish evil on me, but you are not allowed to pity me. Ever." I glance sideways at him. "*I'm* not even allowed to pity me. I mean, I do anyway sometimes, but that's different. Got it?"

I glance over my shoulder when I realize he isn't next to me, and see him standing still as the wind whips his hair back.

"Listen," he says, then waits for me to meet his eyes. "The only people I pity are the ones with hate in their hearts. And you're about as opposite of that as anyone I know." He tilts his head and gazes at me with serious eyes. "Got it?"

An unexpected sunshiny warmth spreads through my body. I smile. "Got it."

*　　*　　*

The jewelry store comes into view, and I turn to Sam. "Let's pretend we're brother and sister this time, instead of fiancés," I suggest. "It could be our parents' fortieth wedding anniversary, and we're going to surprise our mom with jewelry."

"What are we getting Dad?"

"Nothing. We're on a limited income." I pause to look into a gourmet cooking supply store window and see a row of Le Creuset Dutch ovens in various colors. Libby always wanted one but said she could never afford it. My forehead wrinkles in thought as I go over all the ways my marrying Zevi could change her life for the better.

Sam threads his arm through mine and gently but firmly moves me forward. "Control yourself, Superwoman. I know you're dying to go in there and find some poor old woman to hug and exchange childhood stories—"

"I'm not deranged," I say, craning my neck to get one last look. There's one in burgundy, Libby's favorite color.

"You're something."

I look down at my arm and realize Sam is still gripping it as though he doesn't trust me not to run into the store and make a scene. I casually try to disengage myself, but he's got the strength of a Navy SEAL in his prime. "As lovely as it is to be held against my will by a man twice my size, I'm actually not allowed any physical contact with the opposite gender per my religious beliefs."

"Oh shit." Sam drops my arm like it's a ticking time bomb. "Sorry."

"It's okay." I push up my shirt sleeve and examine my arm. "There is a bruise, though."

"*What?* Let me see." He grabs my arm only to suddenly release it. "*Damn it.* Sorry."

"For what?" I say, glancing up at him. "The bruise or your addiction to touch?"

"You don't have a bruise," he says, pointing to my arm. "And I certainly don't have an addiction to touch." He roughly combs his fingers through his hair, causing the ends to stick out. "Whatever the hell that means."

I push my sleeve back down, more than a little disappointed. I've always bruised easily. Maybe something will show up tomorrow.

"I guess it's just me you're addicted to," I say, but he doesn't look amused. His face turns into a scowl as he stares straight ahead, and I can't resist adding, "Or maybe you're one of those touchy-feely people."

His head reels back as though I had slapped him. "I am *not* a touchy-feely person."

His outraged expression makes me want to laugh, but I manage to keep a straight face. "It only becomes a problem," I say, as we reach the front door of the jewelry store, "if you make it a habit of holding women against their will. Society tends to frown on that sort of thing—don't ask me why."

Sam crosses his arm and leans against the door, barring my entrance. "Anything else you need to get off your chest before we go inside?"

"I don't think so," I say, pausing to check my arm again, although there's nothing to see except a slight pink tinge on my skin. "But I'll let you know if this thing turns into a life-threatening blood clot."

"You do that."

Inside, a pretty, fresh-faced saleswoman in a black lace-up top greets us. "Hi there! Come on in," she says, smiling warmly. "It's windy out there, isn't it?" A collection of freckles dusts her cheeks and nose, adding to her cuteness. "I'm Harper. Can I help you find anything?"

"My brother and I are looking for a wedding anniversary gift for our parents."

"Aww, sweet." Her jade eyes focus solely on Sam, as though I don't even exist. "Do you have any ideas, to get started?"

Sam turns to look at me. "Do we, Sis?"

I shrug. "Not really, Bro. We're open to anything."

"I have just the thing. Follow me." She leads us around the semi-circular glass panels, then unlocks a sliding door, and presents two gold bracelets. "Have you heard the story behind Cartier's love bracelets?"

Sam shakes his head. I have of course, but since she seems excited to tell it, I shake my head too.

Harper places the bracelets on a red velvet cloth for us to admire. "A Cartier designer named Aldo Cipullo crafted this piece of jewelry in 1969 as a nod to medieval chastity belts. They're designed to be opened and closed by a special screwdriver that comes with each bracelet." She motions for Sam's arm, and he duly places his wrist on the counter. Under the bright incandescent light of the store, Sam's arm and hand look huge, especially next to Harper's delicate fingers.

"It's a symbolic representation of one's love and commitment."

"Romantic," I murmur at the exact same time Sam says, "Feels like a handcuff."

Harper giggles, taking her time unlocking the bracelet, fingering his wrist longer than seems necessary. "Loving the right person shouldn't feel like a prison sentence."

"The right person isn't always obvious," Sam comments. "Or they are, but other things get in the way."

"Then they were never meant for you," Harper says, staring at him intently. "Sometimes the right person can appear when you least expect it."

I bite the inside of my cheek to keep a straight face. Sam turns to me, possibly for help, but I can't resist adding a little fuel to the fire. Besides, he's single and she's a pretty woman. He'll thank me later. "My brother is still recovering from his last breakup. The sad truth of the matter is that he's lost all faith in women. If only he could find someone that's nice."

Sam shoots me a glare. "Not true. I have lots of faith in wom—"

Harper interrupts with, "Don't let one woman taint your opinion of all of us."

"Exactly." I nod vigorously. "He just needs to meet one of the good ones."

"Like a hole in my head," he mutters under his breath.

I exchange a look with Harper. "That's the trauma speaking."

"Focus on why we're here, Tiny."

Tiny? What happened to Superwoman? And just because he's built like a frickin' NFL quarterback doesn't make me tiny. I'm five foot five—that's legendary for a Jewish girl.

"Whatever . . ." I pause, trying to think of an appropriate comeback. "Big Foot." He does have big feet.

"Really?" His eyebrow lifts. "That's the best you could do?"

"Like *Tiny* is so original," I scoff.

His lips do that thing where they *almost* smile, and my stomach does a small flip-flop in response. He's so serious most of the time that I can't help feeling proud at this small measure of achievement.

Harper giggles. "You guys are such siblings. I love it."

The next half hour passes pleasantly as Sam takes a good look at the store's inventory and asks Harper questions about payment plans. When Harper asks us if we've narrowed down any options, Sam tells her that we're going to take some time to think it over. She takes a pen and scribbles something on the back of a card.

"This is my business card," she says, handing it to Sam. "I wrote my cell phone number on the back if you have more questions. Or . . . whatever," she says, her cheeks turning slightly red as she giggles.

You have to admire the woman's guts: she goes after what she wants instead of waiting around and hoping for things to happen. I try to picture the two of them together, holding hands, but somehow, I can't see Sam dating a giggler.

There's a trash can outside the store, and I see Sam's hand moving toward it with the business card.

"Don't throw it out!" I gasp, glancing back in case Harper is watching. She isn't, thankfully, but would've it killed him to throw it out in a safer location?

He looks at me like I just went from quirky to straight-out cuckoo. "Why not?"

"Because she might see you." *Is he acting dense to drive me insane? Because it's working.*

He shrugs, then takes his sunglasses out of his pants pocket. "So?"

"What do you mean 'so'? Do you *want* to hurt her self-esteem?"

He seems to consider the question as we head past the row of stores. "I'm neutral about it," he says.

Neutral? Ugh! "Just—give it to me." I snatch it out of his hand, because frankly, he's lost my trust. I turn the card over and read it.

I enjoyed meeting you! If you ever want to get a coffee or just hang out, my phone number is 651-699-0350.☺

Eh. Harper may be nice and cute, but she could use help in the creativity department. "I'm disappointed," I admit aloud.

"What did you think it would say?" Sam glances at me with a raised eyebrow.

"I don't know." A gust of wind whips my hair against my face, and I gather and twist it over my shoulder. "Something like *'Meet me in a deserted warehouse at midnight for a night you won't soon forget.'*"

Sam snorts and presses the unlock button from his fob. "Let me give you a piece of advice, Superwoman," he says, resting his arms over the roof of the car. "If you're ever given a note that has the words *midnight* and *deserted warehouse* on it, I strongly advise you to run the hell the other way."

"As if." I open the passenger door and slip inside. "The men I date aren't nearly that imaginative."

But *I* am. I can see it now, this secret warehouse of love: scented candles resting on upturned crates, dozens of rose petals scattered on the floor, leading to a table with a bottle of chilled champagne nestled in a bucket of ice. Lewis Capaldi's voice crooning softly from hidden speakers while a fire hisses and crackles. Sam, sinfully handsome in a tuxedo, saunters forward, beckoning—

I gasp. *What is Sam doing in my fantasy warehouse?*

"You okay?" Sam places his hand on the back of my seat as he reverses the car.

"Fine," I croak. It's not as though I consciously put Sam there. He just kind of showed up on his own. I had *nothing* to do with it. Obviously.

Sam starts talking, but it's hard to concentrate. With his arm resting on the console just a few mere centimeters away and the titillating scent of his aftershave piercing the air, all I can think about is what it would be like to kiss him. To feel his lips pressed against mine, tasting his mouth as his hands travel up and down my body, an electrical current following his every touch—

I take a deep breath and gaze at the passing scenery to ground myself. Let's get something straight—this is not a Sam thing. It's an aftershave thing. A scent thing. It's chemicals.

It's science.

". . . missing much. That's the real problem."

I nod abstractedly. I have no clue what he's talking about, but I do know that he's ruined my warehouse fantasy. Now I have to come up with a whole new one. *Thanks a lot, Sam.*

"What do you think?"

I think I have problems. "Um." I shift in my seat and try to think of something that doesn't give away the fact that I wasn't paying attention because I was too busy fantasizing about him. "I think your logic is twisted," I say, because that seems safest.

Sam scowls. "Trust me," he says, turning the wheel left, "sex isn't everything."

My eyes pop open. *Sex?* Who said anything about sex?

"In fact, too often people mistake sex for love." He sighs. "I know I did. And by the time I realized it, we were already engaged and—" He breaks off, shaking his head. "I don't know. I didn't have the heart to break it off, and I thought maybe we could make it work." He frowns, adding, "Anyway, when you think about it, marriage is nothing more than a business arrangement. There's venture capital, and the statistics for net loss are outrageous."

My head buzzes from this sudden information dump, and it takes me a moment to register what he said. See? I knew it'd be safe to say his logic was twisted. "Marriage is *not* a business arrangement. It's a *re-la-tion-ship*." I enunciate clearly to make sure he understands the difference.

"Initially." He dips his head in agreement. "But not by the end."

"The end meaning death?"

"Divorce," he replies. "It's strictly business at that point." Shaking his head as though to clear his thoughts, he adds, "I don't even know why we're talking about this."

Well, that makes two of us.

"It's you," he says suddenly.

"Me?" I clamp my hand over my chest like the innocent I am.

"You have this way of luring people in—"

I start to sputter in protest, but he continues, "People let their guard down, and within minutes, they've shared secrets they've never told anyone before." His mouth twitches. "It's actually a brilliant marketing strategy."

"I was literally doing nothing but sitting here," I say, gesturing to my seat.

"I've seen how customers open up to you," he adds, tapping his fingers on the steering wheel, clearly on a roll. "And you've said yourself that sometimes you feel like a therapist."

Why do I suddenly feel like I'm being cross-examined in a court of law? "You've taken everything out of context. And besides, what you said wasn't exactly a secret. It's more in the TMI category."

"Still"—he glances at me from the corners of his eyes—"I've never told anyone that before."

I turn to face him. "That you confused sex for love?"

His eyes wince like he's in physical pain. "Don't repeat it."

I cross my legs and smile. "Sorry. I'll pretend you never said it."

"Good."

"It's been wiped clean from my memory."

"Uh-huh."

"It's interesting, though," I muse, tapping my nails against the window pane, "because I always heard guys could have sex without falling in love."

Sam makes a strangling sound. "I thought we had moved on."

"We had," I concede with a nod. "But then we circled back to it because I'm a naturally curious person."

He sighs. "Hey, want some coffee? There's a Starbucks up ahead."

"Are you trying to bribe me?"

Sam switches on his turn signal and looks over his shoulder. "I don't know. Are you willing to be bribed?"

"Not with coffee. That's just insulting."

"Okay, Superwoman," he says as the corners of his mouth twitch. "What's it going to take?"

I grin. So many options—how will I ever choose? Obviously, my mind jumps to jewelry and there's that sapphire ring I love, but no . . . him giving me a ring is too awkward, and actually, him giving me any jewelry is too awkward, so scratch that. I'd accept money except it's illegal and makes me seem like a blackmailer which obviously couldn't be further from the truth. Hmm . . .

"I'm getting nervous," he says.

Ooooh, this will be good. I rub my hands together in anticipation. "Tell me a secret." His eyebrows lift dubiously, so I add, "Or it could just be something that most people don't know about you."

He shakes his head and grins. "I was not expecting that."

"Well," I shrug, "it was this or jewelry."

He laughs, and warmth spreads through my belly. It's hard enough to make him full-on smile, so a laugh feels like winning the lottery.

His eyes crinkle with amusement as he stares off into the distance. "When I was a kid, I'd hang out at the nursing home because my mom was the activities director there, and let me tell you, I learned some mad skills from that place." He pauses to glance at me.

"The nursing home," I repeat, just to make sure I'm not imagining this conversation.

"Yeah." He nods. "I became an expert at canasta, bridge, pinochle, rummy—I can do it all. Rummy's my favorite, though, and we'd play with money. The real stuff—not the fake Monopoly money that they used in the other wards," he says in a serious voice, like he's eight years old again and trying to impress a grown-up.

"Please tell me you weren't playing with people who had dementia," I say.

"I'm not a monster, Penina." He glances at me and grins. "But I did kick a lot of old people's asses. And eventually I became so good that no one wanted to play with me."

My eyebrows lift. "Am I supposed to be impressed by that?"

He grins and the dimple in his cheek deepens. "Hell yes."

I explode with laughter and he does too, and it occurs to me that I haven't had this much fun in a very long time.

CHAPTER TWELVE

"Fashion is instant language."

—*Miuccia Prada*

I made the mistake of speaking to Libby before going to bed last night, and it cost me a night's worth of sleep. She talked about potentially moving to Detroit because of cheaper housing and because Natan has a friend there who's a headhunter. I tried to convince her what a bad idea it was, but then she started to get upset, and I had to backtrack really fast and talked about how beautiful Lake Michigan is.

And Fraydie is a total mystery. Her stomach looks smaller, but then she'll complain how tired she is, *and* I overheard my mother tell Fraydie that it's not healthy to eat an entire jar of pickles in one sitting. And the weirdest part is that no one is talking about it. Not Fraydie or my mom or Libby. I'm starting to wonder if I dreamed the whole thing up.

"Ooh, listen to this," Maya says, glancing up from her phone. Whenever there's a slow period in the store, Maya whips out her phone and reads, out loud, crazy articles, then asks test questions afterward to make sure I listened. Which I do about sixty percent of the time. "'Sign number nine that you're about to meet your soulmate is that you have given up on your urge to control events. It's all about divine timing, and when the Universe wants you to meet, nothing will stop the two of you from coming together.'"

"Yeah, well, I gave up about a decade ago, and look at me," I say, wiggling my ring finger. "Still single."

She shakes her head, then gathers her long blond hair and twists it over her shoulder. She's channeling Barbie today, in a fuchsia jumpsuit cinched at the waist with a black C-shaped belt, and large hoop earrings. I loved this look so much that I posted a picture of her on my feed earlier today, even though it's not something my followers would wear.

"That's because you don't listen to me," she says. "I told you a million times that if you set up a profile on Bumble—"

"Still a hard no," I say. "I didn't save my virginity for twenty-nine years to let some random dude from the internet—"

"You don't *have to* have sex," she interrupts, as though it's the most obvious thing in the world. "Not everyone is on it for that." She puts down her phone and fixes her hair in the mirror. "But you definitely could use some," she adds in an undertone.

"I heard that," I say.

A loud throat clearing startles us, and it's hard to say which one of us is more horrified at seeing Sam leaning casually against the wall, like he had been there for some time. Maya's cheeks turn an attractive shade of rose quartz, and I feel the blood drain from my face. Why couldn't he have snuck up earlier, when we were talking about *The Real Housewives of Beverly Hills*?

"I'm expecting someone," he says, keeping his face carefully blank. "I was going to wait here, but . . ." He pauses and gives a vague hand motion in our general direction. "Please remember that this is a work environment, so keep your conversations appropriate." He glances between Maya and me to see if we object. "I'll be in my office."

Once we hear the click of his door closing, Maya says, "He could use some too."

I nod. "We finally agree about something."

Lately I've been trying to reconcile this idea of who I thought Sam was and the person he is when no one else is around. It's weird, but the times we've been alone, it feels like I'm with a different version of him, the *real* one, where he's playful and funny and even a little vulnerable. But once we're back in the store, he reverts to his scary boss self.

Maya wiggles her eyebrows and grins. "What are the chances that Sam's friend is as hot as him?"

Since Minneapolis isn't exactly teeming with guys that look like models, I reply, "Zero?" When you live in a climate that's cold enough to freeze your nipples off, cellulite is an extra layer of protection.

A few minutes later, a black Range Rover pulls into the parking lot and parks in front of the store. The driver's door opens, and a Victoria's Secret angel emerges. The woman has a movie star face framed by long, wavy hair, and legs that go on for miles. She's in a white blouse, suspenders, and a plaid mini skirt.

She is Hot with a capital "H."

"I *love* her outfit," I say as she makes her way toward the front of the store. "It's quintessential nineties Britney meets Alicia Silverstone from *Clueless*."

"Really?" Maya says. "I think it's more old man meets naughty Catholic girl meets smutty college professor."

And now I have a visual that I could've done without.

The door opens and I put on my professional, but nonthreatening smile. "Hi, welcome to Kleinfeld's," I say. "Is there something I can help you with today?"

"Hi. I'm here to meet with the owner, Sam." She pushes her sunglasses to the top of her glossy dark hair and smiles. "My name's Keila Bergman. He's expecting me."

There's a pregnant pause as Maya and I process that the person Sam is expecting is not only *not* a man, but also hot enough to be a *Sport's Illustrated* cover model.

"Yeah, he said you were on your way," I say, the first to recover. I step around the display case and motion with my hand for her to follow me. "I'll bring you to his office. Can I get you something to drink? Coffee, tea, water?" She smells like the inside of a Whole Food's store—a mixture of herbs and flowers.

"Do you have green tea?"

"I'm not sure, but I'll check." I knuckle tap Sam's door, then open it just as he says to come in.

"Hey, you." He grins, standing up to greet her.

I catch a glimpse of him hugging her as I close the door, and a prickle of irritation runs through me, though I'm not sure why. Maybe I'm annoyed that in the time we spent together, he didn't bother mentioning that he had a girlfriend. I mean, yeah, she could just be a friend and nothing more than that—he did say he has female friends—but shouldn't platonic friends be less . . . I don't know . . . *attractive?*

I make the tea and grab a packet of Splenda and head back to Sam's office. "Knock, knock," I call out, with the hot drink in my hand.

"Thanks, Penina," Sam says as I place the cup on an end table beside the woman. He juts his chin toward her and adds, "Keila is a pediatric oncologist at Trinity."

So she's not only gorgeous but brilliant too. And obviously compassionate because why else would you go into a field like that? I can't imagine anything worse than having to tell parents that their kid has cancer, even if the child does end up being on the right side of the statistics.

"Penina volunteers in the NICU section," Sam tells Keila, like he's a teacher introducing a new student to the class, and he wants everyone to play nicely.

"That's great." She nods, taking a small sip of tea. "What about the pediatric ward? Have you ever helped out there?"

I shake my head. "I guess babies have always been my thing." I feel Sam's gaze on me, and I can only imagine what he's thinking. Except I'd rather not.

"Yeah, I get it." She smiles, putting down the tea. "It's nice of you to volunteer."

The truth is that I get just as much out of it as the babies, but I'm not here to socialize. "Let me know if you need anything else," I say, and close the door.

When I return to the showroom, Maya's frowning and scrolling through her phone, probably checking Sam's horoscope or shopping for shoes. I pull out the bin of jewelry that needs repairs and get to work fixing a men's rotary watch. It's an older model, and it might take a while, so I pull out a stool to get comfortable, when Maya makes a sudden whooping sound.

"Found her!" Maya exclaims, fist pumping the air. "Holy fuck, she's a bikini model. Wait—no, a lingerie model. Whoa—I don't think she's wearing anything in this one."

I glance at her. "Who are you talking about?"

"Sam's *friend*," she says, making air quotes. "Where does he find these women? Do you think he goes to strip clubs? Is she a camgirl? Because, FYI, I'm not into guys who do that stuff."

I shake my head. "I don't think you have the right woman. Keila's a doctor."

"That would explain this then." She holds up her phone, and I see a picture of Keila in scrubs, smiling down at a bald toddler that's fingering her stethoscope, with the caption: *Love my patients! Taking pics for Trinity Hospital's website.* "Wait, she's a doctor *and* a bikini model. Is that even . . . I mean, that's just not—" She pinches the bridge of her nose and draws in a shaky breath. "I am *very* unhappy right now."

"Same," I breathe, and take the phone. No one can fault Sam for his taste in women; Keila is every man's fantasy in one package. I scroll down her Instagram page, which mostly consists of innocent-looking pictures of her and her coworkers, her cats, some food she made, nature trails, and actually not all that many bikini pics, but Maya of course focused on those. "I guess if you've got it, flaunt it, right?" I say, using one of her catchphrases as I hand her phone back.

"No, not right. She shouldn't be posting bikini pictures of herself. It's unprofessional," she fumes, waving her hand in the direction of Sam's office. "*And* she's dating the hottest bachelor around. Like, is there anything in her life that *isn't* perfect?"

The prickle of irritation worsens as I picture Sam and Keila together, and now I'm irritated at myself for getting irritated. "Maybe her furniture is covered with cat hair," I say, winding back the watch's crown. "Or her house is really messy."

"So?" She rolls her eyes. "That's my every day life."

As someone who's visited Maya's apartment multiple times, I can verify that statement. "Maybe she's a hoarder, and her house is covered with cockroaches."

"Better." Maya nods with approval.

The door opens and a customer comes inside, diverting Maya's attention. I continue working on the watch, but my mind is stuck on how perfect Keila's life is. They say no one's life is perfect, no matter how much it seems that way on social media, but what if they're wrong?

I'm so agitated thinking about it that my tweezers accidentally send the dial's watch spinning across the counter. I take a deep breath and try to relax, but the only thing that works is imagining Sam telling Keila that he's just not that into her—that he prefers women who eat regular meals and who choose to lounge on the couch instead of having a good workout.

It's not that I want Sam myself—it's just that I don't want Keila to have him. Which clearly means that I have the maturity of a second-grader.

I'm polishing up the watch when Sam leads Keila out of the store, his hand on her back. Maya makes eyes at me and jerks her head at them, as if to say, *"Told you so."*

I shrug back as if to say, *"Life sucks."* The sad truth is that, those two are *made* for each other. They're equally gorgeous and wealthy. He's a big philanthropist and sits on the board of directors at the hospital she works at, they have crazy chemistry, and they'll probably have incredibly intelligent and freakishly beautiful children. Still . . . I remind myself, it's possible that no one's life is perfect.

I mean, people might look at Libby and think she has the perfect life—a doting husband, healthy children, beautiful home. They wouldn't know of the financial stress that's costing her their house, and how time is running out to save it. They wouldn't know how badly it's affected her marriage or that they might have to move to Detroit because of it. You just never know what goes on behind closed doors. So Keila must have her share of problems too.

Twenty minutes later, a message on our employee's WhatsApp chat pops up from Sam.

Dr. Keila Bergman is being honored at Trinity's annual banquet on Sunday, June 23rd. I've bought a few tables for the event, so save the date and please plan on joining me there.

I take it all back—Keila's life *is* perfect, cat hairs notwithstanding. And not only that, but now the rest of us have front-row seats to watch.

* * *

I finish the NICU's required two-minute hand and arm wash, lift my shoe off the pedal attached to the floor, and wave my hand in front of the motion-sensitive paper towel dispenser. I catch a glimpse of myself in the mirror over the sink and realize how much I look like a surgeon about to enter the OR with my hospital scrubs, gloves, and face mask. There's a nasty virus going around, and because the preemies' immune systems aren't fully developed yet, there's a new rule that everyone who enters the NICU has to be masked and in scrubs.

"Right on time," Delilah calls out as I enter the nursery, patting a baby's back with one hand and grabbing a burp cloth with the other. "This one's getting hungry."

"Perfect." I grin, sitting down on the rocking chair beside the baby's crib.

"Hold your horses, now," she tells the baby, who's showing off an excellent set of lungs. "It's coming, it's coming." She gently lowers the baby into my arms, then passes me the bottle and burp cloth.

I gently wipe away the baby's tears as she sucks greedily at the bottle's nipple. Even though I've never met her before, it feels like the most natural thing in the world to hold this baby against my chest, giving her warmth and nourishment. For a moment, it's just the two of us connecting soul to soul, and all the stresses of the past few weeks fade away to nothingness. Bliss.

But then Delilah opens her mouth.

"How's your love life? Anything new to report?"

I glance up at her and briefly debate whether to tell her the truth about Zevi. Since no one in my "real life" knows I volunteer here—with the exception of Sam—there's no reason not to confide in her. It's not like Delilah will call up my mom or someone in my community and spill the truth.

"Yes. But," I say, rocking the chair slowly, "you have to promise not to laugh."

"I would never," she replies, pressing a hand over her heart and trying to look innocent. "But talk fast because I've only got a few minutes."

"Okay," I reply, then take a deep breath. "Basically, there's this gay Orthodox Jewish man, Zevi, who will give me a lot of money to marry him." I frown. "Hey, you promised you wouldn't laugh."

"Ooh wee!" She laughs, hitting her thigh. "I wasn't expecting to hear that. Sorry, sorry," she gasps. "Keep going."

I wait until she settles down before continuing. Delilah that is, not the baby. "He's doing this because it would make his dying mother really happy to see him get married. And I need the money because my sister is going to lose her house in two months. But"—I pause, readjusting the baby's cap—"besides having to uproot myself and move to New York, I don't like having to lie to everyone, including my own family. And in my community, divorce is one more mark against you, so it would make it even harder for me to find someone to marry for real afterward." I pull the bottle out of the baby's mouth and put her over my shoulder and gently pat her back. "In a sense, it's like selling my life away to save my sister's. I don't know." I sigh. "Thoughts?"

"Wow." Delilah scratches her head, now serious. "That's a lot to process. And why is your sister going to lose her house?"

I sigh again, gazing down at the baby. "It's a long story, but my brother-in-law dug himself into this financial mess, and he used their house as collateral. And there's no way he could come up with enough money to save it at this point unless he won the lottery or something."

"And Zevi would give you enough money to cover the house as long as you marry him?"

"Right," I reply.

"Don't do it," she says, shaking her head. "Worst idea I've ever heard."

"Really?" Her tone implies it's obvious, but I press on. "What makes you say that?"

"Because," she says, glancing at her Apple watch, then pulling up a chair. "Your sister is how old?"

"Thirty-one."

"Exactly." She nods, like I just proved her point. "She's a grown-ass woman, and this is *her* life, *her* problem. Not yours."

"I know," I say, a little irritated. "But she's *my sister*, and I love her. Which is why her problem is my problem."

"Wrong." Delilah shakes her head. "Do you know how poor I'd be if I bailed out my brother every time he asked for money?"

I shrug. In my opinion, helping out your family is more important than anything else.

"Sometimes the best way to help someone," she continues, "is to let them struggle so they can figure it out for themselves. Otherwise, they never learn from their mistakes because they know you'll be there to bail them out. Trust me, it's an endless cycle, and you'll end up broke and resentful of them."

I can't imagine ever being resentful of Libby. Natan, on the other hand, is a different story. The baby starts to fuss, so I put the bottle down and burp her.

"As for Zevi and his mom," she continues, "you should stay out of it. That's not your problem either. It's not up to you to fix everyone's messes."

"Okay, Sam," I mutter.

"Who's Sam?"

"My boss." I glance at the far end of the room, where I had seen him for the very first time. "He's actually one of the big donors here, Sam Kleinfeld."

An alarm goes off, and she holds up a finger. "Hold that thought." When she comes back a minute later, she says, "That alarm must have messed with my head because I could have sworn you said Sam Kleinfeld is your boss."

The baby's warm breath tickles my neck, making me squirm. "Yeah. He is."

Delilah's mouth forms an "O" shape. "Are we talking about tall, dark, and deliciously handsome Sam Kleinfeld? The hospital donor?"

I nod. They say beauty is in the eye of the beholder, but it seems everyone has the same opinion when it comes to him.

"Gurrrl!" She throws up her hands. "You're just getting around to telling me this *now*?"

"Sorry. I forgot you know him." I rub small circles on the baby's back. "And it's not relevant to my life other than that you both think I try too hard to fix other people's problems."

"Back up now," she says. "He's not married, is he? He doesn't wear a ring."

The baby has stopped fussing, so I sit down and offer her the rest of the bottle. "No, but he's dating someone. At least it looks that way." I readjust the pillow under my elbow and ask, "Do you know Dr. Keila Bergman? She works here." Delilah shakes her head. "Well, she's being honored at the gala."

"Sounds like this gala is really about him making a big party to give an award to his girlfriend."

I laugh. "Yeah. Basically."

Delilah shakes her head. "Well, too bad he's taken. All the nurses have a crush on him. Even Ryan," she adds, pointing her chin toward the straight male nurse.

I give a small smile. "You should let him know Sam's off the market."

Delilah stands up and stretches. "Honey, everyone's fair game until the wedding day." She studies me for a moment before saying, "He's Jewish, isn't he?"

"You're Catholic," I say, refusing to play along. "And already married."

If I didn't have a baby in my arms, she'd probably punch me. "Penina, I'm serious. You should go for him."

"Are you really telling me I should try to steal someone else's boyfriend?" I say.

She nods enthusiastically. "Yes!"

I sigh. "Even if he *was* single, it wouldn't work."

"Oh yeah? Why's that?" She puts her hands on her hips and scowls at me. "Because he doesn't have a mommy complex like the last few people you dated—is that a requirement of yours?"

I narrow my eyes. "Below. The. Belt." The truth is there are lots of reasons: I live a totally different lifestyle; I can't give him children; he views marriage as a business relationship; and he's much too bossy. But if I were to say this to her, she'd just argue with me. The baby lets out a burp, and I give her praise, then turn to Delilah. "It's complicated."

"*Your mom's* complicated."

I roll my eyes. Delilah has a twelve-year-old son, and whenever she gets frustrated with me, she reverts to male tween vernacular.

"I give up on you." She picks up the discarded bottle and smiles at the baby. "Good job, baby girl," she coos, rubbing her back, then looks at me. "I've got to document and take vitals. Are you okay rocking her to sleep?"

"Of course. That's the best part."

Delilah laughs and pats my shoulder. "Okay, you enjoy yourself. And while you're rocking, think about what I said about not fixing other people's lives. Focus on living *yours*. Alright?"

"Uh-huh," I say just as another alarm goes off. Delilah heads toward the opposite side of the nursery, where the machine beeps, and I shift the baby to my other shoulder. I close my eyes, breathing in the familiar newborn scent, and focus on the feel of the baby's heart beating against mine. I wish I could suspend this moment in time, where I can pretend, even briefly, that this child belongs to me instead of someone else. Sometimes, the yearning to be a mother is so strong that it literally steals my breath away, and I have to remind myself to breathe. I keep telling myself that it'll get easier with time, that this ache in my chest will eventually stop hurting, that there will come a day when I'll see a pregnant woman and not feel envy, but deep down I know the truth: no matter how many years or decades pass, it won't get easier. I'll never make peace with the fact that I can't be a mother.

CHAPTER THIRTEEN

"Playing dress-up begins at age five and never truly ends."
—*Kate Spade*

I take another bite of the tuna sandwich I had hastily thrown together earlier this evening after receiving a phone call from Gina. She had demanded I return to the store twenty minutes after leaving it because she was suffering from a migraine attack. So now I'm stuck here with a load of new merchandise that needs to be put away, instead of doing something fun, like stalking René-Jean Page on Instagram.

And to make things worse, I'm in this tight pencil skirt, which looked great in the reel I made but doesn't allow for things like bending down, or movement in general.

I click on the "Inbox" icon on my phone and scan past the list of junk mail and advertisements, when I see an email from Zevi.

From: Zevi@zevproductions.com
To: Penina613@gmail.com

May 30, 2022, at 7:32 pm

Hi, Penina

I hope all is well with you. As you're thinking things through, I thought it might be a good idea for you to come to NY and get to know us a little better. I will gladly fly you here and make hotel arrangements (unless you'd rather stay with us). It might help you visualize things so you can make the most informed decision.

Let me know your thoughts and any questions you might have.

Best,

Zevi

The man knows how to apply pressure, that's for sure. Although it's hard to blame him since his mother is dying and dying people are so unpredictable. I keep wishing some miracle will happen where Libby's house is saved, so I don't have to say yes. All I need is for Libby to win the lottery, Zevi's mom to embrace her son's homosexuality, and for Michael Aloni from *Shtisel* to show up at my door, asking me to marry him. Is that so much to ask for?

My fingers hover over the phone, deliberating what to write back. I'll respond later tonight.

I murmur the prayer following a meal, then head to the front of the store and lock the doors. My mind turns over every possible scenario again and again, like a hamster on a wheel going nowhere.

On my way back, I notice a light peeking through the blinds in Sam's office. The cleaning crew must have left it on since Sam is in New York on a business trip. And while I wouldn't say I've missed him, it has been kind of boring without him—although Maya's been especially melodramatic since Keila's Instagram post yesterday, so that's been keeping me busy. It was a group picture of her and Sam and some older people outside the Belvedere Castle in Manhattan, and from the looks of it, his trip isn't *just* business related.

But that's fine. I couldn't care less.

I twist the knob and open the door, then freeze—

A bear of a man stands in the shadows with his back to me. Blood roars in my ears, and a primal scream fills the air, and it takes me a moment before I realize that it's coming from me.

The man whips around, and my eyes blink into focus. "*Sam?*" I gasp, hand clasped over my chest. "Wh-what are you doing here? *Oh my G-d*, he's naked," I add in an undertone.

He gives me a look that implies I played too many video games as a child. "This is my office, Penina."

I know words are coming out of his mouth, but I'm too busy staring at the glorious sight that is Shirtless Sam to pay attention. His body should be added to the list of the Seven Wonders of the World. People would pay money to see this. His shoulders are so wide, so broad, so . . . *big*. And his chest has the most perfect smattering of hair leading toward what must be a twelve-pack. He's all hard planes and ridges and pectorals, not the type of muscles that you get by sitting in yeshiva and studying Torah. When does he even find the time to work out?

"Penina."

I blink but don't tear my eyes away from his chest. "What?"

"Do you mind turning around?"

I glance up at his face. "Oh, sorry." I turn to face the door, which is just as well because my cheeks are flaming up. I can't believe he caught me drooling over him. *How embarrassing.* Especially after my long speech in the car about how he's not my type. He's probably going to fire me now for sexual harassment, in which case, I'll have no choice but to marry Zevi.

My heart is still beating much too fast, but I don't know if it's from the shock of seeing him here or the shock of seeing him topless. I take a big, steadying breath. "Aren't you supposed to be in New York?"

"I came back early."

The sound of pants being unzipped causes my heart to nearly jump out of my chest. "And you're changing here because . . .?"

"It's a long story." He expels a deep sigh. "The child sitting next to me on the airplane had poor aim when he vomited. And the grandmother fondled me under the pretense of cleaning me up."

I press my lips together. *Don't laugh, don't laugh. He thinks you're immature enough as it is.* "I'm sorry to hear that," I manage, then press my lips tightly together. "Why didn't you change at the airport?"

"Because some idiot put my luggage on a plane headed to El Paso."

I bite the inside of my cheek and clear my throat. "Why didn't you just go to your house then?"

"Oh, I did," he says darkly. "But my cleaning lady had decided to move in, and she was high as a kite. She kept calling me Alfonso and then chased me out of the house with one of those small handheld vacuums set on high. And before you ask, my dad was having a sleepover, so there was no way I was going over there." A pause. "For a kind person, you have a real twisted sense of humor."

I'm bent over and laughing so hard that my stomach hurts. I try to say something, but I can't get a full sentence out without breaking into hysterical laughter. Finally, I take some deep breaths. "Are you dressed yet?" I ask.

"I've been dressed for the last five minutes."

"Thanks for telling me." I turn around. He's in a black T-shirt that's stretched tightly against his chest, and I make a concerted effort not to stare, especially now that I know what's beneath it. "Gina had a headache, so I'm taking care of the new shipment," I say, feeling the need to explain why I'm here at this time of the night.

"I know," he nods. "She texted me."

I nod and bite my lip. The only sound in the room is the ticking of the wall clock, and that's when it hits me—the two of us are alone. *Completely alone.*

"Uh, I have to tell you something," I say, rubbing the back of my neck, "and just to warn you, it's going to be awkward." I bite the inside of my cheek as I think of a way to phrase it so he understands. I don't want to come off like a religious fruitcake. And unlike some of the Orthodox laws, this one actually makes sense. "But it's something I have to do."

Sam moves to the front of his desk and sits down, then motions for me to take a seat. "How awkward are we talking?"

"I don't know." I sit down on one of the chairs facing his desk and consider the question. "It's not TMI or anything—it's more like this is going to sound weird."

He leans back and rests his head against his hands. There's a shrewd intelligence behind his narrowed eyes, along with a certain amount of suspicion. "I'd expect nothing less."

I'll pretend I didn't hear that. "Okay, so, you know how we're alone right now, in a locked building?"

One of his eyebrows lifts. He tilts his head, as though trying to gauge something. "We're alone in a locked building," he repeats.

"At night," I add. "No one is coming back until tomorrow morning, right?"

He opens his mouth, but no words come out.

"And the thing is that I'm not technically supposed to be in a locked place with a man." I sigh and rub the back of my neck while trying to figure out how to best word this. "A lot of laws that Orthodox Jews follow are there to prevent sins. So, a man and a woman who aren't married to each other might be tempted to do something . . ." I make a vague hand motion.

"Something?" He leans forward and steeples his fingers. "Could you be more specific?"

Seriously? Moisture gathers in my armpits and on my upper lip. Why is it so hot in here, and why is he deliberately baiting me?

"Just. You know. Physical stuff," I say, wiping the sweat from my upper lip.

"Jumping jacks? Sit-ups? Tai chi?"

I knew he'd make this harder than it had to be. "You *know* what I'm talking about."

He leans back in his chair and crosses his arms. "No clue."

"Do you need me to draw you a picture?"

A slow grin appears on his face. "Great idea."

"Oh my G-d." I stand up and start to pace, shaking my hands to loosen the tension running through my body. I can't do it. I can't stare at the sexiest man alive and casually talk about sexual things. That's above and beyond my skill set. It's like offering someone a juicy steak when they're on a liquid-only diet.

I fan my face with my hand.

He stands up and takes a step toward me. "What were you saying about us being alone in a locked building?"

My body turns tingly, and if he comes one step closer, I can't be held accountable for what happens next. "So, either one of us leaves the building or the doors go unlocked." As long as I don't look at him, everything will be fine.

And I last all of five seconds. *Impressive willpower you got there, Penina.*

Sam plows his hand through his hair, making it stick out every which way. The dark circles under his eyes and haggard expression suggest he didn't have the best night's sleep. "Yeah, that's not happening. But I'll give you my word that no 'physical stuff' will take place," he says, using his fingers for quotation marks. He pauses, hooks his thumbs into the belt loops of his pants then adds in a lazy voice, "Unless . . ." he trails off.

Sweat gathers in unmentionable places and my hands start to shake. That 'unless' is killing me. I feel like a sacrificial lamb about to be thrown into the lion's den. Except the lamb is willing and horny.

Leave it, leave it, don't go there. "Unless . . .?" I hear myself say. *Bad girl!*

His eyes roam over my face, then settle on my lips and he says in a husky voice, "Do you need me to draw you a picture?"

I close my eyes and remind myself of all the reasons why I don't have sex outside of marriage. Unfortunately, my mind has blanked, and now I can't remember any them. The only thing my brain seems to remember is the sight of Sam's chest, which isn't helping. I hear movement and open my eyes to see Sam putting distance between us. Strangely, I don't know if I'm more disappointed or relieved.

"Like I was saying, nothing will happen," he says in a brusque voice, reverting back to his boss self. He powers up his computer and stares at the screen.

Huh? Did I miss something? What caused him to go from flirtatious to boss mode in the time span of thirty seconds? "It's not an honor system. You can't simply promise to be good."

He frowns and picks up a pen and taps it in a staccato rhythm. "So leave."

"I will as soon as I'm done putting away the new shipment. There won't be enough time to do it in the morning."

We have a silent standoff until Sam says, "Last week you were alone with me in the car."

"Well, yes, but the car is different." After a moment, I add, "But only during daylight hours."

Sam mutters something under his breath then pulls out his phone from his back pocket. "I'll call your rabbi. What's his number?"

"He's on vacation now with his wife, so I'd rather not disturb him."

He stands up, plants his hands on the desk, and growls, "You'd rather risk being held at gunpoint while the store is robbed?"

"I don't think this is one of those either/or situations," I say, deftly avoiding the question. Man, am I good. I should have gone into politics.

Sam clenches his jaw as he perches on the edge of his desk. "Look, Penina. There are millions of dollars' worth of merchandise in this store. There's no way I'm leaving the doors unlocked late at night. Besides," he adds, his voice bordering on desperation, "I'm not the kind of guy to wrestle a woman against her will. It's not a turn-on for me, okay?"

Which makes me wonder what does turn him on? Probably something that involves Keila in a bikini and a stethoscope. A pang of guilt hits me as I remember her existence. Not that anything happened. But you'd think Sam would've remembered her existence. *Oh!* That's why he went back to boss mode. Maybe he'll flirt, but only up to a point.

I shake my head as if to clear it. "Don't worry, I know you're not. "I'm not worried about you . . . *doing anything* to me."

Sam cocks his head. "Then what's the problem? Is this about you? Are you having trouble keeping your hands to yourself?"

"No," I snort. But just to be on the safe side, I cross my arms against my chest to keep my hands where I can see them. "That's not the issue. We have to do this because the Torah says so."

Sam smacks his forehead. "And if the Torah said to jump off a bridge, would you do that too?"

"That would be a question for my local rabbi."

"Un-fucking-believable." Sam drags a hand down his face, then begins to pace. "This is absolutely nuts. You do realize, don't you, that this makes no sense?"

"Actually, there's a lot of logic in it," I counter. Does he not remember what almost happened a few minutes ago?

"You just said you know we won't touch each other!"

"Well, I can't know that for sure, can I?" I roll my eyes. "You *might* attack me. Nothing is certain in life."

"That's it. I'm done." Sam reaches into his pants pocket and pulls out a brass key ring. "Catch." He tosses it toward me, but like the terrible athlete I've always been, I instinctively jump out of the way instead of trying to catch it. It clatters onto the floor several feet away as Sam strides toward the door and yanks it open.

"Where are you going?"

He turns to face me, the muscles in his neck pulsating. "You've made me so mad that I can't be here right now."

I cover my mouth with my hand so he doesn't see me laughing. He does anyway. "You think this is funny?"

I press my lips together and shake my head, but a tiny snort escapes through my nose.

"I'm coming back," he warns. "It's just that I started envisioning strangling you, so I knew I had to leave. And if that doesn't prove I'm trustworthy, I don't know what does."

"Um, thank you. I think?" Honestly, I don't know if gratitude is the appropriate response to a person who confesses that he'd like to kill you but is just managing to control himself.

Sam mutters something unintelligible under his breath as he storms out. I head toward the showroom and watch through the window as he climbs into his car, fires it up, and peels away, the wheels grinding against the pavement. If exhaust fumes could curse, the ones from his car would be shouting every expletive in the book and probably invent some new ones too.

I lock and bolt the door, smiling to myself. Sam can be pretty funny when he doesn't mean to be. But now that he's gone, I'm wondering if I shouldn't have said anything. Would it really have been that big a deal to be in a locked office space with him?

I shake my head to clear the cobweb of thoughts. For the next half hour or so, I busy myself with work, inventorying the new shipment of Padparadscha sapphires and collections of taaffeite. I try on some of the new pieces and sing along to the music from the Spotify list on my phone.

I'm putting on a ring when my phone pings with a text message.

Sorry about before

I don't recognize the number, so I type back, Who is this?

The jerk you work for

I laugh. Thanks, but you didn't do anything wrong. I'm sorry for putting you in a bad situation. 😔😣

I lean my chin into my hand, watching the bubbles on the screen.

What are you doing now?

I take a screenshot of my hand and send it to him.

WTF?

I snicker as my phone starts to ring. I'm not quite sure why I find it so fun to rile him up, but it seems to be my new favorite hobby. "Kleinfeld's, how can I help you?"

"You can start by explaining why you're wearing half the store's merchandise."

"I do have a good reason." I pause, drawing out the suspense. "I might be getting engaged soon. But it's not for sure."

There's a pause and the music from the other end of the line cuts off. "What are you talking about?"

I start pulling off the rings, one by one. "A guy asked me to marry him. I just haven't made up my mind whether to accept."

A long pause. "Do you love him?"

Crap, why is this ring stuck? "It's uh . . . complicated."

"How can you even consider marrying someone you don't love?"

"It's like what you said earlier," I say, fidgeting with the ring. "Marriage is basically a business arrangement—"

"You nearly bit my head off when I said that."

"Did I?" I switch the phone off "Speaker" and bring it to my ear. "I don't remember. But we've all said stupid things in the past."

"It was a few weeks ago!" he nearly shouts. "That's hardly the past."

So what if I've changed my mind about marrying for love? I know he'd side with Delilah if I were to tell him the details, and I don't need one more person judging me.

"Well, it's been fun," I say, as the ring comes off with one final tug. "But I better get back to work. Good talk," I add, as though I'm the boss dismissing my employee.

"And put all those rings back," he orders, sounding irritated. "It's not in your job description to play dress-up."

"I know *that*, Mr. Kleinfeld," I say, smiling at my reflection in the mirror, "but it's definitely one of the perks."

"Penina—"

I disconnect the call, then set my phone to airplane mode because he seems like the type of person to retaliate for hanging up on him. I continue working, trying not to think too deeply how taken aback he was to my announcement. I thought he understood that my situation is different and that I'm not in the position to marry for love, that I'd be lucky just to find a companion.

I thought he knew I was broken.

* * *

The following morning, I take a sip of coffee and carefully make my way to the front of the store. I arrived home late last night, and between work and texting with Gina, followed by an even later phone call from Maya, I still haven't gotten around to making a decision about Zevi. I spot Sam's car through the large window in the showroom. He must already be in his office, but after last night's fiasco, I'm not going to personally check. I don't want him asking me questions about my possible marriage, and I don't need a repeat of that weird vibe between us last night.

I tear off a piece of paper towel and put my mug on top of it. Not that he was serious, I've decided. He wouldn't jeopardize what he has with Keila for a quick fling with me.

I survey the showroom, making a last-minute adjustment to the black onyx pendant on display, then head toward the front doors. I undo the locks and flip the curlicue plaque to "Open."

"Hey, sunshine!" Maya bustles through the lobby, clutching a huge wicker basket lined with a red-and-white checked napkin. There's a matching red bow on the handle, and inside are dozens of cinnamon rolls with glazed vanilla icing.

"Hey, yourself." I point to the basket. "What's that for?"

Maya's complexion doesn't quite hide the flush spreading across her cheeks. "Just felt like doing a little baking."

I gaze at her suspiciously. Maya bakes as often as she scrubs a toilet, and with an equal amount of enthusiasm. "Want me to set it in the break room?"

"Nah, I'm good," she says over her shoulder, balancing the basket with both hands. "I'll just say good morning to Sam."

I roll my eyes. The girl gets points for persistence, if nothing else. As I reach for the bin of broken jewelry, my mind wanders toward Sam. I can't help but wonder what it would be like to live in his shoes. I mean, the poor guy must get sick of women throwing themselves at him. If the way Maya acts is any indication of the general female public, he probably gets hit on every time he steps foot out of his house. Even someplace as benign as the grocery store isn't safe, what with all those sex-starved housewives lurking in the produce section.

I'm just polishing the bracelet when Maya returns, lugging the basket by her side. "How'd it go?"

"Not good," she sighs, setting the basket on the counter. "He said they look delicious but he doesn't eat white flour and sugar."

"Jerk," I say, like the loyal friend I am.

Maya shrugs, folding her arms. "Well, he did say he has Celiac disease."

I pause. "Well, he could have at least faked it."

"I know what to do!" She snaps her fingers and smiles in excitement. "I can make some gluten-free ones."

"But you hate baking," I say, because someone has to remind her. One time she bought a motorcycle because some guy made an offhand comment about biker chicks being hot.

"It's fine," she says, tapping on her phone, probably searching for new recipes.

"Okay." I shrug and pat her on the back. "Your funeral."

The rest of the morning is business as usual, and I split my time between talking with customers and repairing jewelry. I glance at the clock on the wall and realize it's nearly lunchtime, when a shrill scream splits the air. Gina and I look at each other, then rush into the cleaning room and find Maya huddled over a work station. Her left thumb is dripping blood, and she's muttering, *"Shitshitshit."*

My mouth goes dry, and a wave of dizziness washes over me. I lean against the doorpost for support while trying to act normal, even though I think I might vomit at any moment.

"What happened?" Gina gasps.

"My fingers slipped when I was fixing that." She nods toward a discarded silver bracelet, then makes a face as she looks at the wound. "Quick! Grab me a Band-Aid, Penina!" Blood drips onto the edge of the worktable while she speaks, and like a train wreck, I'm unable to look away. "Get the whole box."

"S-sure." I take a deep, steadying breath and turn into the hallway. *You can do this, Penina. Keep it together. What's a few drops of blood?*

I place my hand on the wall for support and take another step. My fear of blood is irrational and annoying, and I don't like telling people because no one understands it. *I* don't even understand it. It almost prevented me from holding babies at the NICU on the off chance I might see a blood draw, but it hasn't been a problem yet. And the nurses are good about warning me if one has to be done.

"Hurry, Penina!" Gina shouts. "There's blood everywhere."

Oh G-d. I focus on putting one foot in front of the other, doing my best to forget the sight of Maya's bleeding thumb. My hand trails along the wall for support as my breaths get shorter and shallower. In the background, I hear Gina's voice mingling with Maya's, but I can't make out what they're saying. I propel myself forward, though my legs feel as if they're weighed down by concrete. A faraway buzzing sound rings in my ears, and suddenly, I can't see; everything has become a fuzzy blob of varying shades and sizes. I lose my balance and crash onto the floor.

Someone says my name, and that's the last thing I hear before the darkness swallows me.

*   *   *

I'm in a field of daisies surrounded by talking turkeys. The heat of the sun is overbearing, and I try to turn my face from it, but a huge turkey has me pinned down. Its claws dig against my bare skin—*what the?* Why am I not wearing clothes?

"Can you hear me, Penina?" The droopy skinned beast flaps its feathers against my face. "Blink your eyes once if you can hear me."

Please go away, and take your flock with you.

A lion appears at my other side and covers my hand with his giant paw. "C'mon, Superwoman," the lion cajoles. "You can do it."

The lion's voice is familiar but I can't place it. Somehow I know it's a gentle lion and won't harm me. The turkey, on the other hand, I'm not so sure about.

"Why isn't she waking up?" the lion roars.

"Hard to say," clucks the queen turkey. "They'll probably run a CT scan when we get there."

"What a fucking mess."

I cautiously open one eye and then the other one. *Holy guacamole.* I'm lying on a stretcher inside an ambulance, with a female paramedic on one side and Sam on the other. I don't know for sure, but I think this is a dream. The paramedic asks me my name, then points to Sam. "Is this your husband?"

Why would she think Sam is my husband? "My fiancé is gay," I announce sleepily, "so no sex." I yawn, then add for good measure, "My hymen and I will never part. G'night."

Murmurings of "brain damage" and "concussion" are the last things I hear as I drift back to sleep.

CHAPTER FOURTEEN

"Fashion is all about happiness. It's fun. It's important. But it's not medicine."

—*Donatella Versace*

I cautiously open one eye and try to make sense of where I am. I blink, struggling past the pain and haze of grogginess. I'm on a bed with a thin blanket that smells like industrial laundry soap. There's a curtain partition to my right, and on my other side is a computer with lots of wires, a vitals machine thingy on wheels, and boxes of disposable gloves attached to the wall.

This place reminds me of a nursing home. Or a hospital.

I jerk to a sitting position, suddenly panicked. *Why am I in a hospital? And why does my entire body hurt? And is that . . . Sam?*

He's sleeping on a reclining armchair in the corner of the room, his head resting against the flat of his hand. I watch the gentle rise and fall of his chest, and for the briefest of moments, consider letting him sleep. But then I remember that I'm in a *hospital* and have no idea why.

"Mr. Kleinfeld," I say quietly. He doesn't move, so I clear my throat and say his name a little louder, but all I get in response is a fluttering of his eyelids before he turns on his side, as though to shut out the sound of my voice.

Ruuuude. What kind of boss falls asleep in a hospital room while his employee is gravely ill, possibly on her deathbed for all she knows! I clap my hands and bellow, *"Mr. Kleinfeld! Wake up!"*

Sam jolts awake and, in the process, hits the side of his head against a wheeled tray. He curses under his breath and rubs his head. Poor guy.

"That looked painful."

"It was." He presses his fists against his eyelids and rubs, then blinks wearily at me. His voice has a sexy roughness to it. I shouldn't be surprised—is there anything about him that *isn't* sexy? From his dark, rumpled bed hair to his five o'clock shadow, down to his broad shoulders and expanse of wide chest leading to a flat stomach—

Leave it, leave it!

Sam stands up and approaches the foot of my bed. "How are you feeling?"

My mouth goes dry as I see him coming closer. *Why does he have to smell so good?* His scent should be illegal. "Why am I here?"

Sam reaches for the remote control on my bed and presses a button. "You crashed into my office and fainted."

No wonder my brain is blocking this memory.

"I was—" He breaks off, shaking his head. For a moment, he doesn't say anything at all, just stares into space. He clears his throat, recollecting himself. "We were worried."

I study his face closely, noticing dark circles under his eyes and lines creasing his forehead. It seems that in the time span of one morning, he's aged five years. He's either genuinely concerned about me or terrified that I'm going to sue him for every penny he's got.

The curtain parts and a nurse and doctor come forward, both of whom seem pleased to find me lucid and conscious. The doctor kicks Sam out of the room before doing the exam, then peppers me with questions about my health history.

"This isn't the first time I've fainted," I admit sheepishly. "Sometimes it happens when I get my blood drawn or if I'm given a shot, so they usually have me lie down first. I didn't have breakfast this morning either, which probably didn't help."

After the exam is over, Dr. Bhatt tells me I have a condition called vasovagal syncope, stressing the importance of preventing fainting spells and how it helps to know the triggers, blood, of course, being mine. I guess not having periods is the one silver lining of my condition because that would definitely freak me out.

Sam keeps me company while I wait for the discharge nurse. He listens intently as I repeat what the doctor had said, then gives me an update about Maya. Gina had driven her to Urgent Care, where she was given sutures for the large cut in her thumb. He adds that he told everyone to go home because he can't handle any more casualties today.

A few minutes later, the nurse returns with my discharge papers and instructs me to take it easy for the next few days.

Outside the hospital, we sit in companionable silence on a bench and wait for our Uber driver. A gusty breeze blows my hair, and I absentmindedly tuck some strands behind my ear. I turn to look at Sam, only to find that his eyes are already on me. He gives me a bone-melting smile, and something inside me flutters. My breath hitches and I suddenly don't know where to look. Obviously, I've been reading too many romance novels because I don't do fluttering.

At least, I never had until now.

Get it together, woman. Remember the girlfriend, aka Dr. Sexy?

"You should stay home for the next few days and take it easy," he says. "Come back to work next week."

"Thanks," I say, gazing straight ahead, "but I'll probably feel fine by tomorrow."

"Probably," he agrees. "But you'll still look like a hockey player that lost a fight."

I laugh. He makes a good point.

"Do you have a dress picked out for the gala?"

I shake my head. I think I've been avoiding thinking about it. "Why?"

"You should wear purple. To match the bruises."

I sigh.

"By the way," he continues, stretching his long legs and resting his hands behind his head, "you said some crazy things on the ride to the hospital."

Oh no. First the fluttering and now this. "Like what?"

"You said your fiancé is gay."

I attempt a laugh, but the noises coming from my throat sound more like a seal with indigestion issues. I can't believe I said that. And I still haven't gotten back to Zevi yet. "Hah! That's funny." I glance at him nervously. "Was that all I said?"

"No." Sam pauses. "But for both our sakes', I won't repeat the rest."

He might as well have waved a big red flag in front of a bull. A masochistic one. "Tell me!"

Sam briefly closes his eyes like he's reliving something particularly painful. "I'd rather not."

My face flushes. What could I possibly have said to make Mr. Insensitive so uncomfortable? Well whatever it was, it's only appropriate to relive the humiliation, this time fully conscious. *"Just tell me!"*

He shakes his head and gazes at the sky. "Fine, but don't say I didn't warn you. You said—and I quote: *'My fiancé is gay so we won't have sex. My hymen and I will be together forever.'* End quote."

Hymen? He's got to be making this up. "You're lying."

He glances at me from the corners of his eyes. "I couldn't have made that up if I tried."

I cover my face with my hands. *Please let this be a bad dream.*

"Well?" Sam says.

"Well, what?" I say, my voice muffled from my hands.

"Don't you want to set the record straight?"

I cannot believe he's making me go there. I uncover my face and fix him with a stern gaze. "With all due respect, Mr. Kleinfeld, that's a deeply personal question. Just because I brought up my hymen when I was delirious, or whatever, doesn't mean that you can start asking about—"

"Nononono," he interrupts, the tips of his ears turning pink. "I wasn't talking about *that*. I meant your gay fiancé."

Oh. Although, between the two options, I'd prefer to talk about my hymen. Sam won't approve of the whole Zevi situation, and unfortunately, I've never been a very convincing liar.

Distraction, on the other hand, is a talent of mine.

"Shouldn't the Uber person be here by now?"

He glances at his phone. "Seven minutes." He throws me a pointed glance and adds, "Start talking."

Think, Penina think. "How's your dad?" I ask.

"Great. The guy is tough as boots." He turns so the front of his body is facing me. "Look, I'm going to ask you this one last time, and I want a straight answer. Are you or are you not engaged to a gay man?"

I stare at a tree and don't say anything. With any luck, he'll take the hint and drop it.

"Holy shit," he murmurs, apparently having decided that it is true. "But why?"

I lean against the bench and close my eyes. "This conversation is boring me to tears. Wake me up when the car gets here."

Unfortunately, Sam does not understand social cues. Or more likely, he does understand but ignores them anyway.

"I don't get it," he says, running his hand through his hair. "Did the guy lose a bet or something? And what's in it for you—why would you go along with this?"

I open my eyes and give him my loftiest stare. "For your information, there's such a thing as love without attraction. Two souls can connect with each other on a spiritual level without needing to be physical."

He smirks. "Yeah, it's called a platonic friendship. Look, don't get me wrong," he adds, lifting his palms up, "I love my female friends with all my heart. They add dimension to my life in the way my guy friends can't, *but . . .*" He shakes his head.

"But what?"

"Hell would have to freeze over before I'd *marry* one."

The wind threatens to sweep the front of my skirt, but I smooth it down before my bare legs are revealed. Where is that Uber, anyway?

Sam assesses me with shrewd eyes. "You aren't in love with him."

Why can't he let it go? "Oh, but I am." I nod vehemently. "Hopelessly." I pause, then add, "Desperately."

His eyebrows furrow into a downward "V" shape. "How long have you two known each other?"

My shirt collar suddenly feels stiflingly tight. "Our souls have known each other for centuries."

Sam exhales deeply through his nose, like he's struggling to remain calm. "I'm referring to this lifetime."

The Uber driver is taking way too long to get here. "Technically, I met him for the first time three weeks ago, but—"

"Three weeks?" he yells.

Two nurses strolling by stop and glance over their shoulders at us. "Lower your voice," I murmur. Maybe he doesn't mind causing a scene, but I sure do. "Anyway," I continue, "we got along so well that it feels like I've always known him."

"You're crazy. You know that, right?"

I silently count to ten before responding in true *Big Lebowski* style, "That's, like, your opinion, dude."

"This has disaster written all over it," he declares, shaking his head. "Big mistake."

"Don't take this the wrong way"—I smile tightly—"but please, stop talking."

"Listen, Superwoman," he continues, ignoring my request, "I suggest you run the hell away from this guy. I don't know what's in it for either one of you, but it's obviously not love. And love is the only good reason to get married."

Okay, now I've had it! I jab my finger in the general direction of his chest. *"You're* the one that told me that marriage is nothing more than a business arrangement!"

"But it doesn't fucking start off that way!" he shouts just as an elderly man passes in a wheelchair, a catheter bag hooked onto the side of it. "Only lunatics would do that."

"Leave him for me, honey!" the toothless old man shouts, craning his neck as the orderly pushes him along. "I'll treat you right."

I give him a little wave and smile.

"Is he a religious fanatic, is that it?" Sam stands up from the bench and starts to pace.

He's taking this much worse than I thought he would. "No, that's not it. We just have a really strong bond and want to spend the rest of our lives together. That's all there is to it," I say, irritation leaking into my voice.

He stops walking and turns to face me. "You met the guy three weeks ago. That's not love. That's insanity." Just as I'm opening my mouth to unleash a little righteous indignation, he adds, "Are your parents forcing you into this marriage?"

"Um, no." I roll my eyes. "That sort of thing tends to be illegal in this country."

"That doesn't mean it doesn't happen."

A gray sedan pulls up, and a young man with a blond ponytail lowers the window. "Sorry I'm late. There was a detour. Construction work everywhere."

"It's fine," Sam responds curtly. He opens the back door and gestures for me to get in.

I fasten my seat belt and wonder why Sam cares about my love life—or lack of it—anyway. For someone I didn't know a few months ago, he seems weirdly invested in my life. I send up a silent prayer that he'll sit up front, but naturally he does the opposite of what he should. I inch toward my side of the car, but his frame is so large that it swallows up the space anyway. I glance at him from the corner of my eye, noting the way a shaft of sunlight highlights his chiseled profile.

"Do you guys want music?" Uber man asks, exiting out of the hospital driveway. "I've got everything from classical to Eminem."

"No," Sam replies.

Uber man reaches toward a bag resting on the passenger seat. "I just picked up some cookies from Denny's. Want one?"

"No, thank you," I say while Sam reaches forward to take one.

"Thanks." Sam takes a big bite.

I suddenly recall what Maya said earlier today and turn to Sam in dismay. "Hey! What about your stomach disease?"

He takes another big bite. "You've definitely had a head injury."

"No." I shake my head. "Maya said you have Celiac and that's why you didn't eat the cinnamon buns she made."

Sam takes his time finishing a mouthful of cookie, and I have a feeling that he's the one stalling now. "Here's the truth, Penina," he says, leaning back. "If I had accepted the buns, she would have kept baking. And then the baking would have progressed into presents—"

"What's wrong with free food and presents?" I catch the driver's eye in the mirror and add, "Right?"

"Sure!" He laughs. "I wouldn't mind."

"In my experience, it leads to inappropriate expectations," Sam explains. "But don't mention any of this to Maya, alright?"

"Hold on a second." I put up my hand like a stop sign. "How does one jump from cinnamon buns to inappropriate behavior?"

Sam rakes his hand through his thick hair. "Just trust me." I look at him doubtfully, and he adds, "This isn't the first time a woman has come onto me through baking."

"Full of yourself much?" I smirk. I try to catch the Uber guy's eyes through the mirror again, but he doesn't cooperate this time. In fact, he switches sides.

"I know what you mean, man." The driver nods. "Happened to me once too."

I wish someone would bake for me. These guys don't appreciate how good they have it. "There's a strong possibility that she's planning on baking gluten-free desserts for you."

Sam mutters an obscenity.

"Just a friendly warning." I shrug. "Or," I add cleverly, "you could work it into a conversation that you have a girlfriend."

Sam finishes his cookie in silence, so I guess he doesn't want to talk about his personal life, which is a shame since I'm dying to hear about it.

"Now," Sam says, "explain to me exactly why a gay man wants to marry you."

Uber man glances at me through his rearview mirror but thankfully doesn't say anything. No doubt he's overheard a lot of interesting car conversations, but I bet this one ricochets right off the nutso scale. And since it's painfully obvious that Sam is not the type to let something go, I surrender to the inevitable.

I clear my throat. "To make a long story short, Zevi—that's the guy—comes from an Orthodox family, and his mom is dying. Her biggest wish is to see him married to a nice Jewish girl—that's where I come in."

Sam rubs his thumb at the corner of his mouth. "And what's in it for you?"

"Enough money to save my sister's house from going into foreclosure. And besides," I continue, "the marriage would only be a temporary thing. Just until his mom, you know. . . ." My hand slides across my neck to drive the point home.

Sam rubs his temples. "That has got to be the craziest scheme I've ever heard," to which I shrug. "And completely unethical," he adds.

I inspect my fingernails. "It's a gray area."

The Uber driver snorts.

"Let me break it down for you." Sam pivots in his seat to face me. His knee almost touches my leg, and my traitorous stomach flutters again. "You're faking a marriage and deceiving people. There's no gray in that."

"The gray is fulfilling his dying mother's wish and making his family happy."

"You think ethics should be based on feelings?"

"No. Well, maybe sometimes. Haven't you ever lied to spare someone's feelings?"

"There's lying," Sam says, giving me a look, "and then there's *lying*."

"Preach it, man," Uber man echoes, raising a fist in the air.

"You're only looking at it from one way," I say, frustrated. "Try to see it from this point of view: we've got a dying mother and a son who loves her desperately. He wants her to leave this world happy and reassured that he'll start his own Orthodox Jewish family," I say, ticking off each point with my fingers. Personally, I don't see the harm. "And what if this marriage makes her so happy that she'll have an extra ten years of life. Wouldn't that be nice?"

"That would be great," he agrees. "Especially if you don't mind staying married for an extra ten years."

"It would be an honor," I say, trying not to glare at him.

"Ask yourself this," Sam says. "Would you still be doing this if your sister's house wasn't on the line?"

I open my mouth to say of course I would, but then stop. Would I? Would I really go through all the trouble of uprooting myself and moving to New York to marry Zevi just to make his dying mother happy? The money aspect would be nice, but I like my job, and I've never been someone that craves high-end things. But I'm probably weird like that.

"I rest my case," Sam declares after he catches me scowling at him.

Great. Now, I'm in a catch-22. Either I go through with this and accept the money, or I don't go through with this and am labeled a hypocrite.

"Why do you care anyway?" I ask, exasperated.

"Because," he says after a beat, "you're my friend. And friends don't let friends make dumb decisions."

I snort. "We are *not* friends."

He stretches his legs and hooks his arms behind his head. "You're definitely not one of my nicer friends, that's for sure."

I think there's a difference between being friends and being friendly, but I'm not exactly sure when the crossover is. And I've never been friends with a guy, since my community tends to frown on that whole gender mixing thing unless it's for marriage. But if I were to have a guy friend, I'd probably choose one who was a whole lot more sensitive and much less opinionated than the man sitting next to me.

"When did this 'friendship' start?" I ask, arranging my fingers into quotation marks.

"Probably the first time I took you to the jewelry store. You drove me crazy that day."

I give him a funny look. "*That's* how our friendship started? With you wanting to kill me?"

"Not kill you," he says, a crooked smile playing on his lips. "But some light maiming might have crossed my mind."

I roll my eyes. "Ah yes, the light maiming. The cornerstone of all friendships."

Sam laughs, and I can't help but stare. I can almost see what he must have been like as a kid, before he had a jewelry empire to run and a sick father to take care of. It's not a bad look.

His phone suddenly rings, and he checks the screen before answering it. I lay my head back against the seat and close my eyes, my thoughts drifting back to Zevi. At times like this I wish I had a guardian angel on my shoulder, telling me the right thing to do. Despite what Sam says, the situation isn't as black and white as he makes it out to be. I'm doing this for Libby *and* for Zevi's mom. And I'm finally getting married, even if it is fake.

I think Sam senses my despondency, because when the car comes to a stop in front of the jewelry store, his eyes are resting on me.

"You'll make the right decision," he says.

If only I could get that in writing. "How do you know?"

"I just do," he replies. Seeing my unimpressed face, he adds, "And you're Superwoman. You've got powers that we regular mortals can only dream of."

I smile. "Thanks."

I wish I could say that talking it out with Sam has helped clarify things, but the truth is that I feel more confused than ever.

CHAPTER FIFTEEN

"A great dress can make you remember what is beautiful about life."
—*Rachel Roy*

I think it's fair to say that I'm well out of my league at this silent auction gala, present company excluded. Maya sits to my left, and Gina's on my right, but gazing around the Minneapolis Hilton's ballroom, it's mostly men and women who scream money and higher education and the kind of people who read articles in *The Economist* for fun. I've always felt a little intimidated by people who would prefer to read an article about Kim Jung Un instead of an article about Kim Kardashian's love life.

I wonder if Zevi attends a lot of fundraisers, and if so, whether he'll expect me to go with him. It's fun to get dressed up, but the polite conversations and having to listen to speeches, not so much. I'd rather kick back on my couch with a mug of hot cocoa and watch *The Bachelor*.

"How do I look?" Maya asks for what is probably the fiftieth time tonight.

"Stunning," I reply, just like the other forty-nine times. It's ridiculous, really. I mean, if anyone should be concerned about how they look tonight, it should be me, since I stick out like a nun at a strip club. I'm in a floor-length dress that covers everything from my collarbone to my ankles, and since it's an unusually warm day in May, most of the women here have at least their top half or their bottom half on display. And in some cases, a little of both.

My only comfort is that the green silk works well with my long brown hair and hazel eyes. My Instagram followers loved it, so there's that. And the best part is that my bruises healed, so there was no need to go shopping for a purple or blue dress.

"What about my mascara?" She tucks a wisp of blond hair behind her ear. "Is it flaking?"

I do a quick once-over. "Still perfect," I say, reaching for my glass of water. Maya is one of those rare natural beauties who could turn heads even in grease-stained sweatpants and a hoodie, but she's also the most insecure person I know. And no matter how often I try to reassure her that she looks amazing, it's as useless as trying to fill an ocean using one bucket.

"If you ask how you look one more time tonight," Gina says with a crazy glint in her eyes, "I will take my fork and *run it through your hair*."

Maya's hands fly protectively to her carefully coiffed head. "Why would you do that? I'm not even talking to you."

"But I can *hear you*."

Maya mutters something under her breath just as Sam appears at our table, looking incredible in a black suit and a blue paisley tie. I've seen glimpses of him throughout the night, but haven't had a chance to do anything more than exchange a quick smile since he's at a different table—one with other big-time donors and board members, the CEO, and of course Keila, whom I now know intimately well thanks to Maya's daily check-ins of Keila's social media posts. Maya usually shoves her phone in my face, which is how I know that Keila drinks green smoothies for breakfast, can do crazy Pilates contortionist poses, rescues abandoned animals, is vegan, and rocks a thong bikini like nobody's business. She's basically a hot and sexy Mother Theresa.

Sam nods at us in acknowledgment and thrusts his hands into his pockets. "How are you ladies doing?"

"Oh, we're doing great," Gina purrs, and lifts up her almost-empty wineglass as if to prove it. She gestures toward the table where Keila sits and adds, "Dr. Bergman spoke so well."

Maya raves over everything: the food, the speeches, the center-pieces. Sam answers her questions about the fundraiser, but whenever I glance up, his eyes are on me.

When Maya pauses to breathe, he gestures to my plate and says, "Was the kosher food good?"

It was *exquisite*—and probably a fortune. "How did you know about—wait, did *you* arrange that?" I was shocked when I was handed a take-out box, with my name on it, from the local kosher restaurant in town.

"I figured you'd have nothing to eat otherwise." He shrugs like it's no big deal, when in truth, it's a *huge* deal. That it would even occur to him that I wouldn't be able to eat is incredible, but then to go out of his way to fix it is just . . . *beyond*. Joy hums through my veins, and I realize I'm grinning at him like a lunatic.

"Well, thank you," I say, trying to tone down my smile, to appear more normal. "I really appreciate it."

"And the dessert is from the kosher bakery," he adds with a crooked smile, "so you're covered there too."

My stomach somersaults. Everyone says that the way to a man's heart is through his stomach, but apparently it works for me too—maybe because I can barely manage to feed myself, unless frozen micro-wave dinners count.

For a moment, time seems to stand still as his eyes hover on my face, then run over my dress, as though it's the sexiest thing he's ever seen. His gaze is scorching hot, and I feel myself melting, but I force myself to tear my eyes off his. Everyone at the table has stopped talk-ing and is glancing between the two of us with undisguised interest. Sam either doesn't notice or doesn't care, made further evident when he bends down to whisper in my ear, "Green is my new favorite color."

I feel my face go red, but he's already straightened and is making conversation with the other people at our table. He seems completely relaxed and at ease, while I am very conscious of his hand resting on the upper back of my chair. I have to sit ramrod straight to avoid contact with it, and Maya is shooting me weird glances that have me worried.

"Have you placed bids on anything?" Sam asks, and a man across the table starts talking about the all-inclusive Maldives package.

If one of the prizes had been Libby's house, I'd have spent all my money on it. Of course, knowing my luck, some random millionaire would win anyway, and then both Libby and I would be screwed.

"Is something going on between you two?" Maya says to me in an undertone, her eyes darting between Sam's hand on the back of my chair and my face.

"Between who?" I pretend to look confused, although I am honestly confused. Between that scorching-hot look and the comment about my dress, I don't know what's going through his head. Maybe he's drunk and he thinks I'm Keila.

"You and—" She lifts her chin toward him with wide eyes.

"Of course not," I say, but my voice comes out squeaky, as though I'm lying. "I think he's a little drunk."

She stares at me for a beat. "I think you're lying."

I shake my head, but Maya isn't the type to listen to reason. "You could've said something," she continues. "Friends tell each other things like this."

My chest tightens and it becomes hard to breathe. With Maya's accusations and Sam acting like a male dog smelling a female in heat, I need a moment to myself. To regroup and try to figure things out.

I stand up from the table and murmur something about needing the restroom, careful to avoid eye contact with anyone, including Sam. I exit the double doors of the ballroom and head down the plush carpeted hallway, glancing around for a bathroom sign. It isn't that I have a urgent need to go, but the idea of hiding in a bathroom stall for a little while seems like a great way to pass time and figure things out. I'm feeling . . . unbalanced. Jittery. Between Sam and Libby and Zevi . . . *G-d. So many secrets and no one to confide in.* I'm like a pressure cooker that's been driven to the boiling point and is in danger of exploding.

"Escaping, are we?"

I glance to my right and find a tall, strikingly handsome man, with black hair and sharp cheekbones, smiling down at me. Though not as tall as Sam, the man is still easily six feet, and clearly no stranger to a gym.

"I plead the fifth," I say with a smile, then scan the hallway for a bathroom.

The man approaches, holding a glass of wine, and on closer inspection, his cheeks are flushed, but I can't tell if it's from the alcohol or because he's embarrassed. Although given his easy confidence, I'm guessing it's the wine. "It's okay, I won't tell anyone. I can barely stand those stuffed shirts for more than thirty minutes at a time, and I'm related to half of them."

I laugh, then gesture toward his glass. "At least there's wine."

He grins, displaying a set of perfectly straight white teeth. "True." He transfers the glass to his left hand, then holds out his right. "I'm Henry Chadwick, by the way."

I withhold a sigh. There goes my alone time. "Penina Kalish."

"Exotic name," he murmurs. "Where are you from, Penina?"

"Here. Minneapolis," I say, glancing behind him as an older woman comes around a corner. Maybe that's where the restroom is. "Sorry, I hate to be rude, but I've got to—"

"But where were you born?" he persists, tilting his head, looking at me, confused.

I nearly groan out loud. Every time—and I do mean *every time*—a non-Jewish man hears my name, he immediately assumes I'm an immigrant who recently got off a boat from a faraway land, whereas a non-Jewish woman simply says, "Oh, what a pretty name!"

"I was born at Fairview Southdale Hospital," I answer politely.

He squints his eyes. "The one here? In Minneapolis?"

No, the one in Kazakhstan. I would save so much time if I just wore my birth certificate around my neck, or simply lied and introduced myself as Ashley Johnson. "Yup, the one here."

"That must be why your English is so good."

I inhale deeply through my nose, then exhale out my mouth. "Probably," I agree. "And my parents, grandparents, and great-grandparents were also born in Minnesota, with the exception of one who was born in Nashville."

He raises his eyebrows and mutters under his breath, "Odd."

I suppose my family is odd, but then, isn't everyone's? "Anyway—"

"I'd love to buy you a drink," he cuts in as his eyes make a slow, languid journey down my body. If I were his bro, I'd have taken him aside and been like, *"Dude! Be less obvious when you undress women with your eyes."* But because I'm not, I say, "Sorry, I can't. It's been nice meeting you—"

"Just one," he adds, holding up a finger. "There's a great bar downstairs, and no one will notice if you're gone for a few extra minutes, right?"

"I can't." I start backing away because (A) this guy is starting to give me the creeps, and (B) nothing but the beer will probably be kosher anyway, and (C) even if everything on the menu was kosher, I wouldn't go because of reason A.

"I insist."

I open my mouth to respond, when two hands land possessively on my shoulders. I twist my neck to see who's manhandling me and find Sam's handsome face. Um . . . did he have a concussion recently? Doesn't he remember he's not supposed to touch me?

"What are you doing?" I whisper as Henry comes closer, his lips turned down into a frown.

Sam glances down at me briefly and murmurs, "Just roll with it."

"Roll with what?"

But all he does is give my shoulders a quick squeeze. Of reassurance? As a warning? Of course, if this Henry dude is dangerous and Sam holding onto me is saving my life, then that's totally fine with Jewish law. You can pretty much do anything if you're saving someone's life. My breath catches as Sam's fingers fan against my clavicle, lightly grazing my skin.

"Hey, man, it's been a long time." Henry smiles, darting a quick glance my way. "What have you been up to?"

"The usual. A few things here and there," Sam replies vaguely. I stiffen as his hands slide down my arms, and my pulse quickens when his thumb makes tiny circles on the inside of my arm. It feels *so* good. Amazing, actually. I don't exactly know what's going on, but Sam did say roll with it, and he is my boss, after all, so I lean my head against his chest and sigh. Why does this feel so good? Is Sam secretly a sorcerer of women, or am I that starved for another human's touch?

"How about you?" Sam asks, his voice sounding a little strained.

"Same. Except I'm driving a hybrid now."

My eyelids flutter shut as my body turns to mush. I'm embarrassed to admit it, but yes, I am pressing my entire backside against the front of Sam's. I purr like a contented kitten when Sam's hand snakes around my waist, anchoring me tighter against him. His fingers splay against my dress and the warmth of his hand seeps into my skin.

Thank you, super dangerous man. I owe you one.

"Great." Sam clears his throat. Something is definitely wrong with his voice—he should get that checked out with a doctor.

There's a prolonged silence, and then I hear Henry say, "Is she . . . conscious?"

"Sweetheart," he whispers, lowering his face to rest next to mine. "Are you okay?"

"Mm-hmm," I hum. He's put me into a trance that I never want to wake up from. He is my new cult leader, and I am his most devoted follower.

"She's good," Sam says after a delayed pause, then brushes the pads of his fingers on the space between my ear and neck. My breath hitches, and I arch, trying to give him better access.

"Is this lucky lady going to be wifey number two?"

Sam's fingers abruptly stop moving. "I've been thinking about it."

One eye cracks open, then the other one. Huh?

"If you love her, don't marry her. That's my advice. See you around, brother!"

"See you," Sam calls out, then mutters under his breath, "you worthless piece of shit." His hands drop from my body, and he steps back. "Sorry," he says. "I didn't know how else to—" He shakes his head. "He's not the kind of guy you'd want to find yourself alone with."

It takes me a moment to get my bearings and then another moment to understand the implications behind Sam's words. I swallow. "Yeah, I kind of got that vibe from him." Sam opens the door that leads to the ballroom and gestures for me to go in first. Instead of moving, I say, "Thank you. I really appreciate it."

He shrugs. "I'm a nice guy."

"I wouldn't go that far," I tease, walking backward. "But you're growing on me, Mr. Kleinfeld."

He gazes at me with an expression that's hard to read. "Maybe you should start calling me Sam."

My stomach freefalls, but I try to brush it off. He has a beautiful girlfriend and I might soon have a husband. "Maybe you should give me a raise."

"Don't push it," he says with a crooked grin.

CHAPTER SIXTEEN

"To wear dreams on one's feet is to begin to give a reality to one's dreams."

—*Roger Vivier*

"Hey, guys." I give my mother a quick peck on the cheek and smile at Libby as I dump the grocery bags, filled with cream cheese, cottage cheese, and butter, onto the kitchen counter. Shavuos starts tonight, and as far as Jewish holidays go, this one isn't half bad—unless you're lactose intolerant. Since we received the Torah on a Saturday and couldn't cook because of the no-work-on-Shabbos thing, we stuff ourselves with lasagna, cheesecake, and ice cream.

"I had to go to three different stores for these ingredients," I announce, "but don't feel bad." Although they totally should.

"Three?" Libby's eyes widen as she glances over her shoulder at me. "Why so many?"

I bite my lower lip, wishing I had kept my mouth shut. The truth is that I was distracted because the voices in my head were holding a staff meeting regarding the Zevi situation. I'm starting to think that Sam and Delilah might be right—Libby is an adult. She doesn't need anyone to save her.

To pretend I didn't hear her question, I bury my head in the refrigerator and start putting away the groceries. My mother asks Libby to hand her a spatula and a cup of sugar, and by the time I poke my head out, Libby seems to have moved on.

"What's next?" I ask, knowing there's probably a list of chores a mile long. Since there's no work allowed for the next two days, everything from cooking to laundry, to watering the plants all has to be done before sunset tonight.

"Thanks honey," my mother says, pouring flour into a measuring cup. "Could you set the table? We're having twelve people tonight."

"Paper or real?"

My mother hesitates. Shabbos and holidays are supposed to be celebrated with the finest linens and dishes to distinguish them from regular weekdays, but my mother hates doing the dishes so she sometimes "cheats" by using fancy disposable plates and cups.

"I'll do the washing for you," I say after a beat, then telepathically message: *Please say paper, please say paper.*

"Just use paper," Libby says. "It's easier and no one cares. We've worked hard enough as it is."

I couldn't agree more. Technically speaking, all I did was shop for some ingredients, but still. Did I mention I had to go to three stores?

"Okay, okay. Paper it is." My mother looks up from the cookbook in her hand and turns to me. "We'll have three courses, but keep the soup bowls and dessert plates in the kitchen."

I head to the cabinet at the far end of the room and start pulling out paper plates. "Why is it so quiet? Where are the kids?"

"They're at the park with Fraydie," Libby replies. I raise my eyebrows, and Libby responds, "Desperate times call for desperate measures."

I snort. Fraydie is fine handling the kids as long as A)a friend doesn't call and distract her and B)she doesn't rear end anyone's cars, which C)she's done at least three times now.

I grab a package of fancy napkins and lay them on top of the plates. "And Tatty?"

"Right here," my father says, coming into the room. He holds his arms out to me and places a kiss on the top of my head. My father's beard used to be a stately black when I was a kid, but at some point it transitioned to salt and pepper, and is now a distinguished-looking soft gray. Fraydie calls it a "Santa Claus white" but then, she would. "How are you?"

"Good, thank G-d," I say, stepping back to look at him. There are a couple new creases on his forehead, and I wonder if it's from aging or lack of sleep. Sleep problems run in my family, and my father has it the worst. "How's your insomnia?"

"Not bad. I had a good night," he says, patting me on the head, like I'm still six years old.

"He slept three hours," my mother says, looking up from her cookbook. Libby and I exchange horrified looks. "Three hours? And that's a good night?" I say, shaking my head in disbelief.

"Is it my fault?" Libby asks. "Because you're worried about my house?"

"No," my father says, waving his hand dismissively, but his tone lacks conviction. "Of course not."

I turn to Libby, surprised. "You told them?"

"You know I'm not good at keeping secrets," she replies, which is true enough.

"Do the kids know?" I ask, worried.

"Not yet." She frowns. "I keep hoping I won't have to, but—" A cell phone pings, and Libby glances at her phone. "Penina, can you take over with these cheese blintzes?" she asks, untying her apron. "Fraydie said the baby's getting fussy. I'm going to get them."

Ah, so Fraydie didn't drive. Thank G-d for that, at least.

"I can go," I offer, a hint of panic in my voice. It's not that I'm afraid of cooking per se—it's just that there's some history between us, and none of it is good. Unless, you count omelets. Libby picks up her purse and car keys from the kitchen table. "Thanks, but Goldy needs to go down for her nap."

I glance at the kitchen counter cluttered with ingredients and utensils, and my stomach twists into knots. "I can put her down."

Libby shakes her head. "She's going through a phase right now where she only wants me. But, really, Pen," she adds, seeing my face, "it's not that hard. The recipe is on the counter, and Ma is here if you need help."

"It's never too late to learn," my mother says. "You can add that to your *shidduch* résumé," she says, referring to the list of qualifications matchmakers use to pair people together. When she catches my facial expression, she adds, "It might help—you never know."

Right, because learning how to make potato kugel will make up for the fact that I can't have babies.

"It's my fault," my mother continues. "I should have encouraged you more."

"You encouraged me plenty," I say, then glance at Libby for help.

"I gave up too quickly on you." My mother crosses the kitchen, opens the refrigerator, and pulls out a carton of eggs. "Especially after everyone got food poisoning from your matzah balls."

My father chuckles as he takes an apple out of the fruit bowl. "Remember how Fraydie ran over to use the neighbor's bathroom because all of ours were being used?"

For the record, I am totally innocent. It was obviously a virus that mimicked food poisoning that made everyone sick, but whatever.

"Ma," Libby clears her throat, "the only help Penina needs with *shidduchim* is finding someone deserving of her."

A warmth spreads through me as I smile at Libby and mouth, "Thanks." She's still got my back. Maybe we're so used to saving each other that we don't even realize we're doing it.

I wait for the door to shut, then turn to my mom. "What's the latest news about her house?"

"It's not looking good." My father sighs and pulls out a kitchen chair. "They're in so much debt that the only way to save their house at this point is to win the lottery."

"They could move in with us," my mother says, "but now they're talking about making Aliyah. Natan's parents are getting older and he has more connections in Israel."

My body freezes in horror. Having them move to Detroit was bad enough, but *Israel?* No. Sorry, not happening. I can't believe they're even considering it. And it's all because I've been dragging my feet instead of doing what needs to be done.

"Where are you going?" my mother calls out as I grab my keys and head for the front door.

"I need to do something I've been putting off." I turn around and blow her a kiss.

"But what about the blintzes?"

"The blintzes can wait," I reply, stepping outside. "This can't."

* * *

Zevi answers on the third ring. "Penina?"

"Hi, Zevi." I raise the volume of my car's speaker. "Do you have a minute to talk?"

"You bet. I'm just leaving the gym."

My future husband, the gym rat. Maybe he'll inspire me to become one too. Or better yet, I could cheer him on from a distance, in bed with the TV remote in my hand and a cool drink in the other.

I lick my lips, then clear my throat. "So, um . . . is your original offer still on the table?"

"Yes! Absolutely." In the background, I hear the sounds of traffic and people rushing by. "Are you saying you're interested?"

I take a deep breath, then slowly release it. "Yes. Yes, I am." Silence. "Zevi? Are you still there?"

"Sorry, yeah, I'm here," he says, his voice sounding thick. "I just can't believe this is happening. I'm so grateful to you, Penina. I—" He breaks off suddenly, and I hear something that's almost like a cross between a hiccup and a hyena's laughter. It takes me a minute to figure out what it is.

"Zevi, are you crying?"

"No. Well, maybe a little," he croaks. "I'm just so *relieved*. I honestly don't know what I would have done if you'd said no."

Hearing such pure emotion reaffirms my belief that I'm doing the right thing. Not just for Libby, but for Zevi too. "Don't worry—I'm here for you."

"Thanks. That means a lot. So, how soon can you come to New York?"

"Um, I don't know exactly—"

"I can buy you a ticket for next weekend, if that works. You could fly early Friday morning and head back Sunday night."

"Yeah, I think that will be fine. As long as my boss is okay letting me have that Friday off."

"Cool. And if you get the go-ahead, would you be okay staying at my sister's for Shabbos? The closest hotel is too far away to walk."

Normally, I don't mind the no driving on Shabbos law, but being stuck at a stranger's house for twenty-five hours is a little daunting. "Sure, that's fine. What's she like?"

"Leah? She—she's okay." He clears his throat. "It can take her a while to warm up to people, but she gets there eventually." A beat. "Usually."

The car behind me is too close, so I switch to the right lane. "Is she shy?"

"No," he chuckles. "I wouldn't call it that. Actually, I don't know what I'd call it. It's just that she doesn't take well to outsiders. My grandmother was the same way. If it were up to her, all the cousins would have married each other."

I laugh. "Well, I'll make it my personal mission to get her to like me."

"Don't worry about it, really. And I'll do my best to watch out and protect you as best I can." He says something else but there's a beeping over the line that momentarily cuts him off. "Shoot, I'm sorry. I have to take this call, Penina."

"Sure, no problem."

"Thanks. We'll talk soon."

I hang up and try to figure out what I'm feeling. There's a part of me that's relieved because I know I'm doing the right thing, but there's a slight churning in my stomach that whispers of bad things to come. Things like a cold sister-in-law and having to lie to my family and going into a marriage knowing it will end in divorce, adding yet another strike to my already-doomed dating résumé. Being infertile is one thing, but being infertile *and* divorced is pretty much a guarantee that I'll never get married and be a mother.

I swallow and grip the steering wheel tighter. Not everyone is meant to have the husband and two-point-five kids and white picket fence. And that's okay. I don't need to experience sex or know what it's like to be held by a man I love. I don't need to have children look at me all doe-eyed and hear them call me Mommy. I don't need that, even though I want it.

The fact is that marrying Zevi will provide me with enough money to save my sister's house, and that's that. I'm not okay with them moving to Detroit or Israel, and I know Libby isn't either. I owe this to her. For as long as I can remember, Libby has always been the capable, independent one. She's been the biggest support to me over the years, giving me advice when I needed it or letting me cry and rant while holding me tight. I honestly don't know if I'd be the person I am today without her. I'm lucky to have her in my life, and her happiness means everything.

I turn into the parking garage of my apartment building and park in my regular spot. Everything is going to be just fine. And as long as no one discovers the truth behind our engagement, and Zevi's sister doesn't totally hate me, what could possibly go wrong?

CHAPTER SEVENTEEN

"Gather up your courage like an armful of free clothes at a McQueen sample sale and follow your inner voice wherever it takes you."
—Kelly Cutrone

Everything is going wrong today. First I slept through my alarm clock, which happens only once every ten years, then I nearly got into a car accident because I was speeding to work, and then I realized I left my lunch at home. By the time I pulled into the parking lot, my phone pinged with a message from one of my Instagram sponsors that they were pulling out because they weren't getting enough traction from my posts.

And now I'm in the dragon lady's lair, trying to convince her to give me a day off work so I can go to New York.

"I'm sorry." Gina sets her pen on the desk and assumes an expression of sympathy. It doesn't come naturally to her, so it takes a few moments to arrange her features just right. She settles on placing her hands together and tilting her head. "I wish I could. Unfortunately, it won't be possible."

I silently stare at her, waiting to hear why I can't have Friday off. But then I remember it's Gina I'm talking to, and she thrives on power trips. I'm doomed.

"Could you work in the showroom that day?" I clasp my hands together, prayer style, adding, "I will totally make it up to you. I will bring you back deluxe chocolate candy that has been certified by the most religious rabbi in Brooklyn."

Gina, an agnostic, frowns. "Is that a joke?"

"Not a very good one. But seriously, Gina"—I lean forward in my chair—"is there anything from New York that you'd like?"

"I'm sure that offer would have come in handy twenty years ago," she replies, wrapping a rubber band over a pile of envelopes. "Nowadays, Amazon Prime provides me with all of my needs, plus free shipping."

"Okay," I sigh, scratching my head. How can I convince her? "What if I put in extra hours next week?"

Gina pushes her reading glasses to the top of her head, where they rest like a crown over her stiff hair. She points a French manicured nail in my direction. "I distinctly remember you promising to work extra hours the last time this happened. Which, may I remind you, you never made good on."

What does she mean, *the last time this happened?* I'm pretty sure this is the first time I needed one lousy workday off to go to New York to meet my gay fiancé's family. "I'm sorry, Gina, but I think you're mixing me up with someone else."

"No, it was *you*." She smiles widely, and I notice a slight gap between two teeth. "You went to Duluth for some trivial reason, and then suddenly there was a"—she pauses and shifts her fingers into air quotes—"'blizzard,' and you missed half a week of work. Which, if my memory serves me correctly—and it always does—you never made up."

I smack my forehead. *For the love of—*

"That was two years ago, and it was Sadie, not me. She went for her grandfather's funeral, and the blizzard was so bad that several people died trying to drive in it."

Gina's eyebrows lift up and down a few times. She picks up a pen and taps it in rapid succession on her desk. I can tell she knows I'm right, but will never admit it. "The fact remains that you are needed here that Friday, and that's final."

I massage the crick in my neck. Obviously, I should have just planned on calling in sick that day. Seriously, when has being honest ever worked in my favor?

"What if—" I begin, only to be interrupted by a brief knock. The door opens and Sam walks in.

"Gina, did you hear back from Adir?" Sam's eyes travel down to meet mine and his mouth curves into the smallest of smiles. "Hello, Penina."

Quit fluttering, stomach. We've been over this. There's been a subtle shift in our relationship since the night of the gala. It's like Sam no longer feels the need to maintain his air of authority, and I get to see the real version of him a lot more often now.

I open my mouth to respond, but Gina is faster. "I did hear back from Adir, and I was just getting ready to talk to you, but I've been dealing with *something*." Gina tilts her head in my direction, making it clear that *I'm* that something. "But we've just finished. Isn't that right, Penina?" she says in a clipped tone that makes it clear we are.

I force a smile and stand up from my chair. "I guess so."

Gina pulls open the bottom desk drawer and removes her purse. "Could you grab me a mocha cooler from Caribou? Skim and no whip." Extracting a ten-dollar bill from her Louis Vuitton wallet she adds, "Feel free to grab a little something extra for yourself."

Great. Just great. First, I'm told to get lost, and then I'm told to get Her Highness coffee. Frankly, I'm surprised she trusts me not to spit in it.

When I return to the store, balancing a tray of coffee in one hand and Maya's chocolate croissant in the other, the showroom's spotlights have already been turned on, and the jewelry sparkles from its designated cases. "Looks great." I lower the cup carrier onto the filing cabinet, which is tucked in an unobtrusive spot behind the rare gem display case.

The morning after the hospital gala, Maya called and apologized for being paranoid about Sam and me. Thank G-d she didn't see me pressed against him in the hallway that night, or else that would be one more thing to have to explain.

"Okay, they've *definitely* broken up." Maya grins and passes her phone to me. Her eyes are positively glowing with excitement, and it doesn't take a genius to figure out who she's referring to. "Read this and tell me I'm wrong. *And*," she adds, eying me over the lid of her cup, "she hasn't posted any new pictures of him since New York."

Yes, I know. If only Maya did her dirty work privately instead of dragging me into it too; I'm basically a creeper by association.

Keila's Instagram post is a picture of her doing an incredibly painful-looking yoga pose, in an exercise bra and leggings, against the backdrop of an orange and pink sunrise, with a quote from Robert Frost: *"In three words I can sum up everything I've learned about life: it goes on."*

"See?" Maya is literally glowing as she takes her phone back. "There's nothing else that could possibly mean."

"Actually," I say, trying to keep her grounded in case it's not true, "it could mean lots of different things. A patient could have died or a family member or a friend. Or she had a friend breakup." I think about what makes me feel sad and add, "Or she missed out on a really amazing sale at Zara's."

"No." Maya shakes her head. "Caroline says I should trust my gut, and my gut is saying they broke up."

I turn around so she doesn't see my eye roll. Once Maya brings her psychic into a conversation, you know you've lost.

"Oh, I almost forgot!" she says, reaching for a croissant. "Sam wants to see you in his office ASAP."

"What for?" I straighten and brush a stray wisp of hair off my face.

Maya shrugs. "Beats me. I wish he'd call me into his office. Oh, the things we could do together," she sighs.

And just like that, I picture Sam pinning me against a jewelry display cabinet with his hips, cradling my head with his hands, and angling for a kiss. He runs his fingers through my hair as he gently teases my mouth open with his tongue. *Mmm . . .* He tastes like a freshly cut pine tree with hints of manly pheromones. Moaning with pleasure, I run my hands down the hard ridges of his chest. Frustrated by the barrier of our clothes, he breaks the kiss and rips open my blouse, the buttons scattering to the ground. He takes a step back and stares hungrily at my breasts, the milky tops of which spill over my lacy red bra. Licking his lips, he whispers, "Are they kosher—"

"Pen?"

I blink. "Yeah?"

"You okay?"

"Fine." I clear my throat and smooth down my skirt. "Totally fine. Why wouldn't I be?"

"You had this weird faraway look on your face, and then your mouth fell open a little."

I laugh nervously. "I was just . . . wondering what to have for dinner."

"If you say so." Maya looks at me skeptically. "I'd get a move on if I were you. Sam is waiting."

"Uh . . . right." Moving past the showroom and gallery, I head down the short hallway leading to Sam's office. My cheeks feel hot, and I'm pretty sure I don't normally breathe this fast. I'd like to think I'm just having a panic attack, but I have a feeling it's my body's reaction to having inappropriate thoughts involving my boss. My boss! I should be ashamed of myself. I mean, I *am* ashamed of myself.

But he did say we were friends, so does that make it okay? *No, Penina, it does not.* I guess I'm just not evolved enough to handle a platonic relationship with a good-looking man.

I reach Sam's office and knock on the dark wooden door. *I will not picture Sam naked, I will not picture Sam naked, I will not picture Sam naked.*

"Come in."

Sam sits behind his desk, talking animatedly on the phone. He gestures for me to take a seat, and I take the opportunity to admire the changes in the room. One of the first things he did when he took over the business was to hire a decorator to spruce up his father's old office, and it's undergone an impressive transformation. The furniture and decor are a tribute to modern design and minimalism, with its sharp lines, sleek edges, and asymmetrical layout. A glass-topped desk reigns in the center of the room, and a steel-blue pendant light presides above it. Opposite the desk rests a pair of velvet backed chairs with chrome bases. I choose the one closest to the door in case things get ugly and I need to escape in a hurry.

"Thanks, Clive. I appreciate it . . ." Sam wheels his chair around so that I'm staring at his back. "Uh-huh . . . okay . . . will do." He abruptly disconnects the call, then turns to face me. "So."

There is something so decidedly alpha male about Sam that it makes it difficult to think at times. And because he doesn't look particularly happy at the moment, right now is one of those times.

"So," I parrot because it seems like the safest option.

He leans back in his chair and arches one imperious brow. "About Friday."

Oh no. Here it comes. "Can I just say something?"

He looks surprised but nods. "Go ahead."

"Okay. So, I asked for one day off. It's short notice, and it's a Friday—I get it. But I don't think it's that unreasonable that Gina cut me a little slack here. I covered for her the other week with her gall bladder thingy—remember that?" Sam opens his mouth to say something, but I'm on a roll here, and I can't afford to break my stride. "Do you know the number of times I've put in extra hours because other people had appointments or got sick?"

"How many?"

I frown. It was a rhetorical question. "That's not the point. And you know why? Because I'm not like that—I don't keep track of who owes who. The point is that it would be nice if every now and then the takers would also give."

"Uh-huh."

I cross my legs and notice the way his eyes briefly follow the movement. Not that he can see anything interesting; he doesn't strike me as the type to get excited about a metallic maxi skirt the way my followers did. They loved how I paired it with a simple white T-shirt and gold accessories. "It's like she's a dictator, a female version of Stalin, getting off on starving her countrymen to satisfy her sadistic streak."

The "Stars and Stripes Forever" song begins to play in my head, and I pound my fist on Sam's desk for emphasis (but it took some of the drama away when I had to move the heavy table lamp to clear a space). "Our country is epitomized by freedom and democracy. If Gina doesn't like that, then maybe she belongs in North Korea. A little starvation and forced curfew could do wonders for someone like her."

Sam stares at me wordlessly, and I feel a twinge of guilt for talking bad about Gina behind her back. "I mean, don't get me wrong—she has some nice qualities. For example, she . . . um, she—" I break off, trying to think, but Sam is rubbing his full bottom lip in a thoroughly distracting way. I focus on the wall behind him to concentrate.

"Oh, I know," I say excitedly, snapping my fingers. "She has excellent taste in shoes. Her style is classic and timeless. A little Grace Kelly, a little Lori Harvey." Pathetic, I know, but it was the only thing I could come up with on such short notice.

"And she does have this amazing knockoff red Valentino belt. But she wouldn't tell me where she got it." Which still bugs me. Did she think I was going to rush off and buy the same one? Because I wouldn't have (unless it didn't come in black, in which case I'd have no choice).

"Anything else, or are you finished?"

I do a quick mental checklist of the rest of Gina's wardrobe. "I'm good, thanks."

"I spoke to Gina and we agreed that you should take Friday off."

For a moment, I'm struck speechless. "What? Do you mean it?"

"Penina." Sam leans forward, his warm eyes radiating sincerity. "Rest assured that if I say something, I very much mean it."

The backs of my knees tingle, and my pulse picks up speed. "Thank you. Thank you so much, Mr. Kleinm—oops, Sam." I stand up and move toward the door before he changes his mind.

"Out of curiosity," he says casually, "what's so important about this Friday?"

I hesitate. Based on our previous conversation about Zevi, I know he doesn't think this is a smart idea. Or ethical. Or anything that even remotely resembles a good reason to do this. Not that I asked.

"I'm going out of town." He doesn't say anything, and I add, "New York."

He taps the end of his pen against his desk. "Any particular reason?"

This really is none of his business, I remind myself. I don't owe him an explanation for wanting to use one of my vacation days. Gina and Maya have each taken a day off here and there, and I don't recall either of them getting the third degree.

"It's a nice time of year," I say.

I can tell it was the wrong thing to say, based on the narrowing of his eyes. "Are you planning on seeing Zevi?"

I sigh. He's acting like a jealous husband who suspects his wife is having an affair. "Yes," I reply. "That's on the itinerary."

An emotion flashes across his face, but it's so brief I didn't have time to figure out what it meant. "Never mind. You're needed here on Friday."

My jaw drops. *Is he joking?* "Are you joking?"

"No." He turns his attention to his computer and starts typing something. "Close the door on your way out."

Oh no, he doesn't. I fold my arms across my chest and level my gaze at him. "Explain to me what changed. Because a minute ago you had no problem giving me the day off."

"A minute ago I still thought you were a rational, intelligent human being, capable of making good choices," he says, glancing up from the computer. "Clearly, I misjudged you."

"And clearly, you're an asshole!" I shake my head. "I was starting to think you were nice."

"I am nice!" he barks. "Why do you think I'm doing this?"

The words are out of my mouth before I have time to think them through. "Then I quit. I was going to anyway since I'm moving to New York."

He shakes his head like he refuses to believe what's happening. "Don't do this, Penina."

"It's too late," I say firmly. "I told him I'd do it."

He pushes his chair back and runs his hands through his hair. "Tell him you changed your mind, that something came up."

"What kind of thing 'comes up,'" I say, using air quotes, "that would make someone break off their engagement?" I think of how emotional Zevi got over the phone when I told him I'd go along with the plan.

"How about you finally came to your senses and realized what a stupid idea this was."

"Except it's not."

He stands up and starts to pace. "Tell him you need more time."

"But I don't."

"Tell him you fell in love," he says, gazing out the window.

I laugh at the absurdity. "With who?"

He turns around to face me. "What is it that you really want?"

My eyebrows lift of their own accord. "What do you mean 'what do I really want'?"

"What does Penina Kalish, jewelry associate extraordinaire–slash–social worker–slash–NICU volunteer, *really* want out of life?"

"I want the people I love to be happy." And live in Minneapolis.

"But what makes *you* happy?"

I shrug. How can I explain the pointlessness of it, that this question is better left unasked. After a few beats of silence, I glance up and find Sam studying me. "What?"

He tilts his head. "What are you so afraid of?"

"It's not that I'm afraid." I shake my head. "It's just a matter of being realistic. I accept the fact that real life isn't a fairy tale. People like me don't get happily ever afters." I swallow against the lump in my throat. I can't believe I'm talking about this. *Again.* "And that's okay. I'm happy."

His face turns angry. "What do you 'mean people like you'?"

I play with the gold bangle bracelets on my arm, to avoid looking at him. "Damaged." The silence that follows is so heavy that I don't know where to look. It feels like I just revealed the barest part of my soul, the shameful part, and I cringe, wishing I could take the words back.

"Look at me, Penina."

Control freak. "What?"

His eyes are dark and stormy. "You are not damaged."

Yeah, right. Of course, I'm damaged. And even worse—I'm an imposter. I look like a woman but am missing the most important part of my womanhood. Like an ornate jewelry box that's empty inside.

"A person is more than their reproductive organs." His amber eyes churn with intensity. "*You* are so much more than that."

Sam's voice is so impassioned that it makes my battered heart feel something that's different and scary, and something I don't want to examine. I focus on a picture of him in a graduation gown, flanked by his parents and say, "I don't disagree with you. But the fact remains that I'm still not . . ." I break off, searching for the right word. "*Whole.*"

"Penina." I slowly tear my gaze from the picture and lift my eyes to meet his. "You're more than whole—you're *perfect*. Absolutely perfect."

My breath catches in my throat, and I stare at him in shocked disbelief. How does he believe that? No one is perfect, least of all me. But my defenses are no match for his ardent words, and they knock down my carefully constructed barriers and shine like a rainbow after a long, dark storm.

"How can you say that?" I wonder aloud. "You don't even know me."

"I haven't known you for long," he concedes, "but I do know you. I've seen the way you treat people. You've given a lot to your coworkers, and when you make a sale, it's not just about the commission—the buyer's happiness matters to you." He pauses and tilts his head. "Everyone's happiness matters to you."

"I don't know about *everyone*," I say, thinking of Keila, Gina, and my fifth-grade math teacher. I play with the belt attached to my metallic skirt and add, "But thanks. You're . . . you're a good friend."

There's a subtle change in his eyes, and he shakes his head. "We're not friends."

My mouth opens in surprise, and it feels like someone punched a hole in my gut. A big gaping hole that I hadn't seen coming. "You said we were."

"I lied." He glances away and says, "I've never thought of you as my friend."

"Right." I swallow, blinking against the surge of tears that want to break free. I'm confused and hurt, and I don't know how I'll ever be able to look him in the face again. I turn around so he can't see me, and I twist the doorknob. It occurs to me that I might never see or speak to him again, and if I don't say this now, it'll forever eat away at me. "And as long as we're being honest"—I sniff, my hand on the door—"you should know that square-toed shoes don't look good under any circumstances, and you should burn your black ones."

Then I shut the door and don't look back.

CHAPTER EIGHTEEN

"In a world full of trends, I want to remain a classic."

—*Iman*

I wake up the following morning sick to my stomach. *What was I thinking?* I have a little money saved up, but nothing that will tide me over for more than two months, and who knows when we'll get fake married? In the meantime, I still have to pay rent and buy myself food. Ugh. Adulting sucks.

I squeeze a dollop of toothpaste onto my toothbrush, making sure not to look in the mirror. Nobody wants to see dark circles under their eyes after tossing and turning all night. I gave myself a headache trying to figure out Sam's issues. Why would he say nice things to me, then tell me in the next breath that he lied about being friends? What's the point? It's just mean.

I rinse my mouth out from the faucet and put my toothbrush away. Ever since I met the man, he's yo-yoed between being nice and being a jerk, but yesterday was a record-breaking transition. I'm "absolutely perfect," and oh yeah, he lied. *"I've never thought of you as a friend."*

I turn on the shower and test the temperature. If he does this kind of thing with Keila, then she must be an angel. I can totally see him saying, "I love you. Actually, no—I don't."

Whatever. Sam is in the past, and I'm through thinking about him. In a few more months, I'll be a multimillionaire and never need to work again. What do people who don't have to work do all day? Golf? I hate golf.

The phone rings just as I'm stepping out of the shower, and I wrap a towel around my body before answering.

"Hello?"

"Hi, sweetie," my mother's melodic voice greets me. "How are you?"

"Good. What's up?"

"I know you're getting ready for work, so I'll make this fast. You know Mrs. Hershkowitz?"

I'll tell her later about quitting—after I'm married and rich. She doesn't need one more thing to worry about. "Who?"

"Mrs. Hershkowitz, the old lady from synagogue. She has short red hair and yells at kids to be quiet during service. Small woman, big voice, twitchy eyes . . . ring a bell?"

I put the phone on "Speaker" and place it on a shelf so I can finish drying off. Oh, the witch! I forgot she had a real name. "I know who you mean. What about her?"

"Do you remember her grandson from Israel, Yankeleh? The last time he visited here he was just a kid, but I think you may have played with him once or twice."

"Vaguely." I'm pretty sure he was the kid that stole desserts from the women's section of the synagogue's buffet and brought them to the men's table. "What about him?"

"Well, he's here visiting. And he's just the *sweetest*."

No one can accuse my mother of being subtle, bless her heart. "Uh-huh." I tuck the towel under my armpits and patter back to the bathroom.

"I ran into him at The Kosher Spot. The poor thing was buying jarred gefilte fish instead of the frozen kind. Anyway, I couldn't believe how grown up he is now. And so handsome!"

That doesn't say much, coming from my mother. She thinks her mailman is "a cutie," even though he's missing his front teeth and only has one eye on account of a rabid squirrel attack.

"And guess what?" she continues. "He asked about you!"

Just shoot me now. I squirt some moisturizer onto my legs, then glance at the clock. "I'm sure he was just being polite."

"No," she says. "I know for a fact he wasn't."

A knot forms in the pit of my stomach. "Why do you say that?"

A beat of silence, and then, "Don't be mad, honey, but I gave him your number."

I look up at the ceiling and scream.

"Penina?"

"Ma, you promised to stop doing that!"

"I know and I'm sorry," she says, sounding contrite, like an addict that fell off the bandwagon. "But I figured this was one of those exceptions."

"*Exceptions?*" I grab a fistful of my hair and clench. "Did I say there were *exceptions?*"

"Sweetie, every rule has an exception, or else it wouldn't be a rule."

My head starts to pound, and I suddenly realize the perfect way to shut her down. I take a deep breath and say, "Ma, I'm engaged."

Silence. "What?"

"I'm engaged. Sorry to just blurt it out like that. I meant to tell you earlier." I clutch the side of my head, feeling faint. "But obviously this is why I can't date Yankeleh." A long silence follows, and I check the phone to make sure we're still connected. "Ma? You there?"

"Penina, you're not serious."

"I am, actually." I press the speaker button then head to my closet to get dressed. I open my lingerie drawer and select a hot-pink bra and a pair of underpants with dancing flamingos in choice places. Even though no one sees my underwear—except on occasion, airport security—I still like to have fun with it.

"Is this the rich guy Mrs. Zelikovitch was so excited about? I barely remember anything about him, I just figured it didn't work out between you. Is that the one you're engaged to?"

"Yes, that's him. His name is Zevi Wernick."

"I can't believe this. I can't—why didn't you say something sooner?"

"You know how it is," I say vaguely, snapping my bra clasp shut. "Everything happened so fast."

"So . . . *nu*," she says, using the Yiddish word to let me know she's getting impatient, "tell me everything!"

Ready or not, here comes the interrogation. "He's thirty-six and very handsome and nice."

"What does he do?"

My voice is muffled as I slide a bow-tie chiffon blouse over my head. "He makes movies."

"Religious ones?"

"Um, kind of." His breakout film was about a priest that had been possessed.

"Where's he from?"

I zip up my black pleather skirt, then grab a pair of silver hoop earrings from my jewelry drawer. I'm going to dress for success even though I've got nowhere to go. "Brooklyn."

"Is he divorced?"

"No. This will be his first marriage."

"At thirty-six?"

Already I regret acting so impulsively; it is a truth, universally acknowledged, that a thirty-six-year-old Orthodox Jewish man who has never been married must have something seriously wrong with him. Most men and women are married by their early twenties, since the goal is to have as many children as possible. I bite my bottom lip, trying to think of something that would prevent a man who's almost forty years old from marrying. Something that doesn't involve having no interest in a woman's body. *Think, Penina, think!*

"Does he have a stutter?" My mother asks.

Sure, let's go with that. "Um, yes—how did you know?" I say, hoping she doesn't detect the desperation in my voice. Note to self: Remind my fake fiancé to practice stuttering before our fake wedding. That sounds normal, doesn't it?

"I knew it—I just read about someone like that in the *Jewish Press* the other week. How bad is it?"

"Really bad," I say automatically, pulling my damp hair into a ponytail. Then I quickly add, "But it depends on the day."

"Really? Why is that?"

I lick my dry lips and reach for my lip balm. "I'm not sure. It's . . . complicated."

"But you can communicate okay?"

I start to sweat and decide to add a second layer of my spray deodorant. "Most days, yes."

Silence. She's probably wondering how a marriage is supposed to work if communication only works at random times. Probably better than most marriages. Still . . . I wish I had thought of a simpler excuse, like a fear of commitment, but it's hard to come up with a good lie without advance notice.

"What about sign language?" she asks. "Maybe you could both learn that. Or get a chalkboard for your house or one of those dry erase boards. Remember to add those things to your wedding registry—"

I interrupt with a quick goodbye and a promise to let her know the soonest Zevi can come to town, all of which takes the better part of ten minutes.

In the kitchen, I crack an egg into a glass bowl, then check it for blood since blood is considered *treif*, or nonkosher—and also, I hate the sight of blood. I've never seen any in an egg before, but that could be because I check quickly and with one eye closed. Thankfully, the egg looks clean, so I mix it with a fork, then add cheese and a mini sweet pepper. My mind can't stop circling back to Sam, so I turn on my Spotify playlist and raise the volume to Peter Himmelman's song "Impermanent Things." I was lucky enough to meet Peter backstage after one of his concerts, and he had me laughing the entire time. He's a *nice* man—unlike Sam.

Ugh! Okay, you know what? I'm going to eat, slab on a little makeup, and then I'm going to go somewhere and distract myself. I'll go thrift shopping in Uptown—window thrift shopping, I remind myself sternly. Unless I see an exceptionally good deal, in which case it must be a sign from above that G-d wants me to have it. Obviously.

Thirty minutes later, I unlock my car door and slide the key into the ignition. A year from now, I'll be so rich that I can buy anything I want anytime. Fleetwood Mac's "Landslide" song croons over the radio, and it feels like a sign. With my sunglasses on, I raise the volume and try my best to ignore Sam's voice in my head saying I'm about to make the biggest mistake of my life.

*   *   *

My pulse quickens in excitement as the wheels of the Boeing 737 touch the runway. This past week had been a blur of chores, helping Libby with her kids, dodging Maya's calls and letting her think I'm sick, and one NICU visit where Delilah listed all the reasons why I'm ruining my life.

Good times.

The plane ride gave me plenty of time to think things over, and I've come to a couple of conclusions, the first one being that Sam clearly doesn't grasp the impossibility of my situation. He couldn't, coming from his secular background, especially as more and more people in his world are choosing not to have children.

Second, life is short. I've spent the last decade searching for a husband the traditional way, and it didn't do me any good. I might as well take a chance and live a little. At the very least, it'll make a great story to share with my roomies at the nursing home one day.

And most importantly, I'll be able to save Libby's house.

I slide my window shade up and gaze at the runway. Sunshine breaks through the clouds, casting dark shadows onto the tarmac. The pilot announces the temperature is sixty-seven degrees and the current time is 11:38 AM. I turn on my phone and shoot Zevi a quick text telling him I've landed. A few minutes later, the seat belt sign goes off, and people climb over each other to get to their carry-ons and secure a spot in line.

I make my way off the plane and head toward baggage claim, doing my best to settle the butterflies in my stomach. Because even though Zevi is nice, it doesn't necessarily mean that his family is. The few New Yorkers I've met were knee-buckling intimidating, from the way they swaggered to the way they talked. They said exactly what they thought the moment they thought it. I'm used to the Midwestern way, where you wait until someone's back is turned before saying how much you hate them.

It's so much more civilized.

As I make my way through the baggage claim area, a crocheted flower on my mermaid skirt catches on the wheel of my suitcase, causing me to nearly trip. I bend down to undo the tangle of fabric, hoping nobody tumbles on top of me.

"Penina?"

A pair of red canvas tennis shoes comes into view, topped by denim pants and an even tighter gray T-shirt with the word "ADULT-ISH" on the center.

"Zevi!" I grin, standing up.

"You look great." He smiles, gesturing to my outfit. "I love the skirt."

"I love that you love it," I say, happy to see that he appreciates fashion. "It's vintage Saks that I found at Goodwill."

At the mention of Goodwill, his face turns pained. "How . . . quaint."

"Don't worry," I say. "After the bed bug incident that shall not be named, I learned to wash the clothes as soon as I bring them home."

"Great." He swallows. Pointing to my overnight bag, he says, "Is that it, or do you have something in baggage claim?"

"Just this." I nod.

"You really are my dream woman—a light packer," he jokes, his brown eyes crinkling with humor. "If a gay man could have a female soulmate, I'm sure you'd be mine."

I arrange my hands into a heart shape against my chest. "I heart that comment."

He laughs and reaches for the bag. "Let's head out of here."

At short-term parking, he stows my overnight bag in the trunk of his shiny Jaguar sports car that screams money and opulence. Inside is even more luxurious, with LED lights illuminating the control system, and black-and-red leather bucket seats that feel smoother than butter. When Zevi pushes the keyless button to start, the engine roars to life, its reverberations reminding me of the snarls of jungle cats.

"How do you feel?" Zevi glances at me as he pulls out of the parking space. "Excited? Nervous?"

"A combination of both." I cross my legs. "What about you?"

"Same."

What is he nervous about? He's used to dealing with New Yorkers, and he already knows what his family is like. Unless . . . "Are you worried your family won't like me?"

"No, no." He shakes his head. "Nothing like that. It's more the opposite. I'm worried *you* won't like *them*. I'm afraid a few hours in their company will cause you to run away screaming."

I laugh. "They're not that bad, are they?"

"Not really." He switches to the right lane and merges onto the Grand Central Parkway. "But if you start to feel like you want to bang your head against the wall, try closing your eyes and saying the Hebrew alphabet backward. It usually works for me."

His Channing Tatum profile is as serious as ever, and I get the feeling he isn't kidding. "Thanks for the tip."

A rusty Honda Accord blasts its horn as Zevi zipper-merges into his lane, almost colliding into the Honda. "Fuck off, muthafucker!" the driver shouts through his open window. "I'll kick yo ass!"

I glance over my shoulder to check out the driver. His shaved head and thick neck are covered in tattoos, sporting that whole I-did-my-time-in-the-penitentiary look. He thrusts his middle finger to the center of the windshield, just in case we didn't fully catch his drift. I shrink back into my seat. "I don't think he likes us very much."

"Nah, he's just letting off a little steam," Zevi shrugs. "You'll get used to it. When Jack moved here from Seattle seven years ago, he couldn't stand all the cursing. Now, he barely registers it."

Speaking of Jack . . . "Hey, can I ask you something?"

"Sure."

"How do you explain Jack to your family? Or do they not know he exists?"

"They know about him," he replies, adjusting the rearview mirror. "They think he's my roommate."

I give him a sideways glance. "They actually fell for that? It's not as though you need one, financially speaking."

Zevi smiles. "I did originally. We met several years ago through a Craig's List ad. It was at a time in my life when I couldn't afford my rent, not even some hole-in-the-wall, cockroach-infested place in Queens. I placed an ad for a roommate, and that was the beginning of our friendship."

"But doesn't your family think it's weird that you still live together?"

"Yeah." He sighs, resting his wrist at the bottom of the steering wheel. "The few times they've made comments, I just say that we're best friends, and until one of us gets married, there's no reason why we shouldn't live together," he says, switching on his turn signal. "They seem to accept that."

"Does that mean that Jack is moving out, then—assuming, I mean, when this marriage takes place?" It makes sense, but the idea hadn't occurred to me until now.

He maneuvers the car to the right lane, following the sign for Brooklyn/ Robinson Parkway. "Yeah, Jack and I talked about it. He's going to rent a place nearby. By the way, do you want to pick out your ring, or do you want me to surprise you? I figure since you're a jewelry expert, you probably know exactly what you want."

"Oh, right." The idea of a gorgeous diamond ring on my finger doesn't thrill me the way it did a week ago. It feels . . . not wrong exactly, but not right either. I suddenly recall the intensity in Sam's eyes when he told me I was perfect, the pitch in his tone deepening as he said the words. But we're not friends and we never were friends, *and for the love of G-d, please get out of my head!*

"We can look around today if you'd like," he says, glancing at me, not picking up on the fact that I'm having an existential life crisis. "Which reminds me, I have connections with a few jewelers, in case you want to work after you move here. Whatever you want."

"Sure." I nod, pushing away the image of Sam. Guess we won't be shopping at Kleinfeld's for our wedding-day needs. "That's great— thank you." I need to focus on the here and now—my future. Getting engaged to Zevi and shopping for a ring. Sam's voice comes back to me as he repeats what I said in the ambulance about my hymen. My eyes close in shame; if I were a dog, I'd have been euthanized by now for bad and unpredictable behavior. "So," I say, clearing my throat, grasping for something to talk about, "how's your mother doing?"

"She's hanging in there. She was running a high fever Wednesday night, but she's better now. I thought we could swing by the hospital later today, and I could introduce you to her."

"Great. Let's do that." My voice sounds squeaky, so I clear my throat. "I'm excited to meet everyone."

"The feeling is mutual. Again, I can't thank you enough for doing this." He steers the car to the right to stay on King's Highway. "My family is great and I love them, but"—he shakes his head—"they're very traditional."

I nod. "How do you think your mother would react if she knew the truth about you?"

"I try not to think about that," he says, smiling ruefully.

"Do you think she'd never talk to you again?"

He shakes his head, his fingers gripping the steering wheel. "No, she wouldn't do that. But she'd be devastated. And honestly"—he sighs— "she's had more than enough trauma in her life already."

He's probably referring to his father, though I don't know the details, other than that the guy abandoned his family. I want to ask Zevi about it, but he's got that pinched, closed-off expression people wear when they don't want to discuss something.

"Whoa." I grab onto the dashboard as he makes a sharp turn onto Avenue D and nearly runs over an old woman pushing a rectangular wire granny cart. I hold my breath and look over my shoulder to make sure she's still alive. She calmly crosses the street, as though she hadn't just had a near-death experience. I turn around and inhale through my nose, then slowly release it out of my mouth. I forgot that pedestrians here are treated with the same level of respect as pigeons.

I glance at Zevi. "Don't you ever worry that you'll run someone over?"

"Nah," he says, one hand casually draped over the steering wheel. "Once I felt a bump underneath the car, but I didn't hear any screams, so I kept going." My eyes double in size. Zevi glances at me and laughs. "I'm kidding!"

"Funny," I say weakly.

A few minutes later we pull into the driveway of a rundown, narrow, two-story house. Iron grates cover the windows, and unchecked ivy scales the crumbling bricks. A rusty chain link fence runs along one side of the house, and the small yard is overgrown with weeds.

"My sister's house," he says, hauling my suitcase out of the trunk. "Not exactly the Ritz."

"It's . . . charming in its own way," I say, causing Zevi to hoot with laughter.

"The truth is that I've offered to fix up the house for her or buy a new one, but she's too damn proud, you know?"

I swallow, thinking of Libby. It hadn't occurred to me until now, but what if she refuses the money? She's always been so fiercely independent, I don't know why I never considered that possibility.

But, I reassure myself, if there's one thing that Libby cares about more than her pride, it's her children's happiness, and those kids love their house.

"You'll only stay here for Shabbos," Zevi says. "I booked you a room at the Hyatt for Saturday night."

"Thank you. Although this seems lovely too," I say, sidestepping a headless doll lying on the cracked pavement.

He chuckles and shifts my carry-on bag to his other hand. "You haven't seen the inside yet. Careful! Don't trip." He points to the chipped concrete path leading to the front stoop.

I successfully make it to the door without falling, a real feat considering I'm in three-inch heels, and the booby trap of random objects scattered across the uneven pavement. Zevi follows close behind, then pounds his fist on the door caveman-style. "The doorbell stopped working three years ago, and they haven't gotten around to fixing it yet," he explains with a good-natured eye roll.

A minute later the door swings open, revealing a beautiful woman wearing an apron and black head kerchief. Even in simple clothes and no makeup, she has an arresting presence and a graceful figure. Her manners, on the other hand, leave something to be desired. She doesn't smile or say anything, just eyes both of us up and down with a practiced stare.

"Leah," Zevi sighs, "when you're through staring, feel free to invite us inside."

She grunts but steps back to let us through, then shuts the door behind us. Pointing her finger at Zevi, she barks, "Every time I see you, you look less and less Jewish."

"It's good to see you too," he replies, rocking back on his heels and crossing his arms.

"What's wrong with wearing a nice white button-down shirt and black pants?" She places her hands on her hips. "You should be *proud* to be a Jew. You should declare it from the rooftops. Repeat after me: I am a Jew and I am proud."

O-kay. I'm beginning to see why Zevi doesn't feel he can be honest with his family about who he is. Evidently, the family is still coming to terms with his wardrobe.

"I am proud, Leah," he says, "but that doesn't mean I'm going to voluntarily dress in penguin colors every day of my damn life."

"Language!" she hisses.

"Sorry. *Anyway*," he says, swiftly changing gears, "Leah, let me introduce you to my fiancée, Penina. Penina, this is my charming sister Leah."

I smile and hold out my hand. "It's so nice to meet you."

She stares at my extended hand like it's covered in horse excrement. "We're family!" she declares. "We don't shake hands like businessmen. We hug!" She pulls me into a choking embrace, and I'm not altogether sure she isn't trying to kill me. She releases me after a minute and says, "So, *nu*." She makes a hurry-up motion with her hand. "When's the wedding?"

Zevi answers while I take deep gulps of air to reoxygenate my lungs. "We don't have a date yet. But it will be sooner rather than later. How's Ma doing today?"

"So-so. Her fever is worse, but the coughing went away."

A blond, curly-haired toddler waddles into the room, sucking a pacifier and dragging a book. When he catches sight of Zevi, his eyes light up, and he drops the book and runs to him.

"It's Mordy the airplane!" Zevi bends down and lifts him high in the air. "Penina, can you believe this adorable creature came from my monstrous sister?"

"Uh . . . no. I mean yes." I start to sweat. "Not that your sister is monstrous," I say quickly, fanning myself with my hand. "But yes, he's adorable."

Mordy mumbles something, and his pacifier drops to the ground. Leah bends down to pick it up, spits on it, then dries it, using the corner of her apron, while Zevi and I watch.

"I told you to stop doing that," Zevi says with a groan, then grabs the pacifier from her hand and heads to a different room. "No wonder you guys are always getting sick," he calls over his shoulder. "Is basic hygiene in the twenty-first century too much to ask?"

Leah and I follow Zevi into the kitchen and watch as he turns on the faucet and pumps soap onto the tip of the pacifier.

"If you think that I'm going to be racing to the sink every five seconds to wash that thing, you're crazy," Leah retorts, crossing her arms over her ample chest. "Every time he opens his mouth to say something, it drops to the ground. Besides, germs build up immunity."

"They make pacifier clips," I suggest, but her eyes immediately narrow into slits, and I regret saying anything. "But of course," I say, lifting my palms up, "saliva as a cleaning agent works too."

"Yeah," Zevi says, shutting off the faucet and readjusting Mordy on his hip, "if you're trying to make your kids sick."

"Aren't I lucky to get parenting advice from two people who've never had kids." Leah turns to me and adds, "You got anything more to add?"

I shake my head meekly. Zevi had said his sister didn't like outsiders, but if you ask me, she's not too crazy about her brother either.

"Mordy, want to go zoom-zoom in the sky?" Zevi bends on his knees so he's at eye level with his nephew. The toddler giggles as Zevi lifts him into the air and simulates airplane noises as they fly through the crowded living room.

I look around, taking in the worn furniture and chipped paint. The beige carpet is dotted with stains of questionable origin, and some of the black vinyl couch cushions are peeling near the seams. Bookcases filled to the brim with biblical books line the walls, along with pictures of famous Hassidic rabbis. A bin of toys is partly hidden under the coffee table, and a handmade vase contains a bouquet of wilting pink dahlias.

Although the room could easily be featured as a "Before" picture in a reality TV makeover show, there's something inviting about it. It's undeniably messy and chaotic, but it's cozy and warm. The kids' framed artwork and arts and craft projects are as prominently featured, as though they had designer labels.

I sense Leah's gaze on me and turn to her with a smile. "You have a lovely home."

She sighs, taking in the room like she's seeing it for the first time. "As lovely as a Super 8 motel room. The couch is bad, I know, and the walls could use a paint job too, but you try raising kids in a house the size of a tin can, and let's see if you can do any better."

"Leah," Zevi intervenes, bringing his nephew to a landing on the couch, "she was trying to be *nice*."

Leah's eyes narrow, and I quickly add, "Yes, I meant it as a compliment. Sorry if I came off sounding . . . like it wasn't?" I can feel more sweat pooling in my armpits. *Why is she so scary, and why is she twisting my words?*

Mordy lifts his arms toward his uncle and begs for another airplane ride. "One more, buddy." Zevi picks up his nephew and as he passes, says in an undertone, "She's a little paranoid. Try not to compliment her."

"I heard that," Leah says. Turning to me, she spreads her arms wide. "If you were complimenting me, fine. I thought you weren't. A lot of people are fake, and I don't like fake compliments. If you think my home is a wreck, just say so." Her eyebrows dip to the center of her forehead. "Why are you standing?" She points to the couch. "Sit."

I've never sat down so fast in my life. I open my mouth to reassure her it's a great couch but then remember what Zevi said, so I keep quiet while I think of something to say that couldn't possibly be taken the wrong way. Honestly, though, I have a feeling this woman could twist anything into an insult. Some people are just that talented.

I clear my throat. "The temperature is really nice today."

Leah shrugs and sits down on a beige tufted glider facing the couch. "Yeah, so? The weather is the weather. It'll be bad tomorrow. You're from Iowa, right?"

"Minnesota."

"Same difference."

Not really, but okay.

"You got a dress?"

I tilt my head in confusion from the sudden change in subject. "A dress?"

"A wedding gown," she says. "You're getting married, remember?"

"Oh! Hah!" I laugh uncomfortably. "Of course. But no, not yet. Are there any good stores you recommend?"

"There're tons of them: Wedding Day Princess, Wexler Bride, Couture Modest Bridal. You know," she adds, leaning back in the recliner, "a few nights ago, when Zevi called to tell me he had gotten engaged, I could barely believe it."

"Really?" These abrupt shifts in conversations make my head hurt. "Why?"

"I always wondered a little about him." She shrugs. "Thought maybe he was a *faygelah*."

I panic and pretend to be confused. "A *faygelah*?"

"You don't know?" I shake my head, to which she sighs, then leans forward and whispers, "A gay person. A homosexual."

I'm completely unprepared for this, and my eyes dart around the room as I try to figure out how to respond. "You thought that? That's . . . funny."

"How is that funny?"

I use the back of my hand to wipe the sweat that's beading on my upper lip, then tug my shirt collar. Why is it so hot in here?

"Don't worry, he's not," Leah reassures me, mistaking my reaction for one of concern. "But I did used to wonder."

"Oh," I say lamely, and clear my throat. *Where is Zevi?*

"You hungry?"

I'm about to say no but then realize she'd take that as an insult to her cooking skills. "Yes. Starving."

She nods her head in approval, like I finally got something right. Cupping her hands around her mouth, she hollers, "Zevi!"

Zevi rounds the corner with his nephew's legs dangling over his shoulders. "Yeah?"

"Penina's hungry. Take her somewhere." She looks at me apologetically. "I'd feed you myself, but I don't want to run out of food. For all I know, you're one of those skinny people that eat a ton. Why are you so pale, anyway?"

Taken aback, I gaze at Zevi for help. "I-I didn't know I was."

"Do they not have sun in Iowa?"

"We do." I swallow. "Sometimes."

Zevi crooks his hip against the wall jamb and folds his arms. "Penina, now would be a good time to ignore my sister."

"What?" Leah frowns, standing up from the glider. "Did I say something offensive? I'm not allowed to be concerned about my future sister-in-law's sickly appearance?"

My eyes widen. I have a sickly appearance?

"Stop it. She's gorgeous and you know it," Zevi says.

"I never said she wasn't. All I'm saying is she looks pale and on the verge of dying. *Chas v'chalila,* may she live until one hundred and twenty." She says to me, "I'll give you some vitamin D pills. It'll make you feel better."

No, leaving here would make me feel better. "Thank you, that's very kind, but I don't—"

"I know what I'm talking about," Leah interrupts. "I dabbled in the medical field for some years."

Zevi snorts as he heads to the front door. "Sorry to break it to you, Leah, but working as a medical assistant for a year and a half doesn't mean you know anything about medicine."

"That's *certified* medical assistant, and yes it does!" Leah jabs her forefinger into the center of Zevi's back.

"Ouch. Okay, okay, I take it back." He laughs, sliding the brass chain free from its lock and turning the doorknob. "Ready to go, Pen?"

I nod. Personally, I'm relieved to escape. We couldn't have been here more than ten minutes but it feels like an hour has passed. And I'm pretty sure the armpits of my shirt are permanently stained.

"Take her to Chef Wei's. They have a pre-Shabbos special."

Zevi opens the door, then rests his hand on the doorframe. "I thought that place was condemned. A rat problem, wasn't it?"

"The exterminators got rid of them, and they reopened last week." Leah scoops up Mordy, who's trying to escape. "Go and enjoy."

Zevi and I exchange glances. The sounds of Mordy's escalating whining follows us down the front steps, and she slams the door behind us, double-bolting it.

"Didn't I tell you she was charming?" Zevi wiggles his eyebrows as we head toward the car.

I cover my mouth to hide my laughter in case Leah is spying on us through one of the windows, which I wouldn't put it past her to do. "You did, although I don't think you did her justice."

"It's hard to capture Leah's essence through mere description," Zevi grins, unlocking the car. "Sometimes you just need to experience someone like that firsthand."

I can't help but laugh as I climb inside the car. "How on earth could the two of you be related? You couldn't be more different from each other. One of you had to have been adopted."

Zevi pushes the key start button and buckles his seat belt. "You'd think so. What about you? Are you like your siblings?"

"Not really," I confess, running a hand through my hair. "But maybe that's because I knew I was different—that my path in life wouldn't be straightforward like theirs." Zevi gives me a significant look, then shifts the car into reverse, making me realize my guffaw. "Oh. Same for you, huh?"

"Hell yes." Zevi turns his head as he backs the car out of the driveway. "Living with a secret, knowing you're different from everyone else—it changes a person, doesn't it?"

I murmur agreement. I sometimes wonder how my life would have turned out if I hadn't had fertility issues. Would I have found the love of my life and gotten married at nineteen or twenty like my friends did? Would my days have been filled with carpools, playdates, meals that had to be prepared and served in a house that was in constant need of cleaning? Once the kids were tucked in bed, would my husband and I have had nights that were filled with passionate lovemaking? Might he have locked our bedroom door, then led me to our bed, where his hands massaged the ache in my breasts. Perhaps Sam would have slipped his fingers beneath my—

"Who's Sam?"

I blink. "What?"

Zevi brakes at a red light, then turns to look at me. "You murmured 'Sam' under your breath just now."

If humiliation could cause spontaneous combustion then I'd be dead right now. "No, I didn't."

"Yeah, you did." He grins, shaking a finger at me. "Who is he?"

"No one."

"You said that much too fast for me to believe."

"Is it hot in here, or is it just me?" I press the window control button, hoping the fresh air will return some semblance of sanity. *What in the world is happening to me?* This is not normal. I am not normal. I close my eyes and take a deep breath. Unfortunately, the fetid aroma of chain smoking and exhaust fumes isn't helping to clear my mind.

Okay, it's *possible* that my body might find his body attractive, but it's not a personal thing. I don't like Sam. And the attraction is so small, it's practically microscopic.

"Is he a friend of yours?"

"What? No!" I shake my head and repeat, "We're most definitely not friends."

The light turns green, and Zevi lifts his foot from the brake. "It was just a guess. You don't have to look so horrified."

"I'm not horrified," I reply, fanning my warm cheeks with the back of my hand. "There's nothing to be horrified about." I didn't apply enough deodorant for this conversation.

"Is he your friend's brother?"

I groan and drop my hand. "I think you misheard me. I was talking about . . . um, ham."

"Yeah, I turn pink every time I think about ham too," he says with a grin.

I look out the window. "I'm in the mood for Italian—how about you?"

"Ah," he says, turning the wheel right, "so Sam is Italian?"

I groan and Zevi cracks up. This is what I get for letting my imagination run wild. And though I try my hardest to look disapproving, laughter is contagious, and I start giggling too. And as long as Zevi and Sam never meet each other, I can keep on laughing.

CHAPTER NINETEEN

"When a woman says, 'I have nothing to wear!', what she really means is, 'There's nothing here for who I'm supposed to be today.'"
—*Caitlin Moran*

Zevi and I choose an Italian restaurant and share a lunch of agnolotti and stew with almonds and couscous. The food is delicious, and Zevi entertains me with stories of his childhood. By the time dessert comes, I'm feeling better. Yes, Leah is scary, but she's not the one I'm going to be marrying. And the more I get to know Zevi, with his quirks and self-deprecating humor, the more I can see myself being happy living with him. He talks about his best friend Eli who left Orthodoxy when he joined the Navy, but who has since returned to the fold and is looking to settle down. He tells me the sad story about how his younger sister Ashira had a husband (now ex-husband) who cheated on her with her best friend (now ex-best friend).

"Eli and Ashira could marry each other," I suggest, even though I've never met either one of them.

Zevi chuckles and waves his fork at me. "You're funny."

He shows me pictures of his newly designed Manhattan penthouse, which has five bedrooms, a rooftop garden, a spa, and his own private elevator. Can I handle living in a sweet Manhattan penthouse with a nice man, especially if it means saving my sister's house? Most definitely, yes.

So there, Sam. (Okay, that was unnecessary. Let's pretend I didn't just bring Sam's name up. Sigh.)

We're on our way now to meet Zevi's mother, and I only hope my acting skills are better than what they were in high school. My stage fright was so bad that I forgot my lines, and it took everything I had just to remain upright and not faint. All I could manage was a few stutters until someone took mercy and pulled me offstage. Fraydie thought it was hilarious, but she's sadistic like that.

"This way," Zevi says, and motions for me to follow him down a corridor.

The halls of Mount Sinai Hospital are thick with the fragrance of antiseptic and bleach, but illness has a smell too strong to fully disguise. Zevi's mother has a private suite in a unit called Eleven West, which seems a lot more like a five-star hotel than a hospital. The lobby is all shiny and gold, a mix of traditional and contemporary, with dark maple accents and asymmetrical chandeliers. Areca palms in red and gold oriental planters add splashes of color, displayed in various sections of the room. A black grand piano is tucked in an inconspicuous corner with a waterfall backdrop. Two women stand behind the concierge desk in matching gray vests and blue ties.

"Are you sure this is the right place?" I whisper to Zevi after we've signed in. "It doesn't look anything like a hospital."

Zevi pushes the up button of the elevator. "It better not, given the amount of money they're charging me."

I don't even want to ask how much this place is costing him. Well, I do, but some questions are better left until after the marriage ceremony.

"But," he adds, stepping into the elevator, "it's worth it. My mother likes her privacy, especially now that she's sick. In a regular unit, she'd have to share a room."

I lean against the elevator's handrail and smile at him. "She's lucky to have a son like you."

"Hah." He shakes his head as the doors ping shut. "Thanks, but we both know that isn't true."

I frown. How can he think that? "It *is* true." Zevi is an independent, successful man and a loving, devoted son, a kind brother and doting uncle. He's so much more than his sexual orientation. It's just a small part of who he is, the way my medical condition is only a fraction of who I am.

Sam was right when he said that I'm more than just a woman who can't have kids. I'm a daughter, a sister, aunt, and friend, and a very fine sales associate. Peoples' lives are messy and complicated, and even though we don't always see it, everyone has struggles. You can't be human and go through life without some kind of trauma or pain, but those experiences don't define who we are.

I want to explain this to Zevi, but before I get the chance, the doors open and a middle-aged couple join us. We continue the elevator ride in silence. When we reach our floor, Zevi steps out and holds the doors open for me. "I think," he says, leading me down a hallway, "my mother would have wanted me to do the traditional thing of marrying young, becoming a rabbi, and having lots of kids, even if it meant being poor and living paycheck to paycheck." He leads me around a corner, stuffs his hands in his pants pockets and gives me a rueful smile. "Ironic, isn't it? So many people dream of having the kind of money I have, but the thing I wanted most was to be straight."

"Oh, Zevi." I stop walking and stare at him intently, channeling the way Sam had looked at me that day in his office. "You are perfect exactly as you are."

I must have messed up because instead of seeming touched, he bursts out laughing. "Is that a line from *Barney* or something?"

"No," I frown. "It's an original thought from someone else that was supposed to make you feel better."

"I'm fine, Penina." He chuckles and continues down the hall. "But thank you. It's a very sweet thing to say."

It's sad that he doesn't see his worth the way I do, but hopefully one day he'll come around.

He stops outside a door just as it swings open, revealing a forty-something nurse in turquoise scrubs. She looks tired and overworked and has dark circles under her eyes, but she motions us in with a smile. "Hi, come in." She steps back to give us room, then closes the door. "Your mom is just waking up."

"Thank you, Bea." In a hushed voice, Zevi adds, "How's she doing today?"

"As feisty as ever," she says, pumping disinfectant from the wall dispenser. "She's got a love–hate relationship with her LVAD."

"Oy," he mutters under his breath, then scratches his cheek. "More GI bleeding?"

"Yes," Bea says, massaging the foam between her fingers. "Unfortunately, it's a common side effect. But as I keep reminding her, she's a lot more comfortable with it than without it."

He sighs and crosses his arms over his chest. "And how's her temperature?"

"As of now she doesn't have a fever."

"Good. That's something, at least." He nods as though he's reassuring himself. "Thank you again, Bea."

I have no idea what an LVAD is, but I'm impressed that Zevi does. It sounds as though he's a regular fixture here.

"You're welcome." She opens the door and steps through the doorway. "I'll check in with you later."

"Okay. Sounds good." The door shuts with a gentle click, and he turns to face me. "Ready?"

I don't think anyone is ever ready to meet their future mother-in-law, fake marriage or not, but there's no turning back now. I picture Libby's face and how happy she'll be when she finds out her house will be saved, and I force myself forward.

The first thing that catches my eye is the breathtaking panoramic view of the East River, set against skyscrapers of varying heights. A large double-decker ferry carves a crooked path through the choppy water, and I can picture the captain of the boat with one hand on the wheel and the other holding a glass of bourbon. To my right is a queen-sized bed piled high with pillows and comforters. It takes me a moment to locate the hunched form of Zevi's mother, her figure slight and nearly obscured from view. I watch the gentle rise and fall of her chest before looking away. There's something intimate about watching a person sleep, almost like an invasion of their privacy.

"Hi, Ma." Zevi bends down and places a kiss on his mother's paper-thin cheek. "I've brought someone with me."

Her eyelids flutter open, revealing a pair of almond-shaped eyes in a shocking blue, the color of a clear sky or a hydrangea in full bloom. Her body is all sharp angles and bony slants, skeletal limbs and hollow members, embellished by liberal amounts of age spots. Threadlike wisps of white hair peek from the paisley-patterned kerchief loosely positioned over her head. She looks as tiny and fragile as a duckling struggling to escape its shell. Despite the outward appearance of wrinkles and saggy skin, the shriveled lips and pointed joints, there is a definite presence within her. The bold gaze she levels at me is one of an uncanny astuteness, like a seasoned schoolteacher that can instinctively sort the bull from the crap. Or that could just be my paranoia talking.

"This is Penina," he says softly, gesturing toward me, "the other special woman in my life."

"It's so nice to meet you." I stand at the side of the bed and send up a silent prayer that I don't screw this up. I'm sweating like a mohel about to perform his first circumcision.

She nods and tries to smile. "Sit, sit," she rasps, pointing to an armchair that faces the bed. I settle into it while Zevi raises his mother to a sitting position, then moves pillows behind her and adjusts a large black pouch near her waist. "Stop fussing." She tilts her head to look at Zevi. "I'm fine. Relax and sit down."

The frown lines that bracket his mouth deepen. "What about some water? You look thirsty."

"I have water." She extracts a bottle of Perrier buried under the pile of blankets, then turns to me. "He feels helpless, so he tries to do anything he can think of to make me feel better."

"That's sweet," I say, glancing at Zevi as he moves across the room and removes a folding chair from its hook on the wall.

"So." Her finger traces along the etching of the black pouch. "Tell me a little something about you."

"Sure," I clear my throat and try to channel the cool and calm collected persona of someone effortlessly classy, like Princess Kate. "I'm a homegrown Midwestern girl from Minneapolis—" I break off. Geez, why am I making myself sound like a crop?

"Michigan," she nods. "Very nice."

Like mother, like daughter. The geography blunder makes me want to laugh, but I continue. "I have a degree in liberal arts, but never did much with it. I work—well, used to work at a jewelry store, Kleinfeld's. A Jewish owner whose son recently took over, but he's got serious personality problems and is impossible to work for, not that you heard it from me—"

"Are you divorced?" she interrupts, glancing at Zevi as he places the folding chair beside me and takes a seat.

I shake my head. "No. I've never been married."

"And you're how old?"

Keep it together, girl. Keep. It. Together. "Twenty-nine."

Her eyebrows lift. "Twenty-nine and never been married?"

I know I'm supposed to skirt the truth because Zevi wants his mother to think I'll be able to bear her grandchildren, but there's a shrewdness about this woman that makes me think she can see right through me, straight down to my too-small uterus. "Honestly, I never found someone I wanted to spend the rest of my life with," I say, which is definitely true. Of course, I never dated someone kind and warm like Zevi, or the good version of Sam, handsome, intelligent and surprisingly considerate. The image of his face briefly flits through my mind, specifically his lips. And his body.

G-d, that body.

Leave me alone, intrusive thoughts!

Her fingers brush against the cupid's bow of her mouth. "Hmm."

Hmm? That one little word settles like a brick in my gut. I look at Zevi for help.

He catches my meaning and leans toward his mother. "Penina is a great cook, Ma. Wait until you try her knishes—they're almost as good as yours," he adds with a wink.

Another lie. The only time my knishes are edible is when they come from the frozen food section of the grocery store. Once a person messes up a simple potato kugel recipe, it does something to your self-esteem.

"Is that right?" Zevi's mother asks, her direct stare boring holes into my eyes.

I lick a bead of sweat off my upper lip. "Er . . . not exactly." I lower my gaze and run my fingers over the pleats in my skirt. "I think Zevi's love for me blinds his taste buds."

Zevi throws his head back and laughs.

She tilts her head. "Do you have a date set?"

Zevi and I look at each other. "Do we?" I swallow.

"We've been talking about it," he hedges, returning his gaze to his mother. "But nothing specific yet."

She stares straight ahead, the picture of stoicism, and I can't help but wonder why she isn't acting more happy. Most Jewish mothers would be leaping for joy if their thirty-six-year-old son brought home a bride. Especially after all these years of dating. "Zevi," she says, breaking the silence, "I'm in the mood for coffee. Please get me a cup."

He hesitates. "Should you be drinking coffee?"

"Decaf." She waves her hand dismissively. "It doesn't count."

Zevi looks doubtful but caves in and stands up. "Alright, I'll tell your butler. Hand me the remote."

"No, no." She shakes her head. "I need *you* to get it."

He sits back down and crosses his arms over his broad chest. "You trying to get rid of me, Ma?"

She purses her thin lips together. "Yes."

My foot taps nervously. So much for being coy.

Zevi crosses one leg over his knee. "Look, whatever you want to say, you can say to both of us. We don't keep secrets from each other, so anything you tell her, she'll just tell me anyway." He turns to me. "Right, honey?"

"Right," I squeak, gazing at him with eyes that read, *"Please don't leave me alone with your scary mother."*

"Fine, fine." She sighs and fiddles with the charm bracelet on her skeletal wrist. "Penina, because you're a virgin, there are some things that you need to know about the wedding night—"

"Ma, stop. Please." He rubs his hand over his eyes like he's trying to unsee something. "That's what the wedding teachers are for. There's one in Minneapolis, right, Penina?"

Just the thought of seventy-something-year-old Mrs. Pearlman, with her heavy sweaters and thick stockings and black old-lady shoes with the Velcro straps, talking about sex makes me cringe. "Yes."

She waves her hand dismissively. "I had wedding lessons too, but believe me, there's a lot they don't cover. The kinds of things a virgin should know beforehand. On my own wedding night, for example, I was so shocked, first by the sheer size of—"

Zevi shoots up from his chair so fast that he nearly knocks it over. "I'll be in the library," he calls over his shoulder as he strides toward the door. "Come get me when she's done."

"Um, Zevi, I don't know—" Unfortunately for me, he seems to have developed a sudden case of deafness, and the door slams shut, leaving me alone with the woman who wants to give me advice on having sex with her gay son.

"So, Penina," she says, a ghost of a smile tugging at her lips, "let's talk."

"Sure." I can actually feel each contraction of my heart. *Deep breaths, Penina. You're taking this woman way too seriously.* I cross my ankles and fold my hands in my lap, then refold them.

"This engagement caught me by surprise, mostly because Zevi has rarely gotten further than a second date in the past. Then suddenly, after fifteen years or so of first dates—ta-da! He tells me he's engaged." She closes her eyes for a moment and inhales deeply, like she's gathering courage—or oxygen. "I'm afraid my situation has caused him to have an early-life crisis," she says, opening her eyes. "I'm sure it hasn't helped seeing his father abandon his family the way he did. Did he talk to you about his father?"

"He briefly mentioned wanting to kill him if he ever found him," I say, thinking back. "He said something about his father not being in his life, but no"—I shake my head—"I didn't get any details."

She breaks eye contact and gazes somewhere near my left shoulder. "It was very hard on all of the children when my husband left. But it hit Zevi the hardest. He idolized Seymour, the way boys often do with their fathers. He had plenty of bad things to say about me, but when it came to his father," she says with a half smile, "he could do no wrong."

I nod, already sad. It's that feeling you get when you watch a movie a second time, when you already know it has a tragic ending.

"For months after Seymour left, Zevi refused to believe he'd really gone. Every day after school, he'd stare out the front window, hoping to see his father's Chevy pull into the driveway. I honestly think he believed that if he stared long enough, he'd bring his father home through sheer will."

My throat thickens as I imagine a young Zevi at a window, immobile and staring.

"The other kids would play baseball or ride their bikes and scooters, but not Zevi. Nothing could pry him away from that living-room window." Her eyes well up with tears, and I get up from my chair to pass her a tissue box that's on the wheeled tray. "Thank you." She dabs the corners of her eyes and sighs.

I take a tissue for myself because I feel unaccountably emotional. "How old was he when Seymour left?"

"Twelve. Too young to understand the intricacies of a marriage but old enough to comprehend that it was somehow my fault."

"No." I shake my head emphatically. That doesn't sound like the warm, generous Zevi I know. "He blamed you?"

"Of course." She gives another half smile that tugs at my heartstrings. "I blamed myself too, though I never admitted it. Not out loud, anyway."

"But that's ridiculous. A good man would never desert his wife and children. That is a defect of *his* character." I lean forward in my chair. "Even if you were to blame, nothing would excuse him from abandoning his children."

"True," she agrees. "But it's not our place to judge. When you get to be my age, you realize that judging others and bearing grudges is pointless. Everyone has their reasons for the choices they make in life— everyone does the best they can."

"No." I sit back and cross my arms. "There's no excuse for doing what he did." Then I think of the thriller book I had forgotten to pack and joke, "Unless, he was being chased by the Russian mafia and had to cut all ties to protect you."

Her eyes crinkle at the corners as she laughs. "No," she says, shaking her head. "He eventually wrote me an apology, nearly a decade later, with a West Coast address."

Jerk. "What did he say?"

"It was only a few lines," she says, then pauses to take a sip of her Perrier. "Basically, he was sorry, but he did what he had to do. Apparently, it was that or killing himself."

I pause, stunned. I had assumed he just got tired of being a grown-up with grown-up responsibilities, but maybe it was deeper than that.

She swallows then replaces the cap. "But enough about Seymour. What I want to tell you is that I don't want Zevi getting married for the wrong reason. Do I want him to find love? Of course, I do. Every mother wants that for her child."

"And you don't think he's found it with me?" I ask, afraid of her answer. Does she think I'm not good enough for him, or does she suspect the truth?

She pins me down with her stare. "You tell me. Has he?"

I open my mouth to tell her yes, of course he has, but the expression in her eyes—the penetrative scrutiny mixed with kindness—makes me hesitate. I twist my hands in my lap. What do I do, what do I do? And why on earth did I ever think I could fool anyone, least of all this woman who is clearly a sorcerer of truth? I wish I could go back in time and tell Zevi, *"Sorry, but you're on your own. I'm a terrible actress, and your dying mother is much smarter than you give her credit for and—"*

"Knock, knock," a cheery voice trills, and Bea walks into the room, rubbing her fingers together, the distinct smell of disinfectant tickling my nose. "It's time to change the dressing to your driveline site." She smiles at me and adds, "You might want to step out for this."

Thank you, Bea!

I jump up and approach her bed, and wrap my arms gently around her. "Thank you for confiding in me," I say, pulling back to look into her face. "You're a good mom, and I can see why Zevi adores you." I mean it too. Whether she thinks I'm worthy of her son or not doesn't change the fact that she's an incredible person. Not only has she been through a lot of pain in her life, but she chose to be positive when so many others would have become resentful and bitter, myself included.

She takes my hand in hers. "Think about what I've said."

"I will."

"You're a good girl." She squeezes my hand, then leans back against the pillows and closes her eyes, signaling my dismissal.

I say goodbye to Bea and head down the corridor in search of Zevi. A sign overhead depicts an arrow in the direction of the library, and I turn right. What am I supposed to do now—tell Zevi that our cover might be blown? She was definitely suspicious, but who wouldn't be in this situation? Zevi never found someone to marry after years of dating, and then his mom gets sick, and suddenly he's engaged practically overnight. And why did she pick *me* instead of Zevi to have this conversation with?

"Hey, how'd it go?" Zevi says as I enter the library. He unfolds himself from an armchair and stretches.

"The good news is that she never described the girth or length of your dad's penis."

He cringes and shakes his head. "What's the bad news?"

I plop myself down on a couch and shake my head. "To be honest, she's a little sus."

"Sus?" He gazes at me in confusion.

"Sorry," I say, waving the back of my hand, "that's Delilah's twelve-year-old son's speak for 'suspicious.' I get the feeling she's not buying it."

"Shit, really?" He sits back down in the armchair and crosses his arms. "What happened?"

"She thought it was weird that you're suddenly engaged after all these years." I hesitate, not wanting to upset him, but not wanting to lie either. "And she also brought up your father."

"*What?*" A dark expression crosses Zevi's face. "Why? What did she say?"

"How he, you know, kind of abandoned you guys?" I lower my eyes and wonder if it's normal to be caught in the middle of family politics so soon after getting engaged. But then, there's nothing normal about this situation.

"What the fuck does that have to do with anything?" he says, raising his voice. "Sorry, sorry," he adds, plowing his fingers through his hair. "I'm just so frustrated. I thought she was going to be happy."

"Yeah, me too. But," I add, "who knows? Maybe she is." I chew on my bottom lip in uncertainty. I don't know what to do now. I still desperately need the money to save Libby's house, but now it feels dirty, like I'm tricking a dying woman instead of granting her last wish. "Zevi, I think it might be best if you tell her the truth. I can tell how much she loves you. And I'll be there too, to support you."

He swallows and takes a moment to consider. When he looks up, his eyes are windows of sadness. "I'm not ready, Penina."

My gut twists as I study his tortured face. Though I can't know everything he's been through, it's clear that he's suffered a lot, and there aren't any magic words I can say to cure his pain. All I can do is speak from my heart and show him that I care. "Whatever you need, Zevi," I say quietly, "I'm here."

His eyes well up, and he buries his face in his hands. I waver for a moment, not sure what to do; the only men I've ever hugged are my father and two grandfathers, but my instincts are to go and hug him, and after a moment's hesitation, that's what I do. Besides, I reason, he's basically my husband in that nebulous gray area that Sam doesn't believe in. I squeeze him tighter, and bury my face against his chest, which feels like a brick wall, kind of like Sam's did. *Why is Sam taking up so much of my head space? Ugh!*

"Thank you, Penina," he whispers, patting my back awkwardly before pulling away. "I'm okay now." He gestures toward the door and says in a forced cheery voice, "Let's get this party started."

I put my hands up and follow him out. "Woot, woot."

The rest of the weekend goes by fast and is mostly drama-free. It helped that I said as little as possible to Leah and spent most of Shabbos playing with her kids or walking through the neighborhood with Zevi. Earlier today, I had lunch with him and Jack, and though it wasn't too obvious, Zevi seemed preoccupied with something. On the way to the airport, he tells me that the hospital told him his mother's fever is rising, and she's refusing to eat. And like the selfish person I am, my mind goes straight to the money and whether I'll still be able to save Libby's house if she dies before we get married. Not that I can ask him. Well, I could, but it seems like a jerky thing to do when someone's mother just took a turn for the worse.

So I do what I've always done when things seem hopeless: I tip my head back, close my eyes, and pray for a miracle.

CHAPTER TWENTY

"Fashion has to reflect who you are, what you feel at the moment and where you're going."

—*Pharrell Williams*

"Zone three now boarding."

I grab my purse and head to the back of the line. My ticket is already in my hand, and I use it to fan my overheated, anxiety-ridden face.

My cell phone rings just as the gate agent scans my ticket. "Have a good flight," she smiles, returning my boarding pass.

I head down the jetway and check the caller ID, but don't recognize the number. "Hello?"

"Hey, how are you?"

It takes me a moment to place the deep baritone voice coming from the other end of line. Suddenly, the fog in my brain clears, and my heart rate kicks up a notch. "Sam?"

"Yeah, it's me. Can I ask a question, or are you busy?"

My heart pounds nervously as I step into the aircraft. *Why is Sam calling me?* A flight attendant gives me a thin-lipped smile, and I get the feeling that she's not too happy I'm on the phone. "Um, I'm sort of boarding a plane now, but it's fine."

"Do you know what Ivan Petrov's phone number is?"

The man in front of me stops suddenly to put his carry-on in the overhead bin, and I almost collide into his back. "Um, no," I say, grabbing on to the top of someone's seat to steady myself. "Isn't Gina supposed to have it?"

He sighs over the line. "It's her day off, and I didn't want to bother her."

Apparently, he doesn't feel bad to bother me on vacation. "Are we pretending that I didn't quit?" I say as the line starts to move again.

He ignores that and mutters, "I thought I wrote it down somewhere, but I can't find it."

The woman at the head of the line struggles to lift her carry-on into the overhead bin and flags down a flight attendant for assistance.

"Are you expecting me to show up at work tomorrow?" Maybe he has early onset Alzheimer's.

"Of course," he says.

"And we're pretending that last week was simply . . . what?"

"A much-needed mental health break."

I frown, not loving the way he stressed the words *much-needed*. I glance at the ticket in my hand: 16C.

"Oh, sorry," I apologize as my carry-on bumps into a woman sitting in the aisle seat.

"So, what happened?"

I sigh and switch the phone back to my other ear again. "My luggage assaulted someone."

He chuckles, and the sound of it does strange things to my heart. And my stomach. And other places. "I meant what happened this weekend."

Something brushes against my butt cheek, and the woman behind me murmurs an apology. "Everything went according to plan."

A beat of silence. "So, are you . . .?"

"Engaged?" I sidestep a teenager hogging the aisle and spot my seat two rows down. The two seats next to mine are occupied by a couple that look to be in their mid-sixties. I nod and wave a hand in greeting as I put my purse down on my seat. "Yes. But I still have to get a ring."

"Oh, congratulations!" says the woman beside me. "How wonderful."

The man with the gray handlebar mustache uses his newspaper to point in my direction. "Make sure you get a prenup."

"I'll remember that." I shove my carry-on into the overhead bin, then sit down in my seat.

"I have to go," Sam says. "See you tomorrow."

"Bye." *Well, that was weird.* I hang up, and set my phone to airplane mode. Why does the sound of his voice cause my pulse to skyrocket? Is it stress? Should I get my heart checked out?

I lean my head back and press my fingers over my closed eyes. Is this what it feels like to have wedding jitters? There's no way that it's anything more than that; I mean, even *if* I had a tiny crush on Sam— and even *if* he didn't have a Dr. Jekyll/Mr. Hyde issue—it's stupid to fantasize over him. He's about as attainable as Harry Styles, and it's a serious waste of time to crave someone who's so far out of my league, he might as well be in a different universe.

If he were married, it wouldn't even occur to me to think about him like this—it would be a nonissue. In fact, *I hope* he and Keila are still dating and on the way to getting engaged because then I could get over this sooner . . . whatever *this* is.

"Planning a wedding can be so stressful," the woman next to me says, patting my hand. "But it will be worth it in the end. You'll see."

"Right. It's not like I'm marrying a gay man I don't love or anything." I laugh shrilly. "Or attracted to my heterosexual boss." OMG, I'm totally losing it.

The woman gives me an uncertain smile, then opens up her magazine and proceeds to ignore me for the rest of the flight. Can't say I blame her.

When the plane lands and I switch off my phone's airplane mode, I see that Maya has texted me a series of messages that say **WTF?**, along with a screenshot of Keila's Instagram picture of Sam and her, looking gorgeous and relaxed, leaning on the edge of a boat with the backdrop of a pink sunset. Her caption says:

Always a good time with this guy 😊

A lump settles in the base of my throat as I study Sam's handsome face grinning toward the camera. Keila managed to procure one of his few genuine grins, and I wish I knew what magic she used to cause him to smile like that. Everything about this photo is perfect, from the way his amber eyes are crinkled in amusement, to Keila's amazing body in a red tank top and white shorts. Her legs are tanned and muscular and about a mile long. She and Sam look ridiculously happy, but even more than that, I realize with a sinking stomach, they look like they *belong* with each other.

This is good, I remind myself. Wasn't I just hoping for this very scenario? Besides, I've got Zevi and a five-bedroom penthouse. I bet he'd even let me have a pony if I asked, and no offense to Sam, but not even he can compete with a Falabella.

Makes you want to puke, doesn't it 🤢🥴🤮😩 Maya texts, bringing me back to the present.

I text her back the laughing emoji with the tears, 😂, even though I've never felt further from laughing than in this moment.

* * *

"Hey, everyone." I throw my carry-on into the trunk of my father's ancient Nissan, then climb into the back seat with Fraydie. "It's sweet that you all came to get me."

Fraydie blinks her glittery eyelash extensions at me. "I was told there'd be cake."

I pat her shoulder. "Love your brutal honesty."

Since Minneapolis doesn't have a kosher bakery, it's considered basic decency in our family that when someone returns from a trip to New York or Chicago or L.A. or basically anywhere with kosher eateries and stores, that person *must* bring back food. "I have cookies because it was the only thing I could fit into my overnight bag."

"I accept all sugary donations." She curls her fingers toward her palms in a gimme motion. *"Todah rabah,"* she says in Hebrew.

"You're welcome."

I glance at her stomach, which hasn't changed in size.

"Are you still eating lots of pickles?" I ask.

"What are you talking about," she says, giving me a strange look. "And why are you staring at my stomach?"

"I'm not," I say, skirting my glance away.

"Tell us everything, sweetie," my mother says from the front passenger seat as my father merges onto the I-494. "Do you like his family? Were they nice to you?"

"Yeah." I nod. "Everyone was very nice." Keila, on the other hand, not so much. Between the time the plane taxied to the gate and when I made my way down to arrivals, I've come to the realization that she's not very considerate. Like why does she have to post pictures like that? If I was lucky enough to date Sam, I'd show a little more restraint so the single people in my life wouldn't feel as bad. And if I did post a picture of him, he'd have food in his teeth or be wearing a dorky pair of glasses. *Because I'm nice like that.*

"When can Zevi fly in for the *vort*?" she asks. "I've already figured out a menu."

Oh, crap. My stomach twists into knots as I think about the engagement party, another noose over my neck. *I don't want to get married, I don't want to get married.* Not like this, anyway. "I don't know, Ma. I'll ask him." I sigh and look out the window. "Any news with Libby's house?"

"Nothing good," my father says as his beard ripples in the breeze from the open windows.

"Here's some free advice," Fraydie says to me, crumbs falling out of her mouth and landing on her clothes. "Don't make any jokes to Libby about selling her kids. She doesn't find it funny."

"Imagine that," I say dryly, just as my cell phone rings. It's the same number that Sam called from earlier, and my heart speeds up. *No, bad heart.*

I clear my throat. "Hello?"

"Hey, it's me," Sam's deep voice reverberates loudly through the car.

"Who's 'me'?" My mother's head whips around. "Is that Zevi? I want to talk to him."

I shake my head at my mother. "No, it's my boss," I whisper. "Sorry, Sam, go ahead."

"I finally found Ivan's phone number—"

"Your Jewish boss?" my mother asks.

I nod, putting my finger to my lips. Does everyone's mother butt in on conversations, or is it just mine? "Yay! Where was it?"

"On the floor near my desk—"

"Invite him for dinner this Friday night," my mother interrupts, turning around and tapping my knee.

"Hold on, Sam." I lean forward in my seat and whisper, "Ma, can you be quiet for a minute? I can't focus on anything he's saying."

"Let me just talk to him for a second. I'd love to have him for Shabbos." She snatches the phone from me before I have time to react, and now I'm frozen with terror.

Invite Sam for Shabbos? *Is she trying to give me a heart attack?*

I undo my seat belt and try to get my phone back, but my mother slaps my hand away like I'm some irritating fly.

"Hi Sam, this is Penina's mother. How are you?"

"Give me the phone," I hiss, but she ducks out of my reach.

"Good, thanks. How are you?" Sam's voice is twice as loud now that my mother pressed "Speaker." He doesn't sound concerned that my mother hijacked the conversation, but that's fine because I'm worried enough for both of us.

"I know this is short notice, but we'd be honored if you'd come to us for Shabbos dinner this week. Do you already have plans?"

A sharp pain tingles at the base of my spine and travels straight toward my neck. "Ignore everything she says, Sam!" I yell.

"Tova, stop." My father glances at my mother and shakes his head. "You're embarrassing her."

I appreciate his show of support, but from past experience I know it's useless. Once my mother gets an idea into her head, nothing short of a meteor strike can stop her.

"Thank you for the invitation," Sam replies. "I wish I could, but—"

"This is the first Shabbos that Penina is observing as an engaged woman. Don't you want to help us celebrate?"

I groan. Why would he want to? Why, *why* is this happening?

"Do you think this could be some kind of punishment from the Big Guy Upstairs?" Fraydie whispers and points her finger toward the roof of the car. "He must really hate your guts."

"No more cookies for you," I say, and take the package back.

There's a pause on the other end of the line, and just when I start to think the call got disconnected, Sam's voice breaks the silence. "Actually," he says, "Shabbos dinner sounds great."

Wait. *What?*

What the actual hell?

"How wonderful!" my mother cries with an embarrassing amount of enthusiasm. "I'm so excited to meet you. Penina talks about you all the time."

I grow pale. *Oh my G-d.*

"No, I don't!" I shriek, my left hand nearly hitting Fraydie in the face.

"Our address is 4013 Westwood Drive, in Minneapolis," my mother continues. "Dinner will be at eight thirty."

"Thank you," Sam says. "I'm looking forward to it."

The call disconnects, and my mother, having completed this cruel and unusual punishment, hands me my phone back.

"Ma, how could you do that?" I whine.

"Penina, please. It's a mitzvah." She turns back around and adjusts her seat belt.

"Remember the time she invited her gynecologist for Shabbos?" Fraydie laughs. "He must have thought she was hitting on him."

"No, he didn't." My mother sighs. "He mentioned he was Jewish but didn't know much about it. There's nothing wrong with spreading Judaism to those that are interested."

"Not when a guy is looking at your coochee," Fraydie whispers to me. I stifle a laugh; my sister has a point.

"You would have been a great Jehovah's Witness, Ma," Fraydie muses.

"Eat your cookie, dear," my mother says.

I look out the window and nibble my bottom lip as my heart continues to race a mile a minute. Why in the world did he agree to come? I can't imagine Sam, completely secular in every way, choosing to participate in an Orthodox Shabbos meal. Rituals that are perfectly normal to my family and me will seem archaic and bizarre to him, if not downright ridiculous.

I rub the tender area of my neck. It's a good thing I'm marrying a rich guy because if Friday night goes as awkwardly as I suspect it will, I may be forced into early retirement.

CHAPTER TWENTY-ONE

"A great dress can make you remember what is beautiful about life."

—*Rachel Roy*

Between work, figuring out details and dates for the *vort* and the wedding itself, and announcing my engagement on my media plat-forms, the week flew by faster than I could have imagined. Zevi, to his credit, was really amazing when I finally explained the situation with Libby's house, and he promised to help. All I need to do now is find a good time to tell Libby and hope that her pride doesn't get in the way of her accepting the money. Because it's a little late to back out at this point.

"He's here!" Fraydie announces from her lookout position on the couch.

"Someone get the door!" my mother calls from the kitchen.

"I'll get it," I tell Fraydie as I place the challah cover over the cutting board. Sam was out of town all this week, so I figured there was a good chance he'd want to cancel and relax at home or that he'd even forget about it, so I was surprised when he texted me earlier today, asking what time to come.

I glance at my reflection in the mirror positioned above the credenza. "Everything will be fine," I tell the anxiety-ridden woman staring back at me. "And if not, we'll be dead in a hundred years anyway."

"Does saying that actually make you feel better?" Fraydie says. "Because it depresses the hell out of me."

There's a loud knock on the door. I glance in the mirror and fluff my hair.

"Oh my G-d." Fraydie gasps and shakes her finger at me. "You like him!"

"*What?* No!" I step away from the mirror and try not to panic. Fraydie is like a loose cannon, and you never know what she's going to say, but nine times out of ten, it's not going to be good. "Why would you even think that?"

There's another knock and my mother yells for someone to get it.

"It's pretty obvious. And he's totally your type." Fraydie tilts her head toward the doorway. "You better let him in."

I have a type? Since when? I pause and consider telling her not to do anything embarrassing, but that's like telling a dog to ignore a juicy steak.

Just breathe. Everything will be okay.

I turn the knob and the door swings open. "Hi."

"Hey. I wasn't sure where to—" He stops and stares at me. The Adam's apple that's so prominent on his throat visibly moves as he swallows. The poor man looks shell-shocked.

Alright, confession time: I may have tried a little harder than normal to look my best, but only because . . . well . . . the *why* part isn't important. The important thing to note here is my dress, which, I'd like to go on record stating, is not a bodycon dress, no matter what Fraydie says. It's just that I have an hourglass figure accentuated even more by a petite waist, and it's not my fault that I ended up looking like a red-hot siren. It is simply how G-d made me.

But back to my dress. It's bright red and mermaid style, with sequins on the sleeves and on the heart-shaped bodice (my tailor is a genius for making anything modest if you give her the right fabric). My long, wavy hair is fastened with jeweled combs so it curls seductively over my right shoulder. My makeup is simple, but dramatic: red lips and a hint of mascara. I have a nice four-inch lift thanks to my peep-toe, black patent-leather shoes.

"Wow . . . you look . . ." He swallows. *Please don't say high-class Vegas prostitute,* I telepathically message him. It's bad enough that Fraydie said it, then spent the next fifteen minutes trying to convince me why that's a compliment and not, in fact, a roundabout insult.

"Beautiful."

My heart skips a beat and my stomach freefalls. A range of emotions rush through me, each more confusing than the next. He's made it clear that he's not my friend, that he never was, and now he's standing on my parents' doorstep telling me I look beautiful. "Thanks," I murmur, and motion for him to come inside.

Sam looks and smells like a Hugo Boss model come to life. From his pinstripe button-down shirt and navy regimental tie to the beige dress pants that hug his athletic legs, he's a dangerous combination of charm and testosterone; a tantalizing mixture of spicy and sweet.

Spicy and sweet? I take a few steps back because, frankly, I'm starting to scare myself.

"I'm surprised you made it," I say. "Gina said you've been in Brazil all week."

"I am pretty jet-lagged," he replies. "It's nearly a ten-hour flight, and I got back around three this afternoon."

"If it were me, I'd be dead to the world for the next forty-eight hours," I say.

"I was tempted." A beat. "But more tempted to see you."

The butterflies in my stomach flutter like crazy, and I put my hand over my midsection as though to calm us all down. He chose me over sleep, like an upside-down version of Maslow's Hierarchy of Needs. I lift my eyes to meet his, and a shot of electricity charges up and down my body. Whatever this magnetic pull between us is, it's getting worse instead of better.

"Can I give this to you?" He holds out a wine bag. "I was told it's kosher."

"I'm sure it is." His fingers brush against mine during the transfer, and though it was the slightest of touches, the backs of my knees tingle from the contact.

"Is it?"

"Is it what?"

He arches an eyebrow. "Kosher."

"Oh, right!" *Geez, focus woman.* I twist the bottle around to find the label. "Never mind," I say, and set the wine down on the hallway table. "It's the thought that counts."

"Shit. I'm sorry. The guy said—"

"Some people assume it's kosher," I rush to explain, "but not everyone agrees. There's varying levels, you know?"

"Not really." He shrugs. "But I do feel pretty stupid."

"Stop." I laugh and wave my hand. "It's fine. We're just happy you're here."

"Well"—he sighs, running his fingers through his hair—"if you ever need to buy un-kosher wine pretending to be kosher, Mario at Uptown Liquors can hook you up."

"Good to know," I say, stifling a giggle, although a most unladylike snort comes out.

"Hellooo," Fraydie trills, coming toward us. "You must be Sam."

To his credit, Sam only hesitates a few seconds. Most people who meet Fraydie for the first time take longer to get over the shock, what with the purple lipstick and all-black clothing. Her sense of style is a combination of Goth and Orthodox Judaism with a little *Twilight* vampire thrown in the mix. I often encourage her to broaden her fashion repertoire, but all I get in response is the middle finger waved in my face.

He nods. "And you are?"

"I'm Fraydie, Penina's sister. The charming one."

"Clearly." He grins and throws me an amused look. "It's nice to meet you." He puts his hand out, only to withdraw it a second later. "Oh, sorry—I forgot I'm not supposed to."

"You're fine." Fraydie smiles and adds, "You know, Penina was right about you."

The corners of my mouth tighten. I get the distinct feeling she's about to humiliate me.

"Oh?" He gives me a sideways glance. "How so?"

"She said . . . wait, let me think. I want to remember her exact words." She taps her finger on the side of her head. "Oh yes. She said you were hotter than a ghost pepper crossed with jalapeños on a ninety-nine-degree day."

I laugh because, truly, how does she come up with this stuff? Which is not to say that I'm not going to kill her later because I totally am.

"Really." Sam tucks his hands into his pants pockets and sneaks another sideways glance at me. His expression is hard to read, and I'm much too mortified to try.

"No, no. *Not* really," I choke. "That is so not true." But it's like the more I deny it, the more fake it sounds. A sense of dèjá vu sweeps over me, reminding me of the time I called him sexpot. Why is it so hot in this house? I pick up a magazine from the console table and fan myself. "I mean it's not true that I said it. Not that you aren't handsome," I add as I turn a shade redder and fan myself faster, "it's just that I never *said* you were."

His eyebrows shoot up, but he doesn't say anything. Fraydie pops a bubble from the piece of gum in her mouth and glances back and forth between us like she's watching a tennis match.

"I mean, you're my boss," I babble, waving my hands, "I don't think of you in those terms."

He leans a hip against the doorway as a slow smile appears on his face. "Uh-huh."

Take a bow, Penina. You've officially outdone yourself.

The sound of a key turning in the lock catches our attention, and the door opens, revealing my father. I probably should have warned Sam that Fraydie isn't the only one in the family that dresses differently. My father's knee-length, double-breasted, black dress coat and matching black hat made from rabbit fur aren't the most conventional of fashion choices outside of Orthodox circles.

"Ah, you must be Sam." My father smiles and closes the door. He reaches forward to clasp Sam's hand in both of his. "*Shalom Aleichem.* We're happy you could make it."

If Sam is uncomfortable, he certainly doesn't show it. "It's great to be here. Thanks for having me."

"Of course, of course." My father nods. "Have you met my wife yet?"

"No, not yet."

"Come, follow me." My father takes Sam's elbow and leads him out of the foyer. "Have you lived in this area long?"

As soon as the men are out of earshot, I round on the devil incarnate. "I'm going to kill you."

Fraydie pops a bubble precariously close to my face. "You should thank me. The two of you have enough chemistry to light a fire and burn this house down."

"Lower your voice," I hiss, gazing past her shoulder toward the living room. "First of all, I'm an engaged woman. And second of all, I'm not attracted to him!"

Fraydie rolls her eyes. "That's like someone saying they don't like double whipped cream chocolate mousse pie. No one is dumb enough to believe that."

I open my mouth, then shut it. Fraydie cocks an eyebrow and folds her arms across her chest, waiting for me to respond. It's hard to figure out what I'm feeling, and even harder to put it into words. Yeah, okay, so I might be, a little bit, attracted to Sam. *But* I can't *go there*. I can't start wishing for things that aren't realistic. Putting aside his dual personality problem, he's as secular as I am religious, and he's obviously not interested in marriage because otherwise he'd be taken. A guy like that could snap his fingers and get any woman he wants. Like Keila. And anyway, he'd want to have kids.

Fraydie blows another bubble and it pops.

"It's like . . . well—" I break off mid-sentence and start over. "What's the point of someone admitting they like mousse pie," I say, glancing meaningfully at her, "if they're a diabetic?"

Fraydie's eyes go all squinty, like she's trying to solve a complex math problem. "You can't admit you're attracted to him because you're engaged?"

I hesitate. A part of me wants to confide in her, but a bigger part wants to just forget this whole conversation.

"Yes, that's why." I take a step forward, but she must not believe me because she grabs my elbow.

"Pen, something's wrong."

"Nothing's wrong." I try to shake her off, but she's got me in an iron-clad grip.

"Girls," my mother calls from the other room, "come to the table, please."

"Just a minute!" Fraydie shouts. She lowers her voice and says, "Do you love him?"

"Love him?" I throw up my hands in exasperation. "Of course not. He's my boss, nothing more. Are we done now?"

Fraydie looks at me uneasily.

"What?"

She crosses her arms and her black fingernail polish shines under the hallway light. "I meant Zevi. Your fiancé?"

Crap.

"We were talking about Sam," I say defensively.

She spreads her arms apart. "Only to say he was hot! I had no idea you had feelings for him."

A hot flush spreads across my cheeks and travels to the tips of my toes. "Wow. You are way off."

"Then why can't you admit he's handsome?" Fraydie persists, the whites of her eyes doubling in size.

"Because I'm not like you! I don't go around critiquing how everyone looks—I judge people based on their character, not how good-looking they are."

She takes out her ponytail holder and ruffles her thick, long hair. "I don't judge people based on their looks, but I notice them. And I don't for a second believe that you don't."

"Believe what you want." I shrug, moving past her. "I don't care."

Her arm shoots out and grabs my elbow. "What are you so afraid of, Penina?"

"Nothing." I frown and shimmy out of her grasp. "Sorry to disappoint you, but whatever it is you're looking to find doesn't exist. My life isn't that complicated."

"You can lie to me and you can lie to Zevi," she says, pinning me down with a hard stare, "but don't lie to yourself."

I extract myself from her grasp and head toward the dining room. Lie about what? For a nineteen-year-old girl, she sure has a lot of nerve—acting like she has more insight into my life than I do, the person who's living it. All because I wouldn't admit that Sam was handsome—as if there could be any doubt—and then because she tricked me into saying I didn't love Sam when she meant Zevi. As far as I'm concerned this was a clear-cut example of leading the witness.

Yet . . . there's a tiny nagging voice inside my head that knows better. Fraydie is right—it's one thing to lie to others, but it's another thing entirely to lie to myself. That's beyond sad. I close my eyes and take a deep steadying breath. Here are three absolute truths:

1. I don't want to marry Zevi.
2. There's no way I could live with myself if I don't marry Zevi.
3. And yes—Sam *is* smokin' hot.

*　*　*

"Do you like your balls hard or soft?"

Sam blinks, and I bury my face in my hands. No matter how many times I've told my mother to stop referring to matzah balls as "balls," she never listens. Even after I explained how it sounds, she said no one else thinks such perverted thoughts. Well, from the look on Sam's face, *he* does.

"I said, do you like your balls—"

"*Matzah balls*, Ma," I interrupt, rubbing my forehead. "Please say matzah balls."

My mother gives me a warning look, as though I'm the originator of this double entendre, and I better not corrupt the innocent, pureminded people at the table.

"Either way is fine," Sam says, struggling to keep a straight face.

I stand up and collect the fish plates while my father repeats the sermon he heard earlier from the rabbi. I sneak a peek at Sam, trying to determine how weirded out he is. The evening kicked off awkwardly enough when my mother explained there are special laws on Shabbos, like not using phones or turning lights on or off. Then Fraydie added that he can't tear toilet paper either, but not to worry because there was pre-torn stuff in the bathroom. Sam asked if flushing was allowed. We thought that was hilarious and had a good laugh. Sam looked at us like we were nuts, but in our defense, we never claimed to be sane.

Next, my father blessed my sisters and myself, his hands on our heads, murmuring Hebrew words from centuries past. Each blessing ended with an *amen* and a kiss on the cheek. The recitation of kiddush and hand-washing before challah soon followed, and through it all, Sam acted perfectly at ease—as though all these rituals were the most natural things in the world.

"Careful," my mother says, passing a tray of soup to me, "it's very hot."

I bring the bowl to Sam and point to the matzah balls. "My mom gave you two, one soft and one hard."

Sam lifts his spoon and says with a straight face, "Just the way I like them."

I can't tell if he's kidding or not; maybe my mother is right—maybe *I'm* the one with the problem.

"Would you join me in making a *L'Chaim*, Sam?" My father withdraws a bottle of Glenlivet from the dark mahogany hutch.

"You bet," he replies. "I'm not one to turn down good scotch."

"Excellent. Anyone else?"

My mother and I shake our heads. Fraydie, however, waves her hand. "I'll take a shot."

"Not a chance."

"It's legal in Wisconsin to drink with your parents," she announces.

"But we're not in Wisconsin, dear," my mother replies with a tight smile.

I turn to Fraydie, scandalized. "Please tell me you haven't been drinking—you've heard of fetal alcohol syndrome, right?"

The room falls deathly quiet.

Fraydie's mouth is a perfect "O," and my parents' faces have turned a ghastly shade of white. Sam glances between everyone as he takes another spoonful of soup.

"Fraydie," my mother says nervously, "is there something you'd like to tell us?"

Fraydie starts to laugh so hard that tears run down her face. When she tries to talk, she ends up collapsing into a new round of giggles and bangs her hand on the table. "Oh G-d, I can't . . ." she pants, wiping her eyes. "My stomach hurts."

I say to Fraydie, "Do you want to tell them about the multiple sex partners or should I?"

Fraydie dissolves into a fresh round of hysterical laughter. Guess it'll have to be me. I turn to my parents and say, "She doesn't know who the father is. There were a lot of men."

My parents wear identical faces of horror.

"I've never even"—Fraydie hoots and gasps with laughter—"touched a boy in my life."

I shake my head, confused. "But at the *Lag Ba'Omer* picnic, you were hinting that you were pregnant."

Fraydie abruptly stops laughing. "I wasn't talking about *me*, Penina."

My parents exhale in relief, and then my mother—who never drinks—grabs my father's snifter and tosses back the rest of the contents. And promptly starts coughing.

"I don't understand." I pinch the bridge of my nose and think. "It can't be Libby."

"It isn't," Fraydie confirms.

"Who is it then?" my mother coughs, handing the empty glass to my father.

"I'm not supposed to say," Fraydie says. "But I will tell you that there were three of us in Libby's house that day. And the positive pregnancy test wasn't from Libby or me."

I think back and try to remember a third person, but I'm drawing a blank. Fraydie had been helping Libby with the kids, and she found the pregnancy test in the garbage. At first, she thought it was Libby's but then she—I gasp. *"Mimi?"*

"Bing! Bing!" Fraydie chimes. "We have a winner."

Sam clears his throat and reaches for his wineglass and it occurs to me that this is probably not the kind of Shabbos experience he was expecting.

"Impossible," my mother declares. "My sister would've told me. And Mimi is a good girl."

"She had multiple partners?" I gasp with realization.

Fraydie tears off a piece of challah and pops it into her mouth. "Yup. She has no idea who the father is. I told her to make a spreadsheet next time." Turning to my mother she says, "Great challah, Ma."

"It can't be true," my mother says, shaking her head.

"How old is Mimi?" my father says. "Isn't she nine or ten?"

"Fourteen," Fraydie replies. "She's in ninth grade."

"Yes, she's in a school in Canada," my mother says.

Fraydie shakes her head. "Wrong. She's been home this whole time. They're hiding her until the baby is born."

My mother's jaw drops.

"What about the baby?" I ask. "Are they keeping it?"

Fraydie shrugs. "I don't know."

"What do you mean you don't know?" I say. "Didn't you ask?"

"They're going back and forth about it," Fraydie says, eating and talking at the same time.

"I'm not listening to this *shtus* anymore," my mother says. "Beryl, say a *d'var Torah*."

Fraydie and I exchange glances. My mother must be struggling with reconciling Mimi's squeaky-clean reputation with this new one.

My father fills two crystal snifters with scotch, then hands one to Sam. "This is a very special Shabbos, and we're honored that you could join us, Sam." Sam nods and my father clears his throat. "Our Penina is finally a bride after many years of searching for her soulmate. My dear Penina," my father continues, smiling at me, "may you and Zevi be *zoche* to build a *binyan adei ad*—"

Sam tilts his head at me.

"Merit to build an everlasting edifice," I translate.

"Yes," my father agrees. "But why? Of all the things we could bless a bride and groom with, why do we say this? Anyone want to guess?"

Fraydie raises her hand. "Because Jews insist on being weird?"

My father sighs. "Anyone else?"

"I'll give it a try," Sam says, lowering his snifter. His eyebrows draw together, and he looks as though he's in deep concentration. "The words 'everlasting edifice' must have a deeper meaning than just bricks and mortar. There has to be something beyond that—a symbolism of sorts."

"Yes, yes." My father smiles, seemingly pleased that someone is actually taking him seriously for once. "Go on."

Sam strokes his chin. "My guess is that it means a strong marital foundation. A rock-solid relationship that can weather good times and bad. And it's the everyday things that matter—small acts of prioritizing your partner's needs over your own. Something as mundane as doing a load of laundry, for example, or running to the store late at night helps to strengthen that edifice." He pauses for a moment, then adds, "Then there will be times when stronger action is called for. Maybe you have to defend a family member or stay home from a party because they're sick. That is to me," he concludes, glancing my way, "an everlasting edifice."

A pinprick of yearning tickles travels up and down my body. I don't know if it's the wine or the fact that I'm exhausted, but I suddenly have the strangest urge to curl into Sam's lap like a kitten seeking warmth.

Sam's eyes meet mine across the table. He gives me a brief half smile before turning to face my father. "How'd I do?"

"You took the words straight out of my mouth," my father says, patting Sam's arm. "I'm impressed."

My mother lifts the pitcher of water and pours some into her cup. She raises the glass to her lips and eyes Sam over the rim. "You seem to know an awful lot about marriage."

"I don't know about a lot," he shrugs, "but I guess being married for a few years taught me something."

My mother puts the cup down and tilts her head. "You're not married anymore?"

"No. Not for a few years now."

"Oy, I'm sorry. What happened?" my mother asks, never one for subtlety.

"Tova," my father intones, even though I'm sure he's dying to know too. "Let him be. He probably doesn't want to go into it."

"Or he might," Fraydie, who inherited the tactless gene from my mother, pipes up.

"It's fine," Sam shrugs. He taps the side of his wineglass and says after a beat, "We tried, but I think our foundation was rocky from the beginning. We got married for the wrong reasons."

I think back to that day in his car when he said that marriage is nothing more than a business transaction and how he mistook lust for love.

"Anyway," Sam says, clearing his throat. "I know enough now to realize that I'm not cut out for marriage."

"Who is?" my father chuckles, genuinely amused. "Do you know how many times I wanted to divorce my wife?"

"Not half as many times as I wanted to divorce you, Beryl." My mother grins, looking smug.

Sam turns to me with raised brows, and I find myself smiling. My parents talk like this so much that I've forgotten how strange it sounds. If I didn't know how rock solid their marriage was, I'd have been confused too.

"See?" my father says to Sam, as though my mother just proved his point. "Once you find your *bashert*—soulmate—everything will be fine. Especially if your *bashert* is kind."

Sam gazes across the table at me. "Is your fiancé kind?"

"Excellent question," Fraydie agrees, then waves her spoon. "Tell us more about Zevi."

I lick my lips and try not to panic. Sam knows Zevi is gay and that I'm marrying him to save Libby's house, but my family doesn't. And Fraydie knows—*suspects*—that I'm not in love with Zevi but that I might have feelings for Sam. So, all I have to do is convince everyone that I'm making the right decision without giving anything away.

I pour myself a second glance of wine. Needs must.

"Zevi is kind," I say, which is totally true, "and sweet and generous." My parents smile encouragingly at me, but Sam and Fraydie seem unimpressed. "Loyal," I add.

"Very good." My father smiles and takes a sip of wine.

"What about chemistry?" Fraydie says, an edge to her voice. "Because that's important."

My mother immediately starts in on Fraydie for asking an inappropriate question, and Sam gives me a smirk. My father looks around the table like he's trying to figure something out, then focuses on me.

"Are you okay, Peninaleh?"

No. No, I am not.

"Of course." I start to collect soup bowls, barely noticing what I'm grabbing. Logically, I know I'm doing the right thing. There's no doubt in my mind. So why is my heart filled with such dread?

"Soon you'll be dating," my mother is saying to Fraydie, "and you can't be talking like this."

Fraydie purses her purple lips. "I'm not dating until I reach thirty. End of story."

"Then you'll be considered an old maid, and the matchmakers will set you up with the kinds of men that Penina dates." My mother turns to me and pats my hand. "Mazel tov, again, honey."

I'd laugh if it wasn't so pathetic.

"Fraydie will date when she's ready," my father says, shaking his head. "Don't pressure her."

"Beryl, you know she can't continue like this. She's nineteen. Most girls her age are already dating, if not married."

"Nobody gets married at nineteen anymore," Fraydie argues. "That's an Orthodox boomer thing."

"Boomer?" my father repeats. "What's a boomer?"

Fraydie rolls her eyes. "That is *such* a boomer question."

I exchange grins with Sam as I collect dirty utensils from the table.

"C'mon, Fraydie," I say, and tilt my head. "Help me clear."

"I can't. Someone has to educate the boomers."

"I'll help." Sam pulls his chair back and gets to his feet.

"No, no. You're the guest. Sit and relax." Sam is the last person I want to talk to given the state of my runaway hormones, but short of yelling at him to stay put, there's nothing I can do.

Inside the kitchen, the dirty dishes are piling up. I set the bowls and utensils down in the sink and turn on the faucet. My body becomes aware of Sam's presence before my mind does. A tingling sensation starts from my wrists, then travels to my stomach, where it feels like a primitive drumming. Through my peripheral vision I see Sam putting the remaining bowls on the counter beside me.

"I've never tried using one of those," he says, pointing to the mesh sponge in my hand. "Does it work better than the regular kind?"

I smile, envisioning Sam doing dishes. "They work about the same. We use this one on Shabbos since it's forbidden to press out liquid, and water doesn't get trapped in the mesh."

"What's wrong with pressing out liquid?"

"It's considered a form of labor, and work of any kind is forbidden."

Sam's face is a picture of skepticism. "Pressing out liquid is considered labor?"

"In the good ol' days, it was," I say. "People would squeeze olives to extract their oil or squeeze grapes for their juice."

"Interesting," he replies. After a moment, he adds, "You're lucky, you know."

I tilt my face to look up at him. Even though I'm wearing heels, he still towers over me. "What do you mean?"

"Your family," he says, pressing his hips against the counter and facing me. "They're quirky, I'll give you that. But there's genuine love and a real feeling of togetherness. This Shabbos thing . . ." He shrugs. "It's not as bad as I thought."

I turn off the faucet and grab a dish towel. "That's just the scotch talking."

His dimple deepens as he grins, and the very sight of it makes me dizzy. I'm just going to go ahead and chalk that up to the wine I had. Tomorrow morning, I'll wake up back to normal, and when I see him at work on Monday, my body will not react like this. I will not, for example, study the outline of his lips and wonder how they would feel pressed against my own.

"This no electronics rule is kind of liberating," he continues, crossing his ankles. "I haven't even thought about checking my phone for twenty minutes now, and that's a record."

"It is kind of nice knowing you can't answer the phone or do email," I agree, returning to the sink, where he stands just a few feet away. "Unless you're a workaholic. Then it would be torture." Is it my imagination, or did he just move closer to me?

"What is it like to be so innocent?"

I glance up at him. He definitely moved closer. "What do you mean?"

"Have you ever wondered how it would feel . . ." He stops and shakes his head. "Never mind."

"It's okay," I hear myself saying as my pulse quickens. "You can ask."

He hesitates. "Are you sure you won't be offended?"

I swallow and nod. What if he asks to kiss me right here, in my parents' kitchen? What do I do? I mean, I can't of course. Obviously. But then again, what if this is the only opportunity I ever get—

"Have you ever wondered," he murmurs, leaning forward, "how it would feel . . ."

"Yes?" I can't bear this slow torture. *Kiss me already, you sadistic man!*

". . . to drive on a Saturday?"

I blink. "Huh?"

He leans back and folds his arms across his chest. "Drive on a Saturday." He gazes at me in earnest. "Or eat pork."

Disappointment envelops me like an old blanket ratty from usage. Of course, he never meant to kiss me. How could I be so stupid as to even think that? I'm nothing more than some kind of freak to him. And *hello*? Remember Keila?

Stupid wine. I'm never drinking again.

"Penina?"

I sigh and pick up the sponge. "Yes, I have wondered what pork tastes like, and I did drive on a Saturday once when my sister needed to be seen by a doctor, but it didn't feel any different from driving on a Sunday. Anything else you want to ask?" I say, aware how clipped my voice sounds.

"Shit, I've offended you."

"I'm not offended," I reply stiffly.

"Every woman I've ever met says she's not offended while simultaneously plotting my murder."

I throw my head back and laugh. "Okay, you're right. I'm offended."

"Good." He smiles, making my heart quicken. "That was really brave of you. Now we can move on to the next part."

"Plotting your murder?"

He whistles. "You are one bloodthirsty woman. No, now you get to insult me. I'll give you two chances since I offended you with two questions."

Actually, his offense was not kissing me, but I'm not going to tell him that.

"I'm not going to insult you," I say, folding my arms. "That's crazy. But I do accept the apology you didn't make."

"Uh-huh. So, you're going to give me the deep freeze?"

Something clicks into place. "Is that what your ex-wife did to you?"

He puts his hands in his pants pockets and looks off into the distance. "Pretty much every woman I've ever dated."

"Really?" I feel a pang of sympathy for him. "That's sad."

He shrugs. "They were casual relationships."

"Is that code for 'friends with benefits'?"

He arches an eyebrow and rocks back on his heels. "Possibly."

An awkward silence descends. For all his prying into my life, he's very private about his own. But I'd be lying if I said I wasn't curious.

"Maybe you have commitment issues. You reneged on our friendship out of the blue, after all," I say, trying to appear casual, like I hadn't vacillated between crying and cursing him in my head for days afterward.

He gazes at the ceiling and sighs. "It came out wrong. That's not what I meant."

"It's fine," I say, turning around and grabbing the oven mitts. "Hey, as long as you're here, you might as well make yourself useful. I hope you like kugel, because my mother made three different kinds."

"Penina."

I swallow, steel myself, and turn to face him. "Yeah?"

"I'll try to be your friend. If you let me."

I inhale deeply through my nose, then wave my gloved hand at him. "Fine. But no more of this *'I never thought of you as my friend'* stuff. If I hear that again, we're through."

"It wasn't th—I don't think—" He stops and rubs the back of his neck.

I cross my arms. "What?"

His arm drops to his side, and he shakes his head. "Nothing. You have my word, I won't say that to you again."

"Good." I remove a tray of cinnamon noodle kugel from the oven. "Too bad it's Shabbos so I can't get that in writing."

"Writing isn't allowed?"

I pull open a drawer and put two more trivets on the counter. "It falls under the category of work."

"What if it's not for work?"

I hand him a serving spoon and point to the fried rice. "Mix that. It's still physical labor, right?"

He arches an eyebrow "I wouldn't call moving a pen across a piece of paper physical labor. Is dictation allowed?"

I shut the oven door with my foot and set the tray of chicken on the other trivet. "Ask your local rabbi."

"I'm asking you."

I hold up both of my gloved hands and say, "Do I look like a rabbi to you?"

He stops mixing the rice to give me a slow, full-body perusal, and I silently curse myself because I stepped right into that one. "I'd attend services every week if you were," he says with a crooked smile.

"Perv," I mutter just loud enough for him to hear. His bark of laughter follows me as I stick my head in the fridge to hide my blush.

Sam and I make a good team, and within a few minutes the main course is served. More than once during the meal, I catch Sam's eye and we grin at each other like we're sharing a private joke. I let myself daydream, this time in safer territory, one where Sam and I are nothing more than good friends. Eventually he comes to learn that not all women are crazy, which leads him to falling in love. Not with me, obviously, but someone kind—and preferably with chronic bad breath and an annoying laugh.

Okay, no, that's not nice.

It's nearly eleven o'clock by the time the meal ends. As my family walks Sam toward the front door, he is effusive in his praise of my mother's culinary skills and what a wonderful time he had.

"We loved having you," my mother says, smiling. "And don't worry—I'm going to find you a good woman."

Sam doesn't quite know how to respond, but luckily my father is already speaking so he doesn't have to. "There's a custom of walking your guest several feet past the door, to show hospitality, but my leg is starting to act up, so I'm afraid I won't be able to do it tonight."

"No worries," Sam replies. "I'm fine on my own." Then he pauses, as though a thought just occurred to him. "Actually, Penina could take your place. If that's alright?"

I hold my breath while my parents exchange a look. After a moment, my father nods. "Sure. That's fine."

I feel Fraydie's eyes on me, but I pretend not to notice. "Let me just grab my shawl."

With my shawl wrapped over my shoulders, we step outside and stroll down the front path, beneath the cover of a beautiful night sky filled with stars. It's eerily quiet except for nature's soundtrack, the songs and mating calls of crickets and cicadas. Sam and I walk at a leisurely place toward his car, neither one of us in a hurry. Along the way, I point out which of my parents' neighbors are nice and which ones are so-so, and then the one or two that the rest of us consider borderline evil. All too soon, we reach his car, and Sam pulls out his key fob.

"I had a great time tonight," he says, leaning a hip against the car's fender. The streetlight casts a soft glow over him, illuminating the gold flecks in his eyes. "It was nice of your mom to invite me."

"She loves doing that sort of thing. Inviting random people over for Shabbos." I smile, tightening the shawl around me as a cool breeze passes through. "I'm sure she'll insist you come again."

He twirls the key fob in his hand. "How would you feel about that?"

My stomach flips. "About you coming again?" He nods. "I'd be cool with it," I swallow. "It's been a while since we've had fresh blood. And I mean that in a totally non-vampire type way."

He chuckles and his eyes inadvertently travel to my neck. That dizzying sensation creeps up, and I have to remind myself to breathe. He looks away and clears his throat. "I better go."

I nod. "See you on Monday."

He lifts a hand in goodbye and steps around the car. Before I have time to talk myself out of it, I step forward and say, "Wait, Sam."

He gazes at me over the hood of his car. "Yeah?"

I bite my lower lip, wondering what sadistic spirit is prompting me to do this. "I just wanted you to know that . . . well"—I scratch my neck—"not all women are like your ex."

"I know," he says abruptly.

Okay then. Wrist accordingly slapped. "Okay, great. Have a good—"

"I realized that the day I met you." I stare at him. "Goodnight, Superwoman."

I stand there, immobile with uncertainty, watching the taillights from his car fade into the distance. I gaze up at the sky, trying to put a name to what I'm feeling, this kind of stirring in my gut. The more I get to know Sam, the less certain I feel about marrying Zevi, which is completely ridiculous and really aggravating since one doesn't have anything to do with the other. It's not as though I could swap Zevi for Sam. For one thing, Sam isn't Orthodox; doesn't want to get married again; and most importantly, just because he's said a few nice things to me doesn't mean he likes me in *that way*.

I press my cool palms to my face and start walking back. *Keep it together, Penina—stay focused.* My sister and her family are depending on me, and so is Zevi. It's normal to be nervous; even real couples have cold feet before tying the knot.

I know I'm doing the right thing. So why does it feel so wrong?

CHAPTER TWENTY-TWO

"We don't believe any item of clothing should be restricted to its intended purpose."

—*Chaya Chanin and Simi Polonsky*

Sunday mornings are my time to sleep in, so when I'm woken by the buzzer of my intercom, I'm not too thrilled. I groan and turn over, hoping whoever it is will go away, but this person's finger must be glued to the buzzer. I climb out of bed, grab a knee-length sweater hanging off the desk chair, and hurry to the kitchen. I stub my toe against a table leg and yelp in pain.

"*Ouch!* Who's there?" I croak into the speaker, hopping on one foot and massaging the injured toe of the other.

"Your boss."

My heart slams in my chest, and I wonder whether I'm still dreaming. *Why would Sam be here?* I press the button that lets him into the building, then wait for him by my door. He appears a minute later, looking so handsome that the butterflies in my stomach go from fluttering to a full-on jig, to the Latin style rumba. There's nothing special about his navy V-neck T-shirt and distressed jeans, but the way they cling to his powerhouse body is nothing short of a spiritual revelation. He smiles and the dimple in his cheek deepens.

"Did I wake you?"

I shake my head no, then nod yes. "What are you doing here?"

"Your mom didn't call?"

I shake my head, wondering what my mother has to do with it.

"I stopped off at your parents' house this morning to pick up the sunglasses I left there. Then your mom invited me in for some coffee and we got to talking, and she mentioned that she has this cookbook on hold at the Jewish bookstore. I offered to get it, and we both agreed that you should show me how to get there."

Weird. Weird. Weird. "You couldn't use Google Maps?"

He studies the doorframe like there's nothing more fascinating than a piece of plywood. "This is a team-building exercise."

I stare and wait for him to acknowledge the obvious. "Half the team isn't here," I finally point out. "And besides, I'm not even dressed."

His eyes go from the doorframe to the front of my sweater. "That's a straight-up lie."

"These are pajamas."

"Really?" He gestures to my garish Chanukah pants with large yellow dreidels and my fuzzy slippers with monkey heads. "I thought they were man repellents."

"Yet, here you are . . ." I drawl.

The corners of his mouth twitch as he glances at his Apple watch. "How long will it take?"

"To get rid of you?" I shrug. "No idea."

Instead of appearing insulted, a slow grin lights up his face. "To get dressed."

I briefly consider slamming the door in his face and going back to bed, but this is Sam, after all, and he never takes no for an answer. I take a step back and widen the door. "Long enough that you better come in. But," I add, ignoring the quickening in my pulse when his shirt brushes against the front of my sweater as he walks past, "I expect to be paid overtime for this."

He places his hands on his hips and looks around, his huge frame swallowing up every inch of space. "Keep dreaming, Superwoman."

I mutter under my breath about cheap bosses and pull the latch out to prevent the door from closing.

He gestures to the door with a tilt of his head. "You're sure this is okay?"

Does he want me to call my rabbi and get his permission? "Would you feel better if I left the door wide open? I haven't attacked a man yet, but they say there's always a first."

His eyes slowly run the length of my body, then return to my face. "I'm pretty sure I could handle you."

I search for something to say, but my brain has shut off.

Sam heads toward the bookcase at the far end of the living room and zeroes in on a picture. He studies it, his large fingers curling over the black frame. "Is this you?"

"Yes." I clear my throat. "That was taken at my first piano recital."

"How old were you?"

"Seven."

"Cute." He puts it back and picks up the next picture, the one taken from my bas mitzvah nearly seventeen years ago. My parents flank me, all three of us smiling at the camera. "I hoped you sued the person who did that to your hair."

"That would be my mother," I say, lifting my chin. The truth is that I wasn't a fan of the large bow at the top of my head; it had made me seem younger and definitely dorkier. Still, I wasn't going to push the issue since my mother made it clear the bow was nonnegotiable. "Everyone said I looked adorable."

He squints at the picture for a few moments, then looks at me. "They lied."

"I know." I try to grab the picture from him, but he's at least a head taller than me, if not more, and easily keeps it beyond my reach. I jump, but even that doesn't help.

"I'll give it back," he says, "after you get dressed."

"No, you can't just—" I leap for the picture and miss. "You can't grab my stuff, then hold it hostage." I jump, swipe with my hand, but feel nothing but air. I pause and try to catch my breath. "You were so much better behaved at my parents' house."

He grins. "So were you."

I'm about to lunge again when something grabs his attention, and he pulls a book out from the shelf. One that has a particularly crude cover and is titled *"Earls Just Want to Have Fun."* He taps the spine. "I'll read this while you get ready."

"That was a gift." I yank it out of his hand. "I've been meaning to donate it."

Between the pictures and books, my living room is a treasure trove of humiliation. *Why is this happening to me?*

"Damn," he breathes, pulling out several more romance books, each one bearing a couple more scantily clad than the next. *"My Holiday Cowboy,"* he reads out aloud. *"How to Bed a Warrior, Rough and Ready."* He tilts his head and whistles. "Were these all gifts?"

"I—" I shut my mouth, then open it again. "They are very well written."

"I bet," he says with a smirk.

"Fine." I spread my arms wide. "My name is Penina and I'm addicted to trashy romance novels. Happy now?"

His hoot of laughter follows me as I stomp to my bedroom, the monkey heads of my slippers bobbing with every step. I lock the door, head to my dresser, and select one of my sexier bras, the red one with a diamond front clasp and nipple cutouts. I know it's ridiculous to own a collection of racy underwear when I'm the only one who sees it, but I bought my first pair of panties when I was twenty-four, and I haven't looked back since.

I glance at my reflection in the bathroom mirror and grimace. Did Sam actually flirt with this messy excuse of a woman, complete with frizzy, tangled hair, under-eye circles, and bad attitude? Or was it just my imagination playing tricks with me?

I turn on the shower and shimmy out of my pajamas. I pump some grapefruit and mosa mint shampoo onto my hands and lather it into my hair, angling my neck so the water jets down my back in warm rivulets.

I blame my cavewomen ancestors for my body's inappropriate reaction to Sam. Back in those days, a physically large, handsome man with a great butt signified food, shelter, and mating material. This is nothing more than a simple case of biology. This is *science*.

So what if his eyes churn when he looks at me, and my stomach does somersaults? It doesn't mean anything other than I'm a slave to my genetics and would greatly benefit from the use of a thick blindfold.

I hop out of the shower and dress, swipe a little mascara on my eyelashes and apply some nude lip gloss, all while hearing Sam's laughter every few minutes, which tells me he's enjoying my trashy romance novels a little too much.

I return to the living room, and Sam looks up from the book titled *Seduction and Snacks*. A slow smile spreads across his face as he takes in my shiny pink top and knee-length pencil skirt. "You clean up nice," he says, getting up from the couch.

I don't want him to see me blush, so I turn around and mutter something about needing to find my keys.

"Aren't they over there?" He points to the set of vintage hooks nailed beside my door.

My blush deepens as I realize they were there all along. Being around Sam—especially being *alone with him*—is making me feel off-kilter. "Yes, they are," I say in the perky tone of a gameshow host.

It's a beautiful spring day outside, with cotton-candy clouds floating in an azure sky, and the fragrant scent of peonies and lilacs in the air. A young couple walking an all-American mutt passes us on the left. To the casual observer, Sam and I probably appear like any other couple taking a morning stroll through town. From the outside looking in, no one could tell that Sam has given up on love or that I'm engaged to a rich, homosexual man.

"Explain again why you have this sudden urge for me to come with you?" I ask, sidestepping a puddle. "It isn't hard to find, especially since it's the only Jewish bookstore in town."

"You know what else isn't hard to find? Real literature."

I give up. Whatever his reason is, he's not going to share it with me. "I think we'd disagree on what constitutes real literature."

"Yes." He nods. "Except I'd be right."

I roll my eyes. "Give me some examples."

"*The Old Man and The Sea. Catch-22. The Metamorphosis. The Great Gatsby.*" He pauses and adds, "And obviously anything by Faulkner and Steinbeck."

"So basically," I surmise, "anything written by a male alcoholic during the last two hundred years."

He laughs, and we spend the rest of the walk taking shots at each other in everything from music to movies, to food (he's adamant that Fruit Roll-ups aren't considered fruit, and at one point holds his fist near his mouth and says in a newscaster's voice, "The legendary Fruit Roll-up tree is primarily grown in the unicorn region of Bigfoot and Leprechauns, in the land of Yetis, centaurs, mermaids, and other things that don't exist."

A small strip mall comes into view, and after passing a sketchy-looking pawn shop and a vacuum store, we reach a glass door with the words "Judaica Palace" emblazoned in curlicue white stands against a stonewall brick structure. The display window showcases kiddush cups, candlesticks, menorahs, and a plethora of Jewish children's books.

"FYI," I say, "be prepared for people to assume that we're either engaged or on the verge of getting engaged."

"Why would they think that?"

"Because they like to jump to conclusions and because Orthodox singles don't go out together in public until they're engaged."

"Then where do people go for dates?"

I glance in the window and see a man from my synagogue staring at us. "Hotels," I reply, reaching for the door handle.

"Wait a minute. That can't be right." Sam steps in front of the door, blocking me from entering. "Are you telling me that Orthodox Jews date in hotel rooms? They sit on the bed and talk?"

"No." I bite the inside of my cheek to keep from laughing. "They stay in the lobby."

From the expression on Sam's face, it appears that he still finds the idea strange, but I can't say that I blame him.

The inside of the store smells exactly the same as it did when I was a kid, a combination of tobacco, mothballs, and old books. The avocado-green carpet and heavy brass light fixtures that were trendy fifty years ago have a sad and worn appearance now, and the shelves are coated in a thick layer of dust.

I wave hello to the owner, a sweet-tempered octogenarian fond of bow ties, suspenders, and monogrammed hankies.

"Penina, Penina," he says, pausing to catch his pneumatic breath before he gestures to Sam. "Who's this strapping young man of yours?"

I'm about to explain that he's my boss, not my strapping young man, but Sam cuts me off and extends his hand. "Sam Kleinfeld. Nice to meet you."

The owner enfolds Sam's hand in both of his trembly ones. "Welcome, welcome. Your mother's Jewish?"

Sam looks momentarily taken aback by the abrupt question but quickly recovers. "Yes, sir. Both my parents are."

"It only matters if your mother's Jewish. Don't let nobody tell you different." He pats Sam on the arm and chuckles, "After all, you always know who the mother is, eh?"

My mind automatically goes to Mimi, but as Sam and I head toward the aisles, he murmurs, "Bad news for Adam Levine."

"I'm sure he cries himself to sleep about it every night."

"Okay, Superwoman." Sam puts his hands on his hips and gazes around the store. "I'm trying to find a specific book."

"You mean my mother's cookbook?"

"No, something else. A novel."

I'm immediately suspicious when I notice the corners of his lips quivering, like he's struggling to keep a straight face. "What's the title?"

"*The Bull Rider's Christmas Baby*," he says. "I saw it in your collection and thought, *'Now there's a classic everyone should own.'*"

I sigh, moving through the aisles. He's enjoying this way too much. "You'll never let me live this down, will you?"

"Hell no. I'm going to do my best to work it into every conversation."

I ignore him and continue toward the kids' section. My friend has a children's book coming out, and I want to see if it's here yet.

"Penina," Sam calls, and motions for me to come back.

I turn and when I reach Sam, he points to an overhead sign that says "Family Purity and Marital Advice."

"What does family purity mean?"

"Don't worry about it," I say, then pull out a book titled *Marriage Secrets*. "When's your birthday? Because I just found you a present."

He takes one look at the title, then puts it back on the shelf. "You didn't answer my question—what the hell is family purity?"

"Keep your voice down." I wince, craning my neck to see if anyone heard him. "I'll explain it some other time." I really, *really* do not want to get into a discussion on the laws of marital sex with the guy I fantasize about on a regular occasion. Especially not in the Jewish bookstore.

"I'll just ask bow-tie guy."

I cringe. He would too. I surrender to the inevitable. "Okay, I'll give you the basics," I say, to which he nods. "Family purity is about the laws designed for the Orthodox Jewish couple and their"—I lower my voice and look at the floor—"intimate times."

"Intimate times?" Sam frowns. "Do you mean sex?"

"Shh!" My eyes widen and I put a finger over my lips. "That's a naughty word."

"What word? Sex?"

I nod, color creeping into my cheeks.

"Jesus." Sam shakes his head. "Sex isn't a naughty word."

My seventh-grade teacher, Mrs. Cantor, happens to walk by at that exact moment. I give an embarrassed little wave that she doesn't return, and then, mercifully, she heads to another aisle. In theory, I shouldn't care what an old curmudgeon with untreated OCD thinks about me standing next to a hunky man saying words like *hell*, *sex*, and *Jesus*, but unfortunately I'm not that evolved.

"Let me get this straight," Sam tilts his head. "You're—"

"*Whisper.*"

He crosses his arms over his chest. "Don't you think you're being a little immature?"

"Just humor me."

"This better?" he says, lowering his deep baritone. I give him a silent thumbs-up. "So why are there laws about sex?"

"There are lots of reasons."

"Like?"

"A husband and wife can only be intimate at certain times of the month, so they learn to bond emotionally instead of just physically. And as people get older, there will come a time when intimacy doesn't happen as often. That's why it helps to create a bond early on." I pause, then add cleverly, "Not everyone can be Hugh Hefner on Viagra."

"Wait a second," he says, holding up his hand. "Are you telling me that a married couple can't have sex whenever they feel like it?"

"They can't touch each other at all or even sleep in the same bed, let alone have intimacy. But it's usually just two weeks of the month."

"Two weeks?" Sam pales. "You're shitting me."

The stunned expression on his face makes me laugh. "Nope. Twelve days if you're lucky."

"You're lying."

"Nope."

"That's insane," he says, his voice rising in volume. "I could never do that."

I run my fingers along the spines of the books and shrug. "They say it makes the intimate times a lot hotter."

"If a man needs to stay away from a woman to make the sex hot," he says, pinning me with his eyes, "then he doesn't know what he's doing in the first place."

My cheeks flush and my heart rate spikes. I'm either very attracted to Sam or severely allergic to him.

"How do the men do it?" he continues.

I open a random book and flip pages, hoping he'll take the hint and drop the topic. Unfortunately, I am not that lucky.

"And if a guy is marrying a woman," Sam says, leaning against the bookcase I'm rifling through, "there's already an emotional bond. They already love each other."

I pull out a different book and blow dust off the cover. "In the secular world, yes. But Orthodox Jews don't typically date long enough to form a strong emotional bond."

"Then they have no business getting married in the first place!" he says, a few pitches above a whisper. "This is the most backassward thing I've ever heard."

I shove the book back and turn to face him. "Did you love your wife before you married her?"

"Of course!"

"Great. So, you have that in common with the other fifty percent of Americans who end up divorced."

Sam's eyebrows draw together like two angry storm clouds. "Are you saying that if I had known her *less* before our marriage took place, we'd still be happily married today?"

I nod, though I'm not sure about that at all. "And less intimacy."

He shakes his head and laughs. "You seriously believe that?"

I hesitate. "Yeah."

He stands up straight and points his finger at me. "Then that makes you every bit as crazy as my ex."

I frown. "Just because my opinion is different from yours doesn't make me crazy."

"It does in this case!"

We have a silent stare-down in the family purity section of the store, when a friend of my mother's turns into the aisle, a shopping basket hanging over her arm.

"Oh, hi, Penina!" she says, regarding us with warm eyes. "Mazel tov! This must be your fiancé."

"No," I say quickly, glancing at Sam. "This is my boss, Sam Kleinfeld."

And this time, I can't help but notice, Sam doesn't bother to correct me.

CHAPTER TWENTY-THREE

"I think perfection is ugly. Somewhere in the things humans make,
I want to see scars, failure, disorder, distortion."
—*Yohji Yamamoto*

Sam buys the cookbook but ignores my polite suggestion that I deliver the book for him so he doesn't have to schlep back to my parents' house. Evidently, he isn't the type of man to rely on a gofer to do his work (though he seems to have no problem doing that the rest of the week).

"Listen, I'm sorry I called you crazy back there," Sam says as we approach an intersection. He pulls out his aviator sunglasses and slides them on, then glances at me. "I guess some of those family purity laws made me frustrated."

"Why?" I say, genuinely curious. "You're not Orthodox and you're not married. It doesn't affect you."

He nods and pushes the button for the crosswalk. I get the uncomfortable feeling he's hiding something.

"It's just—" he stops.

I wait for him to continue, but when he doesn't, I say, "What?"

The crosswalk lights up, and he gestures for us to cross. "My friend met this girl." He rubs the side of his face as though he's embarrassed or in pain. "She's Orthodox, and I don't know if it's a lifestyle he could handle. But at the same time, he really likes her."

My stomach plummets as things start clicking into place. His sudden interest in Orthodox Judaism . . . coming over for Shabbos dinner . . . dating questions . . . it's because he's worried about his friend. He's a spy and I've unknowingly been his object of interest this whole time.

I'm so annoyed that it's hard to think straight. My brain slowly processes the fact that he's only been spending time with me because I'm the subject matter of a research project. How could I let myself think, even for a minute, that he might have seen me as a friend, or even something more?

"Penina?"

I lift my head up and blink. "Yeah?"

"Isn't your parents' house that way?" he says, pointing in the opposite direction.

"Sorry, yeah." I swallow and turn around. "I'm a little out of it today. Must be wedding jitters."

He seems lost in thought, and I'm too depressed to make conversation, so we walk in silence for a while.

"Do you think," he says, hesitatingly, "that an Orthodox woman would be okay dating someone secular? Or is that completely out of the question?"

"Out of the question," I reply automatically. "Unless she wants to *frei* out."

"Fry out?" he repeats with raised eyebrows.

A neighborhood cat named Daven prances toward me, and I bend down to scratch his ears. "It means not being observant anymore, as in becoming secular. *Hey, you,*" I coo, as he rolls over so I can scratch his belly. Maybe after I divorce Zevi, I'll get a cat or a dog. That way, I can pretend I'm a mother, and as for a husband, I could get a giant cutout of Regé-Jean Page and prop him against my living room sofa. We'll watch Netflix's *Bridgerton* together, and because he's cardboard, he won't steal any of my popcorn.

"What if they compromise?" he asks, bending down to pet the cat too. Daven turns his face and rubs it against his hand, so I guess even animals find him irresistible.

"How would that possibly work?" I ask, trying not to get too excited about the fact that his hand is so close to mine. "She'd keep Shabbos by herself at home while your friend goes clubbing with his bros, knocking back shots of whiskey?"

The cat sees a chipmunk scurry across the sidewalk, and he jumps up to chase it. Sam stands up and gazes down at me with a condescending sneer. "My friend hasn't gone clubbing since he was in his twenties, and that wasn't what I meant."

I get up and stretch my arms, then fall into step beside him. "What did you mean?"

"I don't know. Maybe . . . he could keep Shabbos and kosher, and in exchange—" He stops without finishing his thought.

"What?" I prompt. If I didn't know any better, I'd think he was embarrassed.

"Those marriage purity laws," he says abruptly. "Are they negotiable?"

I shrug. "Maybe some of them? I don't know."

"Because he'd want to be able to touch his wife more than two weeks out of the month. He'd want to touch her every day."

"Yeah, sorry, I don't know." A thought occurs to me. "Does your friend have a sex addiction or something?"

"What? *No*," he says, sounding irritated. "He's just a normal, regular guy. And it's not necessarily about sex. Maybe he just wants to kiss her goodbye before he leaves for work in the morning. Or put his arm around her when they watch TV. It doesn't have to be about sex, although"—he pauses and gazes up at the sky—"he'd probably want a lot of that too."

"I really have no idea," I say for the millionth time. Talking about sex with Sam is making me think about *having* sex with Sam, and I've already reached my torture quotient for the day. "How's Keila?" I ask, switching gears.

"Keila? She's good."

He doesn't seem to want to add anything, so I say, "That was a great picture of the two of you." He looks confused, so I add, "On the boat."

"Oh, that. Yeah." He chuckles, like he's suddenly remembering something. "Keila's amazing."

Amazing is laying it on a bit thick, but I guess I asked for it. I kick a loose pebble off the sidewalk so no one trips on it.

"Take you, for example," he says after a beat. "You would probably be okay making compromises in a marriage."

"True. I'm moving to New York to marry a gay man," I say lightly as my parent's bungalow-style house comes into view.

"*Why*, Penina?" He stops walking and gives me an exasperated face. "Why would you do that?"

Because I love my sister and when you love someone, you do everything in your power to help them, even if it sometimes means getting hurt in the process. Love is putting your own needs aside to help the other person. Love is self-sacrifice and devotion and loyalty above all else. That's what love is.

I rub my forehead and briefly close my eyes as I imagine my sister packing up the kids' toys and stuffed animals. Of my nieces and nephews fighting within the cramped quarters of my parents' home. Of my brother-in-law's hurt pride that he couldn't provide for his family.

"Talk to me."

I open my eyes and meet Sam's gaze. I don't know if it's due to a buildup of stress or from the memory of being wrapped in his arms by the side of the highway or at the gala or because at some indefinable moment he's become more to me than just a boss, but I suddenly find myself wanting to confide in him. *Needing* to.

So there on the front steps of my parents' home, with the occasional flickering blind from the front windows, I tell him everything—hesitantly at first, then openly and uninhibitedly. From my sister's financial situation to my admission of being set up with men I could never love, to how it seemed like fate when Zevi entered the picture, to the way it feels when I hold NICU babies. His eyes never leave my face, and when I'm finished talking, I feel a little naked and vulnerable, but safe too.

"This isn't something I talk about or even think about, but—" He stops and clears his throat, then releases a deep breath. Whatever it is he's trying to say, it's obviously costing him a lot, and I give him an encouraging nod. "Growing up, my mom was . . ." He shakes his head and runs his fingers through his hair, then starts again. "It was like she only had two settings: distant or furious. My whole childhood was spent trying to be this perfect kid, as if I had to prove to her that I was . . ." He stops and bites his lip.

"Worthy of being loved?" I say gently.

He gives a terse nod and swallows. "Looking back, I think she loved me in her own way. If she even knew what love was." He shrugs and releases a deep sigh. "Anyway, after that car accident she was in—did you know about that?"

I nod, thinking back. "Your dad had mentioned that your mom died in a car crash a while ago." I lick my lips, then add, "I'm sorry."

He bows his head in acknowledgment. "Anyway, once she was gone, I felt like the biggest failure because I had never managed to get her stamp of approval. Can you imagine?" He laughs bitterly. "Twenty-seven-years old and still trying to worm my way into my mother's heart. I had friends, a successful career, was on the board of several establishments—but none of that mattered because it was never good enough for her. *I* was never good enough for her."

"Oh, Sam." I don't know what else to say to such heart wrenching words, so I stay quiet and wait for him to continue. It takes him a few moments, and I can tell he's struggling not to cry. I gaze at his strong, beautiful profile and appreciate that this powerful alpha man is allowing himself to be vulnerable in my presence.

"Then I met Vanessa at a party." He gives me a sideways glance and says, "I had girlfriends in the past, but nothing too serious. Mostly, I used them for . . . you know." I nod because it seems like he wants some kind of response. "Vanessa, though, she was different." His eyes look off into the distance, and it's clear that he's reliving the past. "She had this incredible ability to walk into a room and own it—it didn't matter if she knew people or was surrounded by strangers. She had this magic about her."

"Did she wear a lot of black leather?" I ask, because I've always suspected that black leather lends a certain mystique to a woman.

He blinks. "I don't remember."

"Sorry, it's not important. Keep going."

He stretches his long legs and leans on his elbows. "I think she saw me as a challenge, and I saw her as this incredibly confident, sexy woman that every man wanted and who every woman wanted to be. I never knew the truth until after we were married."

"What was it?"

"That she was a manipulative narcissist who got high off controlling people. She'd make friends and use them, then dump them as if they were nothing. But that's not the point," he says, shaking his head. "I ended up trying and failing to make her happy, over and over again. Nothing was ever good enough."

"Like with your mother," I whisper in understanding.

"Yeah." He's quiet for a few moments.

"So, then what happened?"

"I served her divorce papers after she poisoned River. I couldn't prove it," he says, jaw clenching, "but I know she did."

"Was that your dog?" He nods, and I realize I'm biting my fingernails and drop my hand. "Did River . . . die?"

"Yes."

My brain procures the image of a black, furry dog seizing violently on a kitchen floor while sexy Vanessa, clad in a black leather mini dress with a gold zipper down the back and Louboutin boots, laughs cruelly. My eyes well up with tears, and I blink. Ever since reading *Old Yeller* back in fifth grade, I've been a softy for dogs, and stories like this kill me. "I'm so sorry."

His eyebrows lift in alarm. "Are you crying?"

I press my hand to my mouth and use my other hand to signal I need a minute.

He stares at me. "You are one in a million, you know that?" he says, his voice sounding tender.

"No, I'm not. Everyone hates animal cruelty stories," I say, wiping my dripping nose with my sleeve. *Real classy, Penina.*

"But you take it to the next level," he replies, giving me his trademark half smile. "Listen," he says, his voice low and deep in its pitch. "I'm only telling you this because, even though my marriage isn't at all like what you're dealing with, I also felt overwhelmed and helpless." He pauses, brows furrowed. "I wanted more than anything to fix the problem, but I couldn't. And the reason I couldn't is because it was never my problem to begin with. It was hers." He blows out a puff of air and adds, "I know you love your family and are used to fixing their problems, but maybe it's time to let them figure things out. Maybe they're smarter than you give them credit for."

"They're really not." I sniff, swiping a tear from my cheek. "They need me."

"You're not going anywhere, but you can't keep living like this." He lowers his head and waits for me to meet his gaze. "It's destroying you," he whispers.

I shake my head but can't speak because these stupid tears keep leaking out like I have a plumbing issue.

I don't know how long we were sitting together without speaking—it might've been five minutes or twenty—when Sam suddenly announces, "Everything is going to be fine." His tone is emphatic, and for a second I almost believe him. I glance up and see his eyes soften. "I never say things I don't mean. Trust me, okay? Everything is going to be okay."

"For you," I mutter. He's filthy rich and dating the beautiful Keila. I, on the other hand, will probably end up as one of those crazy cat ladies with nothing better to do than knit sweaters all day. And that prompts a fresh wave of tears because the only thing I suck at more than cooking is knitting.

"No, Superwoman." He shakes his head. "For both of us."

CHAPTER TWENTY-FOUR

"If girls dressed for boys, they'd just walk around naked at all times."

—*Betsey Johnson*

"Thank you so much for coming," I say for what seems like the millionth time as I give my mother's friend a hug. It's eight o'clock at night, and the *vort* is in full swing at my parents' house, and it seems like everyone in my community has stopped by to wish Zevi and me mazel tov and toss back a shot or two of whiskey. My mother and sister spent the majority of the day cooking and setting up for the party, and everything in the house sparkles and shines. The women chat between dainty bites of fruit salad and cake from a buffet table in the living room, while the men sing and eat in the dining room. And Fraydie, being Fraydie, spends the majority of the night in the men's section.

I turn toward the window that overlooks the street and bite my lip. Sam had promised to come, but he's either forgotten about it or decided not to show up. Maybe he's upset because when I arrived to work this morning, I was wearing a huge diamond ring that didn't come from our store. Apparently, Zevi wanted to give business to his cousin, who works in the diamond district, and as he put it, "You could always trade it in for something you like better if you ever get married for real one day."

Hah. Not likely.

"Doing okay?"

I glance up and smile at Zevi's younger sister, Ashira, the one that Jack said looked like me. I don't see it, but I'll take the compliment since she's gorgeous and, even more importantly, nice, someone who could become a real friend. Leah stayed in New York to be with their mother, and though we FaceTimed them at the beginning so they could feel included, Leah spent most of the call complaining how left out they felt.

"Yeah." I nod, pushing the corners of my mouth up into a smile. "Just a little tired."

"Well, as long as you look good, that's what matters," she says, making a hand flourish toward me. "And you look gorgeous. Champagne is definitely your color."

While I was at work, Ashira and Zevi spent the day at the Mall of America, shopping for clothes and going on some rides. They came back with several dresses and outfit choices for me, one of which I'm wearing tonight. It was fun trying on all these designer dresses; I'd normally faint just by looking at the price tags. And yet something inside me felt heavy—like I'm dragging a bowling ball of nerves with me everywhere I go.

"You don't think it makes me look naked?" I whisper. It's form fitting and skin colored and not at all something I would have picked out for myself, but Ashira, Zevi, Fraydie, and even *my own mother* insisted I looked great and should wear it for tonight.

"Only at first glance," she reassures me and pats my hand. "But once your eyes adjust, you realize you're actually wearing clothes."

"Not funny." I laugh and playfully jab her arm.

"Penina!" Fraydie's voice carries from the hallway. "Come *heeeere*."

"Coming!" I call. "Be right back," I tell Ashira, then head to the doorway, careful not to trip in my Cinderella-inspired, see-through heels. "Sorry . . . excuse me . . ." I murmur, threading my way through the crowd, wondering what Fraydie is up to.

I turn the corner and stop abruptly, my pulse hammering like crazy. Sam stands in the front entryway in a simple white button-down, with the sleeves up at the cuffs, and a pair of jeans.

For a moment, I simply drink in the sight of him and what a sight it is. I've come to realize how special a person Sam is, and I'm so lucky to have known him, even for a brief period of time. He's kind and intelligent and has a wicked sense of humor, but he also has an elusive quality that demands respect. When he walks into a room, everyone notices. He's a natural born leader.

"Hi," I say with a dorky wave, forcing myself to relax and keep smiling. "I'm so glad you could make it."

Well, *Sam* clearly thinks I'm naked because his eyes pop out when he sees me, and he spends the next few moments keeping his eyes fixed at some invisible point above my head.

"Where's the lucky man?" he asks, rocking back on his heels and giving me *a look*. The kind of look that says, *"This is a bad idea and I'm disappointed in you."*

"Um." I bite my lip nervously. Sam wouldn't . . . do anything. Would he?

"I'll get him," Fraydie volunteers, a sadistic grin on her face as she hurries off. That girl loves watching reality TV for its drama, so she must be *loving this.*

Maya, in a scandalously short white eyelet dress, heads toward me, holding a shot of whiskey in each hand. "The bride needs to stay hydrated."

I'm more of a straight-up water type of girl, but not tonight. Tonight, I need something stronger to relax and try to forget my troubles, if only for a little while. I take a small sip of whiskey and grimace. *Nasty!* It tastes like cough syrup and snake venom, and makes my eyes water.

She holds up the other shot and gazes around the room. "Up for grabs. Anyone . . . going once . . . going twice . . ."

"Look who I *fooound*," Fraydie singsongs, motioning like a game show host to Zevi. "Zevi, this is Sam. Sam, Zevi."

"Hi, thanks for coming," Zevi nods and smiles.

Sam slaps Zevi on the arm, and Zevi winces slightly. "Congratulations on your engagement. You're a very lucky man."

"Oh, I know." Zevi turns to grin at me, and for a moment I think everything will be fine, but then Zevi murmurs in my ear, "Why does the name Sam sound so familiar?"

I swallow and fiddle with my new diamond tennis bracelet that Zevi gave me as an engagement gift. "He's my boss, so I'm sure I've mentioned his name to you."

"Yeah, makes sense," he agrees, bobbing his head slowly. "But . . . was there an Italian Sam you mentioned?"

Sam arches an eyebrow at me, and with a sudden trepidation, I realize what Zevi means.

Oh crap. Please don't remember, please don't remember.

"Have some cake, dear," I say, taking a piece from Libby's plate and shoving it into his mouth. *Oh my G-d, I'm turning into my mother.*

Sam raises his eyebrows as I shove cake into my fiancé's mouth in the least romantic way possible. Not to blame the victim, but it kind of kills the romance when the person you're feeding keeps shoving your hand away and telling you to stop. I think Zevi got the message to drop the whole "Italian Sam" thing because he skulks back into the men's section. I'm still tense, so I drink from the other shot glass too, figuring the more the merrier.

"Penina?" Libby asks, the sound of her heels clicking against the wood floor. "What's going on? People are wondering where you went."

My eyes travel to the right as Zevi renters the hall, dabbing a napkin at the corners of his mouth.

"Sorry, I got . . . sidetracked." I glance nervously between the two men, suddenly wishing I hadn't invited my boss and coworkers. Seriously, what was I thinking? Sam could easily slip up and say something to Zevi about being gay or Zevi could easily remember why Sam's name rings a bell, and then who knows what might happen? This is a disaster of tsunami proportions waiting to happen. I start to sweat and glance at my watch; shouldn't the party have ended by now?

"Oh, *now* I remember!" Zevi says, snapping his fingers. He turns to me and grins. "We were driving to a restaurant in Flatbush, and you made this sound—" He stops and blinks, then gives me an apologetic look. I'm so terrified that I can't move. My body has become paralyzed with fear.

"What sound?" Fraydie asks, looking confused.

I briefly close my eyes, willing this to be a nightmare.

"No, no. Not a sound. Not exactly." Zevi coughs. He pulls on his earlobe and scrunches his nose. "We were talking about something else, and it rhymed with Sam, but it's not important. So," he claps his hands and looks around the room. "I should be getting back to the men's section. Come on," he says, motioning to Sam. "There's excellent food in there that you have to try. Do you like babka?"

I draw a shaky breath as the men leave, inhaling a combination of relief and anxiety. As the air slowly releases from my cheeks, I notice that Fraydie, Maya, and Libby are all watching me closely.

I frown. "What?"

"Are you okay?" Libby asks, concern etched on her face as she glances at the whiskey in each of my hands. "You seem . . . stressed."

"I'm fine. Totally fine," I lie, then throw my head back and finish the shot. I am the complete opposite of fine—it feels like someone's put me in a box with a lid, and I'm slowly suffocating to death. With all the stress of Libby's house and this engagement and now Sam showing up here . . . it's just *too much*. "I'm going to grab a little fresh air," I say, clearing my throat. Before I start to scream or cry or tear off my clothes and howl at the moon.

"Want me to come with?" Maya asks.

"That's okay." I shake my head and push open the screen door. "I could use some quiet. Don't worry—I'll be back in a few minutes."

I don't plan on going any further than the front steps, but the stillness of the night and the crisp air is so inviting, compared to the noisy chaos inside, that I'm soon halfway down the block. My body feels a little fuzzy, like all the sharp angles have been rounded and it's . . . nice. I lean against a retaining wall and cross my arms, shivering. It's an unusually chilly night for June, and I wish I had thought to grab a sweater. And an umbrella.

I tilt my head back and gaze at the darkening sky with its thick gray clouds. The forecast predicted rain earlier today, but no one was surprised when it didn't happen given our local meteorologist's cocaine habit. And as much as I need alone time, I need to keep dry more. Just a few minutes more, then I'll turn back.

I close my eyes and try to relax. Lately it feels like my life is in a pressure cooker about to explode. So many changes and stressors all happening at once that sometimes I just want to put up my hands and scream. I blame Sam since nothing has been the same since the day I gazed across the NICU and met his tawny eyes.

My eyes fly open at the sound of approaching footsteps.

"Hey, Superwoman."

My heart starts to gallop as Sam strolls toward me, cool, calm and collected, as though nothing's out of the ordinary. As though there's nothing weird about the two of us skipping out on my *vort* or anything. "Did you *follow me here*?"

He ignores my question and stands next to me, with only a few feet separating us. He crosses his ankles and leans against the wall. "A woman shouldn't be walking around alone at night."

I snort and gesture to the sky. "It's not that dark yet, and anyway, what kind of sexist garbage is that? And don't use the fact that you're six foot three million something inches and built like a tank as an excuse. It just makes you easier to shoot at."

He throws his head back and laughs, and the sight of it steals my breath away. Then he does that thing where he tries not to smile. "Have you ever taken self-defense classes?"

I shake my head. "You still haven't answered why you think you're safe to walk around at night."

"My dad was a Marine, and he taught me a thing or two."

My mouth drops open. "Joe was a Marine? I had no idea."

"Most people don't." He folds his arms across his chest and adds, "He doesn't like talking about it, so we mostly ignore that part in our family's history."

"I'm sorry," I say after a moment.

"Don't be." He turns to face me. "I want you to know things about me." He takes a deep breath before he goes on. "And I'd like to know more things about you."

My heart hammers loudly in my chest, and my palms grow slick with sweat. What exactly is going on here? Is Sam saying he's interested in me, or am I reading the signals all wrong? "Because we're friends?"

He nods, then shakes his head, which confuses me even more. "Because I can't stop thinking about you. When I'm driving in the car or standing in line at Target, or even just sitting at home by myself, all I think about is you. And when you're near me"—he swallows—"it's hard to think straight because all I want to do is touch you. And I know it's wrong and complicated because I'm your boss and you're Orthodox, but I'm tired of fighting with myself."

My heart, oh my heart. I'm so shocked and surprised that I can barely make sense of what he said. It feels like a dream that's too good to be true. *He thinks about me? He wants to touch me?*

"And it kills me to see you engaged to another man," he continues. "Even if it is fake."

"You mean—I lick my lips and swallow—"when you said you wanted to touch me . . . like right now, even?"

He looks startled but quickly recovers. "Yes."

"Where?" I ask, my breaths coming out shallow and uneven.

He's quiet for so long that I start to wonder if he's having regrets, but then he says, "I'd start by holding your hands. You have nice hands," he murmurs, his voice coming out low and deep. He inches closer to me, and I get a whiff of his unique scent that seems designed to drive me crazy. "They look like they'd be soft and fit perfectly in mine. Just the right size." He puts his hand next to mine, so close they're almost touching, but not quite.

I feel like I'm under a spell where nothing else matters except this moment in time, the two of us alone, sweet talking about hands.

"Then I'd touch your hair, run my fingers through it. It smells good," he whispers, leaning in. "Like strawberries."

"It's my shampoo," I say breathlessly. "By Suave."

"Mmm," he groans, like I just said something incredibly sexy. "You're killing me."

A small laugh escapes me. "Then what would you do?"

He tilts his head, considering. "I'd rub your earlobes, in small, circular motions."

Earlobes? Seriously?

"Then I'd massage the skin between your ear and neck—" He's so close to me now that I feel his warm breath on my neck. "After that," he whispers, gazing down at my lips, "I'd kiss you. First with my lips, then with my tongue. And then . . . ." He pauses and smiles. "I'd kiss every square inch of your body."

I gulp, my eyes wide and mesmerized, my chest heaving with every breath I take. "That sounds . . . slightly ticklish?" A drop of rain falls onto my dress, then another hits my neck, but it doesn't matter. There's nowhere else I'd rather be than alone in the rain with Sam.

His left eyebrow arches as a slow smile appears on his face. "You ticklish, Superwoman?"

I stare at his lips. "Only one way to find out."

He swallows and his Adam's apple protrudes from the movement. The golden specks in his eyes churn with an intensity unlike anything I've seen before, and slowly, ever so slowly, his lips lower, almost touching—

We both startle as Sam's cell phone rings. "Keila calling," Siri announces.

My mouth drops open, and I stare at him in shock. How did I forget about Keila? And more importantly, how could *he* have forgotten about her?

There's a clap of thunder overhead, followed by sheets of rain. I take a few steps back as he tucks his phone inside the pocket of his jeans, then gazes at me questioningly, as though he senses something has changed. Yeah, no kidding, something has changed! It pains me to even glance in his direction now—the cheater. How is it possible not to appreciate the woman who could easily rival any Victoria's Secret model and hold her own in any intellectual conversation, and loves children? Keila is the compilation of everything a man could ever want, so why would he make things complicated by hitting on me?

"What's wrong?" he says.

"Um, you have a girlfriend, remember?" I say, throwing up my hands. "Did that slip your mind?"

His face registers surprise and confusion, so he's obviously a very adept actor. "What are you talking about?"

"Keila!"

He shakes his head, like he can't believe what he's hearing. "Whoa. You are way off—"

"Don't even try denying it! I've seen all the Instagram posts, the two of you in New York together when you said you were on a 'business trip,'" I say with air quotes. Anger pumps through my veins, and all the frustration and fear I've been carrying inside me bursts like a flood bursting through a dam. "Shame on you for flirting, and shame on me for encouraging it. But," I add, unable to control myself, "more shame on you because you started it." A second clap of thunder rolls overhead, but neither one of us seems to notice.

My breaths are fast and shallow, and there's a tightness in my chest. I clench my hands into fists and realize that I'm shaking.

"Did you cheat on your wife too? Because that would paint a very different picture." His mouth drops open and we're both soaking wet, but I still have more to say. "And what were you hoping to gain by this, whatever *this* is?" I say, my hand motioning between us. "Some cheap thrills? Were you turned on by the fact that you've never had an Ortho-dox girl before? Did you want to see how far you could get me to go? Devirginize the religious freak?"

His eyes are murderous as he puts up his hand. "Stop right there—"

"And even *if* you were single and not a lying, womanizing douche-bag," I continue, my voice rising with emotion, "I couldn't date you! You're not Orthodox! Do you actually see yourself keeping kosher and Shabbos and the family purity stuff? Well? Do you?"

He closes his lips and scowls, but doesn't speak. And that's when I know. This whole thing was nothing but a game to him. *I've been noth-ing but a game to him.*

We stare at each other, radiating mutual loathing, until Sam breaks the silence. "You know what I think? I think you're scared." I make a face, but he keeps talking, "You're scared of letting yourself fall for someone because you have too much responsibility as it is."

"Are you high?"

"You're the on-call babysitter and fundraiser for one sister while putting out small fires from the other one. You think your parents are emotionally fragile, so you shoulder everyone's problems instead of leaning on them for support. You hold yourself accountable as though it's your obligation to figure out a way to save their financial problems or their marriage or whatever, when it's not." His eyes pierce through mine. "You deserve to have your own life. And marrying a gay man is just as cowardly as not getting married at all."

A flash of lightening charges the sky, but neither one of us seems to care if we get electrocuted. His hair is splattered against his forehead, and his designer clothes are completely soaked through, and I'm not in any better shape.

He points his finger at me and shouts over the claps of thunder, "You have no idea how special you are. You have no clue. You've convinced yourself that you're somehow less deserving of happiness because you can't have children. And that is the biggest piece of bullshit I've ever heard. You're the *opposite* of damaged!" he yells, waving his hands. "You have the biggest heart of anyone I've ever met. You're kind and generous and so fucking gorgeous that I can't think straight when I'm around you." Rain drips into his mouth and down his face, and something must be wrong with me, because I've never been more attracted to him than this moment. "Do you think I'm not scared shitless?" he continues. "I swore I'd never let myself fall for another woman, and yet, here I am, like a lovesick idiot. *I am not happy about this either, okay?*" His eyes are bulging and there's practically steam coming out of his ears.

A whole spectrum of emotions surges through me and I have no idea how to process them all. My hair is dripping wet, and my dress is completely soaked and probably see-through, and Sam looks like he wants to kill someone—probably me. "Why are you so angry?"

"Because it would never work between us!"

My eyes well up with tears, and I lift my hands in the air. "Then why are you even here telling me all this?"

"Because I'm an idiot!"

My heart skips a beat as I stare at him, open-mouthed. "What do you want from me? Am I supposed to turn away from my religion to suit your lifestyle?"

He stares at me silently.

I shake my head as disappointment courses through me. That's his solution? "I will *never* change who I am"—I pound my chest—"to please someone else. Not for you and not for any man. Stay away from me, Sam Kleinfeld. You're a liar and a cheater, and Keila doesn't deserve that, even though she is so perfect that it makes me sick," I say, my eyes welling up with tears. "And FYI, I quit! For real, this time!"

I take off my shoes and start to run. Rain splatters into my eyes, mixing with the tears that trickle down my face, forcing me to blink repeatedly to see where I'm going. My lungs are burning as if they're on fire, and I stop running and sink to the ground. I look around and real-ize that I'm at the top of the knolly field across from the library, about a mile from my parents' house, and only then do I remember the *vort*. I'm the worst fake bride ever.

My throat is dry and my head pounds, signaling the start of a migraine—because obviously I needed more misery in my life.

My tears flow unchecked as I gaze up at the inky night sky, feeling sick to my stomach and more alone than I have in a very long time.

CHAPTER TWENTY-FIVE

"My mother was right: When you've got nothing left, all you can do is get into silk underwear and start reading Proust."

—*Jane Birkin*

Last night went down as the most awkward *vort* in history, and I have no doubt that Zevi and I are the talk of the town. My mother started to panic when I didn't come back, so she and the remaining guests started a search party, like one of those murder mystery games that people play. And unluckily for me, I was discovered by Fraydie, who was streaming the whole thing live from her phone.

I hate my life.

The sun peeking through my blinds is an insult to the inner turmoil I'm facing. And I'm facing lots of it. I tossed and turned all night, crying and feeling sorry for myself, although my life is having a moment, to put it lightly. To recap: I no longer have a job; my fiancé, family, and the community as a whole now think I'm a whack job; and there's a huge, gaping hole in my heart at the thought of never seeing Sam again—even though he is a lying, cheating piece of butt.

My ears perk up at the sound of my apartment door opening, followed by my sister's voice. "Hello?"

Ugh, no, a person. Right when I'm introverting.

Libby has a key to my apartment (and obviously too much spare time on her hands), but I only have myself to blame since I'm the one that gave it to her. That's the downside of giving out keys; people assume they can waltz in and check on you whenever they're the slightest bit worried.

"Where's the baby?" I say, sitting up in bed.

"At Ma's," she says, handing me a drink from Starbucks. My heart lifts ever so slightly; I guess it's acceptable to interrupt my introversion time as long as they bring coffee.

"Two Splendas?" she asks, tapping the individual packets against her wrist.

I shake my head. "One's good. Thanks."

She hands it to me and after I say a blessing, I take a small sip and wince. Too hot.

"Well?" she says, making herself comfortable on the other side of my bed.

"Too hot," I say, putting it on my bedside table to give it some time to cool off.

"I wasn't asking about the coffee." She rolls her eyes. "What happened last night? One minute you're smiling and everything is normal, and the next you leave the party, and half the community is looking for you."

I groan and rub my forehead. "It's too early in the morning for this. Can you come back later? Like in three days?"

"No, and ten o'clock is not early." She stands up, moves to the window, and pulls open the blinds. "Now start talking."

I use my hand to shield my eyes from the bright rays of light. The woman obviously missed her calling as an interrogator-slash-torturer. "How did you even know I'd be here and not at work?" I ask, reaching for my coffee.

"I got an anonymous tip."

Maya, probably. I wonder if Sam announced that I quit or if he's waiting to see my next move. I take a tentative sip, then cradle it in my hands.

"It can't be that bad, whatever it is."

Hah! I laugh because it's that or start crying again.

"Tell me, already!"

There is absolutely no way I'm going to tell my sister about what happened with Sam last night. It's bad enough that it keeps replaying in my own brain, and I don't need to go over it with someone else.

"Anytime you're ready, just start talking," Libby says.

"Okay, okay." I sigh. I put the cup on my nightstand, then cross my arms. "Basically, Sam thinks that marrying Zevi is a big mistake, which he's already made very clear to me. When he followed me out last night, we had a big argument, and I quit."

Libby's big brown eyes widen to the size of dinner plates. "Oh my gosh, are you serious?"

I nod. "He's a big jerk, and I hope I never see him again." *Liar.*

Libby lowers her face into the palm of her hand. "This is something I would have expected from Fraydie."

I scowl at her, even though it's true. Fraydie is the impetuous, act-first-think-later person in our family, whereas I've always been . . . not boring exactly, but *steady*. Responsible. Reliable. The complete opposite of rash.

"Penina, what were you thinking?"

"I don't know, but it doesn't matter," I say, rubbing an itch on my arm. It wouldn't surprise me in the least if I end up getting hives from all the recent stress. "I'm getting married in six weeks."

"True." She stares at me thoughtfully. "Why is he so against you marrying Zevi?"

I shrug, picking at a loose thread on my bedspread. No way am I going to tell her what he said. "Maybe because he's had a bad experience with marriage, and he thinks it's ridiculous at how fast Orthodox Jews date and get married."

She sighs and crosses her arms. "Well," she adds, "at least you know he cares. Do you think he gets so passionate about the life choices all his employees make?"

I try to imagine him getting that worked up if, instead of me, it were Maya engaged to a gay man, but somehow don't see it. "I don't know. Maybe," I say, not meeting her eyes.

"Do you think he likes you?" she asks, tilting her head.

I almost choke on my drink and try to act shocked. "What is this, second grade?" I snort and roll my eyes.

"A lot of men don't mature past second grade," she replies, lifting her hands in the air, "so yes. It's possible. And besides, how could he *not* like you? You're kind and funny and beautiful. Fun to talk to. And loyal. Of course, he likes you. It makes perfect sense to me now."

I laugh at the fiery seriousness in her expression. Every girl, every woman, every *human* deserves to have a sister like Libby—the kind that sees the best in you and builds you up instead of tearing you down. "I love you, Libs."

"I love you too." She stands up, then abruptly sits back down. "Are you sure that's the only thing bothering you?"

My mouth goes dry as I fight down the urge to confide in her, the way I always have. I so badly want to tell her the truth about Zevi and how terrifying it's been that she might lose her house. Libby doesn't know it, but Natan has agreed to meet with Zevi and me after dinner tonight, so he can go over the exact numbers with Zevi. "Yes," I nod. "That's it."

"Okay then." She moves to the bedroom door and places her hand on the knob. "I'll see you later?"

"Yup." I smile, putting down my cup. I lay my head against my pillow, listening to her soft footsteps on the carpet as she makes her way out. The apartment door opens and shuts, then I hear the key turning the lock.

I'm doing the right thing by not telling her. I'm not selfish enough to risk her knowing the truth just because I want her advice.

But apparently, I *am* that selfish because the next moment I'm flinging the bedspread off and jumping out of bed, not bothering to put on my slippers. I race to the door, unlock it, and dash into the hallway, running toward the elevator. Disappointment courses through me when Libby isn't there.

The stairs! I totally forgot that Libby likes to take the stairs. I throw open the door and shout at the top of my lungs, "Libby, stop!"

A woman coming down the staircase shrieks and clutches her heart. "Oh! Oh, you scared me," she says. Normally, I'd immediately apologize, take her pulse, invite her back to my place, and make a pot of coffee, but I'm too deep in my own problems right now.

"Penina?" Libby's voice floats up from below the stairwell. "What's going on?"

"I have to talk to you," I holler. "Can you come back?"

Silence. And then she says, *"Okaaaay."*

The woman I frightened passes by, muttering something about millennials. "Sorry!" I call after her, but other than that, I feel no desire to go out of my way to make it up to her. *Take that, Sam. So much for me being responsible for other people's happiness.*

Libby laughs when she sees me. "No wonder that woman screamed. You're a mess."

Once we're back inside my apartment and I look in the mirror, I know exactly what she means. My cheeks are stained with black eyeliner and mascara from last night because I was too depressed to do anything except change into pajamas and climb into bed.

"So, what changed between now and two minutes ago?" Libby asks, dumping her purse on my couch and sitting down.

I swallow, suddenly nervous. Now that she's here and I made the decision to tell her, I'm seized with uncertainty. "Do you want something to drink?"

She shakes her head and pats the cushion next to her. "Come talk to me. You know you can tell me anything, right?"

"Yeah, I know." I sit on the couch, and turn to face her, pulling my legs underneath me. "I didn't tell you the whole story about why Sam doesn't want me to marry Zevi. This is a big secret, so you absolutely can't say anything to anyone, but—" I take a deep breath and say, "Zevi's gay."

"Gay?" I nod, but she shakes her head. "Are we talking about *your Zevi*, the one you're marrying in six weeks?"

"Yes. That one." I watch as her face changes expressions, from shock to confusion, to uncertainty.

"But you don't know that, right?" she says, tilting her head, the way a dog does when he hears the word *treat*. "You just suspect it."

"No, Libby," I say gently. "He is. And I've met his boyfriend."

She stares at me, puzzled. "I don't understand."

I start to explain the situation with his mother and everything, but she cuts me off with an impatient, "But why did *you* agree to do this?"

"Zevi has a lot of money. Like, a lot." I scratch my neck and add, "Enough to . . . save a house."

It doesn't take long for Libby's face to register understanding, and her eyes fill with tears. "You idiot," she mumbles, reaching for the tissue box on my coffee table. "No, Penina." She cries and shakes her head. "No. Absolutely not."

Like a chain reaction, I start to cry, even though it's a miracle that I have any tears left. "It's the only way," I croak.

"But it's a lie." Her face is anguished and flushed with pain. "A really big one. It's not right."

"But think of the kids, Libby. How traumatic it would be for them to leave their friends and all of us and move to a strange place they've never been before."

Her phone pings with an incoming text. She reads it, then looks at me with a funny expression.

"What? Why are you looking at me like that?"

"Pen," she says slowly, "have you ever thought about adopting a baby?"

My breath catches. What? "W-what?"

"You love children," she says, looking excited. "It's the perfect solution. This is so amazing, I can't believe it didn't occur to me earlier. Of course, it's only been a few days since she changed her mind, and with everything going on, it simply never occurred to me, although I need to make sure it's okay with her, of course. But how perfect it would be!" She stands up, beaming, then says, "Listen, I need to make a private phone call, and you absolutely cannot eavesdrop, okay?"

Things start clicking into place. "It's Mimi's baby, isn't it?"

She sighs. "Yes."

"You knew she was pregnant the whole time?" She nods. "Why did she tell you?"

"I used to babysit her when I was in high school," Libby reminds me. "She feels comfortable with me."

I'm still having trouble wrapping my head around the fact that my quiet, soft-spoken, modestly dressed cousin was living a double life. I didn't see that coming at all. Fraydie, yes, but *Mimi*? I don't know her too well given our age difference and because she's so quiet, but still. A fourteen-year-old having multiple sex partners seems like a cry for help. "Can you make sure Mimi sees someone?"

Libby nods. "I'm working on it."

My heart refuses to slow down, even though I keep reminding it not to get my hopes up. Mimi could very well change her mind about keeping the baby.

"Would she be okay with me being the one to potentially adopt it?"

"That's what I'm going to find out," she says excitedly.

I laugh when she breaks into a run—which, I should point out, I haven't seen her do since we were children. Then I hear the click of my bedroom door lock. Adopting a child had always been something I'd wanted to do, but it seemed about as likely a dream as winning the lottery because (A) it costs a ton of money to get the child in the first place; and (B) raising him or her costs a ton of money; and (C) it would break my heart if I wasn't able to provide for a child properly.

But everything is different now because I'm marrying a rich man. I draw a deep breath as I realize how absolutely perfect this is. My eyes well up with emotion as I picture Jack, Zevi, and me coparenting. This child will be so loved and cherished. It would be a dream come true, a dream I barely allowed myself to think of, but now—I can definitely picture it now.

The bedroom door opens, and I suck in a deep breath. It feels like my life is riding on whatever Libby is about to say. Her footsteps are slow, which is probably a bad sign. My heart deflates, but there are tons of children in the world that need a home, I remind myself. I don't need this mystery baby, even though I've already grown emotionally attached to it in my head.

Libby comes into the living room and sighs. "She said she needs time to think about it. Which isn't a no," she adds. I get the feeling that she's trying to make herself feel better, that she was just as excited as I was, if not more. "She doesn't want to give away any details about her, you know . . . situation. Unless, she decides yes, of course."

I nod, disappointment welling up inside me. "I get it."

"Yeah," she says with a small smile, and shrugs. "We'll just wait and pray that she makes the right choice for the baby." She gazes at me for a moment, then sits down on the couch. "We never finished what we were talking about earlier."

"But actually," I say, thinking out loud, "I need to marry Zevi in order to adopt any baby."

"*What?* No, you don't," Libby says sternly. "There are lots of wonderful single-parent families—"

"That's not why," I say, rubbing my neck. "I don't make enough to support two people."

"Hold on—let's think about this," she says, her lips pursed in concentration. "I've got *plenty* of hand-me-downs to give to you, not just clothes, but equipment and baby toys too, and all that will save you tons of money right there."

"Okay, but childcare is expensive, and I don't see Gina or any manager being okay with a baby hanging around. Oh, never mind." I deflate. "I don't even have a job."

Libby hesitates and taps her chin. "You'll find another job. And I'll watch it."

"From Israel?"

"We're not going. In the end, we decided to move into Ma and Tatty's for the time being, until we land on our feet. Besides," she grins, "it won't be so bad having three babysitters around. See? Solution solved."

I consider for a moment. "Maybe it could work," I say slowly.

Libby nods. "Children don't need lots of toys and shiny things. They need love and a stable, safe environment. It's going to be fine. Better than fine." Her face turns serious, and she adds, "But Penina, you need to call off the engagement."

I stand up and start to pace, my hands on my head. "I don't know, I don't know."

"Is lying to a dying woman the right thing to do?"

"I don't know!" I throw up my hands. "Maybe? In this case."

"No, Penina." Libby's voice is firm. "It isn't. Everything about this situation is wrong. Zevi needs to come out to his mother, for his own good."

"So, she can get angry and die hating him?"

Libby stands up and shakes her head. "A real mother always loves her child. *Always.* She might disagree with the way he lives or the choices he makes, but she wouldn't hate him."

"She might," I say, my heart beating rapidly. "You don't know that."

"You're right. I don't." She picks up her purse. "But I know that if she chooses hate over love, then she never truly loved him in the first place."

Maybe that is exactly what Zevi is afraid of discovering, I realize suddenly.

She gives me a tight hug, then steps back. "I know you'll do the right thing. For Zevi, and for *you*."

CHAPTER TWENTY-SIX

"Be the designer of your own destiny."

—*Oscar de la Renta*

I recheck the time on my phone and nibble my bottom lip. Zevi was supposed to be at the coffee shop ten minutes ago, and I'm pretty sure that every moment that passes without his arrival causes irreparable damage to my heart.

A hot mom with expertly woven blond highlights and designer label clothing sashays past me, one hand clutching a Stella McCartney purse and the other cradling her stomach, which looks as though it's been stuffed with a basketball. Her face pinches in concentration as she reads from her phone. Without lifting her gaze, she maneuvers through the maze of furniture in the room and dumps her purse on an empty table before settling into a chair; all in all, an impressive display of balance considering her four-inch stilettos.

Louboutins in case you were wondering. I glance down at my outfit and wonder if it's good enough to post on Instagram. A simple three-quarter-length-sleeve a striped navy-blue Michael Stars T-shirt, hot-pink skirt, and wedge espadrilles that've already caused blisters, based on the pain of my pinky toes. I pulled my hair into a loose, high ponytail that sticks out through the hole of my Minnesota Twin's baseball hat.

The shop door opens and I crane my neck to see if it's Zevi, but it's just a couple of teenagers. I take an unsteady breath and try to sort through the barrage of emotions that have been plaguing me these last few hours. When Zevi first entered the picture, everything seemed so simple: marry the gay guy and fulfill his mother's dying wish then pass Go, collect the money, and save my sister's house. But at some point along the way, things got a little hazy. As much as I want the money to save Libby's house, I know now that living a lie isn't the right way to go about it. And while I like the idea of fulfilling a dying woman's wish, Zevi might have regrets if he never tells his mother the truth, because a love based on conditions isn't really love at all.

And then there's Sam, stubborn and insightful, arrogant and much too handsome, whose face frequents my dreams at night and who's the one I wake up thinking about. But while I was slowly falling in love with him—at least, the person I thought he was—he was just plotting ways to cheat on Keila.

Not that he doesn't have his good side. The first time I saw him, he was being led around the NICU with other philanthropic bigwigs, though he's never talked or bragged about it. And if I were to bring it up, he'd probably just raise an eyebrow and ask what my point is.

He's a good listener too. I remember how his head was bent in concentration when I was pouring out all of my secrets, never once interrupting me. And I'll never forget how he looked when he opened up to me about his marriage. He was my friend, I realize. And putting aside the cheating aspect, I *like* who he is; I could spend hours talking to him.

I take a sip of my almond milk latte as a shadow crosses my peripheral vision, and Zevi steps into view. Today he's sporting the *Brokeback Mountain, Jewish Edition*, look with a black felt Stetson tipped low on his head, a plaid shirt tucked into whitewashed jeans, and a pair of traditional cowboy boots. If I didn't know any better, I'd think he'd just came from rounding up a herd of cattle or branding some pigs.

He sinks down into a leather armchair, removes his hat, and places it over his knees, exposing a tiny suede yarmulke in neon tangerine. I swiftly recategorize him, from Heath Ledger to a Jew with avant-garde fashion taste.

"Hey," he says, looking tired. I can immediately tell that something about him is different today, and I realize after a moment what it is—he's lacking his customary joie de vivre that I've come to expect. Maybe he has a hangover. Or maybe he senses that I'm about to call off the engagement.

"Dark roast okay?" I say, handing him a Styrofoam cup.

"Perfect. Thanks." He reaches for some sugar packets and taps them on his other hand. "I've been worried about you."

"I know. I'm really sorry about last night," I say, leaning forward, hoping he can tell how much I mean it. "I don't know what came over me. Well, actually, I do." I laugh awkwardly and rub the back of my neck. "But that's why I wanted to meet with you."

"Okay," he says slowly, looking like someone who was just told they need a root canal.

My stomach clenches with nerves, and I find myself wavering; I hate letting people down, and even though I know it wasn't a real engagement in the sense that we didn't love each other, I had still promised to marry him.

"I can't go through with it." I meet his gaze and whisper, "I'm so sorry."

He shakes his head like he's struggling to process what I've said. "But why? Did I do something wrong?"

"No, no," I say quickly. "It's nothing like that."

His eyes dart around the room, like the answer is pinned on one of the walls. "It's because of Sam, isn't it?" he asks. "Everything was fine until he showed up. What did he say to you?"

I stall for a moment by taking a drink of my coffee, then do the classic Jew move of answering a question with a question. "Do you really think your mother would hate you if you came out?"

He tilts his head toward the ceiling and groans. "I don't want to go there."

"Zevi, I don't want to tell you how to live your life, because I know how that feels and it's awful." I pause. "But sometimes we *need* that. We need to hear the things that hurt us because those are the things that help us grow."

"It's not that—" He stops abruptly, and I notice his eyes look watery. "I'm not afraid of her hating me. It's more that—he pauses and swallows hard—"she's been through enough in her life, with my dad leaving and Ashira's divorce and everything. I just . . . I don't want to be the one to add any more pain, you know?"

My own throat gets thick as I think about what a hard life she's had. So, that's what it's all about in the end. He doesn't want to be another disappointment; he simply wants to make her happy by giving her what he thinks she wants. "I know. But Zevi," I add, "I think you're not giving your mom enough credit. I mean, do you think she's happy with all the choices Leah has made? Or Ashira?"

"It's not the same," he growls, and I nod in understanding. It isn't the same, but I guess I have more faith in his mom than he does.

"When I was a kid," I say, "I once fantasized about these red tennis shoes I saw in a store's window display, but my mom said no because I already had a pair of tennis shoes." I stop to roll my eyes, because that type of logic never flies with a fashionista, not at ten years old and not at eighty. "I longed for these shoes. I planned what outfits I'd pair them with, told all my friends about them. They were my *dream* shoes." Zevi takes a sip of coffee and nods, but looks bored. "Anyway, by the time I earned the money to buy them, it was too late. The season was over, and they weren't getting any more in. I was devastated. But then, a pair of red cowgirl boots on a display shelf caught my eye and well"—I clutch my heart—"obviously, they were way cooler than the tennis shoes."

"Why are you telling me this?" Zevi asks tersely.

"People are adaptable. Your mother will be okay." I clear my throat and smile. "You just have to be strong enough to give her the chance."

We're both quiet for a while, lost in our own thoughts. "What about your sister's house?" he asks abruptly. "Did something happen that she's not losing it in the end?"

"No," I say, shaking my head. "She's going to lose it."

"And you still want to call it off?" he asks in a disbelieving voice. "Give up the five million dollars?"

"I don't *want* to," I admit, meeting his gaze. "But I have to. I can't accept blood money."

Zevi shakes his head, signaling his disagreement. A toddler runs up to Zevi and giggles, but he doesn't seem to notice. I wish I knew the right words to convince him to be his authentic self, no matter what his mother's reaction is. Because living a lie isn't really living—it's just existing.

"Here," I say, pulling the ring off my finger and handing it to him. He takes it wordlessly and drops it into the pocket of his plaid shirt. "I hope you can forgive me one day."

He doesn't reply, doesn't even look at me, but I get it. I'd be pretty upset too if I were him.

I stand up and pick up my purse and coffee. "Let's keep in touch, okay? For real. I'm not just saying that. You're my friend and I care about you." With a deep sigh, I turn to leave, but in the next moment, I remember to add, "And thank you, Zevi."

He lifts his head from the hand that was cupping it. "For what?"

I can't even begin to encapsulate how much this experience has meant to me. How do I explain that meeting him was a turning point in my life? That because of this fake engagement, I've learned to trust that my family will take care of their problems. That I've realized it's okay—no, it's *essential* to focus on my own needs. That being part of his family, even briefly, was an honor, and that those memories are forever etched in my brain.

"For all of it."

CHAPTER TWENTY-SEVEN

"Real fashion change comes from real changes in real life. Every-thing else is just decoration."

—Tom Ford

I wouldn't say I feel *happy* as I leave the coffee shop. It's hard knowing that I let Zevi down, even if it was for his own good. I hope he'll come out to his family and tell them the truth about our engagement, but I have a bad feeling that he might just make up another outrageous lie instead. Perhaps he'll say he found me in a compromised situation with some Italian dude named Sam. *If only.*

My chest tightens as I think about last night. I cross the street, head toward my parked car, and pull out my keys. I literally lost my mind—first by almost kissing Sam, then for screaming at him like a total lunatic. Not saying he didn't deserve it, but I shouldn't have lost my cool like that. My father always says that the moment a person raises their voice, they've already lost the fight.

I unlock my car door and get inside. I still need to come clean to my parents about Zevi, and my stomach churns knowing how disappointed they'll be. I hope they'll be able to see past the deception part and focus on the reason behind doing what I did, but still . . . a lie is a lie, and they raised me better than that.

I turn on the car and reverse out of my tight parking spot. But first, I need to ask—perhaps beg—Sam for my job back, at least until I can find somewhere else to work. There's no way I can stay there long term after what happened.

I head onto the main road and instruct Siri to call Sam. It rings and rings, until it finally hits his voicemail. I almost leave a message but then decide against it. This is going to be one of those situations where you have to read a person's face to feel it out; that way if I get a bad vibe, I'll know not to ask. Worst-case scenario: I can't find work and am forced to move into my parents' house along with Libby's family. Not ideal, but at least I'd have food to eat and a roof over my head.

I brake at a red light and start to laugh because it's so pathetic. My poor parents had talked about downsizing and moving into an apartment, but it doesn't look like that'll be happening any time soon. I laugh so hard that my stomach starts to hurt, and the car behind me honks to let me know the light is green.

If Gina tries to give me a hard time when I get to the store, I'll explain how I've been a faithful employee of that store for over six years, so I deserve one day of playing hooky. And what a fun day it's been, I think, and giggle some more.

After parking in my usual spot, I open the front doors and see Maya, whose eyebrows shoot up to the center of her forehead. She calls after me, but I'm on a one-track mission, and nothing is going to slow me down. I knock on Sam's door, but when I don't hear him answer, I turn the knob and go inside.

It's empty. I look around confused, turning in a circle, trying to figure out why his desk is clean and all his pictures and mementos are no longer there.

"He's gone," Maya says quietly.

I startle, not realizing she had come in. "What do you mean?" I ask slowly, a bad feeling stirring in my gut.

"He came in this morning and announced that his father missed working, and that Joe is taking over. Sucks, doesn't it?"

My mouth drops open. "Joe's coming back?" She nods. "But what's Sam going to do?"

"That's the weird part," she says, lifting her hands. "He said he needed time away. He wants to travel the world and all that." She collapses into a chair and mutters, "Did he offer to take me with him? No, he did not."

Travel the world?

I put my hands on either side of my head and start to pace. I can't believe this is happening. I mean, yes, I screamed at him, but who quits their company to travel the world because their feelings were hurt? *The very next day? Who does that?*

And what about—

"What about Keila?" I ask, stopping my frantic pacing to look at her. "Is she going too?" Though I can't imagine her leaving the job she loves so much for an impromptu vacation, even if it is around the world.

Maya frowns. "Why would she? Do you not remember our conversation from two days ago?"

Obviously not. "Refresh my memory?"

"I *knew* you weren't paying attention! You were like 'Uh-huh-ing' the whole time," Maya says as she takes out her phone and starts tapping. "Luckily for you, I'm a forgiving person so I won't hold it against you . . . one second . . . here it is."

I take the phone and peer at the Instagram post from Keila's page. It's a picture of her in the red tank top and white shorts, but instead of Sam next to her on the boat, she's in the arms of a tattooed man who's planting a solid kiss on her lips. The caption says *Can't imagine life without you @spike_duran.* My heart accelerates as I swipe the screen to see the other pictures attached to the post. There are a few group pictures, plus the original one she posted of her and Sam together on the boat. I'm starting to get a really bad feeling now, the kind I get when I've seriously messed up. "Maybe she's dating both of them," I say, grasping at straws.

"No one's *that* lucky," she replies, rolling her eyes. "Besides, she and Sam are cousins."

Cousins? I collapse into a chair next and stare at her in shock. "How do you know?"

Maya makes a "give-it-here" hand motion and takes her phone back. "I figured it out by checking out this one girl that commented on the boat picture, because she did the hashtag #PrettyGenes, so then I was, like, *say whaaat?* Then I looked at her account, and she's got some family reunion pictures. Remember that picture in front of Belvedere Castle with Keila and Sam and some older people?"

I nod, already hating where this is going.

"It was their grandparents' big anniversary party. And she put all these annoying hashtags with it, like #Family and #Grandparents and #ThreeGenerations and a lot more. The girl has a serious hashtag addiction—"

I groan and bury my face in my hands. *"Why didn't you tell me?"*

"I *did*!" she says, her eyes huge with innocence, "but you were all stressed out and self-absorbed." She tilts her head, scrutinizing me. "What's going on with you?"

I need to get out of here. I need to talk to Sam. Preferably sooner rather than later. I jump out of the chair and race to the door before realizing I have no idea where to find him and I seriously doubt he'll answer the phone for me. "Where is he now?"

"Sam?"

Who else? "Yes, Sam," I say through clenched teeth.

"Probably the airport."

My head whips back. *"Already?"*

"He said his plane leaves this afternoon." She stands up and places her hands on her hips. "What is going on with you?"

"I'll tell you later," I call over my shoulder and run down the hall. Unfortunately, I nearly collide with Gina, who looks like she wants to kill someone, and I'm pretty sure that someone is *me*.

"There's a *customer* in the showroom, *Penina*." Her nostrils flare, and her voice burns like acid on my skin. "Get out there and do what you get paid to do. And *where is Maya*?"

I could stop and explain, but that would take precious seconds away from my current mission, and frankly, I'm just not feeling cooperative today. "Bye Gina," I say, picking up speed.

"What do you mean 'bye'?" she says, her voice rising in volume. "Don't you *dare* walk away from me! Get *back* here."

"Someone will be with you shortly!" I call to the bewildered customer as I blaze past.

I try not to hyperventilate as I drive, but it seems like everyone behind the wheel today is over the age of ninety, and it's making the drive twice as long as normal. *"C'mon, c'mon,"* I moan, hitting the steering wheel in frustration. And to make things worse, Sam's phone keeps going straight to voicemail, and I have no idea what I'm going to do once I get there—I can't just waltz in the airport and chase him down.

But I can call the airport!

"Call airport," I shout to Siri.

"Which one would you like to call?" she asks in that fake, syrupy voice of hers. *"I found fourteen."*

Of course, she did. That bitch. She *knows* which one I mean. I grind my teeth as I pass a dairy truck, then tell her Minneapolis–St. Paul International Airport. The third time is the charm, and after a few more steps, I'm finally talking to a live person.

"Hi," I say breathlessly, "I need you to stop someone named Sam Kleinfeld from getting on a plane."

There's a brief pause. "Do you suspect this man of posing a threat to others?"

"No, no, nothing like that," I say quickly before she gets the wrong idea and alerts security. "It's just that we had an argument last night, and I said things I didn't mean, and now he's getting on a plane, and I never got to apologize, and he's not answering his phone—"

"All I can do is page him, ma'am. What's his name?"

"Sam Kleinfeld," I say, merging onto highway 5. Three more minutes to go. *Please, please let them catch him in time.*

I follow the signs for the airport and switch lanes following the "Departures" sign while on hold. I hate myself sometimes—I really do. How could I throw all those accusations at him without even giving him an opportunity to respond? I was prosecutor, judge, and jury, declaring him guilty based on my own misguided thoughts.

I slow my car down to a sedate thirty-five miles per hour because the cops here are like hawks. Bored hawks. Am I still on hold or have we been disconnected? I glance at my phone and see the seconds ticking by, so it isn't that. I move to the slow lane to buy me some more time.

"Ma'am, are you still there?"

My heart jumps into my throat. "Yes!"

"I'm sorry, we weren't able to locate him."

I squeeze my eyes shut as despair consumes me. *Why didn't I see this coming?* Why didn't I prepare for something like this to happen instead of allowing myself to get my hopes up? But it wasn't supposed to happen this way. I was supposed to track him down and apologize for the awful things I said, and then he was going to forgive me, and . . . and. . . . Everything was going to be okay.

But *now?*

My eyes fly open at the sound of a car honking from behind me. "Get moving," a cop with a whistle shouts, making wild hand motions at me. With a start, I realize there's a line of cars piled up behind me, and a couple of people on the sidewalk are throwing disapproving glances my way.

I put on my signal and merge into traffic, brushing the tears from my cheeks.

"Can I help you with anything else, ma'am?" says the woman on the other end of the phone.

"No," I whisper. "Thank you." I end the call and let my tears flow unchecked. I drive blindly, not sure where I'm going or what to do next. Within the time span of twenty-four hours, my life has turned upside down, and I'd give anything for a redo. There's an ache in my chest, but this time I know it has nothing to do with indigestion or eating too quickly.

It's the pain of my heart breaking in two.

CHAPTER TWENTY-EIGHT

"I can't concentrate in flats."

—*Victoria Beckham*

Several weeks pass in a haze of disappointment and sadness, and every day that passes where I don't hear from Sam convinces me that whatever short-lived thing happened between us is long over and done with. He's moved on, and I have no choice but to do the same. The only problem is that it isn't happening. People say that time heals all wounds, but they never specify a time line, do they? What if I never get over him? What if I end up being like one of those sad old ladies in the nursing home who never got married because her boyfriend was killed during the Second World War and she was never able to move on?

Not that I plan on marrying. I've completely given up on that and had an honest, assertive conversation with my parents, in which I informed them that I was done dating. It went as well as could be expected, meaning my father patted my head and walked back to his study while my mother burst into tears and said I was ruining my life. I was glad I had dragged Libby along to help buffer me.

If only there was some antidote to heartbreak or an amnesia pill that could wipe out the memory of Sam. Why hasn't anyone invented that yet? What are all these genius scientists with the long ponytails doing anyway?

I pull up into my parent's driveway and park next to Libby's minivan. I grab my purse and climb out of the car. My parents and Libby know I haven't been the same since the night of the *vort*, but I can't handle their well-meaning advice. They think I'm going through a phase because of what happened with Zevi, who I am admittedly worried about. He still hasn't answered any of my texts or calls, and I'm starting to lose hope that he ever will.

And as for Mimi's baby that I grew emotionally attached to, Libby says she wants her parents to raise it, even though they're older and not in the best of health. So, there goes that. And according to my research, adoption cost in Minnesota is typically twenty-three thousand to twenty-five thousand dollars, and I can't even fathom ever having the ability to save up that amount.

"Hello?" I call out, letting myself through the front door. "Anyone home?"

"In here," my mother responds, her voice coming from the kitchen. "Are you hungry, sweetie?"

I set my purse and keys on the table in the hall, then glance at my reflection in the mirror. My face looks thinner than normal, and there are dark circles under my eyes. It's been a while since I've had a normal appetite, and as a result, my clothes hang loosely around my frame. Even my followers on Instagram have noticed and made comments. One person said I was getting obsessed with my weight, and another person said I must be sick, and someone else said I had gotten lipo. Then a big debate started about fluctuating weights and judging women's bodies.

But no one guessed the truth.

My mother thinks the solution to all problems, besides getting a good night's sleep, is only one meal away, and has been trying everything she can think of to fatten me up. "Sure," I say, coming into the kitchen, since that's the only answer she wants to hear.

"Good, what can I get you?" She comes over and places a gentle kiss on the top of my head.

"Whatever you're planning on making for dinner is fine," I say, pulling out a chair to join Libby at the table. "Hey, Libs." Through the kitchen window, I spy Natan and the kids playing a game of tag.

"Hey, Pens." She looks up from her phone and automatically frowns. "This isn't funny anymore. You have to eat at some point."

"I do." Not nearly the amount I used to, but my appetite is gone. Before Libby has a change to argue back, Fraydie walks into the room, and I give a startled gasp.

"Don't be so dramatic," she says to me, rolling her eyes. "It's fake."

I exchange a glance with Libby and my mother. "Which part? The piercings or tattoos? Or the hair?"

She pulls off the blue wig and tosses it onto the table. "All of it."

"She's having a meeting with Mrs. Zelikovitch this afternoon, and she thinks this will help her out," my mother says, an edge to her voice, as she sits down next to me. "What she doesn't realize is that it will ruin all future chances of getting a good *shidduch*. This is a small community, and if another matchmaker calls around to get information on her, it's over."

Fraydie perches on a counter and grabs an apple from the fruit bowl. "My entire life just flashed in front of me," she says cheerfully and takes a big bite.

"Don't be *chutzpadik*," Libby says in the same tone she uses to scold her kids. "Ma's just looking out for you. I know you don't appreciate it now, but one day you'll see that she's right and that wearing costumes isn't going to help you in the long run."

"None of you get it—this is *my life*," Fraydie replies, then gestures to my mother and Libby with her apple. "Not yours or yours, so stay out of it, and if I have regrets in the future, then that's okay, because at least they were *my choices*—"

"We want to save you from having to have those regrets," Libby cuts in.

"*I don't want to be saved!*" Fraydie says, her voice lifting with frustration. "Why is that so hard for you to get? Just because you've always been Miss Perfect doesn't give you the right to judge me. And don't think I haven't noticed that you always fly to Penina's defense, but when it comes to me, you're brutal."

"Penina is an adult," Libby says startled, but Fraydie cuts her off.

"Guess what, Libby? I'm legally an adult too."

"Then why don't you start acti—"

"Guys." I stand up and clap my hands. "I'm learning to trust that you guys will make good choices, but clearly, this is an emergency." I pause and gaze between Libby and my mother. "Fraydie is an adult and capable of making her own life choices. Despite her strange, at times disturbing, bizarre fashion choices—"

"Right here," Fraydie says.

"She'll always be quirky," I continue, "and I guess that makes her seem immature, but that's just who she is." I smile. "Okay?"

Libby nods while my mother says, "Absolutely not."

I sit down and shrug. "I tried," I say to Fraydie as Libby gives her a big bear hug.

Fraydie pats Libby's back awkwardly. "One out of two isn't bad," she replies, pulling away.

A tennis ball hits one of the kitchen windows, followed by my nephews' shrieks. I turn to Libby. "When do you guys move in?"

"Oh, um." Libby looks at my mother for a moment, then clears her throat. "There's been a change. The truth is . . . it's been taken care of. We get to keep the house in the end. So, that's great." She smiles, but it's the kind of smile you'd have if someone held a gun to your head and told you to smile. Forced and terrified.

I stare at her, trying to figure out if this is some bizarre prank meant to . . . meant to . . . I have no idea. Why would anyone do a prank like this, least of all Libby? I glance at my mother and realize that she must have known too because she's not acting surprised at all, though how she managed not to tell me is the real secret. I suddenly feel as if I boarded a plane to go to Nashville but landed instead on planet Mars and am surrounded by aliens having a tea party. I am *that* confused.

"What?" I finally manage to get out. "*What?*"

"I know." Libby nods, drumming her fingers on the table and not meeting my eyes. "It's really great."

"*When?* When did this happen? *And why didn't you tell me?*" I say, my voice rising.

My mother's chair makes a loud scraping noise as she abruptly stands up. "I should start dinner. I'm going to heat up Shabbos leftovers and repurpose them. Now, where did that cookbook go? Oh, that's right—I left it over here." She opens the cabinet drawer, then slams it shut. "Wait, why isn't it here? Shoot."

I frown, trying to tune out my mother's babbling and focus on Libby. "Well?"

"I meant to. I was going to," she says, scratching her neck, "and I did. Just now."

I don't often get upset with Libby, but I suddenly feel like shaking her. "But Ma knew," I say through clenched teeth. "Why would you tell her and not me?"

"I knew too," Fraydie adds, crunching noisily on her apple.

My mouth drops open. How could Libby tell everyone but *me*? A small voice in my head whispers to let it go, that it's not important and I should just celebrate the wonderful news, but another voice is, like, *Something weird is going on and I don't like it.*

Libby glares at her before turning to look at me. "I'm sorry. Things have been so chaotic lately that it slipped my mind."

"*It slipped your mind?*" My veins burst with adrenaline. "Are you kidding me? You knew what I was prepared to do to save your house!"

Libby swallows and glances at my mother, whose back is conveniently turned. "I'm sorry, okay? It was an accident."

"And honey, you were so busy with your engagement," my mother adds, tying the strings of her apron.

She couldn't have chosen a worse defense, and I lift up my hands. "*Because I was trying to save her house!*"

My mother's eyes light up as she heads to the pantry. "Oh, of course! I put it in here."

I dip my head and groan.

"I'm sorry I didn't tell you sooner. It was a terrible mistake," Libby says. She gets up and gives me a quick hug and murmurs, "Thank you, Penina, for everything. You're the best sister ever."

The knot in my stomach loosens a little, and I hug her back. "I know."

As Libby crosses the kitchen, I realize something. "Wait!" I shout. "You never told me—what happened? How did you save the house?"

Libby goes to the sink and fills up a glass with water. "It's a new program Natan found, but I don't know the exact details." She takes a few gulps, then tilts her head. "Did you hear that?" I stare at her blankly because it's completely silent inside the house. "I think someone's calling me. I better go see."

There wasn't anyone calling for her, and what program? Something doesn't feel so kosher here, but I can't put my finger on it. I turn to my mother. "Tell me about this program."

"I think it's through the government or something," she says vaguely, flipping through pages of the cookbook.

"When did you find out about it?"

My mother's shoulders stiffen. "Last week."

"Why didn't anyone tell me?" I say with mounting frustration. I know there's something they're not telling me. *I can feel it.*

Fraydie has a stupid grin on her face, clearly enjoying the drama, and I narrow my eyes at her.

"It was an oversight." My mother puts on the bifocals that hang from her necklace and consults the recipe. "Zahtar . . . darn it. I think I'm running low on that. Check for me, would you, Penina?" She smiles and adds, "I'm making a recipe from the new cookbook Sam got me."

A sharp pain stabs my chest at the mention of Sam's name. I had hoped by now that I'd be able to hear his name and not be affected, but I guess that was overly ambitious of me. I sigh and grab some saffron from the seasoning rack. "Ma, hold on. You have to know something about this program. I need details."

"I don't know anything," she murmurs.

Fraydie snorts and I whirl around to face her. "Tell me what you know."

"I can't," she shrugs. "I was told my life is in danger if I tell."

I gasp. *I knew it!*

"Fraydie!" My mother narrows her eyes in warning. Turning to me she says, "Please look for the zahtar, sweetie. You gave me saffron."

Screw the stupid spices! Something weird is going on, and I refuse to be the last one to know about it.

"Natan will tell me." I square my shoulders and glare at them with an air of defiance. "Otherwise, the kids will be next. And yeah, in case you were wondering," I add, putting a hand on my hip, "I would stoop that low."

* * *

"What do you mean you can't tell me?" I yell, every muscle in my body clenching in outrage. "You've clearly told everyone else!"

"I said this was going to happen, Libby," my brother-in-law mutters, his accent deepening as he becomes agitated. "You never listen!"

"What do you want from me?" Libby spreads her arms wide, barely missing hitting her toddler in the face. "An 'I-told-you-so' trophy?"

"To listen!" Natan says, raising his voice. He stands up from the Adirondack chair and starts pacing the patio. "Why it so hard to keep secret? Tell me. Tell me why this is."

My niece waddles over and raises her hands to me. I pick her up and plant a kiss on her squishy cheek. Because Natan is Israeli, everything he says sounds like an accusation, even when he means it to be complimentary. The first time we met, he told me with one raised eyebrow that Libby had told him "many things" about me, and even though he was smiling, the inflection of his tone implied that these "many things" were far from good.

"So, it's fine for you to tell your entire family, but I can't tell one person?" Libby's voice rises to match his, and her eyes flash with anger.

"You choose one person who tell entire world!" Natan's eyes bulge like a goldfish's, and his face flushes an apoplectic shade of red. "Telling your mother is like announcement on internet! Same thing."

"Whatever, Natan."

My niece chooses that moment to shove her fingers inside my mouth, and I taste something salty. I grimace and pull them out. "Anyway," I continue, trying to get the conversation back on track, "since pretty much everyone in the whole world knows, what's one more person, right?"

"See, Natan?" Libby gestures toward me with the back of her hand. "She still has no clue, so he has no reason to be upset."

He? "So, not a program. It's a person," I murmur to my niece. "Excellent. We just have to narrow it down from the nearly eight billion people on this planet."

Natan slaps his hand against his forehead and strides toward the gate's door. "I no longer can stand this. I going for smoke."

"You told me you quit!" Libby shouts.

"Yeah, and now I starting!"

An awkward silence descends as Libby and I watch Natan storm off. My niece shimmies down my legs, then pounces on the collection of toys on the patio.

I settle into the vacated chair and turn to my sister. "I'm sorry, Libs." I'm not exactly sure why I'm apologizing, perhaps because I was the impetus to their fight. But if in doubt, I always apologize because that's what being raised in the state of "Minnesota nice" does to a person.

"It's not your fault." She drags a sigh that sounds like it comes from the very bottom of her shoes. "Natan's right. I shouldn't have told Ma."

"Maybe not, but I get it. It's hard to keep things inside. And it isn't good for your health." I should probably feel bad for still trying to draw the secret out of her, but it seems my conscience is having a sick day.

"But that was the *one* condition we were given. He didn't want anyone to know that he was the benefactor."

"Okay. I can respect that." And I can, except—"But as long as everyone else knows in the family, what's the harm in telling me? You know I'll keep it a secret."

"I-I just can't. I'm sorry, Penina." She lifts her eyes to meet mine, and I can tell she genuinely feels bad for holding out on me. She puts down her magazine and reaches out to squeeze my hand. "But it's such an amazing, wonderful thing. Let's just be happy about it, okay?"

"Sure. You're right, that's the important thing." And it is, of course. Their house is saved, and that's a huge burden off everyone's shoulders. Whoever did it—obviously a very kind and rich, not to mention humble, man—isn't the point.

"Did Zevi call Natan?" I ask. I had given Zevi Natan's number the day of our *vort*, and I'm impatient for the two of them to connect since Zevi promised to help Natan find a job.

Libby shakes her head. "Not yet."

Dang it. I'm sure it will happen eventually. I take a deep breath, and my mind circles back to this mysterious person no one will tell me anything about. Anyway, I remind myself, it isn't important. Their house was saved, and that's what matters. So what if I don't know?

I lean back in the chair and close my eyes, trying my best to relax, even though I'm as tense as a coiled spring. *Stop thinking, Penina. Just focus on breathing. In and out, in . . . and out.*

From somewhere up high a bird sings, and I smell the scent of freshly mowed grass and blooming flowers. My nephews have abandoned their football game and are playing on the swing set while my niece babbles to her toys, barely pausing for breath. My muscles slowly begin to relax, and I'm proud of myself for being so mature.

Then a thought occurs to me.

I crack open one eye. "Hey, Lib, would you tell me who it was if I gave you fifty bucks?" She pretends not to hear me and flips a page in her magazine. "Seventy-five? A hundred?"

"That's it. I'm leaving," she declares, getting up from her chair, grabbing her magazine, and heading toward the house.

I turn and look at my niece. "Should I have offered more?"

CHAPTER TWENTY-NINE

"I want people to see the dress, but focus on the woman."
—*Vera Wang*

"You look stunning," I tell Libby a few nights later, admiring her navy wrap dress and bright pink shoes. I'm here to babysit the kids while she and Natan celebrate their ninth wedding anniversary, but so far Libby hasn't left her closet, much less the house. Discarded dresses lie at her feet, and several pairs of shoes litter the floor. Marie Kondo would have a heart attack if she saw this mess, And the rest of the house is in even worse shape because the boys have friends over. Toys and food are strewn across the furniture, rugs, counters, and walls. And the noise— dear G-d, the *noise*. As Natan would say in Arabic, it's *fauda*, or chaos.

"Really? I don't look bloated and fat?"

"Not at all," I say, careful to maintain eye contact and not to blink so she doesn't think I'm lying.

She places her hands on her hips and swivels from side to side in front of the full-length mirror. "Natan thinks I always have to have something to worry about. He said that since I don't have to worry about losing the house anymore, I transferred my anxiety to my weight."

Sounds about right. "Did you?"

"Did I what? Oh my gosh, look at me! I look pregnant," Libby frowns, pressing her hands to the small of her back, gazing in the mirror. "I literally look like I'm in my second trimester. With twins."

"It's probably water retention," I say, trying to calm her down. "It's not real."

She swivels her head toward me and gasps. *"So I do look fat!"*

Crap. "No, you don't. Now step away from the mirror," I command, putting my hands on her shoulders and gently steering her in the other direction. "One step at a time. You can do it."

"I can't go out like this!" she exclaims, frantically combing through clothes. "People will wish me mazel tov."

"That's not a thing. People don't do that." People in my community, anyway, preferring to wait until after the baby is born to say mazel tov.

"Whatever—they'll say *beshaah tovah*. That's not the point. The point is th—"

"Libby!" Natan hollers from the floor below. "Let's go already. *Yallah*," he adds, as though a prompt in Arabic will get her moving.

"Tell him I need ten more minutes." Libby raises her voice over the sound of hangers clattering against the wood floor. Which in Libby-time means twenty more minutes, if not more.

I head downstairs and find Natan in the kitchen, making train noises and guiding a spoon of mashed sweet potatoes toward my niece's mouth. I grab a clementine from the fruit bowl on the counter and explain Libby's wardrobe crisis to Natan as I peel it. He predictably slaps his forehead, which is his go-to method of dealing with stress. Honestly, I'm surprised he's lived this long without slapping himself into a concussion.

"A million times I say I *like* her body, I like curves, like a Renunsence woman, but does she listen? No. So? What am I supposed to do, already?"

"A Renunsence woman?" I repeat, popping a piece of clementine into my mouth.

"Yeah," he says, looking impatient, "naked women paintings. Michelangelo."

"Oh," I laugh. "A Renaissance woman. I get it."

"Yeah—she looks like that. Natural and beautiful."

I smile and nod. That's a nice way of putting it.

"Not skinny like pole or sticks," he adds, then says to me, "no offense."

I start to cough as a piece of the fruit goes down the wrong way.

Natan continues, "I like her round and soft. Like a matzah ball."

"I'd skip the matzah ball part and anything else that even remotely sounds doughy, but she'd probably like hearing you compare her to a Renaissance woman."

"Yeah?" Natan says, puffing up with pride.

"Totally," I say, nodding, just as two of my nephews run past, arguing loudly about some Nerf gun while the youngest boy complains he's being left out. I act as peacemaker between them, then turn back to Natan.

My niece grabs the spoon from her father's hand and throws it to the floor. He sighs, reaches down, and picks it up. "No matter. If it not that, it be something else. She always complains about something. Why she can't go one day just be happy?" It must be a rhetorical question because he cuts me off as I was about to offer an explanation. "We have good news about the house, healthy children, friends, good family." He picks up a napkin and tries to wipe my niece's cheeks, but she protests, turning her head away. "Sam saved the house, yes, but he can't make Libby happy. So, what am I supposed to do?"

My head reels back. "What?"

Natan pushes his sleeve back as he glances at his wristwatch. "What?"

My heart starts to pound, and I suddenly feel lightheaded. I pull a chair out from the table and sit down. "What did you say about Sam?"

"I said he can't make Libby hap—" He breaks off suddenly and slaps his forehead for the second time in five minutes. He looks me straight in the eyes and says, "I said nothing."

My pulse races and the pounding in my chest builds to a crescendo. *Sam saved their house*—he's the mysterious donor? But . . . it doesn't make sense. Why would he do that, and why did he not want anyone to know?

"Tell me," I plead, my eyes wide with urgency. "Please. I promise I won't say a word to anyone."

"Stop." Natan removes the highchair tray, places it on the kitchen counter. "Nothing to tell."

"I *heard* you, Natan. You said Sam saved the house." I unbuckle my niece from the highchair and place her on my hip. "You can't unsay it."

He tears off a piece of paper towel from the roll and wets it under the running faucet. "Check on Libby. Maybe she ready to go now."

"Fine." I shift the toddler to my other hip. "I'll just ask Sam myself." The truth is that I've come so close to dialing his number over the last few weeks, but never got farther than the area code before chickening out. What would I have said? *"Hey, Sam, I'm going to drop my religion so we can be together?"* That's not happening. Besides, he's probably moved on by now with some beautiful woman. Someone beautiful *and* fertile. I bet she's pregnant already—with twins. And they're married and shopping for a villa to buy in Rome.

"No no no *no!*" Natan whirls around and shakes a finger at me. "You do no such thing."

"I will do such thing!" I say, accidentally matching his broken English. I'm determined to get to the bottom of this mystery. Why would Sam, of all people, pay my sister's mortgage? What could it mean? And why did he not want anyone to know? "Right now, in fact." I reach for my phone, located in my shirt pocket, and unlock the screen.

"Stop, Penina! This no joke!"

"Who's laughing?" My niece shimmies down my leg and waddles away. "Ah, here he is . . . Sam Kleinfeld."

He yells something in Arabic and lunges for my phone. Luckily, I have quick reflexes, and I run for the stairs, taking them two at a time. I race into my sister's bedroom, slam the door shut, and quickly lock it. Seconds later, Natan's fist bangs on the other side. "Open the door!" he shrieks. "I tell you everything. Don't call!"

"Penina?" Libby emerges from her master bathroom in a pink sheath dress with a pleated fold at one side. "What's going on?"

"Libby, open the door!" Natan yells.

Ignoring her husband, she turns to me with a bewildered expression. "What's going on?"

"I know it's Sam who gave you the money for the house," I say in a rush, still slightly out of breath. "Natan said so."

"Liar!" he slams his hand against the door. "Open this door or I break it down."

Libby must believe him because she hurries to open it. "You owe me a big apology, Natan! And my mother too."

He points an accusing finger toward Libby, advancing into the room. "This is what happens when you don't let me smoke. I not think straight!"

"Oh no, you don't. Don't you dare try to blame me for this," Libby retorts. "Admit that you have a bigger mouth than my mother. Put on your big boy pants and own up to it."

Natan's eyes resemble storm clouds, and his thick caterpillar eyebrows slam together. "Only if you put on big girl skirt and let me smoke."

Libby gesticulates wildly like a bird trying to take flight. "Of all the things I've ever heard you say in our nine-year marriage, that is the absolute dumbest, *stupidest*, most idio—"

"Time-out, time-out," I interrupt, stepping between the two of them and holding up my hands. "You guys can fight about this later. Right now, someone needs to tell me why Sam gave the money in the first place and why he didn't want anyone to know."

"He didn't want *you* to know," Libby corrects. "I don't think he cared if other people knew, but he didn't want it getting back to you."

"But this is so bizarre. I feel like I'm in the twilight zone." My throat feels dry, and I swallow. "Why? Why did he do it?"

Libby and Natan exchange a glance. "He said that he likes our family and we're nice people," she says, "and he doesn't want us losing the house."

I start to pace, even though I feel slightly dizzy. "When did this even happen?"

"It was a day or two after the *vort*."

I bite my lip, thinking back. I remember confessing everything to him, like how I had to marry Zevi to pay for my sister's house. He told me everything would work out, but that's what everyone says to people when they're having an existential life crisis. No one actually makes it *work out*. It's a euphemism for G-d's sake!

"She looks like she going to faint," Natan says, pointing to me. "Maybe then she wakes up and not remember anything."

"Oh, be quiet," Libby chides him. She guides me to the loveseat positioned at the end of the bed. "Do you want water or anything? I know this is quite a shock."

I shake my head. "I'm fine. But I still don't understand why Sam didn't want me to find out."

"I don't know," she shrugs. "He never said why, just that it would be better this way. It was his only request."

Natan crosses his arms. "If Penina don't say anything, he will never know."

"You know what? Maybe it's good she knows," Libby muses, glancing at her husband. "Either way, it's not the worst thing in the world."

I look between the two of them, who seem to be engrossed in some kind of telepathic conversation. "Why is it good if I know? What exactly am I supposed to do with this information?"

"Do?" Natan breaks eye contact with his wife to face me. "You do nothing! Let things still, like sleeping dogs."

Normally, Natan's incorrectly conjugated analogies make me laugh, but all I can manage now is a weak smile. "I won't say anything, *bli neder*," I add. The literal translation being "without a vow," which means that if I break my promise, it's not considered as bad as breaking an actual oath in Jewish law.

"I'm actually glad that you know." A slow smile appears on Libby's face. "I've wanted to thank you for the longest time."

My hand flies to my chest. "*Me?* I'm not the one who forked over the money."

"I know, but none of this would have happened if you hadn't told Sam about our situation. And I still can't believe you were going to go ahead with a fake marriage just to save our house." Her eyes fill with tears, and she puts an arm around me. "Promise me you'll never sacrifice yourself like that again."

I swallow against the sudden lump in my throat. "You would have done the same thing for me if our roles had been reversed."

"But—"

"What other mess are you planning on getting into that would involve me marrying a rich gay man?" I say, putting my hands on my hips.

Libby laughs. "None."

"See? I rest my case."

Little Ari suddenly bursts into the room. "Mommy, Abba, come quick!" he exclaims with a wide grin. "Binyamin just kicked Yehudah Leib in the nuts, and Sholom tackled Dovid, and I ran away because Asher is trying to wrap everyone up with duct tape!"

Natan mutters a long string of Hebrew curses as he strides out of the room with a gleeful Ari trailing behind.

"Have fun babysitting tonight," Libby says sardonically and pats my hand. She stands up from the loveseat, adjusts the fold of her dress, and sighs. "I feel so much better now that you know."

I nod, lost in thought. Sam and his family are known for being philanthropists, but I never would have guessed that he'd take it upon himself to do something like this. I feel humbled that such an amazing man liked me, even for the small amount of time it was. And maybe it's okay if this pang of loss never goes away, because it will remind me one day when I'm old and lonely that, for a short time, I didn't merely exist, but that I lived.

CHAPTER THIRTY

"The way I dress depends on how I feel."

—*Rihanna*

As I drive home later that night, exhausted from refereeing the four very energetic boys, my phone rings with a FaceTime request from Zevi. I'm so shocked and thrilled that I pull to the side of the road and put my car in park. I click "Join," and my mouth drops open when I see the screen. Zevi's mom is in her hospital bed, flanked by Zevi on one side and Jack on the other. For a moment I'm filled with excitement because I assume this means that Zevi has come out, but then I remember that Jack has always been around the family because he's Zevi's "roommate." To be on the safe side, I just say, "*Heeeey*! How are you feeling Mrs. Wernick?"

She grins and her bright blue eyes shine with joy. "I'm feeling very grateful to you, Penina."

Jack and Zevi exchange smiles, and my heart fills with excitement and hope. *Oh my G-d. Does she know? I think she knows!*

My hand flies to my chest in surprise. "Me?"

"Yes," she nods. "If it wasn't for your encouragement, Zevi wouldn't have come out."

I hadn't been aware I was holding my breath until this moment, and I let it out in one long exhalation. "And you're . . . okay with it?" I say, tapping my foot nervously in the car.

She lifts a hand and says, "G-d made Zevi exactly the way He wanted. Who am I to argue?"

Wow. "I like that," I agree.

"The way I see it," she continues, "is that we all have our hardships and our struggles, but we're all G-dly souls. And my job as his mother is to love him unconditionally." She kisses his cheek and adds, "And our job as Jews is to see the G-dly spark in everyone. Not to judge each other."

"You are so cool," I tell her, and grin. "Will you adopt me?"

They laugh and Zevi takes the phone from his mother. He has tears in his eyes and he says, "The funny part is that my mom suspected it all along, and I just realized that it wasn't my mother's judgment I was afraid of—it was *mine*."

"Oh, Zevi," I shake my head.

"Anyway." He grins. "You were right and I was wrong."

"You would've been a good husband," I say, laughing.

The phone transfers to Jack. "I love you, dollface."

"I love you too." I blow a kiss. "I love all you guys!"

"Come visit us anytime," Zevi calls out. "Our penthouse doors are always open."

"I like the sound of that," I smile. "Okay guys, I better go because I'm parked on the side of the road, but keep in touch."

"We will! Bye!" they say merrily.

I pull back onto the road and drive, and only when I reach home do I realize that I'm still smiling.

* * *

I wave goodbye to Delilah, then sign off in the volunteer ledger. I love her of course, but only in very limited doses. For some reason, she goes into interrogation mode every time she sees me, although it's hard to blame her since my life has gotten pretty interesting lately. And she agreed that I did the right thing by calling off the wedding, even though the money would have been nice—she mentioned something about the two of us going on a kosher cruise to Alaska, which to be perfectly honest, I didn't even know was on the table.

I wave goodbye to the security guard and head down the long corridor. I keep replaying the FaceTime call with Zevi because it's like an instant shot of serotonin straight to my brain.

It's nice when things work out for people. Libby gets to keep her house and is now in charge of the family's finances. Mimi has her beautiful baby boy. Zevi knows how much his mother loves him. Maya is in love with her plastic surgeon boyfriend. Sam is probably shopping for furniture with his new lingerie model wife. And me? I will continue on my current trajectory of withering into old maidenhood like a dried-out flower that was never plucked.

Oh, and I no longer do social media. Or fashion. I rotate three different outfits because it's easy and I don't care. I can't even remember the last time I put on makeup. The other day I came to work in flats, and Maya cried.

I stop walking to shrug off my sweater and tie it around my waist. Fall is here, and with it come all the preparations for the High Holidays. Normally, it's something I look forward to, tasting the traditional sweet foods like honey cake, fresh fish, and apples and honey, as well as spending quality time with my family. I've always appreciated the idea of starting over, with a fresh, blank slate, that the Jewish New Year brings, the focus on moving forward instead of the mistakes made in the past.

But this year, it's different. I just want to stay home in bed and sleep the holidays away. Some days I miss Sam so much that it hurts, a constant ache in the pit of my stomach. All I have left are my memories, and I play one after the other, like TikTok reels. I feel horrible that I never thanked him for saving Libby's house, but I don't want to risk getting Libby and Natan in trouble, even though I can't figure out why he doesn't want me to know.

I turn a corner, and murmur, "Excuse me," to an orderly pushing a supply cart. Sam's dad is back at work, but he's not in the store as often as he used to be, and when he is, he never mentions his son.

I suddenly notice two men in suits coming down the hall, and one of them *looks exactly* like Sam. It's freaky, to be honest. Does he have an identical twin that he forgot to mention? It can't be Sam because Sam is traveling the world, and Joe would've said something if he had come back.

But I'm starting to think, *It is Sam*. Am I hallucinating? Is this what losing your mind is like? I screw my eyes tight and count to ten before opening. A group of nurses block my view, but when they pass, the look-alike is still there and getting closer by the second.

Stay calm, stay calm. There's no reason to freak out, even if it is him. Just . . . be cool. We had a minor attraction, a little flirting, a few secrets spilled, but so what? Technically speaking, one of us fell hopelessly in love, but whatever. No need to get technical.

Shit! He sees me!

I instinctively drop down and bend forward, and semi-crouch, semi-walk behind two elderly women, trying to blend in like a chameleon. Maybe he won't recognize me, or maybe he'll think he's hallucinating, or maybe I actually am—

"Penina?"

I freeze. Shit just got real. I cringe and slowly straighten, then pretend to be surprised, as though we hadn't made eye contact ten seconds ago. Or that I was hiding from him. "Oh, wow! Hi," I laugh, tucking some hair behind my ear. "I didn't know you were in town."

He nods and does that crooked smile thing that makes my stomach flip. "Since last week."

"Oh, wow. Okay," I repeat, careful to keep my face super happy. Even though he had plenty of time to contact me. He could have easily picked up the phone or dropped a quick text or camped outside my apartment building like a stalker, but he didn't. He didn't, and that's the bottom line.

I'm precariously close to tears and need to escape before he sees me cry. I'd rather eat spinach-flavored tofu than have him witness the aftermath of how hard I fell for him, whereas he moved on within twenty-four hours. I start inching backward. "Sorry, I've got to run—I'm late. For a thing . . ."

"Are you okay?" he asks, peering closely at me. "You look different."

"You must be referring to the fact that I've lost my will to live." I laugh shrilly, although he doesn't join in. I clear my throat. "My plant died." *Shut up, Penina, shut up!*

"Your plant died," he repeats.

He, of course, is a picture of health and male perfection, and even more handsome than I remembered. So yeah, that's great.

"I'm fine. I'm wonderful," I ramble on, focusing on the top button of his shirt. *Don't cry, Penina, you're talking to a button, not the man who stole your heart, then trampled all over it.* "Really wonderful." *Who even uses the word* wonderful? *You sound deranged.*

He looks like he's about to say something, then changes his mind and clears his throat. "I'm a little tied up at the moment," he says, gesturing toward the man in the suit that's patiently waiting for him, "but if you—"

"Of course, same here." I nod and grin like a maniac. "*So* nice running into you. And I've got things to . . . you know," I say airily, waving my hand, "*do*. Lots of things. Anyway, ciao!"

I turn around and speed walk toward the bank of elevators, dodging past people, hardly registering where I'm going. *Ciao, Penina? Really? Ugh! Why am I so awkward?*

When I reach the elevators, there's a group of people already waiting, and I fold my arms and tap my foot impatiently. I won't think about Sam. I won't. I won't try to dissect what his face meant when he said I looked different. It wasn't a compliment, though—I could tell that much.

Where is that elevator?

About one eternity later, the elevator doors slide open, but a patient moaning and strapped to a bed is being pushed inside by an orderly, followed by a janitor and his cleaning equipment, then a family of four, leaving no room for me. Unfortunately, I'm desperate, so I ignore the grimaces of my fellow passengers and pack myself in anyway.

The doors start to close, but then—in a total horror movie–type way—a large hand suddenly shoots between the few inches of space, and because I'm already so wound up, I scream. My heart races as the doors slide open to reveal the one person I don't want to face. *Sam.*

"Penina," he says in a firm voice, "we need to talk."

Oh, now he wants to talk? He goes radio silent for almost three months and is in town for a week, and doesn't think to talk then, but now that he's accidentally run into me and insinuated that I look terrible, he insists on having a discussion?

I. Don't. Think. So.

"You have my number, Mr. Kleinfeld," I say coldly. "You could have used it. Now, if you'll excuse me, I have somewhere to be." I jab at the "Close" button and lift my chin with all the dignity I can muster. Unfortunately, nothing happens and I realize I pressed the "Open" button. Stupid arrows.

"Penina, please. Come out so we can talk."

I make sure to press the right one this time, and as the doors begin to shut, I say, "Goodbye, Mr. Kleinfeld."

First, his leg, then his entire body slips through the closing doors and into the already crammed elevator. *What is he doing?* No one says anything, even though it's totally claustrophobic, because this is Minnesota nice and we keep our aggression strictly to the road.

I swallow, trying not to notice how the side of his body is pressed against mine and that he smells like tantalizing man soap. We both stare straight ahead at the doors, and when the elevator finally moves, it's painfully quiet inside. Even the groaning patient stopped making noises, so he either died or doesn't want to miss a word of our argument.

"How's your family?" Sam murmurs.

I pale—I never thanked him for saving Libby's house. How could I forget, even for a moment, everything that he's done for my family? I was so caught up feeling rejected that I forgot to thank him. But I was told not to say anything because he didn't want me to know. This is torture. This is hell on earth. This is fire and brimstone, cockroaches and tarantulas, polyester plaid shirts and old lady Velcro-strapped shoes. What do I do?

"Good." I swallow. "Thank G-d."

The doors open and the man with the patient on the wheeled bed says, "This is our stop, excuse me."

Sam makes room for them by crushing the front of himself against the front of myself, and all things aside, it's *excruciatingly sexy*. Our hips and chests are pressed against each other's, and his breathing tickles my neck. I can't help but shiver as I remember the night of my *vort* and how we almost kissed.

His face is close. So very close. I catch the quickening of his breath as he studies my lips like they're a work of art, and I envision what it would be like to kiss him, to explore his mouth and taste his essence. My nipples harden at the thought, and I wonder if he can feel the change since he is, after all, pressed against me.

"Damn," he whispers. So that answers that.

The doors ping shut and the elevator starts to move, but Sam hasn't. "You can move now," I say, glancing away. No way am I falling for that trap again, a few cheap thrills that don't mean anything to him.

He exhales deeply and steps back. I risk a quick peek at his face and am surprised to see how flushed it is. And there's something odd about the way he's staring at me.

"I'm sorry I was rude before," I say. "I'd love to talk to you." I owe him that much, at least. But at the first mention of his baby mama, I'm outta there.

His eyebrows lift in surprise, but he nods. "Want to grab a coffee?"

"We can just find somewhere quiet to sit. Unless you want coffee?" I add politely.

He shakes his head, and once the elevator doors open to the first level, he leads me down the main corridor, pausing every now and then to make sure I'm still there. I had forgotten how fast he walks. When I realize he's taking me to the parking ramp, I say, "Wait. Where are we going?"

"Somewhere quiet."

My heart skips over itself at the thought of the two of us alone. I swallow and feel my hands dampen with sweat. I'm not sure I trust myself to be somewhere quiet with him. Unless it's the library; I can't imagine doing anything naughty there—the librarians would never tolerate it. Except wait, aren't there conference rooms with locks on the door? Ooh.

No, bad Penina, bad! I shake my head and resist the urge to smack myself as I follow him up a flight of stairs. Apparently, five minutes with Sam is all it takes to forget three months of rejection, and *that's not okay.*

He holds the door open for me, and I walk through the doorway into the parking garage. I glance at Sam with my peripheral vision and steel myself not to say anything about Libby's house. Not even if he brings up the subject of their house. Not even if he straight out asks me about the anonymous donor.

He catches me staring, and his mouth curls into a grin.

That's it. I can't keep it inside me any longer. "I know I'm not supposed to know about this, but I just want to say thank you, from the bottom of my heart, for saving Libby's house."

Sam's footsteps falter for a moment. "I didn't realize Natan and Libby were so untrustworthy."

"Only Natan," I clarify, tossing him under that bus. "But it wasn't intentional—it just slipped out."

"I see." He frowns, pulls out his fob, and presses the "Unlock" button.

He's mad, but I still don't get why. I can understand wanting to be anonymous, but then why is he fine with everyone else in the family knowing? Why was I the only one who couldn't know the truth?

For the first time ever, Sam opens the passenger door for me, and normally I would find that sweet except for the fact that he looks like he wants to kill someone. I assume that someone is Natan, but in case it's me, I decide to apologize as he gets behind the wheel and turns on the car. "I'm sorry. I shouldn't have said anything."

"When did you find out?" he asks, reversing out of the parking spot.

"About a week or two after you gave them the money."

He shakes his head in disgust but doesn't say anything. I'm so uncomfortable at this point that I stay quiet for a good ten minutes and stare out my window. It's only when he merges onto the highway, that I turn to him and say, "Why didn't you want me to know?"

A muscle in his jaw clenches. "Isn't it obvious?"

"If it was, would I be asking?"

He sighs. "Here's the thing, Superwoman. You have an overdeveloped sense of responsibility. How many people would have been willing to marry someone just to save their sister's house?"

I shift uncomfortably in my seat. "I didn't go through with it in the end, so it doesn't count."

"It does."

Nice to know he hasn't lost a drop of arrogance since I last saw him. With his arm draped over the wheel, he looks so classic Sam that for a moment I allow myself to simply drink in the sight of him. He has this casual confidence, an alpha male vibe that's different from most men

I've met who try to project confidence but get it wrong. They laugh a little too hard or move when they should be still or have trouble maintaining eye contact, or their shoulders are stooped.

But this man was born to be a leader.

"I never wanted you to feel obligated to do something you didn't want to do," he says after a moment, glancing at me from the corners of his eyes.

Like what? I get the feeling that he thinks I know what he's talking about, when in reality, he might as well be speaking in tongues. "Can you be more specific? Because I literally have no idea what you're talking about."

He inhales deeply, blowing out forcefully as he exhales. "I didn't want you to feel obligated to date me."

My heart slams in my chest as I try to process what he just said. *Date him? How could I have dated him? Was he planning on having a long-distance relationship as he globe-trotted? Is this a trick he's using to seduce me? Because it's working.*

I lick my lips and swallow, keeping my eyes straight ahead. "But you left, Mr. Kleinfeld." As long as I call him Mr. Kleinfeld, I can keep the facts separated from the fiction. Fact: He's my former boss, not a former boyfriend. Fact: He left and never once tried to contact me in the three months he was gone. Fact: He saved my sister's house but didn't want me to know. Fact: He was here for a week and still never contacted me.

"Because, Ms. Kalish," he says in a quieter voice, "I was falling in love with you."

I stop breathing. *Did he actually say what I think he just said, or am I hearing things?*

"And," he continues, "I didn't think it was fair to either one of us if I couldn't handle being Orthodox. That's why I needed time and distance. I've been in London."

I close my gaping mouth and turn to look at him. He glances at me for a moment too long, and a car behind us honks. Sam murmurs, "We were supposed to be having this conversation when I wasn't driving."

I put my hand over my chest to steady my breathing. "Um, why London?"

"My good friend lives there. He grew up secular but became religious and married an Orthodox girl. I wanted to learn about Orthodox Judaism from someone I was comfortable with, who had a similar background, and he was happy to help."

Wow. Here I was thinking he'd have already moved on with someone else, when really he'd been studying Torah this whole time.

"And I loved it. I started seeing the beauty and the richness of the lifestyle instead of the restrictions. Everything made sense. Well, not everything," he pauses. "I still don't like the family purity stuff, but my friend said some of that is negotiable."

My face flushes and I can't think of a single thing to say. Family purity stuff is for married couples, so . . . what is he saying exactly?

He puts on his turn signal and switches to the right lane. "I'm not completely there yet, but he said to do things at my own pace. I started keeping Shabbos and some form of kosher, but I'm not praying three times a day or wearing a yarmulke. But I did buy one." He flips open the center console and pulls out a simple black velvet yarmulke, and puts it on his head. "What do you think?"

I think I've never seen anything sexier in my life. "It looks great. You look great." *I love you.* Then I blush again because I can't seem to stop. "Why didn't you tell me you were back in town?"

He puts the yarmulke back in the console as we exit the highway. "I needed to figure out some details," he says vaguely.

"Details," I repeat.

"Yes," he replies, as though that answers everything. He's quiet for a few beats, then clears his throat. "I need to ask you something, but I want your honest answer—not what you think you should say or feel obligated to say."

"Okay." I swallow, my eyes never leaving his beautiful face. "What is it?"

"Well, you know how I feel about you," he says, glancing my way, "but I don't know how you feel about me. The last thing you said to me before I left was that I was a lying, cheating, douche—"

"Yes, yes, I know," I cut him off, mortified that he remembers the exact words I used. "I'm really sorry, by the way. I said a lot of things that I didn't mean that night. If I had asked you about Keila instead of blowing up, I would've found out she was your cousin." I sigh. "Will you forgive me?"

He glances at me and smiles. "Always."

"The truth is," I say quickly since my heart is racing so fast it'll probably go into cardiac arrest any moment, "that I fell in love with you a long time ago. Maybe I'm not supposed to tell you that because it's too soon, but it's the truth. You're incredibly loyal and kind—not in an obvious, obnoxious-type way, but in a quiet, humble way, and you have such a strong moral compass and you helped me see the truth about Zevi, even though I didn't want to at the time, and you're so handsome that it hurts to look at you, and you always smell really, really good—like, seriously, what soap do you use? It drives me *insane*—where do you get it?—because I want it all over my body, and is it just me or did this conversation just turn really awkward?"

He laughs and turns into a parking lot. "I love it when you talk awkward to me. Do you recognize where we are?"

I look around and my eyes widen in surprise as he parks in front of the first jewelry store we ever visited together in Edina. "Of course. This is where we posed as a couple to spy on their merchandise and prices."

"That's what *I told you*," he says, smirking. "But I could have easily found out all that information on their website."

I gasp and point my finger at him. *"You lied!"*

He shrugs, not looking the least bit remorseful. "How else was I supposed to get to know you?"

"Um, by asking me out?"

"Absolutely not," he says, turning off the car and opening his door. "I don't date people I work with." I snort, but he doesn't notice because he's coming around to my side. He opens my door and adds, "Wasn't that one of the reasons you fell in love with me—my strong moral compass?"

"Yeah, but it's getting hazier and hazier by the moment," I say, trying not to smile, but failing. "So, why are we here?" I ask, following him to the entrance of the jewelry store.

He arches an eyebrow as he opens the door, gesturing me to go inside first. "Patience, Prude."

I roll my eyes. A male salesman greets us warmly, but I'm disappointed that it's not the nice woman with the babysitting problems.

What was her name, again? "How can I help you guys today?" the man asks, with a brisk clap of hands.

"Is Carly here?" Sam asks.

That's it! Sam has an awesome memory.

"Yeah, she's in the back. I'll go grab her for you." He points to a desk with two chairs. "Make yourselves comfortable."

"Remember how worried you were that we wasted Carly's time because she'd never get a commission?" Sam says as we sit down.

That I remember clearly. "Yes."

"Well, don't worry," he says. "I more than made up for it."

I'm trying to wrap my head around everything, but I'm starting to feel like Alice when she fell down the rabbit hole. Did Sam buy me something? I mean, if a man says he loves you and then brings you to a jewelry store, what else is a girl supposed to think? But shouldn't we go on a few dates first? I wonder if it's going to be a pair of earrings or a bracelet. I hope it's not a necklace, because I'm very picky when it comes to necklaces, and I don't want to hurt his feelings, at least not on the same day he tells me he loves me—

"*Pruuuude!*" Carly calls from the back of the store as she comes forward.

I turn my most withering glare at Sam, and he whispers, "Sorry," even though he doesn't *look* sorry. He's wearing the biggest grin I've ever seen him with. I guess being in love with someone doesn't change their sadistic sense of humor.

"It's been so long," she gushes as she takes a seat across from us. "How have you been?" We catch up for a few minutes, talking about fashion and babysitting, but I can feel Sam growing restless with each passing second. I think Carly can too, because she turns to him and says, "Now, Sam, I know you're eager, but remember I said it was going to take a little while longer because—"

"Right, I know," he interrupts. "But you still have it here, don't you?"

She looks at him disapprovingly. "You really want to show it to her now?" He nods, and she says with a shrug, "I had a feeling you were going to say that. Here it is . . ." She pulls a small box out of her pocket and places it on the table.

I blink and swallow and struggle to breathe. *That's a ring box! But . . . but, that makes no sense. Maybe it's a pair of small earrings placed inside a ring box? Because there's no way he could be proposing. Absolutely no way. The very idea is absurd. It's probably earrings or a—Whoa! Whoa! Whoa!*

Why is he getting down on one knee?

"Penina"—he swallows, lifting his eyes to meet mine—"the first time I ever saw you was in the NICU, holding a baby, and I kept think-ing that I'd never seen someone more beautiful." He pauses and clears his throat. "The way you looked at the baby, your smile—it could have been a painting. I was mesmerized."

He was mesmerized? By me holding a baby?

"I told myself to look away because you were probably someone else's wife, but I was drawn to you like a magnet. It wasn't just because you're beautiful—I think it was . . ." he breaks off, "I don't know how to describe it. It was almost like there was a halo of light around the two of you." He shakes his head ruefully. "I didn't hear a word anyone said after that. They could've been talking Mandarin, and I wouldn't have noticed.

"Then you smacked into me in the hallway, and I was so happy, and I tried to figure out a non-creepy way to ask you out, but you ran away before I could. I thought about asking the nurses for your name, but . . ." he trails off. "Then when I saw you again at the store and real-ized you were my employee, I was in shock. I tried to play it cool, but inside I was panicking."

"Why?" I breathe.

"Because I hadn't been able to get you out of my head, and there you were on my first day as the new boss. It felt like fate."

I shake my head. "You don't believe in fate."

"I didn't want to, which is probably why I came off like an asshole at first. My father had just reached remission, and I was finally putting my messy divorce behind me and learning a new business. The last thing I ever wanted to do was to fall in love, but there you were anyway. Funny and smart and beautiful. And so damn kind."

There's a whirring sensation in my stomach, like someone set a load of wash inside. My lips split into a grin. He pauses and points to my cheek, "I love your smile. You have a double dimple right there."

I'm so full of happiness right now that all I can do is stare at him, afraid that any moment I'll wake up and discover this was all a dream.

"I love you, Penina Kalish, and I want to spend the rest of my life with you. Please say yes and be my wife."

"Y-yes. A million times over yes!" I didn't even realize I was crying until a tear drops onto my hand, followed by another, and Carly—I'd almost forgotten she was here—hands me a tissue box.

Sam's eyes look shiny, and he clears his throat. He starts to stand up, but Carly stage-whispers to him, "Show her the ring."

Sam startles, like he can't believe he forgot. He resumes his position on the floor and opens the box.

My mouth opens and shuts. OMG. *He remembered the ring I loved, the one I almost said I would have chosen for myself if I was a real bride instead of posing as one.*

"Do you remember it?" he asks.

"*Yes!*" And now I *really* start to cry and shakily reach for it.

This is too much. I can't believe I'm still upright and breathing. First, Sam comes back out of the blue, telling me he's Orthodox-ish and that he loves me, and then to top that all off, he *proposes with the ring of my dreams.*

The band is too big and the diamond turns upside down, but I don't care, I'm never taking it off.

"Hey, Carly!" the first salesman shouts. "Babysitter on the phone."

"I promise, I only get these types of calls when you two are here." She laughs, standing up. "I'll be right back."

The word *babysitter* douses over me like a pitcher of ice water. "Sam, wait. I just remembered—you want children one day, right?" I shrug, to make it seem like his answer isn't a big deal either way. "I mean, of course you do. Most people do."

"Absolutely." He nods vigorously. "I don't know about me, but *you* were definitely meant to be a mother."

A harsh laugh spills from my lips. How incredibly funny. He remembers the smallest details like one silly comment about a ring but completely forgets the most important things. I slide the ring off my finger and replace it in the box. "I bet we made a new record for shortest engagement in history," I say, my eyes filling up with fresh tears—sad ones this time. "I thought you would've . . . Sam"—I swallow, unable to look him in the eyes—"I can't give you babies."

"Penina." His eyes are confused as he shakes his head. "You misunderstood me. The world has enough babies, but not enough parents," he says softly. "I was thinking we could look into adoption."

It takes me several seconds for his words to register, but as soon as they do, I start to really cry then, like full-on cry, not the delicate sniffles of a lady, but the wracking sobs of someone who's been to hell and back, then to hell and back a second time. I never even knew this type of happiness *existed*!

After all the paperwork is signed and we're back in the car, we agree on a three-month engagement.

I turn to Sam and say playfully, "You seemed very sure I'd marry you."

"Not at all." He grins. "Which is why I wanted to have the ring on hand in case you needed some extra convincing."

I shake my head. "You are a bad, *bad* man."

"In three months from now," he says, throwing me a wolfish grin, "you'll get to see just how bad."

I throw my head back and laugh.

And that is how I, Penina Kalish, began my very own Happily Ever After.

*　*　*

"Holy crap, how much is this thing worth?" Fraydie exclaims, examining my five-carat ring.

"Shabbos table!" my mother trills, slapping her palm against the dining room table. This is code for (A) no swearing and (B) no talking about money on Shabbos, two rules my sister managed to break in just one sentence.

Pretty impressive, even for her.

"My bad," Fraydie says, raising her hands. "What I meant is how many *challahs* would need to be baked to be equal to that ring?"

Natan, seated at the far end of the long table, seems amused. "That bad English."

"No offense, hon," Libby says, working the stopper from the wine bottle, "but you're not exactly fit to criticize other people's grammar."

"Nu?" Fraydie prods, angling my hand so the diamond sparkles under the chandelier's lights. "Give me a number."

"Frankly, I don't know, and I don't want to know." I extract my hand from Fraydie's grasp and pick up my fork. That's not technically true, but every time I think of the price I start to feel dizzy, so I try not to. "The important thing is that Sam and I are very happy, and we can't wait to spend the rest of our lives together. The value of the ring isn't relevant."

Sam's lips bow into a smile and he whispers something so naughty into my ear that I can't help but flush. His newest hobby seems to be how often he can make me turn red.

"Look how cute they are together." Libby elbows Natan and nods her head in our direction. "Remember when we used to be like that? It was ages ago, but still."

Natan reaches for a slice of challah and breaks off a piece. "Yes. By second date already, you could not stop touching me."

"You touched before you were married?" Fraydie says, wiggling her eyebrows.

"Her hands always on me," Natan replies. "What could I do?"

"*Natan!*" Libby shrieks, slapping his arm. "That is so not true! You're the one that first touched—"

"*Shabbos table!*" my mother singsongs, reminding us of rule C: no sexual references.

"Ma, why do you always have to cut people off just when things get interesting?" Fraydie protests, waving her hands.

"Try these knishes, everyone." My father, ever the peacemaker, holds up a large oval tray of dough dumplings filled with mashed potatoes, fried onions, and mushrooms.

"Pass them to Sam," Libby says, then adds, "I think you should offer him more scotch too. Do you want more, Sam?" she asks.

"No. But thank you."

"Can I pass you anything?"

"I'm still good, thanks."

I lean toward Sam and whisper, "Libby hero-worships you. It's kind of annoying."

He lowers his wineglass and turns to face me. "And you?" he asks, lifting an eyebrow. "Do you hero-worship me?"

"Nope." I shake my head and try to hide my smile under my hand. "Not even a little."

"Liar," he murmurs. "You know you worship me a little."

"I *tolerate* you, Mr. Kleinfeld. But only because you're easy on the eyes."

"What are you guys whispering about?" Fraydie asks.

"Fraydie . . ." my father intones.

Sam gives me a look that implies we'll finish this conversation later, and I laugh. He steals a meatball from my plate in retaliation.

"Can I ask you a question, Sam?" Libby says, her finger tracing a bead of moisture down a can of soda. Without waiting for permission, she continues, "Why didn't you want Penina to know you saved our house? It would have helped your cause."

Sam swallows the piece of food in his mouth and arches his eyebrows. "My cause?"

"You know what I mean," she replies, batting her hand. "Getting Penina to fall in love with you."

I smile, already knowing what he's going to say since we've been over this several times.

He places his arm over the back of my chair and glances at me. "As we all know, Penina has an overdeveloped sense of duty, and I didn't want her to feel like she owed me anything. I didn't want that for either one of us."

My mother's eyes shine with joy. "Unbelievably sweet."

"I'd like to make a *L'Chaim*." My father raises his snifter and looks around the table. He pauses a moment, waiting for everyone to hold up a glass, then turns to face Sam and me. "Mazel tov on your engagement, Penina and Sam. Tonight happens to be a special night on the Jewish calendar, the fifteenth of the month *Av*. During Temple times, the unmarried daughters of Jerusalem dressed in white gowns and danced in the vineyards for eligible men. Afterward, the men would select their future wives—"

"Why didn't the men put on virgin white pants and dance for the women?" Fraydie cuts in. "This is so disgustingly patriarchal it makes me want to puke."

"Finish eating your salad, Fraydie," my mother says.

320

"As I was saying," my father continues, stroking his graying beard, "this is a special time in our calendar for love, and although you two found it in a somewhat unorthodox way, there is nothing unusual about the mutual affection you share. May we continue to share in more happy occasions until the rebuilding of the Temple, speedily in our days. *L'Chaim!*"

"*L'Chaim!*"

Sam and I look at each other and smile. Ever since he proposed, I've been walking on air, feeling an all-encompassing joy that touches every part of me. He is, without a doubt, the kind of man that dreams are made of, and certainly not the type I ever imagined myself being with.

Life still has its day-to-day challenges, and a part of me will always mourn the biological children I couldn't have, but for the first time in my life, I can honestly say that I'm more than just happy. I am whole and complete.

And really, what more could a girl want?

EPILOGUE

"A woman is never sexier than when she is comfortable in her clothes."
—*Vera Wang*

So, this is what it feels like to be Princess Kate. I sit on my makeshift throne, flanked by my mother and Sam's aunt, and gaze down at the crowd of women in line to see me, my cheeks already sore from the constant smiling. It's the first part of the wedding, the *kabolas ponim*, where female guests wish me mazel tov, and I murmur the occasional psalm from a prayer book. Every now and then, my eyes seek out the dark haired, blue-eyed infant in the crowd, the one in a tiny suit that's being held by one of my mother's friends, and my heart squeezes at how perfect he is.

My pulse quickens at the knowledge that Sam is merely in the next room over, and I hear the men's lively singing and jovial shouts as they congratulate him. According to tradition, we haven't seen or spoken to each other for the last seven days, but we've been giving each other messages through Fraydie—and like the game of Telephone, I'm pretty sure she's been adding her own unique spin to them.

I gaze at my wedding gown, arguably the most important fashion decision of my life, and sigh happily. It's elegant and timeless, and very

"Grace Kelly meets Eleonora Mararo." The sleeves and collar are French Chantilly lace, while the bodice and skirt are ivory silk. The best part is the incredibly long detachable train that screams high drama, although my Cinderella-inspired shoes are a close second.

My Instagram followers loved all the pictures I posted of it, and I'm glad I made the decision to return to social media—especially after I gave everyone a long lecture about body shaming. This time around, I try to include plus and petite options, so that women of all shapes and sizes can copy the looks I put together.

I gingerly touch the diamond tiara resting on my half-up, half-down hairdo with loose tendrils framing my face, which Maya and Libby both insisted I needed to get since it perfectly complemented my gown. It takes a moment to spot Maya, but not too long since her head-to-toe sequined gown makes her stand out from the crowd like a stripper at a convent. She grins at me, holding a plate full of hors d'oeuvres in one hand and a glass of wine in the other, and I blow her a kiss.

At first, it was a little weird between us when I told her that Sam and I had feelings for each other, especially because she seemed to take it personally that I hadn't said something earlier. But she herself is engaged now to the plastic surgeon that gave her mom a facelift, and lives with him in his gorgeous condo off Lake Bde Maka Ska. And the best part of living with a plastic surgeon, according to Maya, is that she doesn't need to exercise ever again because she gets an unlimited amount of liposuction.

Someone reaches for my hands, and I look up from my prayer book to see Mrs. Zelikovitch. "What a beautiful *kallah* you make, Peninaleh. And Sam, your *chosson*," she adds, bringing her fingers to her lips and making a smacking sound, "prime cut of beef. Top of the top. *Mazel tov, mazel tov.*"

Libby waits until Mrs. Zelikovitch is out of hearing range before leaning down to whisper, "She's still as creepy as ever, isn't she?"

"Tell me about it," Fraydie's voice pipes up from behind my chair. "Is it safe to come out yet?"

"It's almost time for the *bedeken*, so you'd better," my mother says from the seat next to mine, twisting around to see Fraydie.

Sam's aunt leans toward me, her hazel eyes round with curiosity. "What's the *bedeken*?"

"That's when the groom covers the bride with a veil."

"Oh, got it," she says, nodding. "And what's the meaning behind that?" Ever since Sam's aunt Lainee showed up this weekend, she's been asking about every tradition, big and small.

"It's supposed to show that the guy isn't solely interested in his bride's looks which will fade with time, but her inner beauty which she will never lose."

"That's lovely." She smiles. "What a nice message."

"I know at least a handful of women who didn't have looks or personality," Fraydie says, poking her head between us. "But their grooms still covered them with a veil. So how does that make any sense?"

"*Fraydie,*" my mother says in her warning voice. "Why don't you go make yourself a plate."

Fraydie gives me a mischievous wink and heads off. I continue murmuring psalms, stopping here and there to smile with people and pose for pictures.

The men's singing draws closer, and my stomach somersaults. I swallow, but my mouth is dry from fasting, and my tongue sticks to the roof of my mouth. The wedding planner, a four foot ten woman with the voice and mannerisms of a drill sergeant, comes barreling through the sea of women and shouts, "Make room, the men are coming!"

My heart crescendos as Sam enters the room, leading the procession. He breaks into a huge, very un-Sam-like grin when he sees me, and I feel myself blush under his gaze. My eyes travel down the length of his traditional white garment, hugging him in all the right places, and he's wearing the Hermès tie I picked out for him.

It's crazy noisy from the live band and all the singing and clapping, but when Sam comes forward to cover me with the veil, then puts his lips next to my ear and says, "I love you," my eyes fill with tears, and the moment feels suspended in time, as though it's just the two of us. My father comes next, places his hands over my head, and recites the blessing in Hebrew, that one that says I should be like my great Jewish matriarchs, Sara, Rivka, Rochel, and Leah, each of whom had unique qualities that played an essential role in the future of the Jewish people.

With my mother on one side of me and Sam's aunt on the other, we wait for the wedding planner's cue before heading to another room, where a beautiful wedding canopy stands, surrounded by lanterns and flowers. The ceremony is long, and there's an awful lot of bodies in a tight space, but the moment finally comes when Sam's shoe shatters the glass cup—because no occasion is ever completely happy until we're reunited in Jerusalem with the Third Temple—then Sam and I are whisked through the crowd amid shouts of "Mazel tov!" and more singing.

The wedding planner leads us down a short hallway and stops outside a doorway. "Eight minutes," she barks, her eyes bouncing between Sam and me. "And don't get too cozy. Pictures are right after this, and I don't want anyone's makeup getting ruined."

Sam and I exchange an amused look. Since the *yichud* room is where the bride and groom can touch for the first time, this woman has probably seen it all. And from the way Sam's looking at me, I don't blame her for being nervous.

Sam places his hand on the doorframe and gives the wedding coordinator one of his most intimidating stares, the kind that closes business deals without compromise or negotiation. "Twenty minutes."

"Twenty?" she squeals, clutching her chest. She shakes her head and starts to protest but Sam is already closing the door. The lock clicks, and then he turns around to face me.

For a moment, we simply stare at each other, drinking in this moment; the two of us alone as husband and wife. *Finally.*

His eyes take a languid journey, starting at my face then lingering at the bodice of my gown and its hourglass shape before returning to my lips. My heart quickens as he approaches, one deliberate step at a time.

"Are you hungry?" I point to the table in the corner, piled high with food to break the traditional wedding day fast. There are chicken kabobs, steak crostini, lamb skewers, salads, and drinks, but even after fasting all day, the butterflies in my stomach have replaced any appetite I'd normally have.

"I'm starving," he says, taking a step toward me. "But not for food."

A shiver of excitement races through me, along with some fear. "The thing is," I say, swallowing and gathering my breath, "I've never done any of this before, and I don't know where to put my hands or my tongue or, or . . . teeth."

His eyebrow lifts as though he's slightly taken aback. "Let's keep teeth out of it," he suggests lightly. "As for everything else, just try to relax. Do what feels natural."

Right. Do what feels natural. I place my hand along the arm of a couch and inch backward.

His lips curve into a half smile. "Sweetheart."

"Yeah?"

"It might help if you stop moving."

"Right." I gulp. "Makes sense."

"I'm scared too, you know," he says, running a hand through his hair. "It says in our marriage contract, the—what's it called again?"

"Kesubah." I smile, knowing where he's going with this.

He unbuttons his traditional white garment and tosses it onto the couch. "Doesn't it say in there that it's the husband's duty to give pleasure to his wife? Not the other way around."

"True," I acknowledge, relaxing slightly.

"The pressure is all on me," he continues, shaking his head and placing his hands on his hips. "It's enough to make weaker men buckle."

"Or less arrogant ones."

He shrugs. "It's a tough job, but someone's gotta do it."

I take a small step toward him. "Do you have some kind of strategy, or are you just going to wing it?"

His eyes drop to my lips. "I've got some ideas, but I'm open to suggestions."

I take a moment to think it over. "I don't think I'd like handcuffs or whips," I say. "Not even the cute-looking ones with the fake fur attached."

His eyebrow lifts as he takes a few steps toward me. "I don't even want to know."

"There's a place in Uptown called Smitten Kitten. I just happened to be in the neighborhood," I say innocently.

"Uh-huh," he murmurs, closing the distance between us. "Of course you were."

He slowly lifts his hand and stares into my eyes, giving me time to say no. I smile my consent and close my eyes as his fingers graze the side of my face. Every nerve and synapse in my body comes alive, hyperaware. He inhales sharply and I can tell he feels it too, this charged energy between us. It's weird and strange and deliciously wonderful.

"So damn beautiful," he murmurs. He cups my face between his hands and gazes at me like he can't believe I'm his. My veins hum with happiness, especially because I can't believe I'm his either.

His lips brush against mine, soft and innocent at first, but after a little while, his tongue parts my mouth, and the kiss quickly turns fiery. He's like a starving man at an all-you-can-eat buffet, and it causes parts of my body that I didn't even know existed to tingle. My hormones kick into high gear, and I curl against him like Glad Cling Wrap, moaning into his mouth.

A low growl emits from his throat, and he grasps the back of my neck, angling it to deepen the kiss. "You're killing me," he pants, reaching around to the back of my dress. "Shit! There's a hundred buttons. Who the hell designed this thing?"

I blink and try to focus. "Uh, Vera Wang."

"Vera should use zippers." He looks around the room and scowls. "I need scissors. You don't mind if I cut it open, do you?"

"Two more minutes," the wedding coordinator yells from the other side of the door.

Sam mutters a string of expletives and releases me. He runs his hand over his face, then shakes his head and grins. "Damn."

"What?" I smile. I'm not used to seeing him like this, with rumpled hair and heavy breathing. He's normally Mr. Cool, Calm, and Collected, and I can't help feeling some perverse satisfaction knowing that a few minutes alone with me has left him flustered and dazed.

He flashes me one his trademark smirks. "You're a fast learner."

I match his smirk. "Obviously," I say with a wave of my hand. "As if there was any doubt."

He chuckles and reaches for me again, like he can't bear not to touch me. "I love you, Superwoman."

"I love you too, Mr. Kleinfeld. Or is it okay to call you Sam now?"

"Only when we're naked."

I smile, reveling in the fact that this gorgeous, kind, smart man is my husband. Libby's letter came to fruition after all, though it took a while to get to this point. A few weeks ago, I got the phone call that I've always wanted but never dared to dream of.

"Penina, are you sitting down?" Libby had said.

My eyes widened in panic. "Who died?"

Libby laughed. "Always so paranoid. No, this is good news. Really good news."

I breathed a sigh of relief and went back to the seating chart for the wedding. "Tell me."

"Mimi and Uncle Tzvi and Aunt Peshie talked and decided it would be best if you adopted the baby," Libby said. "That way he'd be raised by family and they know he'll be well loved."

My heart stopped and I was afraid I hadn't heard correctly. "Can you repeat that?"

"Mimi wants you to have the baby. He's a month old and way cuter than any of my kids were at that age."

"She wants me to have it, as in . . . to keep?"

"Yes," Libby laughs. "To keep. Mazel tov, Penina! You're a mom now!"

I sat down and covered my mouth with my hand. Then I laughed. And cried.

I had driven over that very night to get him because A)I already loved this child with all my heart, and B)I'd already been separated from him for a month.

I was nervous to tell Sam because of the timing. It was ridiculous, really. What newlywed couple is thrown into parenthood straight away? I was afraid Sam would say it's too soon, that we'd need a few years for ourselves first, so I employed the same strategy he used when he proposed to me—I took the baby to visit him in person and when Sam picked him up and the two of them looked at each other, it was love at first sight. I've basically been third-wheeling ever since, which is fine by me.

We named him Rafael after Sam's grandfather because, eerily enough, he resembles him. Sam and Rafael are everything I could have hoped for and then some.

* * *

"Time's up!" the wedding coordinator hollers and knocks on the door.

"Ready?" Sam asks.

I nod and take his hand. "Ready."

ACKNOWLEDGMENTS

They say it takes a village to raise a child, but it took two continents and several hundred people to get this baby into print. (Okay, maybe not several hundred people, but definitely a lot!) Thank you so much to my fairy godmothers, a.k.a. agents, Hannah Schofield and Claire Friedman, for taking a chance on a newbie. Like the Mafia, we'll be together for life.

A *huge* thank-you to my American team, Toni Kirkpatrick, and everyone at Alcove Press, along with my editor, Emily Beth Rapoport. Thank you Rebecca Nelson, Dulce Botello, Madeline Rathle, and Jill Pellarin.

Another *huge* thank-you to my UK team, Emilie Marneur of Embla Books, and editors Hannah Smith and Cara Chimirri. Thank you Jane Snelgrove, Jennifer Porter, Anna Perkins, and Hannah Deuce.

Thank you to Leo Daniels, for answering my jewelry questions; Estee Silver, for your expertise on infertility; and Chavie Bruk, for information on adoption within the Orthodox Jewish community.

Thank you to the following authors, who took time out of their day to encourage me: Abby Jimenez, Jean Meltzer, Goldy Moldovsky, Carly Bloom, and Cara Lockwood.

Acknowledgments

Julia Carpenter, meeting you changed my life. This book wouldn't exist without your constant guidance, and one day soon, we'll go on book tours together.

Thank you to all my past and present critique writers: Skye, Karl, Kara, Paula, John, Ned, Lynn, Ellie, Kerrie, Schujaa, Emily, Dvora, Larry, Gregs 1 and 2, Barbra, and Sheryl.

Thank you Jennifer Ebner for promoting my writing!

Thank you to my first fan who wasn't related to me by blood, Kristi Oman, owner of the historic Semple Mansion.

Love to my besties, Kim and Sarah, and hugs to my family; my sister, brother, sibling in-laws, nieces, nephews, cousins. Thank you, Dr. Joel Shertok, for distracting the children so I could write, and to my parents, Dr. Michael and Rae Ann Wexler for your unconditional love and unwavering belief in me. To the people I birthed—Asher, Esty, and Ari—and the guy I married, Daniel, there's no one else whose underwear I'd rather fold.